CLAR

HALIFAX CLARION CYCLING CLUB 1896

By Ruth Enright

First Published in 2023 by Blossom Spring Publishing

ISBN 978-1-7394532-3-7
E: admin@blossomspringpublishing.com
W: www.blossomspringpublishing.com

Dedication – To Halifax, my home town. The hand-chiselled inscription on the top of Albert Promenade rocks, 'J.H. Henderson, C.J. Raynor, 1896', was the inspiration for this book. I always wondered who they might have been and why they stopped to chisel the inscription there, with that particular date. The Clarion Cycling Club's history suggested a possible story for them in this work of fiction.

Chapter One

There were twelve of them. Twelve cyclists in the newly established Halifax Clarion Club. Some of them were acquainted already, others only through this fledgling organisation. They were a loose alliance of young people who had come together to combine the pleasures of cycling in the countryside with sharing the *Clarion* newspaper's broadly socialist ideas of the day. Published in Bradford by former Halifax man Robert Blatchford, it was the inspiration for all the popular Clarion Cycling Clubs springing up in industrial towns and cities in the last few years. The groups' members were called 'Clarionettes'.

It seemed unlikely that socialism, however vaguely conceived, was the reason for some of the people in this group to be there, but the activity was something new and daring which enabled the classes and sexes to mix, and in a physical exercise outdoors which was frowned on by the respectable. For those who did take the club's founding ethic seriously, the presence of those who did not was going to be irksome, but for the present they were young, new to it and enjoying their first group cycle, men and women together.

The Halifax Clarionettes were mill workers, a minister's daughter, a teacher at the Crossley and Porter Orphan Home and School, and one or two were even the children of mill owners. Younger sons and daughters, they had some sensibility about how their own prosperity and the reasons for it contrasted with the positions of others. They were possibly freer to consider it, since they would not be the direct inheritors of the family wealth. One of them, however, Noel Ogden, was already a rich heir. Always at the forefront of anything unorthodox and an eccentric individual, he had come into his factory-born money young. He indulged himself in extravagant theatricals and was always busy remodelling his mansion as the fancy took him. His favourite costume, in which he had been photographed, was worn for playing Oberon, King of the Fairies. Dressed in this, he sat in a gilded throne, was much garlanded with flowers for a crown and wore a slashed doublet, silk stockings, fancy buckled shoes and the expression of a poet and aesthete (neither of which he really was).

The Clarionettes had alighted on the top of Albert Promenade, a long pavement on an escarpment with views across the Calder Valley towards the hilly fields of Norland. Trains on the railway line below produced the only smoke in the air, for it being Sunday, the mill chimneys of Halifax, and Sowerby Bridge further along, were not fired up today. Sitting on the black, millstone grit crags, they had paused for their picnic refreshments at lunchtime. Two friends, monumental stonemasons who worked together, were engaged in chiselling their names and the date of this visit into the obdurate dark rock – 'J.H. Henderson, C.W. Raynor, 1896' – where they might last as long as the stone and marble memorials they made for the graveyards.

"This is a public promenade, you know, John and Cyril," said Ellen Rastrick, worried they were transgressing.

Ellen was the youngest daughter of a bobbin factory owner. She was here with her maid, Libby, who was accompanying her on a Sunday off and so could join her privately.

"The rocks don't belong to anyone, Miss Rastrick," said John in his loud, cheery voice. "And that wants to be noted down."

They all laughed, as the group's secretary would say this of any point of action or particularly meaningful statement made at meetings. Proceedings had to pause while he laboriously did so. George Holroyd had learned to read and write after his retirement from the Pellon Lane Mill and was proud of the achievement, so that the others, respecting this older radical, let him take his time.

The more genteel walkers who were strolling along the promenade today looked askance at this unruly group of cyclists at rest, their bicycles lying beside them in a mechanical heap. Ellen had read about the Clarionettes in the newspaper and talked to Libby of them when she was having her hair dressed for yet another tame neighbourly visit. Together, they had gone to some meetings under the pretext of Ellen being accompanied to one of the charity bazaars, of which there were always many.

***

Libby's manner outside the house was quite other than it was with her servant's cap on. There was a subtle lack of deference in it which showed Ellen that she and the family were probably far less respected as the maid's employers than they thought they were, even if she and Libby *were* on quite friendly terms at home. It came as something of a surprise to her seventeen-year-old self, for all her egalitarian notions. Libby's confidence when speaking at a meeting also surprised the slightly younger Ellen, who found herself a bit inhibited by the gatherings and also by the gruff directness of the working people present.

The Clarionettes had formed a club to finance the purchase of bicycles to be shared between those who did not own them. In this way, those who were young ladies could enjoy the participation without being suspected of harbouring dangerous notions about emancipation. Socialism had begun with those who could contribute more to this by doing so, the working members paying a weekly sub to offset the outlay. This in itself formed a bond between them, as did the fact that, in a sense, this was a clandestine expedition for many of them.

Each of the young ladies from the better social classes were supposedly engaged in some other reason for being out and about. For the working people, it was safer not to be too open about it either, as they might be suspected of views leading to subversive activity in the workplace. The shared bicycles were stored in a disused Sunday School building attached to a small Methodist Church, of which the retired group secretary was now the caretaker and graveyard gardener, for a small remuneration. While you could work you did work, the mills not providing any pension and the wages not offering the opportunity for savings.

Among the Clarionettes, the working men and women present had an instant camaraderie which made them more at ease in the company than some of the others, apart from Noel, whom nothing ever did constrain. Sarah Greenwood and Hannah Robertshaw were mill workers together in Dewhirst Dye Works. Their companion, Albert Dewhirst, was a son of its owner. There was an underlying familiarity between the trio which puzzled Ellen and Jane. Jane Ellison was a minister's daughter and, like Ellen, had little notion of what that familiarity might be. Albert was turning Sarah and Hannah about in different positions on the rocks, saying they would make a tableau in his photographic studio and he would picture them as nymphs in the woods of holm oaks growing on the slopes below.

"Or, I could set up my box camera and picture you here in situ," he said. "We can return one private afternoon, the three of us."

"Do tell us more of that, Albert," said Ellen, overhearing him. "I should like my portrait taken with a bicycle. Mother *would* be pleased," she added jestingly.

The two mill women exchanged an amused look, again suggestive of secrets between them and a little mocking of Ellen's naivety, but Albert raised his hat and said, to a ripple of laughter from them all, "I should be delighted, Miss Rastrick. I am only an amateur, though, and would probably fail to do you justice."

Noel jumped in to call across, "Albert, I would be happy to pose for you in any attire or disarray you care for! I hear you have a penchant for the inner chimney sweep in us all and especially in your portraits of the ladies in their native dirt!"

This arch and outrageous statement made Hannah and Sarah smile at one another again. Before Albert could retort, however, attention was distracted by Peter Lumb, who was returning from a short leg stretcher along the promenade, loudly pointing out the lantern-topped pinnacle of Wainhouse Tower to them all.

"Look at that!" he derided. "For summat that never needed building and all for spending money on nowt. Two hundred and fifty-three foot of a mill chimney what never *were* a mill chimney and now stands there like a stick of rhubarb for all the world to see."

"Oh, no, I disagree," said Noel. "There is every need for a folly in this dismally pragmatic world here."

"Nay. Money squandered, I say," grumbled Peter, who was feeling these things particularly since, as everyone present knew, he was out of work recently because the flour mill he worked in had burned down after a fire in the drying room.

"You should come in with me," his friend Stanley Jagger said now, and not for the first time that day or previously. "Crossley Carpets are manufacturing for all over the world. And they do some good, don't they? The orphanage they built, and the land given for the Moor Field below it to make clean air and a green space for the public choked with smoke?"

"They do, Stanley," said Eustace Horsfall with a smile. A quiet man who took life seriously, he taught in the orphanage residential school and was particularly wary of Noel Ogden and his dilettante ways.

"What? Work on those looms? I'd be as deaf at twenty as you are, cloth ears!" joked Peter to Stanley.

"Cheeky beggar!" reposted Stanley.

"Besides," Peter went on indignantly, "Dean Clough Mills are t' only ones won't go for that new four day August break t' Chamber of Commerce 'ave just agreed for mill workers every year. Ah'm not working theer!"

"Wakes week, you mean," countered Stanley with a grin.

Peter rose inevitably to the bait with, "Nay, that's for Lancashire's mill folk. We want a proper good Yorkshire name for ours!"

Desultory cheers and ironic clapping met this truculent statement. Although they were still in high feather about such a watermark concession by the employers, it was a Clarion Club campaign to press for this holiday, so recently won, to have a title fitting for its locality. So far, however, it was still going to be 'Wakes Week'.

"Why not 'Wainhouse Week'?" suggested Noel flippantly, pointing up at the tower which had been the subject of Peter's strident objections. "Did you know that several parties who set out to mount to the top of that tower were never seen again? Its central staircase winds and winds in the dark with only a slit window here and there to let in the light of the world and you lose your way. It's like a maze in there."

"Rubbish, Noel," said Albert trenchantly. He knew Noel well and had no scruple about giving the lie to his romancing. "It was built for a dye works chimney over twenty years back. My father often tells the story of Wainhouse and Henry Edwards coming to daggers drawn about it. Edwards boasting nothing would dominate the landscape like his mansion at Pye Nest and Wainright swearing down that Edwards would have no option but to look out at his chimney every morning from his windows."

"I know why it was built, Albert. A great notion for a factory chimney," said Noel.

"Aye but it were never finished as that or used as one," said Peter in his dour manner, churlish about it as an excess to be disapproved of, which was rather how he viewed Noel himself. "And when the dye works was sold, that monstrosity was left out of the purchase. They say it will be sold off again soon to a private owner but I don't know who'd want it."

"*I* want to have it," declared Noel flippantly. "I can grow my hair long and lean over the balcony at the top like Rapunzel. Which of you would climb up to rescue me? You can bring the Neptune fire engine from Victoria Mill with its ladders, gentlemen."

"Not I!" said Peter hotly, disgusted by this effete talk and looking rather aggressive. "We're not 'ere to listen to daft prattle from t' like of thee about summat serious!"

Peter Lumb, John Henderson and Cyril Raynor were all volunteer firemen and there were plenty of blazes for them to attend in the area, brave and risky affairs. Noel's flippancy about that clearly offended him too.

"I thought we were all friends together here, Peter," laughed Noel, pleased to have nettled him because he had that kind of sly, puckish humour.

"I think you would look beautiful, Noel," said Ellen, who admired Noel very much and was envious of his carefree flouting of conventions.

"I would, Ellen," replied Noel complacently. "With a

cascade of this grown rippling down the wall for some strong young man to climb up and get me. Can you imagine?"

He ruffled at his loose ringlets of dark gold, fondling them in a satirical way that made the other young men look at one another and laugh, for in spite of his words and posturing there was nothing particularly effeminate about Noel's manner or voice, although he wore his hair longer than they did and dressed for effect wherever possible. He was a tall, athletic young man who might easily become burly from self-indulgent living if he did not exercise as fanatically as he did everything else, while the fad lasted. For the present, it was the Clarionettes and cycling. He wanted the company, liked the frisson of mingling with the lower orders and enjoyed any opportunity to shock or irritate.

"I may try to find out who owns it now and put in an offer for it," he went on. "We can climb to the top and halloo all below to our hearts' content. Do you know that it has four hundred and three stone steps in its circular staircase inside?"

"Oh, do buy it, Noel! I think it's a marvellous idea," said Ellen.

"Hardly a contribution to the Clarion Club though, Miss Ellen, is it?" said Libby, crushing Ellen's enthusiasm as Libby liked to do when they were among this group. Besides, Ellen's clear admiration of Noel Ogden was a gauche thing and flattered his considerable vanity. "I don't know so much about photographs of nymphs either, Albert," she said, but when she spoke to Albert it was in a lighter way because he was handsome and she liked him. "We are all comrades together in the Clarion Club, aren't we? Real people. Men and women together."

"That's true," he conceded. "And it is how I like it.

Men and women together." He met her eyes flirtatiously with his own, rather fine, dark ones and flashed a grin of his even white teeth (a rarity in that area). "But it does not prevent us aspiring to art. If *you* were to be a nymph, Libby, you would bring some sense into the proceedings, I'm sure."

"I am sure I would," she agreed.

Hannah Robertshaw and Sarah Greenwood exchanged that private look, with another of those conspiratorial smiles, which suggested their own connection with Albert outweighed any other flirtation. Libby felt this and eyed them with disfavour.

"Look. There's grass growing all over them 'ills opposite," remarked Stanley Jagger. "On Beacon Hill behind Dean Clough Mills it's black as soot all t' way up and not a twig or leaf anywhere on it!"

"We must get more of your fellows to join us!" said Jane. "Feel how sweet the breeze is up here and how fresh the air is to breathe!"

"You could be preaching that in your father's Sunday School instead of being out with us enjoying yourself, Jane," said Noel, with a teasing smile which did not take the sting out of his words.

Jane flushed, sensitive to being found priggish, moving Eustace Horsfall to say, "I think it's a fine sentiment, Miss Ellison, Jane, I should say, and very well said."

"Here, here," said John Henderson in his deep voice and he stood up to invite Jane to look at the inscription he and Cyril had made. "Take my hand over the wall there" – (a low wall edged the pavement) – "and see this view below, Jane. It is even finer from this escarpment. There's a narrow way to climb down the rocks too if we dared it one day with a rope, Cyril. Good practice for our drills."

Jane accepted, grateful to be saved from a reply, for she never knew how to parry Noel's little sallies. She and the two men peered down the twisting break between the rocks forming a narrow, dark column to be squeezed through. John and Cyril discussed climbing up and down the tall rock face with grappling irons and ropes as training for their firemen's duties.

"We should produce leaflets," said Eustace to the others, "to give out in the mills you all work in. Invite people to join us as Jane suggested."

"Like I said at t' meeting, Eustace, most folk can't read, so there's no point in that," answered Peter Lumb in his downright fashion, always ready with a reason why not before he found a reason to agree to something.

"No," said Eustace, blushing but pressing on. "Although we can speak to people outside when they leave the workplace perhaps? And we should try to offer them a chance to learn to read."

"*You* could, Eustace, and Albert and even Noel over there. Some of the ladies might. Not us working men and keep our jobs."

It was a circular discussion but Eustace, being the dogged sort, kept coming back to his point when the opportunity offered. Noel had languidly got up and stepped over the wall to look at the view too and, with him out of earshot, Peter said, "If we'd known that great ninny would inflict himself on us like this so much, we'd never have agreed to Albert there inviting him in, would we?"

"I knew he would pay up towards the bicycles you all needed," said Albert. "Noel has his own money and the rest of us don't have such access to funds. Besides, Noel loves a grand, quixotic gesture and I knew he wouldn't be able to resist. He isn't a bad sort when you get past all that carry on. Noel has too much money and is bored.

Other people have too little money and they are bored with the monotony of earning it. We meet in the middle here, do we not, to address the imbalance?"

"Oh, aye, nicely put, Albert" said Peter drily. "Some of us haven't got a means of earning it, if you'd forgotten."

"I hadn't," said Albert, "for you keep reminding us. But Stanley has offered you a remedy. I too could get you a place in the Dewhirst Dye Works. You only have to give me the word."

"I had a place by my own merit and skill. Ely Bradbury's will get back up and running again; meanwhile, my brother-in-law's got me took on next week at the abattoir. But thank you."

His thanks were given grudgingly because Albert had spoken with unwitting condescension, which was resented.

"Ellen, would you consider teaching some of the people in a night-class to read and write, as one of our first projects for the Clarionettes?" asked Eustace, still determined on some worthy outcome for this healthy cycling excursion.

"Oh, I, I don't know," said Ellen, rather shrinking from the idea of it because she felt instinctively that she was no match for the down-to-earth pragmatism of the workers.

They might laugh at and possibly scorn her as a 'do-gooder', which she was sure Libby did behind those clear-sighted hazel eyes of hers. They were wide set in a face as fresh as a lily, in which her soft, pink mouth was prettily defined. Libby had a puff of strawberry blonde hair from which small tendrils wafted when it was put up in a twisted, fluffy bun. These were all features which Ellen, who had troubled skin, flat hair and indeterminate colouring, envied greatly. Her own slenderness of figure was not in vogue and she had not yet filled out properly, whereas Libby was all mature, creamy skin. For Ellen, the confidence she had hoped to build by joining the Clarionettes had not yet arrived, but she loved the freedom offered her by cycling in the open air and in the company of young men who were not her brother, especially Noel's. When they all addressed each other by their first names, it was like finding a new taste in your mouth, to be handled carefully. The Clarionettes had decided they should be on an equal and informal footing with one another but they were still unused to it.

Noel had been posturing on the clifftop, putting a hand to his brow and peering out theatrically across the horizon. Now he turned to them all to say, "Time to get on, Clarionettes! The Hipperholme Sunny Vale Pleasure Garden awaits and I mean to treat you all to tickets for the boating and a ride on the train and the donkeys, not forgetting an ice each!"

"You see," said Albert, to Peter and Stanley in particular. "He does have a generous heart."

"Aye. He's all right," said Stanley, which in this locality was virtually an enthusiastic accolade.

Mounting their bicycles once again, the Clarionettes set out for the long downhills through town and then the steep uphill to the pleasure gardens. Tickets purchased, they all ambled about the place, rivalries and undercurrents subsiding as they boated on the two lakes and enjoyed all the facilities available to them for the afternoon. Not to be outdone by Noel, everybody who could made some little contribution to the proceedings, a cup of tea here, or pennies towards payments there, and these offers were received with delicacy by those who had enough money themselves to pay for anything they wanted. The day over they returned, tired and pleased with their time, cycles put away in the Sunday School building or ridden home by those who owned them.

On the rocks of Albert Promenade, the chiselled letters – J.H. Henderson and C.W. Raynor, 1896 – left an enigmatic record of their visit on that summer day, one which was still visible to others strolling there a hundred years and more later. People would wonder who they had been and why they had come there, and what occasion it was which they had marked by chiselling out their names so clearly for posterity.

Chapter Two

Ellen Rastrick's family lived in one of the mansion villas at the bottom of Saville Park below the Moor. The tall gateposts were topped by perfect stone spheres which had looked as big as a world each to Ellen as a child. Like everywhere else hereabouts, the golden sandstone of the building was tipped with sooty black from industrial smoke, with white mortar, thickly wedged against weathering, standing out against it. Situated here, the building was not as entirely encased in grime as those in the town centre were. The decorative carvings on the town hall's clock tower were already virtually invisible. Ellen occasionally fantasised about one of those gatepost tops rolling off and crushing a particularly tiresome neighbour passing through the entrance.

She wished it especially this afternoon, when Winifred Butterworth might have been silenced before making her visit. Ellen would have spared Kenneth, Winifred's son, because Kenneth actually noticed Ellen and included her in conversation, not being so entirely transfixed by the vivacious Sylvia, her older sister, as most young men were. Sandwiches and home-made pickles were being served for afternoon tea, delicately presented with the crusts cut off and made with what Ellen's mother never failed to refer to as 'best butter', the implication being that no other kind was on offer at *her* table.

Sylvia herself, being in demand, was mainly indifferent to her many admirers of course. This seemed especially unfair to Ellen, a far more tender-hearted and introspective soul who already despaired of ever being loved. This was not helped by having a crush on such a person as Noel Ogden. Feeling it was entirely to be expected that any love of hers was likely to be unrequited, Ellen pined for him secretly, in as far as that was possible. Mrs Butterworth was in the middle of making conversation as the food and the tea tray were being brought in, a dangerous time, especially as Ellen had noticed the look of expectant glee on her broad gossip's face. Sure enough, Ellen's heart sank as she found herself to be the subject of a strange sight encountered the other day by Mrs Butterworth's neighbour.

"Yes, Mrs Rastrick! Positively riding about like a hoyden. On a bicycle! And in mixed company too," she said, twinkling as if this were said in the friendliest fashion. "Shy Miss Ellen. I was astonished indeed. Had it been her sister, or her brother…"

"It would have been nothing remarkable at all," put in Ellen's brother Leonard, trying to come to her rescue (for having lent her his own bicycle for the excursion, he was party to her secret membership of the Clarion Club, not that he really understood anything of its politics, for she had downplayed that aspect).

"And with none other than, you will never guess it, ma'am, Noel Ogden!" continued Mrs Butterworth, who had not yet finished and had no intention of being prevented from delivering this coup de grâce. Mention of Noel had Ellen blushing hotly, made mute with resentful embarrassment.

"A *bicycle*?" Ellen's mother frowned, looking puzzled.

"Oh, really, Mother. It's hardly as if she were riding an elephant, is it?" said Len, laughing. "It was mine.

"Yours, Leonard? Whatever was going on, Ellen?"

"A bicycle ride," muttered Ellen.

"But – with whom?"

"Not alone, Mother," said Ellen, more crimson than ever. "I was with a group. For exercise and health."

"Noel Ogden, Mrs Butterworth said," commented

Sylvia slyly, for Ellen's crush was, naturally, far less of a secret than she supposed.

"Well, if Len was with you…" began Mrs Rastrick, choosing to assume that Ellen's brother had also been there somehow, but here there was an interruption as a dish of sliced beetroot slid from the maid's tray.

With unusual clumsiness, Libby also overset the jug of milk and spilt it on to the best rug. Sufficient consternation was caused by the fuss in cleaning that up, and in ensuring Mrs Butterworth's dress was sponged clean, for the heat to have been taken out of the moment. Mrs Rastrick took advantage of the diversion, not wishing whatever the full account of the occasion was to be aired in front of Winnie Butterworth, a noted tattler. Ellen knew that Noel was seen as somebody risqué due to his flaunted eccentricities. To be found in his company at all was to be noticed with raised eyebrows. Nevertheless, as a man of considerable wealth, he was also viewed as being an eligible bachelor by those who thought convention would eventually prevail in his life. Kenneth rose to the occasion too by addressing both Leonard and Ellen.

"I must say, I rather envy you. I have never tried one of the new two wheelers," he said pleasantly.

"I am sure we are all surprised that Ellen has done so," remarked Sylvia mischievously.

"Don't tease her, Syl," frowned Leonard, exclaiming, "Good heavens, Libby, how much scrubbing can a carpet need?" on being made to move his feet yet again out of her industrious way with a bowl and a cloth.

"Sorry, sir," said Libby, scrubbing briskly, her presence hindering the tea-party from resuming immediately.

Proceedings were so disrupted that since Mrs Butterworth was deprived of full satisfaction she soon made a move to take whatever her other news was off elsewhere, having made at least some small hit here. Before leaving, Kenneth lent Ellen a book he had thoughtfully brought for her to read and asked Sylvia if she would care to take a walk with him one day, as the weather was so fine. Like all gentlemen, he was not immune to her charms.

"Certainly! But why don't you ask Ellen too?" Sylvia answered teasingly. "And you can talk about your *book*."

She spoke as if that would be the funniest thing in the world for a man to want to converse with a young woman about on a walk – certainly not a pretty one like herself anyway. Kenneth simply smiled, however, answering, "Naturally, I assumed your sister would join us. I will bid you both good day for the present, then."

Like Eustace Horsfall, Kenneth was quiet, but he had a presence about him which modest Eustace did not possess. Somehow, without him having indicated it in any way, it was clear that Sylvia, rather than seeming flirtatiously provocative, had disappointed his opinion of her. Moreover, Sylvia herself looked, very slightly, as if she might regret her answer. Serve her right, thought Ellen as their guests left, for trying to show her up about Noel Ogden in the company and cocking a snook at Kenneth's kindness in lending her plainer sister a book! Sylvia had no doubt expected him to laugh and demur at inviting her sister too. Ellen was glad that he had not, for Sylvia was far too used to being chased after.

"What group of people was Mrs Butterworth referring to, Leonard, that you and your sister were with the other day? I would not object to your asking Mr Ogden to call in for tea one day, you know," resumed Mrs Rastrick now that their visitors had departed.

"Oh, it was an impromptu moment among a few people I know," pretended Leonard with a wink at Ellen.

“Didn’t you remember that I have taught Ellen to ride my bicycle, Mother?”

“No and I am not sure it is fitting that she should do so. But if she is with you and Mr Ogden is a party to the occasion then it must be socially appropriate. These are more modern days we are coming into. There are machines everywhere you look!” she vaguely observed of this very industrial age.

“I am not sure that socially appropriate and Noel Ogden go together, Mother,” he replied with a laugh. “But I will be sure to tell him.”

“If you bring Noel to tea, he and I will have great sport,” said Sylvia. “For I find him very amusing. I have a light opera duet just arrived which I am sure he would enjoy singing with me at the pianoforte.”

This clearly went down well with Mrs Rastrick, if not with Ellen, who couldn’t eat another bite of bread with best butter for fear it would choke her. Leonard just laughed very heartily and agreed that it would indeed be great sport to have Noel Ogden in the house. No more was said of it. Leonard had no interest in the blue stocking company which he thought, from Ellen’s account of it, the infant cycling club was likely to offer, except to ask her later how on earth Noel had come to be there – although he added that anything Noel did was never to be guessed at. When Ellen said that she did not know, he merely commented that he must have known somebody and taken a fancy to join them. Ellen quietly agreed that he must have done. When she had the opportunity, she thanked Libby (who had been roundly scolded for her clumsiness by cook) for her intervention. Libby shrugged.

“Had to be done, Miss, in case Mrs Butterworth knew about me being there too. If that came out your mother would smell a rat then, sure as eggs is eggs. I could lose my place."

"I wish you'd got that beetroot to land in Winnie's hair," giggled Ellen. "That would have been a very fine mess indeed!"

"That it would," agreed Libby, laughing too. "Best be about my business, now, Miss Ellen. Cook's fair on the rampage because staff standards reflect on her being in charge from the kitchen standpoint, or so she says."

"Mother was glad. She didn't like me being talked about by Winnie Butterworth any more than I did."

"No, but her son's all right. Kindly, like. That's nice in a man, I think."

"Do you?" said Ellen, wrinkling her nose a little. "Yes, but…"

"Oh, I know. He's no Noel Ogden in your eyes. You know what attaching yourself to him will bring you? A broken heart, that's what."

"I don't know what you're talking about," said Ellen and Libby smiled.

"Oh, yes you do, Ellen. Vain as a peacock for attention and too busy getting it to give his to any other. Right, that's your hair brushed as nice as anyone can make it for the night. Shame it's still so lank but keep it under your cap or your hat and who's to know, Miss Ellen? You'll grow out of it."

"It shines when it's washed," said Ellen, ruefully.

"Well, let Mr Ogden come to tea and I'll do it with egg yolks to give it a gloss," said Libby. "And I'll make a lemon juice wash for your skin too. Not that you should be bothering looking your best for him in my opinion."

"Thank you," said Ellen meekly, who wanted to do so, naturally, whatever anybody else said about Noel.

***

There would not be another Clarion Club meeting for several weeks, when a sought-after woman speaker was said to be due to address them, a passionate advocate of cycling for women. Meanwhile, Ellen found reasons to accompany her brother into town if he was going, in case Noel Ogden might also be there for any reason. He might have a fancy for a new hat or, as they were doing today, be taking a turn around the Piece Hall, the colonnaded Georgian market square where woollen cloth was bought and sold across the district. She walked along the first floor's balconied outdoor corridor in front of the shops, arm in arm with Leonard. Ellen was sure, for no good reason at all, that since Noel was so much in her thoughts they were bound to come across him. Leonard had designs on expanding the bobbin factory's reach to one of the worsted mills and was amusing himself by gaining skills in what the best cloth would be to produce for the most profit.

"Father is almost persuaded." He did his best to persuade himself instead, while explaining it all to Ellen. "Old Stanger is ready to retire any time and he has no heir to inherit when he dies. I could update that mill in the valley bottom there and have it produce only the finest of materials for an exclusive market."

"Mmm," said Ellen, only half paying attention. "But you will have to take over the bobbin mill from Father already."

"The bobbin mill may have had its day by then. It's a case of seizing the moment."

"Yes, but…"

"What?"

"Are you quite sure you know what you're doing?"

Leonard had never shown a great deal of interest in any business before and, knowing the mill he meant, an old one with an ancient waterwheel, she doubted it to be as viable a prospect as Leonard seemed to think.

"I will do, when it comes to it," he assured her.

"Anyway, he *has* got an heir. Or an heiress. What about Carrie?"

"Carrie Stanger's forty if she's a day and keeps house for her old father. What would she want with it?"

"To inherit it, perhaps?"

"I suppose I could marry her," speculated Leonard, carelessly insulting.

"Len! You're only twenty!"

"True," he said, laughing at the idea of it because he had not been at all serious, and probably wasn't about the mill either, really, Ellen thought. It was only that he was bored by being a spare part in the family business which his father had such competent control over.

"Can I borrow your bicycle tomorrow?" she asked. "I'd like to practise my riding."

"Yes, if you like," he answered carelessly. "Don't tell Ma, though. She's all right if she doesn't know about things, or doesn't have to look as if she does, but she'll put her foot down for form's sake if she has it put in front of her."

"I know," agreed Ellen.

Just then, much to their mutual consternation, Carrie Stanger and her elderly father came out of the cloth merchant's, which happened to be behind them on the balustraded paved walkway. Ellen and Len had stopped to chat together outside its open door whilst looking down on the other people busy in the square below. Their conversation would have been entirely audible from within, they realised.

"Miss Stanger, Mr Stanger," said Leonard, recovering himself and raising his hat. "I hope we find you well?"

"Tolerable, I'm glad to say," replied old Stanger gravely. Leonard had the grace to blush and Stanger gave a slight, dry smile. "If you have any proposal to make, Mr Rastrick, to either one of us, my daughter and I can usually be found at home."

"I – I will certainly call to give my regards to you both," said Leonard hastily.

"If I'm spared," added Stanger astringently, replacing his hat. "Good afternoon."

Carrie Stanger, who had a characterful face and self-command in her gaze, studied Leonard during this exchange in such a manner that it made him blush all the more with shame. Ellen smiled to see it, for like Sylvia, Len was good-looking enough to be sure of himself with the opposite sex in most circumstances. She was enjoying seeing him at a loss.

"Good afternoon," replied Leonard. "Miss Stanger, I – I do beg your pardon," he concluded, much discomfited and knowing full well now that his incivility had certainly been overheard.

"I suppose I could grant it," she said, in exactly the same tone he had used about marrying her, to his even greater embarrassment.

Then Mr and Miss Stanger walked away. Miss Stanger had a good figure and upright carriage, carrying herself off with dignity and style, Ellen thought, as she and Leonard were left standing at a loss after this scathing exchange. Ellen laughed.

"Serves you right, Len," she commented and he laughed back, agreeing that perhaps it did.

"Well, I shall have to call upon them now, of course!" he added brightly, "So I may manage to get a foot in the door, so to speak, about the mill, discreetly managed."

"Ha-ha, I think that particular horse has already bolted, Len," said Ellen. "But I think I might invite Miss Stanger to the Clarion Club."

"I would. She looks the sort," said Len, at which Ellen smiled, knowing full well what sort he meant. "I can see her riding a bike and talking literature," he added, confirming this.

They did not stay much longer and Ellen never saw any sign of Noel Ogden anyway during these visits to town. The next day she had taken Leonard's bike out and was freewheeling down a hill, getting bolder with her riding, when the gradient became too steep for her to manage any control and, like a horse bolting, the bike went juddering over the cobbles, faster and faster. Ellen's teeth jolted in her jaw. Towards the bottom a loose cobble made the bicycle jump and she was thrown over the bars to land in a stunned heap. Her hat was gone, her hair fallen out of its pins, her face grazed and her head bumped, her palms bleeding where she had thrust them out ahead to try and break her fall. She had landed outside a walled yard of some kind, in front of its open gate, and somebody came running out to her.

"Miss Rastrick! Ellen!" It was the deep, loud voice of John, the stonemason, who picked her up with tender care to lead her in, shaken, to a building full of blocks of stone and carved memorials in the making. "Mr Ogden!" John called out.

Much to Ellen's surprise and dismay at being discovered in such a condition, Noel appeared to help escort her in to have her cuts and grazes tended. Her poor chin was raw and bleeding. She was too shaken to be as embarrassed as she might have been.

"Noel!" she exclaimed.

"You wonder to find me here. Do not be concerned. It is not my gravestone he carves but only my effigy."

"Aye. I'm doing him as a knight laid out on his tomb," said John drily, fetching a basin of warm water, a towel and gauze from somewhere.

"Did you know, Ellen, that John is a very fine sculptor? Yes, he is modelling me! I am to be Alexander the Great, for my hallway. I could not convince him to carve me as Michelangelo's *David* – although I think my physique would have stood it!"

He was talking on both to shock and distract Ellen from her wincing distress, as John Henderson gently swabbed at her cuts and grazes.

"It's not as bad as it looks," John encouraged her.

"Would that he said that of his model," sighed Noel.

"I'm not having *you* standing about here posing nekkid," said John, with a frankness startling to Ellen, who had had no idea how risqué Noel was being. "You'd catch your death for one thing. And for another I'm not trained for it. Draperies I can do in marble. Cyril and I do plenty of angels and urns."

Noel swished his Grecian tunic and admired his own sandaled legs in a mirror propped against a wall to amuse Ellen, who was trying to hold back the tears which had sprung to her eyes from the sting of iodine which John was now dabbing on her chin and forehead.

"Ellen, you need to rest a little and recover. John, are we nearly done with my sitting?" Noel asked.

"I need to sketch an arm again to check my lines are carved right and then, yes, for now."

John went to empty out the bowl and dispose of the things he had cleaned her up with, leaving one hand, the palm worse grazed, wrapped in a gauze bandage. Most of the cuts were superficial, although the shallow scrapes were sore. Ellen sipped at the glass of water she had been given, watching on. Noel posed, arm upraised as if holding a torch, sword or standard, while John competently sketched out a well-rounded, muscled arm and hand from the less athletic limb before him. She was impressed by John's draughtsmanship and shocked that the word 'nekkid' had been mentioned in front of her, even if said with amused scorn to Noel. She looked under her eyelashes at Noel and thought of what he had said about Michelangelo's *David*, wondering what kind of statue that might have been. Something nude and unthinkably immodest, she presumed, finding herself blushing again with her recent self-consciousness in the male presence. She looked away from Noel, unsettled by the proximity of him in such a costume and with his legs on show below the tunic. Noel spoke to her, as if aware of her thoughts.

"Ellen, I will be dressed properly in a moment and will escort you home. I have my chaise today. Whose bicycle have you destroyed? Not one of our noble Clarion Club's, I hope?"

"No. Leonard's."

"Your brother's?"

"Yes."

"It'll mend," said John. "Leave it wi' me, lass and I'll bring it back if you'd be in bother for damaging it or riding about alone."

"I would," said Ellen. "I will be when Mother sees me like this."

"I will make your excuses for you," offered Noel. "And I am sure all will be well."

Possibly it would be, if her mother saw Noel bringing her home, given her earlier words to Leonard about him, thought Ellen. The bicycle remained with John for repair. He laughed when she again thanked him for cleaning up her grazes, saying, "Nay, I'm used to it. I've plenty of little brothers and sisters I've dusted down after a tumble."

She was grateful to him for making it seem that he had tended her as he would have done such a sibling, rather than as a young lady finding herself in an indelicate social circumstance amongst men.

"What will I say happened?" she asked in sudden consternation. "Mother will never let me borrow Len's bicycle again if she realises that I have been out on it and fallen off."

"Never fear, I'll bring it back in secret for you." John smiled and he said that he would return it a week on Wednesday, after dark, when he would wait on the road outside the house gates for her, so nobody would know about it. "And I'm sure you can rely on Noel's powers of invention for a tale when you return home now."

Noel merely smiled, having reappeared restored to his dandy grandeur in a well-cut suit and waistcoat, with a flourishing cravat about his neck like a crimson flower. He offered Ellen his arm. She took it to walk out to the carriage with a sense of wonder, feeling almost as childlike as the younger brothers and sisters John had referred to. Arriving back in style with the flamboyant Noel Ogden caused as much interest in the household as might be expected. Her mother was at home with her sister. Leonard was at the bobbin factory with their father.

"Now, pray do not be alarmed, Mrs Rastrick. Ellen was out walking upon the Moor above. A small dog being exercised ran across her path unexpectedly and she tumbled upon the ground, grazing her hands and face a little from the suddenness of it. Fortunately, I was taking a turn around the Moor in my carriage after paying a visit and saw the occurrence, so I have brought her straight home to you."

Ellen hastily removed the gauze bandage and put it in her skirt pocket, realising its appearance was not covered by this account.

"Oh, my dear girl, you must go straight to your room and I will send Libby to see to cleaning the grazes."

Ellen had to give in to this while Noel was welcomed into the sitting room. Not long afterwards, while telling Libby her wounds were already cleaned up by John

Henderson and how her fall had come about in reality, Ellen heard the strains of the piano being played and two voices in harmonious duet. Noel had a mellow tenor, her sister a clear mezzosoprano and, most annoyingly, they sounded very well together. She went back downstairs and joined her mother, who was making a very appreciative audience. The duet ended and Mrs Rastrick applauded as if she were present at the most charming musical occasion she had ever attended.

"What a voice you have, Mr Ogden!" she praised. "Of course, we hear of your home theatricals."

She said this as if it were quite daring of her to even know of them.

"I should be delighted to have you see them. I am always happy to invite participants, Mrs Rastrick, in the neighbourhood, and your daughter has a fine performing voice too."

Sylvia gave a rippling laugh.

"I believe it would be amusing, Mr Ogden."

"Oh, I am not sure…" Mrs Rastrick demurred.

"Mr Dickens, you know, was always a great one for home theatre productions," prompted Noel. "One of our nation's greatest writers!"

"Oh, well, in that case, er, I am sure we could consider it. You will stay to take some tea, of course, Mr Ogden?"

"Of course!" he agreed gladly and Mrs Rastrick rang the bell. He looked most delighted when it appeared, saying, "I do so love a sugar biscuit!" as if they had presented him with an exquisite dainty, which charmed everyone.

Noel held court like a minor Sun King and soon had everybody laughing constantly, although they barely knew at what because he created such a lively atmosphere about himself and was a natural raconteur. He had a particular story about remodelling a hill behind his house into a set of terraced gardens which he was presently about, imitating the gardener's stooped walk and caveats about this or that as he told the tale.

"I assure you that I *will* have a sundial placed there *and* a carp pond, whether he tells me it will be in as much shade as during a full eclipse, or he does not!" he concluded with a flourish.

"I should be delighted to see it one day," said Sylvia.

"And so you shall!" cried Noel. "In fact, I will invite you all to come."

"Oh, I do not go out very much myself these days," said Mrs Rastrick untruthfully. "But Sylvia might go, if Ellen went with her."

Ellen felt embittered. Naturally, she was to be chaperone and Sylvia the star of the occasion.

"Then we are agreed," Noel said, giving a comical bow to amuse them further.

After Noel left, Mrs Rastrick said, "Well, for all people say of Mr Ogden, he has plenty of natural graces and is quite conscious of the social decencies, is he not?"

Ellen had wanted to show that she knew Noel better than they did by asking him if he still intended to buy Wainhouse Tower, but that would have given away the occasion of their Clarion Club meetings and she did not want to be prevented from going to them. Sylvia was now going out to pay calls herself and so Ellen was left reluctantly listening to their mother's complacent remarks about how nice it had been to hear Sylvia and Mr Ogden singing together. Libby was in and out during the visit, bringing in the tea and then coming in to clear up the tray. When she was brushing Ellen's hair out for bedtime she remarked, "Well, are you happy now, Ellen? You saw your precious Noel today."

"No," said Ellen. "And he's not my precious Noel." Libby just laughed and she pulled Ellen's hair as she brushed it, which Ellen thought was no accident. "*You'd* be happy to see Albert Dewhirst, Libby," she accused in retaliation.

"Well, maybe I have," teased Libby.

"And maybe you haven't," said Ellen, who knew the maid had not had any time off since she had been out with her on the bicycling Sunday.

"Goodnight, then. I hope you get out of the right side of the bed tomorrow," said Libby, which made Ellen apologise, easily made to feel in the wrong and now on a different kind of footing with her maid after the Clarion Club meetings anyway.

Ellen fell asleep despondent. She had looked at her very worst today and Sylvia, naturally, being someone who nearly always did, had looked her very best. Ellen's affection for Noel seemed even less likely to be returned, however much she had thoroughly enjoyed his company earlier.

***

No word of the home theatricals came along in the immediate future, however; although Sylvia was invited to join Noel at a concert in the evening to be held at the Halifax Theatre, a very popular and fashionable venue. Such was Ellen's jealousy that she could not rest until she was bought a ticket to be there too, entirely forgetting that John Henderson had arranged to bring the mended bicycle home to her on the same night. And so, he stood patiently waiting in the dark of the road outside the Saville Park house gates after his day's work was done, while Ellen was in the red plush balcony seats of the concert hall, taking turns with opera glasses and delighted to be seated beside Noel Ogden.

Noel must also have forgotten, if he had listened to the arrangement John had made at all, Ellen thought when she remembered the following morning. She gave a little gasp at breakfast, saying, "Leonard – I must speak to you before you go out today." She took him aside to tell him that a man called John Henderson would have come last night to give back the bicycle but she had gone out and missed him. She told Leonard now that Noel hadn't found her on the Moor at all and that she had fallen off outside a sculptor's workshop where Noel happened to be for a commission. "There was a bit of damage to the bicycle and Mr Henderson offered to mend it and bring it back privately. They both covered up for me so Mother would not prevent me going on it again. Would you be able to go down at all and tell him I am sorry?" she asked. "I cannot go myself today as Mother has me tied up with her and Sylvia."

"It was kind of him to offer that and rude of you to forget," said Leonard. "Especially when he came to bring it in secret direct to you. I could have gone down for it. Why did you not tell me?" Again, Ellen shamefacedly muttered that she had forgotten, for indeed she had, taken up wholly with Noel bringing her home and then Sylvia's intrusion into everything since. "I will offer him something for his trouble in mending my bicycle for me. It must have taken time of his for no reward," said Len.

Ellen thanked him and felt better about it. Of course, being with Noel had been rather bittersweet anyway because he and Sylvia had laughed together all the way through the interval over their refreshments and she had felt rather de trop. She asked Leonard in the evening later on how it had gone with John.

"He was very polite about it and said it was no trouble but of course we knew it must have been. He wouldn't take anything from me, though. Said it was his pleasure. You mustn't take advantage of the generosity of a working man again, Ellen. He can't afford his time for no pay." Ellen felt that, of all of them, it was she who should have known this thanks to her membership of the Clarion Club. She told herself that she would make a point of speaking to John about it the next time she saw him there. Leonard turned back to her with a smile. "There's a statue he's making of Noel – he was almost finished with it – an astonishing thing altogether. So at least he will be paid for something."

This made Ellen decide that she would visit John in person at the studio workshop because, who knew, she might find Noel there again too and Sylvia would certainly not be present. Leonard being at work and her mother and Sylvia out, she took the bicycle again and arrived at the studio without incident this time, now knowing where it was. John and Cyril were both there together today, working on different things – Cyril on a cross, down which lilies were draped, and John polishing up a life-sized marble pug on a tasselled marble cushion.

"Here is Ellen come to see us," said John, putting down his cloth as she put her face tentatively round the door. "Come in. I'm glad to see you whole on arriving today," he said humorously in his loud, hearty tone.

"John, I have come to apologise to you for – for not being at home on Wednesday night."

"Think nothing of it," said John. "Your brother explained you'd been called on to go to a concert with your sister and Noel Ogden. Trust *him* to have forgotten about it!" he said, with a laugh.

Ellen was grateful that, unjustly, she had come out of it better than she deserved thanks to Leonard.

"He is not here today?" she said tentatively, looking around for Noel.

John and Cyril exchanged a sympathetic glance, seeing how it was with her, but John answered kindly, "No, his sittings are finished. I don't doubt you'll be invited to see the unveiling. Noel has some party occasion in mind. Here's the almost-finished article."

He undraped a statue on its plinth and it did, indeed, bear a remarkable resemblance to Noel, although he had been given a classical symmetry of feature and a straight, perfect nose which he did not quite possess in reality.

"Oh, you have made him beautiful!" exclaimed Ellen, impressed by it.

"I've made Alexander the Great beautiful," said John matter-of-factly. "Because legend has it that *he* was."

Ellen laughed as he had intended and turned her attention to the pug dog. "Oh, look how sweet and touching that is!" she exclaimed, unable to prevent herself from stroking the smooth stone head of it.

"That little dog was as precious to its owner as the child Cyril is making a memorial for was to her mother," John said, shaking his head slightly at the extravagance of such a monument. "And when there are children lost every day and parents lost to them too in this town! Still, the dog may have replaced such losses of her own," he added, not wishing to judge his customer unfairly, for all his musings.

"You see, John's a philosopher as well as a sculptor," commented Cyril in his lighter voice, "and sentimental with it," he teased.

"Get along with you, Cyril," said John, laughing.

Ellen saw a large book on a table full of engravings and drawings, with tissue paper carefully laid between the pages.

"Are those your templates for working?" she asked. "May I look?"

"Certainly," agreed John and she went across to turn the pages carefully, coming upon several images of the classical statues and one, titled Michelangelo's *David*, a male nude of such proportions that she stood completely shocked and blushing all over at the recollection of what

Noel had said.

Ellen turned over the page again before she could be caught looking at this enthralling and disgraceful creation, safely studying a garland of stone flowers when John came over to see what she thought of the pictures.

"If you are interested in the work, Ellen, you may call in at any time to watch us, and even draw and try carving yourself if it were something that you would enjoy learning."

"Oh, I can scarcely draw a straight line." Ellen blushed, diffidently unsure of herself as usual.

"Nobody can at first." John smiled. "You're welcome any time you fancy trying."

Ellen smiled back and thanked him, saying that she should not be in their way of working any longer today.

"I should be in trouble with Leonard for it," she said ingenuously. "He pointed out how much time I had cost you with the bicycle here."

"Rest assured, you're in none with me," John said easily.

Ellen left feeling a lot happier about her lapse than when she had arrived but with a mental image of Michelangelo's *David* in her mind which, conflated with that of Noel Ogden, was very disconcerting indeed in a new kind of manner. What had John said about not having him standing about 'nekkid' posing for his own statue? In addition, she realised that a whole other world existed beyond the prudery of her upbringing, thinking too of Albert Dewhirst photographing the two mill girls. Perhaps because it was art it was acceptable, she thought, although she did not think that her mother would agree. Ellen returned home feeling even more daring, cycling out to call upon men from the Clarion Club alone! Not that, being comrades together, that mattered anyway between them, she assured herself.

Chapter Three

The looms of Crossley Carpets, like giant threshing machines, thundered in the great complex of buildings below Lee Mount, the tall crown of its high factory chimney standing out in the smoking, busy landscape. Every day Stanley Jagger, among his fellows, tramped down the steep cobbled sets in his clog-soled boots to reach it. He counted himself lucky, in spite of a couple of fingers lost to the machines, in having such a secure employment. He had a sister married in Manchester whose husband worked producing Town Gas and he had even better conditions, for if you died in service (a not unlikely event) they provided you with your coffin, an expensive item for a working man's family.

Stanley had his own concerns about this, for lately he had experienced night sweats which might suggest the onset of consumption. He had told nobody and hoped the fresh air outings provided by the Clarion Club might save him from it, as cycling certainly worked the lungs. Today, his shift done by mid-afternoon, he was meeting Peter Lumb, who had just finished at the abattoir (another pre-dawn start), joining one another to nurse a half of mild in the Royal Oak during a long chat. True to form, Peter was loathing work at the abattoir. On a summer day, or with the wind in the wrong direction, the stench of the boneyard drifted all over town. Today was one such.

"One thing abaht it," commented Peter with characteristically grim satisfaction. "Them in their grand houses 'ave to smell it the same as the rest of us. I reckon I need to leave before I get blood poisoning there."

Both of these young men, while unmarried, had a great deal of family responsibility, with widowed mothers and younger siblings still at home to keep who were not yet old enough to bring much wage in themselves.

"I've told you, come in wi' me," said Stanley.

"Nay but, again, thank you. If I'm to be in a mill, I'll be back in my own bakery trade when Bradbury's gets back on its feet."

"That could be a long while, if ever. It were a bad fire, that one. Swallow your pride, man. Young Albert Dewhirst made you a good offer. The dye works isn't so bad as a temporary fix." Peter, who was wavering, Stanley knew, thought about it and shrugged. "How about we take a walk down there now and take a look at it?" Stanley suggested, to prompt him further.

Peter being agreeable, they finished up and began the mile or two's walk along the valley bottom. As they neared the factory, the water in the Hebble Brook was lurid with violently unnatural colours, the air filled with a chemical stink from aniline dyes. A bubbling brown foam pooling at the sides and clogging up the water suggested that, these days, you wouldn't find any speckled trout in it. Arrived at the factory gates, Stanley struggled a little for breath, coughing and wiping his face.

"What's up wi' thee?" asked Peter, frowning.

"Nowt. Just hot from walking," Stanley answered. That and being pink-cheeked from the exertion made him look the picture of health, so Peter just nodded at him. "Any road. We're here now," added Stanley.

They arrived as the working day was finishing. The factory gates opened and a crowd of men, women, girls and boys came out, the women and girls wrapped in shawls pulled over their heads. There was a great deal of lively chatter on their release and among them the two men saw Hannah Robertshaw and Sarah Greenwood, arm in arm and swinging along together. Peter and Stanley hailed them loudly.

"What's both of thee doin' dahn 'ere?" asked Sarah,

greeting them with pleased surprise.

"Just came to look at the place," answered Peter. "Albert said – about a job 'ere," he concluded roughly.

"Oh, yes. I remember."

"How is it? Here, like?"

"All right. They pay us, don't they?"

The two women exchanged their complicit looks and laughs.

"Come home with us if you want to talk to him."

"To Albert?"

"Hannah and me, we rent and keep house together."

"Wages must be good, then," commented Stanley.

"Aye but for what?" said Peter with a grin. "None of our business anyway," he hastened to add. "Albert – he'll be at your house, will he?"

"He'll call in a bit toneet. We always know when to expect him in the week."

The two women smiled at one another again and the two men exchanged a glance of their own. The bohemian set-up with Albert had not been commented upon by the Clarionettes for several reasons. It was not overtly spoken about, out of modesty and also because the Clarion Club prided itself on being a modern, forward-looking and free-thinking organisation. Besides, practically speaking, both girls came from among the town's many orphaned working children and so needed to look out for themselves as best they could. If Albert abandoned them, and either or both had a child themselves, they would still have each other going forward in life. Perhaps, too, he would not leave them to marry respectably elsewhere. Rumour had it among the Clarionettes that he meant to buy a house and set up with them both living in it with him, as his servants as far as the wider world knew. Stranger things had happened. He was not yet in his majority, though, and such possibilities remained in the future.

Stanley and Peter walked with the two young women down into a private kind of yard off a back ginnel where a small, one-time weaver's cottage stood slightly apart from any neighbours, offering a kind of privacy. It had heavy stone slabs for a roof and small, narrow windows along its side, showing its age and original purpose. Inside, it was very neatly appointed for a poor millworker's place, no broken chairs around the kitchen table and a dresser with a display about which the visitors exclaimed.

"You've a full matching tea set!"

"And a canteen of cutlery!"

Such grand things were only acquired as a rule following a wedding. There were other things on the walls of the downstairs rooms which they tried not to look at too closely – in the hall, in the kitchen and in the little parlour of which the door was ajar. Framed photographic plates of the two women appeared over and over, some with them dirty from the day's work and in mill clothes, others more daring. In one, there was a profile view of a girl stepping into a slipper bath with a fall of long hair covering all but one rounded buttock and the glimpse of a breast. It could have been either of them and neither Stanley nor Peter, fascinated as they were, wanted to be caught staring too long. In another, which the men scarcely dared to glance at, the two women lay together nude on a bed with gauzy drapes in a canopy around them and in what seemed to be a languorous tangle of limbs.

The intimacy of the photographs and the fact that they were on the walls showed that only one other person usually visited here. It was not long before they heard his key in the lock, another signifier of his proprietorship in the house. Peter and Stanley sat drinking tea in the kitchen with the two young women. Hannah and Sarah both looked so ordinary, still dressed for work, that it was almost impossible to think of them as the subject of those erotic poses.

"Peter Lumb's come for a word, Albert," Hannah explained as he came in and stopped in surprise, frowning at this unexpected invasion of his Seraglio.

"The office would have done," he said shortly.

"Aye, would it? Cap in hand, I suppose," retorted Peter, his quick ire rising.

"I didn't mean that," said Albert, visibly striving to accommodate the principles of the Clarion Club with finding the two working men making themselves at home in what he considered to be his kitchen, if not actively making free with his women. Subduing the arrogance it had come naturally to him to address them with, he came forward to shake hands and said more cordially, "I am pleased to see you both. It is only that – I was surprised to find you *here*."

"They were waiting at the gate when we came out, Albert," said Sarah. "So, we brought them home."

"Of course you did. Quite right," he said, but both Stanley and Peter had perceived his social struggle.

"Not quite the same finding us on your doorstep, is it, Albert?" said Peter, manfully avoiding the pictures on the walls and looking Albert straight in the eye.

"Peter…" cautioned Stanley but he too looked chagrined.

Albert chose to pretend he did not understand so as to try and recover the situation between them.

"What a grand time we all had together in Sunny Vale Gardens, didn't we?" he reminisced with a cheerful grin. "I hope we Clarionettes may do it again very soon! Now, Peter, let's you and I go into the next room to speak and the ladies will give Stanley another cup of tea whilst we do so."

Peter stood up to go with him, looking more amenable now he had been spoken to without any edge. They returned a short time later with Albert saying, "I will speak to the foreman myself and you may start as soon as you please, Peter. Father will not object if I say you come highly recommended but I can't say how it will go after that. I'm not in charge of who gets laid off if business goes slack."

"Understood. All reet. Monday, then. I'll have to complete this week out at the boneyard so's not to let my brother-in-law down." Albert's glance now passed between the two men and the two women. Peter gave a short laugh. "No-one will hear it from me," he said without elaborating. "Not but what I don't doubt folk already know."

"We are not seen together at the factory," said Albert. "That's all."

"Oh aye, that's all, is it?" said Peter laconically.

"Now, then!" said Albert, turning hearty and rubbing his hands together. "Are we all finished here?"

"*We* are," said Stanley neutrally, so that a faint note of disapproval hovered momentarily in the air.

Then he and Peter took their leave, politely thanking Hannah and Sarah for their hospitality. The two friends began the long tramp back along the valley bottom to town and their back-to-back homes. After a time, Peter observed, "A rum do, that lot."

"Aye. That it is," Stanley agreed and they continued on their way with neither choosing to speak further about Albert's ménage, for they were both, after all, Methodist raised.

***

Jane Ellison was with Eustace Horsfall at the Crossley and Porter Orphan Home and School, wondering if she should have come. There was an evangelical fervour about his approach to the ideals they discussed which made her fear a narrowness in him, that kind of pinching disapproval of pleasure for its own sake which could be so crushing in life. Jane had a shy but sensual nature which was already confined enough. She felt now rather like a sheep which, beckoned towards freedom from an enclosed field, found itself instead shepherded into what was really an even smaller pen which would be barred behind it. Jane could not fault Eustace's sincerity or commitment to improving the lot of these unfortunate orphan children. Nor could she wonder, he being a teacher and she a minister's daughter, that of all the Clarionettes, she would be the one he had asked to come. She simply did not wish to find herself being courted by him. Jane feared that an assumption might be made by association which would become accepted. One which would undoubtedly be approved of by her father.

Physically, she was attracted to Albert Dewhirst's looks and excited by what she had begun to guess passed between him, Hannah and Sarah. She was shocked, envious and curious all at once. Eustace was not striking and stuttered a bit when speaking, which made him spit unbecomingly. Once she had noticed this, whilst feeling for him, Jane was also rather repelled, which made her ashamed of herself. Altogether, her feelings seemed more complex than the situation warranted. Because she would have preferred to avoid him, she had guiltily acceded to his invitation to volunteer as a teacher helper at his side in the orphanage where they were always short staffed, it being a taxing, underpaid and demanding environment. Now, a scabby-headed boy, hair shaved for the lice he had scratched at, sat reading his letters with her, stumbling over them awkwardly and picking his nose without any shame at all, unconscious of it being bad manners. Jane, wishing she were a better person, felt quite revolted.

She had joined the Clarion Club seeking the freedom it espoused, not this. Bowling along in the open air in the mixed crowd, or being part of them at a meeting talking of great things, excited her. This, however, was just more of the womanly good works which she had been raised to be expected to do and Jane found that she did not want to do them. Eustace returned to the classroom a short while later and released her from the unpleasant child.

"Come and walk in the grounds, Jane. Have you seen the building's architecture? It is a marvel that so much work was put into creating such a beautiful place for these poor children to live in. Visionary. Not a hideous, punitive workhouse!"

Again, Jane could not find anything to disagree with. What he said was admirable and yet she could not find real pleasure in his company. It came to her, after a while strolling with him and being impressed indeed by the features of the building which he pointed out (its fine clock tower, the carved stone balustrades surrounding it, the generous amount of light provided by many windows), that it was because of his personal gravity, a certain stiffness of demeanour. Her horror of being found priggish herself extended to others and she saw it, rightly or wrongly, in Eustace. Perhaps due to this she turned the conversation now, perversely, to those who intrigued and titillated her interest among the Clarionettes, unable to prevent herself.

"Hannah and Sarah were orphan girls too, weren't they?" she remarked casually, to lead into it. "I wonder if *they* were sent here?"

"To Crossley and Porter's? They have never said so," he answered vaguely, looking aside. She could tell that he shrank from talking of them to her, out of delicacy no doubt, given her far more genteel situation.

"If they were, then they have not been made humble and ashamed by it, have they? They are not afraid to stand out."

Eustace glanced at her, trying to read from her expression how much or how little she might have guessed about the two women's circumstances with Albert.

"You mean, of course, their courage as working women in joining the Clarion Club?" he suggested.

"As to that, I imagine Mr Dewhirst brought them in, as he did Mr Ogden," she answered with provocative daring.

"Or, 'Albert' and 'Noel' as we are told we should speak of them," he said with a smile, turning to lighter aspects of the Clarionettes' unconventional ways. It still felt quaintly peculiar to be so familiar with one another's forenames.

"Albert, yes," she said, pleased to speak his name.

A smile touched her lips as she did so. Eustace looked away for a moment, instantly conscious of the reason for it. He flushed uncomfortably, his next words less fluent because of that and obstructed by the spitting stutter due to all the 'tees and esses' in them.

"Albert...Albert is not moved in his actions only by ideals, I think," he said.

Jane saw the fine spray of his spittle in the air and tried not to wince.

"Ideals are not just ideas, Eustace. They are to be lived by and there is bravery in that," she found herself declaring.

He paused for a moment and collected himself before answering quietly, "Only in those put at risk by it and who might suffer for it."

Now it was Jane who flushed at hearing Albert criticised by default, answering rather recklessly, "There is no liberty of any kind without risk! Or we should not be members of the Clarion Club at all."

"It is indeed a braver thing for all the ladies amongst us to be members of it than it is for any of we men," Eustace said, speaking more generally. It eased the awkward moment and obscured Jane's oblique reference to illicit love. "I look forward to hearing our next speaker," he continued. "I am sure she will be a firm believer in the freedom of cycling in the open air for women."

"I am sure she will be," Jane agreed on this safer topic.

They passed on to talk of other things before Jane left to go home to the parsonage again. She went away thinking of how Albert's dark eyes had flirted with Libby when she challenged him on the promenade and wishing it had been her whom he smiled at instead.

Albert featured disturbingly in her dreams sometimes, as did the two women. Sometimes she was a part of things with them, vague things, things that woke feelings in her which remained, restless with longings, in the morning. Once, in her dream, they were all strolling together and Albert put his arm about her waist, which she felt so distinctly that it still seemed like a physical reality the next day, so much so that she felt the strength of her reaction to it would make her shy when she saw him again.

***

Ellen and Leonard set out to visit Mr and Miss Stanger one afternoon, not by bicycle but in their father's chaise. The Stangers lived several miles out of town in a big house called Heatherfield. It was built of dark stone with side turrets, set at an angle in the dank valley bottom of the road to Rishworth, along from the old mill which Leonard said he wanted to take over. The house looked half-sunk into the hillside and as if its floors would run with water from the fern-filled slopes of the steep green fields above it. Ellen had never been here and nor had Leonard, but politeness now dictated that he ought to and he would not do it alone.

"We must both make amends," he said. "Even though it was I who spoke the words."

"Perhaps they will not be at home," said Ellen hopefully, a girl who hated the dreary tedium of obligatory afternoon calls in general.

"Perhaps not. Then I may just leave my card and have done with it," said Leonard, equally hopeful as they got down from the carriage and approached the front door.

Father and daughter were both at home, however, and the two guests were ushered into a sitting room looking out on to the green slope of the hill rising directly outside it. Square panes of glass in the big sash windows soon ran with rain as they attempted to begin conversation and keep it going. No refreshments were offered, but more as if it had simply not occurred to either host to do so than it being due to an intended snub. Mr Stanger was the uncommunicative kind, planted four square in his chair with his hands on his knees and answering Leonard's pleasantries in dry monosyllables. He looked quite comfortable all the while as Leonard and Ellen became more and more ill at ease. Miss Stanger, either from respect or in a quiet revenge upon Leonard, chose to remain in silence, looking at her father to speak. Possibly it was because she too was not one to trouble herself to be social. A book had been laid aside to which her eyes strayed, as if her reading had been reluctantly interrupted. Ellen could sympathise here and asked if it were a novel.

"No," replied Miss Stanger.

"Oh…I…I enjoy novels," said Ellen.

"Indeed?" enquired Miss Stanger mildly.

Another silence fell.

“I wonder, Miss Stanger,” Ellen burst out in desperation, “if you are interested in cycling?”

“Ellen is quite an enthusiast for it,” Leonard came in eagerly to say, a subject having been found that the two of *them* at least could converse about.

“Cycling,” repeated Miss Stanger without inflection.

“Oh, yes. It is most invigorating. And, and I am a member of a discussion group with other ladies present if it is at all the sort of thing which…” Here, Ellen trailed off.

“Miss Stanger has already said she does not read novels,” Leonard teased her.

“I do not think I did,” said Miss Stanger meditatively.

“No, no, Leonard, she merely explained that the book she was reading is not a novel.”

“I was not reading it,” said Miss Stanger.

The conversation faltered awkwardly again.

“My accounts,” said Mr Stanger. “We were perusing them together.”

“Ah,” said Leonard.

“They are quite healthy you know, Mr Rastrick.”

“I am delighted to hear it,” said Leonard, blushing.

Mr Stanger said, “As am I”, and chuckled to himself. Leonard expressed himself equally delighted to hear this too. “New-fangled ways,” said Mr Stanger, stroking his chin thoughtfully. “You had some in mind.”

“Well, I – I was merely speculating about modernisations in general.”

“Ah. In general,” observed Mr Stanger, taking no pity on him whatsoever and continuing to look at Leonard as keenly as before. “Then it is hard to comment on.”

“I think we have disturbed you quite long enough. Many thanks for receiving us,” said Leonard, who could endure no more by this time. “Come, Ellen, I think it has stopped raining.”

Miss Stanger looked out of the window and stated, "No. It is still pouring down. Your chaise is open to the elements. I think you must remain a while." So the awkward occasion stumbled on until the moment when the rain became drizzle and brother and sister exited in a great relief.

"I declare, that was the most difficult call I have ever had to pay!" said Leonard, as he roused the horse to a brisk trot homewards. "Never again!"

"Indeed not!" agreed Ellen and they laughed about it together as they went along, glad to have escaped.

It appeared that things had not been seen in the same light by the Stangers, however, for quite unexpectedly, Miss Stanger paid a call herself the following week, finding Ellen, Sylvia and Mrs Rastrick at home. Miss Stanger sat in the same way as she had done before, mainly silent and making short enough answers to small talk. She remained composed as Mrs Rastrick, in ever more rattled efforts to entertain, pressed more tea and biscuits upon her and spoke with increasing desperation of the weather. After what seemed an age, Miss Stanger consulted the clock on the mantel.

"I believe my hour is concluded and I must take my leave." She nodded and looked satisfied. "My return visit is paid," she said, as though describing an unwelcome obligation. "Oh" – She turned back as she put her gloves back on and made to leave – "you may tell Mr Leonard Rastrick that Father will be pleased to see him at any time. As will I. Good afternoon, ladies."

"Extraordinary woman!" exclaimed Mrs Rastrick as soon as the visitor had safely left the house. "Why on earth would Leonard wish to see Mr Stanger, or Miss Stanger for that matter?"

"Leonard has been talking to Father about their old worsted mill along the valley, Mother."

"Oh. Business matters," Mrs Rastrick said, sounding relieved.

"Did you consider it an affair of the heart, Mother?" laughed Sylvia.

"Of course not, silly girl!" blustered their mother, laughing at the very idea.

Ellen, though, wondered what was in Miss Stanger's mind, for she seemed a lady whose way of being was unusual and who saw nothing strange in being silent if she had nothing in particular to say. Their next caller that Saturday was Kenneth Butterworth, who arrived to ask how Ellen enjoyed the humorous book he had lent her, *The Diary of a Nobody* by George Weedon Grossmith. Ellen was amused by it but preferred the writings of Mrs Gaskell. She didn't add that *Mary Barton*, about working-class families, had been part of her inspiration to join the Clarion Club, whilst *Wives and Daughters*, which she was reading now, chimed with her own situation, a plain Molly to Sylvia's glamorous Cynthia, she felt. It was a pleasant enough afternoon outside and Kenneth next suggested again that a walk might be enjoyable. Both being invited, both sisters agreed, Sylvia making no quips this time. They set out to stroll along from Saville Park along the avenue of trees on Birdcage Lane and through to the woodland path below Albert Promenade.

"It will be dry enough underfoot today," Kenneth said, thinking of their ladies' shoes being less waterproof than his own boots.

They walked through dappled shade among the twisting branches of the holm oak wood. Last year's fallen leaves and exquisitely tiny acorns were underfoot. Treasures for pixies, Ellen had always thought them, collecting them up as a child. A black stone wall made a buttress at the side of the steep hillside above and below the straight path, where great rocks were tumbled slabs on the slopes. Tree trunks were vivid with lichen, rounder stones at their feet plumply mossed. Hooded crows made cawing, clicking calls in the canopy above and an earthy tang rose from the ground, mushroom damp under the leaves. As they went along, the voices of men could be heard, one in particular being loud and deep, resonating strongly.

"Watch the rope there, Peter! It's caught – let me come down to you to free it!"

There were men with ropes and grapple hooks climbing down the sheer, flat face of the craggy escarpment, without any support other than their wits. The hobnailed boots of the man who had spoken scraped on the stone as he walked himself down towards the man clinging on with upraised arms to the narrow ledge like the cornice of a mantelpiece, which he was stuck on due to his rope being caught on the boulders above. Reaching at a perilous-looking angle, the man descending strained to reach the rope and unhook it. Below, another man was trying to work the ropes as pulleys to support them.

Ellen had at once recognised the voice of John Henderson and realised that they had come upon the volunteer firemen doing a drill as suggested. It had not occurred to her that she would meet any of the Clarionettes while with her sister and Kenneth and she felt completely flustered as to what to do. Naturally, their trio stopped on the path, partly in sympathy and partly so as not to distract the men at such a dangerous moment. They stood watching as the little drama unfolded. Instructions were shouted back and forth from the ground by those who had a better vantage point than the men on the rocks and finally, after some tense moments when one or both looked likely to fall with serious consequences to them, the rope was unhooked and the two climbers succeeded in scrambling down the rock face. Kenneth applauded.

"Bravo!" he cried with impressed relief.

Invigorated, flushed with effort and the success of a daring attempt, the group of men turned, smiling. John Henderson, Peter, Stanley and Cyril among them, all saw Ellen standing by her companions, applauding too. Kenneth had walked forward to shake hands cordially with them all, impressed, so luckily the moment of recognition was covered by his enthusiastic greeting and asking why they were climbing there. Introduced to the volunteer firemen of the Neptune, he talked to them of having read many an article in the local paper about their brave actions. Ellen, beside her sister, smiled shyly at the men she knew but they did not give her away.

Kenneth politely introduced Sylvia and Ellen to them as Miss Rastrick and Miss Ellen Rastrick. John Henderson, in particular, looked admiringly at Sylvia, so that Ellen knew he had been struck by her pretty face and good looks in general. Ellen herself had been noting Kenneth's manner and wondering if he might prove to be a recruit to the Clarionettes if she were to invite him to a meeting. If she got a moment with him alone, she decided that she would do it. Not in Sylvia's hearing, though. Her sister would enjoy tormenting her by bringing her club membership out into the open. Len was one thing in the family and Sylvia quite another. Perhaps it was because he had seen Sylvia and wanted to prolong the moment that John Henderson now called after them, as they made to continue on their walk, "Miss Ellen, I hope you are quite recovered from your accident today?"

The three of them stopped and Sylvia gave her gracious, thrilling laugh.

"Great heavens, Ellen, did you have to be rescued by firemen when you fell off Len's bike the other week?"

"Her tumble happened near our stonemasons' yard,

didn't it, Cyril?" Cyril frowned at him for exposing Ellen but nodded. "I helped her up, that's all."

"But, surely, it was Mr Ogden who brought my sister home?" exclaimed Sylvia. "What a dark horse you are to be sure, Ellen!"

"It was Mr Ogden," John agreed hastily. "He'd just finished sitting for his statue with me when he drove Miss Ellen home after her tumble. I've been sculpting him as Alexander the Great as a piece for his entrance hall."

"Really?" exclaimed Sylvia, seeming artlessly impressed. "How interesting to find an artist amongst us!"

"More artisan than artist, Miss Rastrick." John laughed modestly, but he looked pleased nonetheless.

"I am quite recovered now, thank you, J – Mr Henderson," said Ellen, only just preventing herself from using the first name she had found it so hard to be easy with when the Clarionettes first started addressing one another informally.

Ellen's superficial grazes were mostly healed over, only her knuckles still bearing scabs on them and her chin, thankfully, no longer marked by the fall.

"I'm glad to hear it." He smiled.

"I am pleased to meet you, Mr Henderson, as my sister's other rescuer," said Sylvia, dipping her head charmingly.

John Henderson returned the civility with a slight bow himself.

"I'm delighted to make your acquaintance, Miss Rastrick." He turned to include Kenneth and Ellen, saying, "I'll be delivering Mr Ogden his statue later on today and I'm sure he'd be very happy to have callers coming to admire it."

The speech humorously incorporated a knowledge of Noel's likely vanity without mocking him for it and effectively offered another opportunity for John to see Sylvia again. It was deftly done but Ellen was disappointed by it. If he became one of Sylvia's admirers, however distantly, Ellen would never feel a friendship of any kind with herself was for her own sake again. She had begun to feel an affinity with the Clarionettes and especially for those like John and Cyril, whom she had come upon outside of that by chance and who had treated her so kindly after the cycling accident he had referred to earlier.

"Is that so? What hour will that be, do you estimate?" asked Kenneth. "I will be happy to bring the ladies once Mr Ogden has had a chance to establish it in place."

"Oh, probably about four o'clock. We've finished our drill for today and I've only to take it up in the cart with Cyril to lift it inside."

"If it is life-sized, I think more than two of you might be needed!" said Sylvia, lightly mocking.

"Not quite that, Miss Rastrick," said John, amused. "We'll manage him between us."

"Then we will meet you there. Mother does not have use of the carriage today and I will take you there and back in time for your dinners, ladies," Kenneth assured them, reasserting his own position by offering both of them his arm to continue strolling along, for which the path was wide enough.

With a backward half-smile at John, Sylvia took one and Ellen, saying goodbye, took his other. Kenneth turned to Ellen and spoke to her more about books, partly perhaps to show Sylvia that her flirting left him unmoved, although clearly, it had not. There was a certain tension in his manner now and Ellen knew he was not really listening to her answers. Still, it annoyed Sylvia to be ignored, however slightly, and that was always to the good, so Ellen was happy to answer as they continued along the woodland path, back up the cobbled sets to the top path and down the top of Albert Promenade to conclude their walk.

By this time, Kenneth was speaking to Sylvia of the view's clarity today. When they paused to admire it, Ellen looked for where the names of John and Cyril were carved into the rock for posterity, finding them half-concealed under a tussock of grass which had sprung across. Of the men themselves there was now no sign, nor the sound of John's resonant tones, so they must have left already in the other direction. Ellen smiled to herself about the secret alliances she had, and thought with pleasure of seeing Noel again unexpectedly today, thanks to John. Her spirits lightened at the prospect because one of the things about Noel was that he liked to play the goat and most of the others, herself possibly included, were on the serious side in the Clarionettes. Sylvia, however, had something to ask her.

"Ellen, surely Noel told us he picked you up on the Moor and yet Mr Henderson has told quite a different tale?"

"I fell quite heavily and I asked Noel not to alarm Mother," replied Ellen with hasty untruth. "I was quite grazed and they bathed the cuts before Noel brought me back, so it did not look so bad by then."

"I expect, being firemen, they are quite used to being in the rescuing business," said Kenneth supportively, for which she was grateful and Sylvia, for the present at least, left it at that.

Again, Ellen seriously considered asking Kenneth Butterworth to come to the meetings, not only for his own interest but to provide a buffer between her day world and that one. She was sure he would keep her council if she asked him to. There was Libby's position to consider, though, too, so perhaps she ought not to rush into it. Kenneth returned with the carriage as promised no more than an hour or so later and took both Sylvia and Ellen with him. Leonard joined them on his own horse and they travelled the couple of miles or so to Noel's hillside house, an exuberant gothic pile which he was adding to with extra towers, follies in the grounds and various garden projects. The terraced rockeries at the front as you approached up the drive now tumbled with flowers. A fountain played in the forecourt, plump dolphins with arching tails blowing trumpets of water up at a cherubic child in the centre. A cart stood outside, so that it seemed John and Cyril had already arrived with the promised statue.

Their party was welcomed in with great good cheer to admire the statue's ceremonial placing to perfection, which Noel was orchestrating as they arrived. John and Cyril were setting the plinth and then the statue to best effect beside the grand staircase, where Noel could hold court in image as well as in person. Cyril was ticking Noel off quite familiarly for insisting on moving its angle from where he thought it looked best himself. Noel seemed to take it in good part, while John laughed genially at the pair of them. There was something about this which seemed intimate and Ellen was puzzled by it for a moment, this not being something she had observed before. Of course, though, Noel had been to the stonemasons' yard to pose for the statue and no doubt on frequent occasions.

"Now then," said John, "that'll do. Leave it bide now and take another look at it later."

But this did not do for Noel, who insisted that everybody should come outside and look at it from the entrance and the side windows, a large arch of coloured glass on each side illuminating the hallway.

"You see, Cyril," he said plaintively. "If it were turned

just slightly, that terrific profile John has carved would be on better view."

"I don't agree," Cyril retorted. "It's set just right as it is for the light on it. You look *almost* heroic."

"*Almost*?" protested Noel, but Cyril gave no quarter.

"That's what I said," he answered refusing to flatter.

Noel laughed in amused reproach. "Very well," said Noel, surveying the statue critically. "Let Alexander stand there for the present and I will consider him again later. Come in, come in, everyone! We will take tea and I am sure I can persuade Miss Rastrick to play and sing with me to entertain you all!"

Noel had a grand piano in the drawing room and Sylvia was certainly soon persuaded to perform with him in another of the pretty duets in which they harmonised so well. Later, people relaxed together or strolled to admire the grounds Noel was working on. Ellen, walking round a corner with Leonard, came upon Noel and Cyril close together and in animated conversation. Cyril looked a little pettish and Noel placating, but their expressions smoothed as they turned to smile at Leonard and Ellen.

"Where is the other delightful Miss Rastrick?" Noel enquired. "I must let you all take a turn in the maze I have had constructed of yew hedge. Box, I am told, will not thrive in this harsh climate."

"Not much point in that," returned Cyril. "It is hardly grown. And we can all see *exactly* where we are," he added, looking at Noel meaningfully.

"I would love to see it," Ellen hastened to say, sensing discord and pleased to be at least one of the delightful Miss Rastricks. Noel sent Cyril to muster up the other guests, as much because it clearly irritated Cyril to be asked to do so as for any other reason, it seemed. As host, Noel monopolised Sylvia. Leonard, Kenneth and Ellen walked behind them, mingling with John and Cyril,

Kenneth telling Leonard all about their earlier encounter together in the woods and that John and Cyril were volunteer firemen. This occupied the conversation, so that Ellen was able to covertly observe Noel and Sylvia, both effusive together as they strolled along, aware of being watched. Ellen noticed that Cyril's attention was also upon the couple, a slight strain showing in his expression. All at once she realised he was jealous too, as she was. She had not realised that Cyril was particularly Noel's friend but he had certainly been pushed aside in favour of Sylvia being given precedence in Noel's company today. She supposed that he felt put out given their comradeship together in the Clarion Club on equal terms, and also because Noel was certainly lording it about. John Henderson and Kenneth were too much the masters of themselves to show whatever their own feelings were with regard to the attention being shown to Sylvia. It was probable that neither of them took Noel Ogden very seriously in any case.

The visit concluded with further general admiration of the statue, everyone drawn up in an admiring circle before it, then taking their departure. John Henderson received many compliments on his skills, which he accepted without any vanity about them. Then everyone left and Kenneth drove Ellen and Sylvia home, chatting pleasantly to both of them. Sylvia was now being quite as gracious to Kenneth as she had been to Noel. There was no reading her for any attachment of her own, any more than there ever was. There was a veiled neutrality about Sylvia which, whilst it did not make her demeanour cool, left everyone guessing at her inner self, attractive as her looks and vitality were.

Ellen was left thinking, with her usual dissatisfaction, of how she was always put in the shadow of her sister. Resentful, she gossiped with a reckless freedom about it all to Libby later on, having spent an evening looking out at a sky turned as dismal as her thoughts while wishing that Noel had bothered with her too. Leonard was out, Sylvia had gone visiting somewhere with their mother, which Ellen had declined, and Father was in his study. It was raining and so she had to stay in now herself. Libby was going efficiently through Ellen's wardrobe for anything with a button missing or needing another repair, while Ellen sat talking to her from the edge of her neatly made bed, spilling out her distresses from the day to her confidante, who made little of them. Libby had already been busy putting a box pleat in the back of two of Ellen's old outdoor skirts, so that she and Ellen could wear them when secretly out on their bicycles. 'Rational wear' it was described as, to enable women to cycle more easily. They had tried the skirts on shortly before, and Libby had just hung them up, hidden away among Ellen's other things.

"Never mind, Ellen. We'll soon be at the next Clarion Club meeting and hearing our speaker. You'll be with them all on your own terms then."

Ellen smiled, glad that Libby understood how different this was for her outside the house. Libby had been interested to hear about the statue's success and remarked that Mr Henderson might be a man to make his name one day if he could get a good patron for his sculpting, in Mr Ogden to begin with.

"Do you like him, Libby?" asked Ellen.

"I like him well enough," replied Libby, which did not seem like much of an answer at all to Ellen. Libby critically held up one of Ellen's dresses to the window after noting its hemline was down, from a heel that had caught in its skirts unobserved by Ellen at the time. "This needs mending. I'll take it down with me. Well, if you saw John Henderson making eyes at your sister, he's not the only one, is he? He's not a flirt like Albert Dewhirst though." The mention of Albert made her smile. "Now he *is* a rare one, all right."

"Libby!" exclaimed Ellen. "Have you met Albert alone?"

"How would I do that, do you reckon?" asked the other young woman, laughing. "Besides, I've got my place here to think of!"

"What would you think of me asking Kenneth Butterworth to join the Clarionettes, Libby?" asked Ellen next.

Libby considered it, putting away the last of the clothes and picking up those to be mended.

"He's young but he is not as wide-thinking in his attitudes as all that, from what I can see."

"He admired their being firemen and praised John's sculpting."

"As a gentleman, though, I imagine."

Ellen thought about the encounters.

"Yes, I suppose so. All right. I will not say anything to him. I don't want to be prevented myself from going if Sylvia finds out. Kenneth talks much to her when he can."

"Yes. That's one young lady I would never be telling my secrets to, Ellen, even if she is your sister," said Libby. "Right, I've work to get on with. So I'll bid you goodnight."

Ellen felt almost envious of the servant's tedious task of mending, for at least it was an activity, even though she loathed embroidering and hemming handkerchiefs herself. She had nothing to do and did not feel at all like reading. It was at times like this that the freedoms which the Clarion Club seemed to offer, a different way of life which did not immure you in society's given expectations of you as a young lady, were most attractive to her. After all, wasn't she falling into those limitations herself anyway, fretting over her feelings about Noel when she could be learning so much about other matters? The difficulty was that since they were all young, the attractions between them held more sway than the ideals they might be aspiring to and Ellen was quite perceptive enough to know it. Sighing, she got out the newspaper articles which had inspired her to join the club in the first place from her drawer and read them again for encouragement.

Chapter Four

Leonard was out frequently during his leisure time. It seemed, against all the odds, that he was managing to persuade old Mr Stanger and that his ideas for modernisation of the outdated worsted mill were gaining ground. Conversations over the dinner table also featured lively discussions between Len and his father about investing in new machinery for the bobbin mill. The advantage to employers was a smaller workforce. Len was promoting this with Mr Stanger as his example. Ellen, seeing which way this wind was blowing, put in some cautionary words. She knew, from heated discussions at the Clarion Club meetings, how hard it would be for an older person to gain any new employment if they lost their positions and Stanger's people had been with him for many years.

"Leonard, you speak as if there is no loss to anybody in all of this. But what of the older people who do not have the skills for the new machines and who have tended his looms all these years, tying warp and weft by hand on them? How will they live if they are turned off?"

"Why, they cannot work forever, Ellen and must finish one day soon. Better with some small benefit to them being paid off now to live on than find themselves unfit to continue such hard labour."

"Will he pay them any pension?" she was emboldened to ask, this being something that featured in the Clarion Club's discussions about working people's needs, so as not to become destitute once they could not work. If they had nobody to care for them financially in their families, as many were too poor to do, they were in danger of it.

"Where are you acquiring these odd notions?" laughed Leonard. "Those bluestockings of yours, no doubt."

"Bluestockings?" enquired their mother sharply.

"Ellen has little enough advantages without consorting with such women."

"Mother!" exclaimed a mortified Ellen.

"Well, you will speak of books, Ellen. It is not a thing most young men like to hear about."

"Let her alone," said her father, who of all of them had more sympathy with Ellen's temperament, being a reflective sort of man himself. "Leonard is right, though. A man can't pay his workers for not working. Where would he be then? He can, however, look after his tenants. Which is why I favour these model villages being built, so workers can live healthily. It is better for everybody and productivity together. I would be prepared to put money into such a thing myself one day, should profits lend themselves."

"But what will those workers do when turned off in their age by Mr Stanger?" persisted Ellen.

"If they have saved for their older years, and been as prudent as they ought to have been, then they will not be at any risk of penury, especially if a benefit is paid to them," remarked Leonard, spearing a peach from the fruit bowl to eat, his own cheeks scarcely more marked by life as yet than the fuzzy skin of the fruit itself. "I think Stanger is being more than generous. As a matter of fact, Ellen, Miss Stanger herself has raised that very same question, given that their workforce has remained so loyal to them in the valley."

That was interesting, Ellen thought. She had to leave the discussion there because her remarks were rather subversive as it was. She was always conscious of the need for discretion in order to get out to the Clarion Club meetings again. She found it even more interesting when she attended the next meeting of the Clarionettes and discovered that the woman speaker and advocate of cycling for women was none other than, of all people,

Miss Stanger herself! She announced that she was a member of such a group on the Lancashire side of the valleys and was quite eloquent on the subject of the benefits of its freedoms which, given her laconic style in general, came as some surprise to Ellen. It seemed that she was simply not a woman for small talk but, where there was something to say, she expressed herself quite freely.

Miss Stanger's club preferred to ride as women separately, she explained, as it caused less of a frisson amongst the general public. This allowed them to travel about more freely to support the cause of women's emancipation and suffrage for all under its guise. There was a strong movement for that in Manchester, to which her own cycling group was affiliated, she said. She had seen Ellen among the seated crowd listening and came to speak to her afterwards, her characterful face still coloured with the stress of public speaking, which it was clear did not come easily to her nature.

"I was highly amused when you asked me about cycling, Miss Rastrick, on your visit to our house that afternoon. For a moment, I had a notion that you knew my secret but then I perceived you did not. I'll warrant you were surprised to find me on the platform today in front of you. I take it your own appearance here is as little known to your family and your brother as my own activities are to my father and, until tonight, this district? I had not expected to find the sons and daughters of our local mill owners among this gathering. I was invited on the basis that this is a new group."

"We are quite new and I am not usually the only one of us, Miss Stanger. Noel Ogden and Albert Dewhirst are members."

"I do not know them well personally and I doubt they would remember me particularly," she answered. "Let us remain private about our membership in the circles here."

Ellen smiled, saying, "Leonard would be shocked, wouldn't he? Mind you, he thinks we are all bluestockings at my cycling group."

"My father likes him and it is well he will have somebody to take an interest in his mill in future years. I certainly will not but I am sure Leonard will be quite amenable to me leading a separate life if I do not embarrass him locally. And that I will not."

"Separate life, Miss Stanger?"

"Our engagement will not trouble either of us and is only to please my father while he is alive. He is not, in spite of what he says, in full vigour now. I'm afraid that he fails with some slow ailment the doctor warns him of being weakening as time goes on, although he is in no distress. It would make him happy to think my future secure with a man."

"But – do I understand that you are to be…you are engaged to my *brother*?"

"Oh, yes, it is quite understood between us. In private, of course. I would not wish to alarm your mother and father. The money is left to me, you understand, only if I am expected to marry. I will allow Leonard his portion to be as proactive as he wishes in the mill in due course. My own share will fund other activities."

"You, you do not intend to marry one another then, do you mean?" asked a totally bewildered Ellen.

"Oh no, not unless it becomes unavoidable for any reason. But we do not expect that to happen."

Ellen thought of her conventional mother and a small snort of derision passed her lips.

"It is to be hoped that Sylvia can supply Mother with her grandchildren, then. For she has certainly no hopes of it with me, not in her view."

"There is more to life than childbearing, Ellen, and

more chance of surviving to enjoy it without that burden," said Miss Stanger in her odd, dry way. "You must join me at one of my own meetings one day and learn more of it. There are many projects in view for women, education and labour."

"Leonard did say that he supposed he might marry you," Ellen reflected, rather rudely, still shocked.

"Yes. He did. Didn't he?" said Miss Stanger with a practical smile. "A most useful reflection when I came to consider it. Goodnight, Miss Rastrick." She left Ellen's side, drawn back into the main company of the people who had invited her to speak and who seemed to know her differently.

"Peculiar sort of woman and with peculiar notions," remarked Peter Lumb of Miss Stanger's speech to the Clarion Club. He and Stanley came over to say hello to Ellen, most of their usual group being missing from the occasion.

"Don't you believe in votes for women, then, Peter?" asked Ellen, as Stanley excused himself to speak to somebody else across the room, leaving them together.

"Can't say as I do or I don't," he said stoutly. "There's things that matter first afore that. Not having folk clemmed for lack of work for a start."

"You know," said Ellen, moved by these words to speak of it to him. "Miss Stanger's mill, well, her father's, is going to be modernised. It's one of the few old loom mills still working and if it is…"

"…Then plenty of folk will be laid off," Peter said. "You see what I mean, Ellen?" His face darkened. "Them as puts fires out know how to start one and all," he muttered, more to himself than to Ellen.

Ellen looked at him in surprise, connecting things instinctively. "Peter – that fire in the drying room at your flour mill…?" she asked, speaking low.

“Weren’t meant to tekk hold like that,” he answered defensively, with a startled jerk of his head at realising he had rashly spoken his thoughts aloud in the heat of the moment. “It were intended for a warning,” he answered, trying to keep his own voice down. “How could I know the Neptune didn’t have enough in her pumps for a blaze like that? Went up too fast for us to hold it and we weren’t near enough to watter for getting it brought fast enough. I got us there the minute it sparked up, raised the alarm myself.”

Ellen remembered how he had been hailed a hero, embittered one that he was, furious against the flour mill owners for cutting back on their wages due to what they called a shortage in demand, which none of the workers there believed in. There had been no doubting his equal distress at the catastrophe that had befallen Bradbury’s Mill and his fellow workers there due to the fire. His reactions to everything seemed to blaze up as strongly as any flame, unable to hold himself back from saying what he thought. Often, when he spoke up in the Clarion Club, they were angry thoughts, on his and everybody else’s behalf. He clearly realised now that he had given himself away to her as the fire-starter.

“You’re one of us in ’ere, Ellen,” Peter said now, looking at her intently. “What’s said between us in t’ Clarion Club stays in it.”

He had taken a great chance in admitting the truth to her given her position in life, as he staked this claim to Ellen’s loyalty. But it was his clear belief that he had it already as a comrade which moved her unexpectedly. Peter seemed a chaotic, driven sort of person. Ellen was rather wary of him in general but she found his intense gaze at her now compelling. She was suddenly very aware of him as a young man. This consciousness was something new to her and Ellen feared it might show, instantly embarrassed. Flustered, she hastened to assure him.

"I won't say anything. You know I won't!" To change the subject and because it was relevant to whatever his state of mind might be, Ellen asked, "Are you working again now, Peter?"

"Yes. Albert Dewhirst has found me a job in his father's dye works."

Here, Albert himself appeared,

"Sorry I was too late for the talk tonight. I have come to collect Hannah and Sarah to walk them home. How was it?"

"Do you know Miss Stanger, Albert?" asked Ellen. "Her father has one of the worsted mills along the valley." In her confusion, she was scarcely conscious that she had already gone against Miss Stanger's request to keep her identity from the factory-owning people they might both know.

"Stanger? I don't think so."

"She was the speaker."

"Aye, all about the emancipation of women. Yourn could have learned a thing or two," Peter suggested, with an ironic nod at Hannah and Sarah.

"Manchester's a bit different from Halifax, sounded like," said Hannah wryly. "Mebbe one day."

"You are free enough, Hannah, aren't you?" said Albert, with his engaging smile.

"Depends, dun't it," Sarah answered instead, rather bluntly. She and Hannah exchanged one of their private looks.

"Libby, I am glad to see you," said Albert, turning aside from this as Ellen's maid, who had been talking to John Henderson, returned to her side. "And you too, of course, Ellen."

He shook hands with them both, Ellen noting that, as

ever, she was the also ran where a comelier girl was her companion. She was disappointed not to see Noel Ogden tonight. Libby smiled back in a composed way which Ellen envied. Somehow, Libby also conveyed that her interest might be won if Albert worked at gaining it and he strolled aside with her for a moment, pointing out some bill posters on the wall which he said he had not seen before. Hannah and Sarah exchanged their inscrutable smile together about it and then John Henderson came across to speak to Ellen too. Now piqued, she interrupted his greeting with, "Before you ask me, John, my sister is quite well, thank you."

"Your sister is no part of the Clarion Club, Ellen," he said calmly. "I came to ask how you do yourself. No more tumbles from your brother's bicycle, I hope, since I saw you last?"

"No, none, thank you," she answered.

"Then I should like to ask you to ride out with me one day. For a practice. You could do with that," he added drily, with a smile she found herself returning.

"I'd like that, John. Thank you," she answered.

"I'm free tomorrow afternoon if you are and the weather's set reasonable."

"Reasonable," she laughed.

"Best we get round 'ere!" he answered, putting his cap on. "I will wait outside the gates for you on the road. Two-thirty suit you?"

"It would," said Ellen, pleased to be asked.

This agreed, the meeting began to break up. Albert collected Hannah and Sarah, Libby returned to Ellen's side and everybody said goodnight. Ellen looked at Libby curiously but knew she would be told to mind her own business, so did not ask what Albert had spoken to her about. In return, she made no mention of John's invitation to her for the following day. Returning to the house and each to their own quarters, Ellen went to see if Leonard was at home and found him there, just emerging from their father's study after some further discussion.

"Len, may I borrow your bicycle again tomorrow afternoon?" she asked, stopping him in the hallway.

"Certainly. I have no need of it then," he answered.

"Thank you. I have a fancy to practise again on it, for our next group ride will be coming up on a weekend soon. Len—?"

"Yes?"

"Miss Stanger. I happened to see her at my bazaar tonight and she suggested, hinted, well, stated, in fact, that you and she are, to be engaged?" she said in an urgent whisper. Looking at her fresh-faced older brother, it seemed wholly unlikely to be true.

"It will not be announced. A private understanding only, her father being old fashioned."

"But, Len!" protested Ellen.

"Needs must when the devil drives," he said with a grin. "She's a character, Miss Stanger. Quite forceful and persuasive when you get to know her. It is to help her as much as me to get on. Oh, you wouldn't understand at all, Ellen. You are such a romantic with all your reading."

"You can't *marry* her, Len!"

"She gains respectability by our engagement and I gain a mill. What's wrong with that arrangement?" Ellen stared at him. "Oh, we shan't go through with it. Once her father, well, not to be coarse about it, is no longer with us, we shall please ourselves what we do. Miss Stanger will be a woman of independent means and I will have shared in them. He won't leave it to her without that. Thinks a mill's for a man to run. Fortunately, so does Carrie." He laughed. "What a face! And on the girl who thinks herself half in love with Noel Ogden!"

Ellen blushed furiously.

"I have never said that I was!" she declared.

"I know you too well for you to need to," he said. "I warn you against it. Noel is certainly a man who will marry to advantage when he does."

"Why doesn't *he* marry Miss Stanger, then?" she retorted.

"She'd eat him alive. Besides, Noel will seek someone to look as well by his side as he considers he does himself," said Leonard kindly.

"Like Sylvia, you mean!" said Ellen hotly.

"Just like Sylvia," he answered. "But it wouldn't be for her own sake. Listen, Nell, you'll come into your own one day. You are the youngest of us. Give yourself a chance to grow up first. Have a bit of fun going out with your bluestockings and don't waste your time fretting over some pointless fellow or other. I worry for your heart more than any of ours, truly I do. Sylvia and I can take care of ourselves but I am not sure that you can."

Just then, their father came out of the study and they all went together to join their mother and Sylvia for a light supper before bedtime, as was their custom. Ellen wondered if their mother and father knew of Leonard's arrangement. Somehow, she doubted it, for it seemed rather too cool an affair to be approved by either of them, but her father she was not so sure about. He was certainly more of a financial pragmatist than her mother. Ellen decided to keep out of it.

Her bicycle ride with John Henderson was an exhilarating one. He had them push up narrow, steep cobbled pathways and walk part way, until they reached the height of Beacon Hill overlooking the industrial mass at the bottom of the valley, talking as they went of how they felt about life in general. The other side of the vista looked across towards Bradford.

"It is hard to believe our pleasure gardens lie just over

that hillside at Sunny Vale, is it not?" he asked, as they reached the smoke-blighted crest of Beacon Hill, scant of greenery.

"And the estate of Shibden Park and its woods over there," pointed out Ellen.

"John Lister has created an industrial school at Shibden, you know," said John. "An enlightened kind of man. I think we're lucky to have some in the richer classes who do have these philanthropic views in the area."

"If you were to become a rich man too, John, what would you do?" asked Ellen.

"Continue that good work in my home town and create the best sculpture that I can," answered John. "I'd be freed from knocking out gravestones at least, even though there's always plenty of business in *that*."

The grim humour was typical of the West Riding they lived in and not said in any heartless way.

"Those are grand ambitions to have," said Ellen, who had already said that she felt she had done nothing with her life yet.

"And you, Ellen?"

"I don't know. When I think of what's expected of me, it feels stifling. Or I can't imagine anything about it at all. And then, when I think of real possibilities for independence of some kind, I can't picture that either. It makes me feel stupid and frightened, as if I won't be fit for anything worthwhile."

She spoke with touching candour.

"It's only as you haven't been taught to imagine it, Ellen," John said kindly. "None of us have. That's why we all have to reach out for it ourselves. The Clarion Club gives us that starting point – a vision together will lead to a vision for our own lives and those of others."

"Do you really think so, John?" asked Ellen. "I just

see a bit of a muddle and vanity, and vying for position among people, the same as there is anywhere."

"Now what you're up against there is human nature." He laughed. "We're all up against that, in ourselves and in others. Let's hope we can rise above it, or we won't do any good at all really."

"How serious we are," she remarked next. "Sylvia would have you laughing. I expect you would prefer it." She spoke casually, for she had seen his reaction to her sister of course. Then she turned to him and said, "I thought I would introduce her into the conversation before you did, John, to save you the difficulty of it."

He gave a rueful laugh.

"Am I so obvious, Ellen? How rude of me."

"No, you have not been so at all but you have never invited me out before and I knew you would have a reason for it beyond assisting me with my cycling practice."

"Well, then – as you mention her yourself. I wondered if – if there were any kind of understanding between your sister and Mr Butterworth, who was with you both the other day?"

"There is no understanding between Sylvia and anybody as far as I am aware, and it is of no use to ask me what Sylvia's feelings are towards any person, for I have no more knowledge of them than you do."

She knew her tone was sharp and he withdrew a little, feeling it.

"Thank you for telling me," he said coolly.

"You are welcome," she said, brusque because even though she had brought Sylvia up herself, her sister had intruded upon the occasion.

"I hope we're friends, Ellen," John said next, studying her expression. "I'd not thought...given your own preference for," he said with delicacy, "someone else perhaps, that…that I might give any offence," he finished lamely.

Ellen's face flamed up, taking his meaning at once that he thought her offended because she might have a liking for him too and she was mortified by it.

"You do not!" she said roundly, and seizing up her bicycle, she got back on it and set off to begin riding back down.

"Ellen, take care! It's too steep here!" cautioned John. "Damn it all!" she heard him exclaim in exasperation, heading after her. "Wait! Stop if you can!"

Ellen realised he was right and not wanting a worse repeat experience, managed to steer off towards a sooty stone wall before the curve took her down the precipitous decline. She skidded to a halt and dismounted. John got off beside her. She looked down, biting her lip.

"I'm sorry," she said, having frightened herself as well.

"No. I am," he said. "I'm not usually as clumsy as that, I hope. I didn't mean to express myself so badly and I apologise to you, Ellen, as one Clarionette to another. Shake hands, won't you?"

The comradeliness of the gesture, putting them on an equal and friendly footing, let her raise her face again and she shook hands gladly enough.

"I want to be friends, John," she said, hoping to sound as mature as she intended and not like a girl jealous over her sister's good looks and the inevitable attention men gave her.

"Then so we are," he averred, "and nothing shall prevent it between us."

"Good," she answered. "I am glad of it."

Let him court Sylvia if he wished, and Noel and Kenneth too. Let the whole world get on with courting Sylvia. She would make her own friendships, lasting ones, with both men and women, Ellen decided, feeling better for their exchange now. John had shown he valued her as a person to stand shoulder to shoulder with, as they had spoken of earlier and that, surely, was something good to strive for? It was a different thing though, she realised, and would never be enough for her going through life ahead. Still, being a Clarionette made her a better person than Sylvia was, didn't it? Although, after all, since Sylvia's inner self was so veiled, this was hard to determine. Awkwardness over, Ellen and John enjoyed the rest of their cycle ride together and were able to laugh about clattering over the cobbles on the solid tyres and how it made their teeth chatter.

***

A change in the weather to dismal and blustering deferred the proposed group cycle, so that when it finally took place it seemed a very long time since their first ride out together. There was excitement in the air because Noel had invited everybody to take part in his next theatrical 'extravaganza', if they wanted to have a role in it or be involved in putting it together. For Noel, it was never too soon to revisit his role of Oberon and, besides, he knew the part and could concentrate on production, he claimed, plus there were lots of roles for extras, scenery makers and shifters, prompts and so on. There was amusement among the working men at the prospect but also some interest. Ellen had expected Eustace to frown and find it unsuitable for the Clarionettes' more serious aims, but in fact the teacher in him exulted in the chance to be involved in Shakespeare. Jane Ellison wanted to know who would be Titania.

"That will be earmarked for my sister, Sylvia, I do not doubt," Ellen said, "if she agrees to it."

"Oh."

Jane looked a little disappointed. Noel wanted to turn

the world upside down, though, by having the mill workers playing nobles and the rest cast as rustics.

"I'm not pussyfooting round the place in costume!" declared Peter Lumb. "What is it, any road? Sounds plain daft the way you described it. What do you think, Stanley?"

Stanley was struggling with a bout of coughing and breathlessness after the exertion of the hill ride and walk and just shook his head. They had gone this time via Hebden Bridge right up to Heptonstall, where weavers' cottages built of dark stone blocks clung to the topmost hillside after a steep climb, with the Clarionettes mostly pushing their bikes up the packhorse road to it. It was a forbidding sort of village, old, heavily built to withstand the weather and with something implacable about it. The views across from it were spectacular, however.

I have Albert in mind for Bottom," said Noel archly.

"Have you?" said Albert, laughing. "I don't think so. No speaking parts thank you."

He was exchanging admiring glances with Libby, both looking attractive in the outdoors, her soft hair blowing loose from its knot and his face smoothly browned by summer sunshine. They were the kind of glances that suggested attraction and Noel remarked it.

"How is your photography these days, Albert?" he asked. "Any new subjects posing for you?"

"Never mind my photographic plates. What's this about a statue of you as Alexander the Great?" retorted Albert.

"Oh, yes, indeed there is! And I intend to hold an unveiling party to show it off."

"I think enjoyment should certainly be a part of our club, but we should set ourselves to work too, shouldn't we?" said Eustace. "Jane has already helped me with our orphans but it might be something others of you might care to…"

Here, he looked around them with his characteristic frowning anxiety, full of earnest intent.

"God bless you, what a dear sort of man you are!" said Noel, with a rather false warmth. "I will happily come and feed your orphans, or whatever it is you do with them. I will send chocolates! I doubt they have many."

"That is kind but I was thinking more of their education."

"Slates?"

"Teaching them, Noel," said Eustace gently.

"I know! They can all come and be fairies in *A Midsummer Night's Dream*. You can never have too many of them in a cast."

"I think to see and be a part of a Shakespearean play would be a wonder to them and that is very kind also. But—"

His demur, whatever it was to have been, in order to pursue engagement in his work from the others, was drowned out by Noel declaring, "There we are, then! We have plenty of ladies amongst us to shepherd them about, do we not?"

"You missed our speaker last week, Noel," said Ellen with unusual mischief. "She has filled our heads with ideas of female emancipation, so I do not think that looking after children is our aspiration, is it, ladies?"

Hannah and Sarah looked at one another.

"Don't mind it, so long as we don't have to visit any orphanages. We haven't long got out of one," said Sarah bluntly.

"I am sorry!" Eustace hastened to say, conscious of a gaffe on his part.

"Yes. Some of us weren't blessed with a silver spoon to suck our porridge off," said Peter. "That's why we're here. Not that you didn't mean it well."

"I think you all have enough hard work in your worlds," said Noel more soberly. "I mean to offer you a diversion from it as my contribution."

"When is your unveiling party to be, then, Noel?" asked John Henderson. "I want the world to see my masterpiece."

"Soon. You are one and all invited to that! I plan it for a couple of weeks' time, when I have my provisions and drinks in."

"Well, we can't all come," said Libby. "I'll be on duty. Others will be on factory shifts."

The realities of other people's lives not being something Noel could do anything about, he left the conversation there for the present. Ellen said to him that she thought it was a splendid idea and this pleased him, for even Noel was looking a little uncomfortable about the dichotomies in people's situations which his largesse was pointing out.

Stanley had recovered himself now and said, "I think it would do everybody a great deal of good to get a look at something else in life. A play. A party. Life's too short as it is."

Although nobody knew his suspicions as to his own health, his bout of coughing and sweaty pallor after it had brought him more than one glance of concern. They had all halted for longer than anybody else had needed to let him recover himself.

"Are you all right now, Stan?" asked Peter, clapping him on the back encouragingly.

"Aye – just carpet cough," said Stanley. "All that wool flying about gets in a chap's lungs."

"Well, this fresh air will clear it out beautifully!" said Jane.

"Aye," said Stanley again, nodding over at John and Cyril to add drily, "I don't want to be giving those two characters extra work any time soon."

John and Cyril laughed at this sally, robust humour being needful at all times to ward off bad luck among the lives of the workers, or real ill-health in anybody. Stanley being young and well-built, strong from the work he did too, nobody thought him at any real risk and in truth, he did not himself. It was not to be admitted to. Noel teased Ellen about her little speech.

"I shall have to tell Sylvia where her sister is getting her ideas from!"

"Don't give me away, Noel! I will be prevented from being a member of the Clarion Club."

"Oh, no – I like our little secret," he said, which pleased her by making her feel that there was at least something private between them.

Remounting their bicycles, they rode along and back down to Hebden Bridge, stopping to buy bakery refreshments which Noel and Albert paid for. By now, the other people who had no money accepted this without prickly refusal, for they were all hungry and, again, it had been both stated and tacitly accepted that this was a part of what the factory-moneyed people owed to their comrades to offer. Jane and Ellen had little actual money because they were dependent on their fathers, a situation which made them, although far better dressed, less adult than the mill women workers with their company. There were inconsistencies in everybody's freedoms, with the most independent and free individual of all, Noel, trapped in his own invention of himself. Even Ellen could see that keeping up the constant performance must be something of a strain for Noel, although far less of one than putting actual food on your table to eat, of course. Ellen overheard a crabby little exchange between Cyril and Noel.

"Just because you *can* afford to please yourself

doesn't mean you ought to," said Cyril.

Although she did not know what it referred to, Ellen wondered if it related to Sylvia, and Noel's growing flirtation with her. There was a covert tussle between those two men somehow, which she had observed a couple of times now. Ellen was worrying over how it would work if everyone were invited to the theatricals and feared that her acquaintanceship with people from these entirely different spheres might come out. Jane was looking anxious too. Ellen wondered if this was on the same account, but on noticing Eustace hovering at Jane's elbow and seeing how she attempted to sidle away towards Albert's laughing group (Hannah, Sarah and Libby), Ellen realised it was not.

"Proper little harem he's building up," said John Henderson with disapproving amusement, while Eustace shook his head, troubled by it.

"I – I feel it is not right. Not at all right. We meet as friends and the ladies ought to be treated with equal respect."

"I agree with you," said John, frowning. "At least, Ellen, you seem to be immune to the general infection."

Ellen recognised that he was still proffering olive branches in recompense for his male presumption at their last meeting. She smiled slightly saying, "I think Eustace is quite right. It is a shame you were neither of you present to hear Miss Stanger at our last meeting."

"I felt," said Eustace diffidently, "that it would be more enabling for those women wishing to hear her to be present with less men crowding out the room. Given the subject."

The idea of Eustace, slight and uncharismatic as he was, being intimidating, was rather touching.

"That was kind but, in fact, I think it is important for us to share our views together."

"I agree with you, Ellen," said Eustace, after a considering pause.

"I do too!" declared John. "I braved it."

"You found it interesting?"

"I did – but I have to say it was a middle-class lady speaking, one with the leisure to give to action, and probably the money to do it, too," said John.

"John," Ellen found herself saying, as Eustace, nodding politely, his attention still on Jane Ellison really, moved aside to join her in the other group, "Miss Stanger has entered into an agreement with my brother Leonard – to do with…"

"I know about that!" interrupted Peter Lumb in his hasty way.

"Oh. Peter," Ellen cautioned.

She had not realised he was in earshot but, het up, he went on, "You know I do! And I don't like it! I know things have to move on but we have to find ways to do it without the ordinary folk being out of their livelihoods."

John Henderson was looking at Ellen curiously, realising she had been interrupted before she could confide something else but had obviously thought better of it now.

"How are you finding working with the dye works dynasty?" John asked Peter, trying for something more humorous to distract the man, but this too was not the right tack with tricky Peter.

"I don't like having to be grateful for it!" retorted Peter bluntly. "Stanley and me 'ad to go to that house where he – where he keeps his womenfolk. No better than a brothel."

"Peter…" his friend, overhearing, cautioned him.

"I know. I won't say owt more of what we saw," said Peter truculently.

It left an impression of libidinous secrets too dark to

be described, which had the colour coming up in Ellen's face like a shameful stain, ignorant as she was of what they might be.

"All right," said John, aware of her discomfort and closing Peter down. "Come on folks, we need to be getting back along the valley now, or poor old George will be standing fretting with his keys in his hand by that outhouse shed."

Libby and Albert cycled side by side, swooping along the road and laughing, Hannah and Sarah behind them like a watchful pair of guards. Noel and Cyril had paired off too, with Eustace valiantly attempting to remain by Jane Ellison's side. Peter and Stanley came next and Ellen and John, by default, were bringing up the rear together, but she did not go back to telling him about Leonard and Miss Stanger. John, though, was watching Libby and Albert and he said quietly, as they cycled side by side, "Libby, away from our group, is your maid, Ellen?"

"Yes."

"Would you feel able to caution her?"

"She would not respect my opinion about it."

"Then that is a pity," he said.

John, it seemed, was not the only person to be taking note of the butterflies of bright feeling fluttering into view between people. When they had reached the gloomy portals of the small, plain old church where George waited for them to return their bikes, and had wheeled them through the lychgate and snicket path into the graveyard, Peter and Eustace were both speaking to Libby. Peter spoke first.

"You're one of us, Libby. What are you thinking, girl?"

He did not mean one of the Clarionettes, as Libby knew, her throat flushing with temper. He was referring to their being working class.

"Oh? Are Hannah and Sarah any different from that?"

"Nay but *he* is!" said Peter, with a bitter vehemence.

"We cannot stand by and see you exploited," Eustace said more discreetly.

"*To spread good fellowship is the most important work of the Clarion Cycling Club*, quoted Libby, with flippant disregard of his meaning. "*Through enjoyment of a day out together*."

"But, Libby – Albert's way of living," Eustace cautioned, feeling his way delicately but evidently moved to speak out, his own morals outraged. "He takes advantage of you with his attitude. Surely you see it?"

"Are you Clarionettes or chaperones?" asked Libby crossly. "Am I at liberty to enjoy exercise among my fellow men or am I not?"

"He's got more exercise than cycling in mind!" said Peter crudely.

"Libby," cautioned Eustace. "What we observe, others will, and from your working life."

They all glanced over at Ellen, who of course had heard most of the conversation being only just behind them with John, but he had the presence of mind to say quite loudly, "No, Ellen, it's the high obelisk over there which I point out to you. He was a man who travelled to Egypt and brought back many wonders here, an antiquarian."

"I see it!" she replied, as if her attention were upon nothing else. "Your monument?"

"Indeed it is and it was a long and intricate inscription to make too."

Albert himself was looking as sunnily delighted with life as ever, laughing with Noel, Hannah and Sarah now as the bicycles to be stored were passed back through into the outhouse shed. Peter threw him a dark look of which he seemed unaware and then said to Ellen that he hoped she would keep them informed as to any plans for the working mills she knew of. She guiltily agreed that she would. The others within earshot had not been present at the conversation when he had spoken so openly of his views and how he was prepared to act, however, so none took him up on it.

"We must distribute the *Clarion* and spread the word," Eustace said. "Shall that be our next meeting and excursion?"

The Clarionettes were in agreement, since this activity was one of the founding principles of the clubs. Libby did not return home with Ellen this time as she still had time off until the evening and was going to visit her married sister, she said, and so Ellen cycled home alone, wondering if that were really where she had gone. She was having disturbing visions of Libby, Hannah and Sarah involved in some photographic tableau with gauzy draperies and naked limbs, for Stanley and Peter had talked of what they had seen together on the walls of the house and she had heard them. Ellen and John were cycling directly behind and the wind had brought their words clearly back to her ears. John had not paid any heed and she wondered, given his occupation and how loudly he spoke, if he were a little hard of hearing, for her glance at him showed him to be entirely oblivious to the other men's conversation together.

Upon her return to the big house in Saville Park, a full-blown family row was in progress in the drawing room. Leonard's plans had been discovered, or revealed to some extent. Their mother was looking distracted, their father evasive and Leonard defiantly dogged. Sylvia looked as if she were thoroughly enjoying all the sturm and drang going on around her.

"Never mind, Mother. I have an invitation in my hand

from Mr Ogden to a supper party later this week. Surely that pleases you?"

"Naturally but – oh, Leonard! How can you make such an announcement?" their mother exclaimed, handkerchief fluttering at her eyes to demonstrate just how upset she was.

"I didn't," said Leonard. "You asked Miss Stanger a direct question and she gave you a direct answer. That is her way, I am afraid."

"Now, then, Mary," soothed their father. "A young man must make his own decisions. I dare say you have not heard the full story yet."

"To hear it on the open street!"

"Actually, Mother, it was inside, since we had gone to look at the newly opened Borough Market at the time and were admiring the ornamental clock in the centre. You should go to see it, Ellen. It all looks very elegant, we thought. You were in there too, Mother, and came directly across with Sylvia to address us!"

"Naturally, seeing you unexpectedly with that lady on a Saturday afternoon."

"What was it that Mother asked?" enquired Ellen innocently.

"She asked if there were a reason for our new association together and Miss Stanger answered that it was because we are engaged to be married." (Sylvia here gave a snort of laughter which encompassed what she saw as Miss Stanger's shortcomings.) "Handsome is as handsome does," said Leonard, interpreting this correctly. "And Carrie has got money. I have plans as to how to use it."

"Now we get to it!" crowed Sylvia. "This is why Father is looking as cool as a cucumber, no doubt."

"Mother – Carrie and I have an understanding and the plan is for a lengthy engagement until we see if our future is suited. She has no plans to leave her father."

"No plans to...? Then, I hope I understand you correctly, Len?" said their mother, her brow lightening.

"Creaking doors," said Sylvia exultantly. "Len could be stuck with it for donkey's years! Well past his eligible best. It would serve him right for being so cold-blooded!"

"Then let us hope that you and Mr Ogden find yourselves suited sooner, or that somebody does," answered their mother crisply, for Leonard, being the boy, was of course her undeclared favourite.

"Oh, don't leave the responsibility all to me, Mother," said Sylvia with languid malice. "There is always Ellen to fall back on."

"I shall never marry anyone!" declared Ellen roundly. "I have higher aims in life."

"That will do – from everybody," said their father, sighing and folding up his newspaper as an abandoned pleasure unless read in solitude. "I am going to my study. You may inform me when it is time for dinner."

"I couldn't eat a thing!" said his wife. "And I am astonished that you can consider it!"

"I can face it with resolution, my dear," answered her husband drily. "And a good saddle of mutton I can face better than many things in life. I will have the courage for that, you may be certain." Leaving his family to their discussions, he went out of the room and when Leonard made to follow him he said, relenting in face of his son's discomfort, "Come with me, then, lad, and tell me more of what's in store for Stanger's Mill."

"Gladly!" said Leonard, leaving with him.

The three women were left looking at one another.

"Where have you been, Ellen?" asked Sylvia. "Was that Len's bicycle I saw you arriving home on?"

"Ellen going on a bicycle is the least of my worries," said their mother. "But I will get to the bottom of this other business with Leonard. He cannot avoid me forever!"

***

Jane found herself knocking on the little almshouse door with guilty fear, as if her arrival were as loud as a fanfare to the neighbourhood. There were several of these gothic little stone cottages with narrow, arched windows and doorways on the road below the woods of Albert Promenade, meant for the aged workers who had once worked in a long-closed calico factory along the valley bottom. They were now part of the Dewhirst property portfolio gained through inheritance, and this one Albert had acquired the use of for his artist's studio. He had assured Jane that sitters of all kinds came here to have their pictures taken and she need have no anxiety on that score. Naturally, she did, for although she was ostensibly here solely for the purpose of a seated portrait, she would be alone with Albert and her heart beat faster at the thought of that in itself, even if nothing happened between them. There had been no suggestion from him, by so much as the flicker of an eyelash, that anything would.

All had been arranged previously at the cycling meet in a most business-like fashion, although they had stepped covertly aside to speak of it. Jane had initiated the idea that she would like to sit and Albert had answered as if it were the most natural thing in the world for her to wish to do so. It was to be a present in a silver frame for her father's forthcoming birthday. Albert said he would choose one suitably sized for her expensive gift. This gave the escapade, as she could not help think of it as being, a respectable motive.

Jane thought Albert looking very handsome as he opened the door, smiling, to invite her into his studio. The downstairs sitting room was full of props, painted backdrops, ornate chairs, a white wrought iron garden bench and ornamental draperies of various kinds. It gave her the sensation of entering a magically unreal realm and stepping into a new world with different boundaries.

"Is this where you take all your photographs, Albert?" she asked.

"Not all," he said, with a smile at which she dropped her eyes in confusion. "This is where I take my formal portraits, such as the one I will make of you. Sometimes, I venture out into nature."

It was a simple word, nature, and yet it seemed to hint at more racy proceedings than a walk in woods. When she looked at him now, his dark eyes were quite steady and she could read no hidden meanings in his expression, and yet she knew he hinted at something. It made her look around and say, "I hope Hannah and Sarah are not here." At which he laughed aloud.

"No, Jane. I assure you that we are quite on our own. Now, let us set about choosing your setting." He studied the dress she was wearing, her best of course, and she had corseted her waist in to look as neat as possible. "I think the garden bench and the backdrop with a painted apple tree behind you."

"No! I would look like Eve about to tempt Adam. Father would certainly not approve."

"I had not thought of that," he said gravely but with a hint of mischief that she tried not to respond to. "Then, let us have a formal décor, where all will be as it ought."

He pulled forward a gilt chair and set it before, this time, a draped stand which made a backdrop with a vase on top of it. Jane took her place on it nervously while he stood behind the box camera and looked through it, then came out to suggest she moved her hands to clasp in her lap. He adjusted her position gently, moving her shoulders, and lifting her chin. The brief contact with his warm fingers was disturbingly intimate to her, dispassionately done as it was. He returned under the cloth of his camera to consider his shot again.

"Try to relax. I shan't come out to bite you. Or perhaps I will," he said, popping his head out from under the curtain and giving a mock growl, so that she half-smiled while trying to keep still. "That's much better!" he said. "Stay like that."

A few minutes later the portrait had been taken. Albert said he would develop it and frame it for her as promised. Next, they looked at a selection of frames he had and she picked one she liked. This concluded, the sitting was over. Albert made no suggestions about offering her any refreshment to prolong proceedings so, rather disappointed that everything had remained as seemly as it purported to be, Jane went to retrieve her outdoor coat from the back of the door. Albert politely held it so she could put it on. This drew them closer together and she could feel his breath on the back of her neck as he said, "There, all ready to face the world again." But then he stepped back.

Jane thanked him, saying that she would look forward to getting the portrait, after which he showed her out and she left to walk back to the vicarage. When it appeared, the picture would show a collected, rather serious young woman. It gave no sign at all of her actual feelings at the time and the fluttering of desire she had felt. When she did see it and realised how self-contained she looked, she wondered if he had simply not thought her interested but, recalling his semi-flirtatious words, she knew that he had felt her attraction. Perhaps her respectable position in life was enough to deter him. She had jealous thoughts about how he had ridden alongside Libby and laughed with her at the last cycling meeting whereas, inconsistently, she managed to put thoughts of Hannah and Sarah quite aside. She could barely imagine the reality of his situation with them, it never having been openly stated among the Clarionettes in her presence.

***

Ellen and Peter were out distributing the *Clarion* newspaper together. The club had drawn lots for who would ride in pairs and on what days that could be managed. Ellen had drawn Peter and today was their turn. She found him difficult. That resentment compacted in his core was always ready to burst out about something and often did. Yet now, without the others jarring at his class sensibilities, he was lighter, brighter company. Influenced already by Peter's conviction and carried along by his belief that they were sworn allies as Clarionettes, Ellen was swayed by his assumption that they were in natural agreement about things. And so, a conversation began today which drew her into an unintentional decision.

"Are you still at the Dewhirst Dye Works, Peter?" she asked politely as they set off on their way.

"No," he said shortly. "Laid off. Last in, first out. Can't complain." (This said as if he had every right to do so and everyone should know it.)

"Oh, that is a shame! Can't Albert help you again?"

"*Him*? Wouldn't ask it!" he said violently.

"Oh," said Ellen again.

"You know what he does with them women's wicked, don't you?" he stated, as if she were bound to agree. Ellen bit her lip and looked uncomfortably away. "He should get his comeuppance for exploiting his situation. That maid of yours will be next. And the vicar's daughter makes her eyes at him too. Disgusting, I call it. At least *you* don't do that, Ellen."

"No," she found herself agreeing with him compliantly, while wishing she hadn't sounded as if she was equally judgemental of Albert's flirtations.

"You're with the Clarion Club for the right reasons, Ellen: to make a difference to the common man."

"That's right," she agreed, with more confidence.

"Not like them other toffs. Noel Ogden, for instance," he said, with a curl of his lip, "I wouldn't like to say what *he* wants out of his fellow man!" He gave a harsh laugh. "Oh, I shouldn't talk like that to you. I know you don't understand, Ellen."

"No. I don't," she answered truthfully.

"Well, don't you worry, you're with me today and I'll look after you like a comrade should. Just like you'll look after me."

"Thank you," said Ellen uncertainly.

"Now – tell me again what's happening with that Stanger's worsted mill."

"Erm, well, Len and Miss Stanger are going ahead with modernising the machines."

"And you don't like that, do you?"

"No, I don't," she agreed, again truthfully.

"No more do I. Want to put a stop to it?"

"I don't want anybody put out of work, of course," she agreed.

"Well, I already am!" he cried hotly, as if stung afresh by the grievous injustice of it.

"I know. It's terrible," she agreed, hoping to calm him down.

"Here's what we do, Ellen. You and me will give out these papers down that way and go along to the mill there next. Then – you get down old Stanger's ear yourself. Tell him what they're up to behind his back."

"But – I cannot! And I think he has agreed."

"Not to all he's worked for being turned out to grass so Miss Stanger can go flouncing off on her bicycle with some rich women wanting more of what they have already! What, and your brother just takes the money without even marrying her?"

"Well, I – I didn't say they wouldn't."

"You did!" he said indignantly. "You told me before it was all agreed between them two, a false engagement."

"Well, I – yes, I suppose I did," admitted Ellen, wondering just how she had come to confide in unpredictable Peter about it all. His strength of character and direct way of getting straight to the blunt point, with such different manners than she was used to, made her feel she had to answer just as openly. And besides, Peter always sounded so convinced.

"You did right to tell me," he said roundly. "And now we can do the right thing about it. Try to slow things down. Together. Comrades making a stand."

His determined expression made her anxious and what he said confused her. What did he intend by it? He seemed to have come with a plan already. Ellen told herself that she did not know what he meant to do but of course she remembered his confession to her about Bradbury's. A growing dread gnawed within her as the papers were given out and they did cycle down to the old mill along the valley. Its chimney was quiet because it was no longer running at its full capacity every day, left behind by more modernised competitors. Peter, it seemed, had already known the mill was not in operation that day.

He had a rough knapsack tied to the back of his bike and he gestured at Ellen to get off quietly and follow him down the track to the mill. There, at the side where the delivery shafts led up and down the building, he broke through the lower door to set tinder, as he called it, and did the same at the bottom of the mill chimney itself. He poured flammable liquid over old rags stacked against bales of packed shoddy and dragged some into the mouth of the chimney's base. She opened her mouth to ask him what he was doing but said nothing because, of course, she realised she knew.

"Now, Ellen," he said, turning to her with a wild, warm smile of encouragement, "it's *your* turn to take part. Here's a box of matches. We'll both strike one and set the fire – there'll be no danger to life and limb, you may be certain, for the place is empty and I saw no watchman about the place. This is to cause small but effective damage, nowt too serious, I promise you. We have a duty to act where we can as members of the Clarion Club." Ellen hesitated. "Quickly! Or we'll both be caught here. A proud moment for you, Ellen, striking a blow to save a worker's job for them!"

His clear assumption that she was already convinced, fully committed to a shared decision they had implicitly made together in wanting to prevent the loss of people's jobs here, made her feel there was no turning back. She must prove herself as a genuine comrade, or earn his disgust forever for nailing false colours to the Clarion Club's mast and pretending to deserve its respect. Ellen alone shared his secret about Bradbury's, and because she had kept it she felt guilty by association about that fire already. Now, with the strength of Peter's conviction flooding through her too that this was a rightful cause, already believing herself to be embroiled in Peter's rebellion by default, Ellen struck the match. With a sense of disbelief, she set fire to the pile at her feet. The blaze took hold.

Peter took the matches and said eagerly, "My turn! We're in this together, Ellen! A blood pact with no blood spilt!"

He lit the other side of the pile and then knocked the blaze down to a slow smoulder, assuring her things would take hold slowly.

“We cannot let it burn down, Peter!” cried Ellen.

“We won’t! I’m a fireman, aren’t I? You cut along home now and I’ll be the one to send a message that the Neptune must come out! It’ll be enough to delay matters, this fire, so that no new work in there can begin before you alert old Stanger.”

“But – Peter – how will I do it?”

“Not in person. Write him an anonymous letter, lass, sealed and marked personal business so that there’s no danger of his daughter opening it. I take it he does all his own office work?”

Ellen thought of the rain-smitten windows in the drawing room, looking out on the steep green hillside which had run with water. No other ledger had been in the room but the one old Mr Stanger had brought out to work on with his daughter and no other letters had been there. Hadn’t Leonard complained of how close the old man played all his business cards to his chest and the hours he had to spend privately talking with him in his study?

“I believe so,” she answered reluctantly.

“Do it, then, the moment you return home and we will have done something to salvage people’s livings from the rise of any more machines!”

“When you spoke at meetings like this, people said the Luddites were long ago and lost their cause, Peter. Isn’t this the same act?”

“It’s the only act a man like me can make and to write that letter is the only one a young lady like you can make! None shall know your part in this action here, I promise you that, but *you* will know you did it, Ellen!” He expected her to feel proud and for one moment, a fleeting one, she did and nodded back with a reflection of his exultant smile. “Well, then! Now, let’s go,” he urged and they wheeled their bikes back along the path.

Ellen set off in the direction of home and Peter towards the town when their ways diverged again. She had glanced back, heartened to see no smoke rising behind and half-imagining that nothing would really happen. Upon her return to the house, she made haste to write the letter, anonymously, as Peter had told her to do. Len's engagement felt wrong to Ellen for so many reasons that a part of her wanted to do it for Len's own sake, however much she knew she should not. She simply wrote that Mr Stanger needed to question the engagement between his daughter and Mr Leonard Rastrick and would discover the real reason being the acquisition of his mill by Mr Rastrick alone, and that no marriage was planned of any kind. This too felt like something unreal, even as she hurried to post it unseen from somewhere away from the house. She felt she had washed her hands of something dirty that she could put behind her and pretend had never happened, certainly that she had never colluded in. All was quiet as she sat over her postcard album when her mother and Sylvia returned, chattering excitedly (in her mother's case) and both fresh from taking tea with Noel Ogden, it seemed.

"Oh, and he is to have a party next week for his new statue, Ellen, so you will be invited too and need not feel at all left out!" said Mrs Rastrick, unaware of the wound she was stabbing through her youngest daughter's heart with the hatpin she was pulling out of her headgear and pointing towards her with as she spoke.

Shortly after this the doorbell rang and an urgent request was made by the messenger for Leonard, who was still at their own mill with Mr Rastrick.

"What has happened?" asked Mrs Rastrick, concerned.

"It is from Miss Stanger. A fire at her father's mill has taken hold and she has asked for him."

"Great heavens! What a misfortune. Of course he will

go to them. Ellen, send our man at once to Rastrick's with the carriage for him."

"I will go too, Mother. I know Miss Stanger better than you."

"Oh, certainly," said Mrs Rastrick, relieved and having no liking for the discomfiting woman whom Leonard claimed to be engaged to. "I am sure I should only be in the way."

Ellen's face felt as if it were burning as fiercely as the fire might be as she hurried on her way for Leonard, and then with him towards the blaze she herself had helped to set in motion. As they neared, a black plume of smoke was clearly visible and a pall of it hanging in the air showed how long it had been burning. There was a great clamour of activity, the red fire engine Neptune there, pumps going and men up ladders precariously near to the smoke and buried in billows of it as they worked. Leaving the man with the carriage at enough of a distance for the horse not to be spooked, Leonard and Ellen got as close as they dared to. Miss Stanger came over.

"I have left Father at home – his health would not stand the shock and the smoke."

"How bad is it?" asked Leonard

"At first, the men thought it could be quickly doused. A cyclist passing earlier had noticed some smoke from the building and raised the alarm – he is one of the firemen too, so that was a very lucky chance for us. Even so, the wool packages have caught fiercely and the chimney is well ablaze. They are trying to save it and at quite some danger to themselves!"

Shielding her eyes, Miss Stanger gazed into the smoke, smuts all over her face from it already. In heart-thudding suspense, Ellen looked too and, among the shouts of those on ladders up the tall chimney, she could hear the strong, deep voice of John Henderson directing action. Water was being vigorously pumped out through the hoses and then, as she and Leonard went nearer, they could see other men at work there. Cyril was manning the pumps below, and he turned on seeing them.

"No closer!" he shouted. "The chimney is unstable now and may come down."

"Beware below!" shouts came from above as masonry began to collapse, the dressed stones hurtling down like red hot boulders from a giant's catapult.

"Get down! Peter! John!" Cyril was shouting up.

"One last try!" came the call back. "Keep pumping!"

Cyril handed over to a waiting fireman and stood back to get his breath.

"Ellen!" he exclaimed, surprised.

Leonard turned.

"You know my sister?" he asked, surprised in turn.

"Oh, Len, from when I fell off your bike!" she answered. "He's a mason with John Henderson up there."

"I see," he answered, distracted again by the blaze and Miss Stanger's increasing concern, both moving further away to see those tackling the blaze on the building.

"Ellen," said Cyril urgently. "You were giving out the paper today with Peter, weren't you?"

"I was, yes," she answered.

"Did you see this with him?"

"I – no," she answered.

"And yet – he raised the alarm," said Cyril slowly. "Just as with Bradbury's…"

Did Cyril suspect now, Ellen wondered? She felt a horrid jolt of panic.

"Do not even think of accusing him!" Stanley interrupted, coughing desperately as he spoke. Retreating from the smoke, he had heard what Cyril said. "Peter raised the alarm both times because he's a fireman like us. We see if there is risk of a blaze from smoke somewhere strange. He risks his life up there again to stop this one if he can, same as before! A man with no job at all to pay for injury if he falls!"

"Stanley, I do not accuse him," apologised Cyril, alarmed by the state Stanley, coughing so terribly, was in. "Calm yourself. And the Clarion Club will help with support for any of us who find we are in need. We all collect, don't we? And those who can do so give generously."

Stanley, overcome enough to step away from working on the fire himself and bent over now with the paroxysms he was enduring, just nodded.

"Get that man aside, he is made ill by the fire!" Miss Stanger cried, seeing him from where she was standing further away. She gestured urgently to her own carriage driver and called, "Take him up to our house and get him seen to with water. I think I must go back too and send for the doctor for my father as it is, Leonard. And he may look over all these men working here afterwards."

As she left and Stanley was taken aside with her, a cry went up and the men on the ladders trying to save the chimney were called out to, desperately, to come down. Ellen, looking up, saw Cyril run back and begin a scramble up from the bottom with a rope in answer to the alarm from above that a man was caught. She could not hear anything now over the noise of the fire. The smoke cleared enough to see a man high at the top pushing stones aside and down, trying to control their collapse to protect the man below him who dangled unconscious in the loop of the rope he swung in. He was caught beneath his arms and round his chest, having fallen already or been knocked out as he worked. The man at the top was John and the one hanging so helplessly was Peter!

It was a nightmare version of what had happened on the drill Ellen had seen them doing on the rocks of the

Albert Promenade woodland. Cyril and another man got to Peter and began to manhandle him below while John, high above, still tried to push debris down to the ground and aside from them. The water continued to spout out over all of them but clearly the blaze had got pretty out of control.

"John! Get down the ladder now! We have him!" bellowed various men up at the figure so dangerously at the top, still working like a man possessed. Finally hearing, above the uproar of the fire, that his comrade was safely below, John Henderson made to come down too.

Ellen found her heart in her mouth as the unconscious man was brought, soaking wet, alongside, to be put in the cart brought along now for any wounded. Peter's distinct features and taut expression were slack and pale. She gazed up through the smoke as John clambered down, hampered and now with masonry collapsing all about him. He had stayed too long, his partial deafness preventing him from hearing the men calling up to him to stop because Peter was rescued. Part way down, the ladder rungs gave way, burned through by the smouldering fire all about, and he fell.

Ellen cried out along with everyone as the smoke blew over. It was impossible to see what was happening or to get near because, at that moment, the fire engine was being urgently drawn back from the danger too and everyone was being shouted at to get aside. There was a thunderous noise as the chimney collapsed and then a terrible silence as the fallen stack settled, the mill building still standing alongside and afire. There were cries of, "My God!", "He's buried there!", "Find him!" and a frantic rush forward was made by all the men, but then another great shout went up as a figure miraculously staggered forward from the wreckage.

"They can wait till I'm proper dead to bury *me* under any stones! I'll not have a mill chimney be my monument!" John bellowed with a kind of mad relief as he was grabbed in a hero's welcome by the waiting arms of his fellow volunteer firemen, soot covered and his head and face running with rivulets of blood and water. His hands and fingers were ragged ruins. But he was alive and still standing!

"John!" cried Ellen. "I am heartily glad to see you safe!"

From the stress of the moment and the great burden of guilt she was naturally feeling, she burst into floods of tears. Her brother led her out of the way to their carriage saying, "Come, Ellen. It's the shock. We are only in the way here now and should go to Heatherfield."

The firemen were all brought up to the house as well, to be given brandy and water and have their injuries reviewed by the family doctor. Miss Stanger had summoned him on her earlier return to the house. Ellen had pulled herself together and found Leonard talking urgently to Miss Stanger of how bad the damage was.

"We must speak to my father," she was saying. "He seems to have had some other blow tonight. He spoke of a letter which came after I was called out to the mill fire. He has been most affected by it but says he will not discuss it until we are alone."

"Whatever it is, it cannot be as grave a matter as what has just befallen the mill. Let us tell him the worst is prevented and we will see in the morning what has become of it all. It is dark now and too dangerous to go near."

"I agree. We must not distress him further. Let us have these men seen to. They risked their lives for us. One remains out of his senses altogether and must be taken to the infirmary, the doctor says. I will pay for his care as it is our responsibility."

Ellen bowed her head in shame, for all of it was his own responsibility, of course, both Peter's and hers. John was having his hands dressed and the doctor shook his head over the burns as being very damaging and ones which would take long to heal.

"The sinews will shorten and the fingers may claw, I fear. What is your work?"

"I am a sculptor, doctor, and a monumental mason."

The doctor looked at him with compassionate concern and said, "Time may heal." But John's face revealed how much he recognised the gravity of the situation, although he bore up stoically.

"Aye, that it will," he answered, steadily enough.

John and Peter were both, as the worst wounded, taken off to the infirmary for the night to be watched over and to receive pain relief from morphine there. John's scalp wound would need stitching once he got there, the doctor said. Ellen went to John before he was taken out and said, "I am so, so sorry!" in the most heartfelt of tones, at which he tried to smile.

"No worse than a fall off your bicycle. Don't worry about me," he answered, making her feel even worse as he was taken off, Peter on a stretcher beside him.

The badly coughing Stanley was told to go with them too and the doctor asked him if he realised what ailed him, at which Stanley said that he had suspected it. When Stanley had gone and the doctor was leaving too, Ellen asked what he had meant by that. The doctor shook his head and said, "Consumption. Advancing. He'll not make old bones, poor lad."

Ellen thought how sad it was that two of the nicest people she had met at the Clarionettes were hearing terrible news about their futures tonight. One of them she could have done nothing about and the other's plight she was directly responsible for! She could not give Peter away by confessing herself because he would hang for that and if anyone died there would be deaths on their hands as well as the fire. She heard talk of staff having rushed to the mill at first and not everyone having been accounted for. It was a nightmare outcome for Peter's rebellious act that he had meant for bravery and she was equally implicated in the blame for it all. Ellen did not know how she would be able to bear it.

Chapter Five

News from Heatherfield the following day was that, while the damage was extensive, the mill chimney had been the main casualty. Thankfully, none of the workers who rushed to help *had* been caught up in it and everybody had got out safely, which eased Ellen's mind on that score at least. Leonard received an urgent note at breakfast and set off on his horse to the Stangers immediately. He spent much time there over the next several days and when at home had an urgent and private meeting with his father, the result of which neither disclosed to the rest of the family. Then one morning, dressed rather in their best for a working day at their own Rastrick Mill, Leonard and Mr Rastrick set out in top hats and serious looks. Mrs Rastrick, weeping, took to her room. Nobody would tell Ellen or Sylvia what was going on. What had happened as a result of her letter to Mr Stanger? It had not been spoken of. When Mr Rastrick returned alone that evening, it became clear what that was. The family was gathered in the drawing room for him to inform them, and he did so briefly.

"Your brother Leonard has been forced to honour his earlier engagement to Miss Stanger by marrying her this morning. I gave the bride away with Mr Stanger's agreement. The poor man is bedbound and sinking due to the double shock he has received of his mill being half-burned to the ground and an anonymous letter making an allegation that the engagement was a false one. Miss Stanger risked losing her inheritance entirely, such was his anger that his trust was being betrayed by them both, and he was set to alter his will in favour of a male cousin. Of course, Leonard and Miss Stanger, Carrie, I should say, as she is now another daughter, were able to reassure him by making their vows."

"Good God!" exclaimed Sylvia, breaking out into appalled laughter.

"Where is Leonard?" asked Ellen, stunned by yet another unlooked-for outcome of what she and Peter had done together.

"With his bride and his father-in-law at his future home. I will have his things sent to him tomorrow."

"Oh!" cried Mrs Rastrick in distress.

"Come, my dear, do not take on so. You will see plenty of your son."

"But not *his* sons!" exclaimed Mrs Rastrick bitterly. "How could you condone it, Harold? She is so much older than Leonard!"

"She is his wife, Mary. And as such will be made welcome here whenever she wishes it."

"Rastrick and Stanger's, Father. It has a ring to it, does it not?" observed Sylvia with cool mockery.

Rallying, Mrs Rastrick said, "And how much better will Rastrick, Stanger and Ogden's sound together?"

Sylvia just smiled her private smile while Ellen burst out with, "How *can* you, Mother?"

"Why, what is the matter, Ellen?" asked Mrs Rastrick in surprise.

"Ellen is rather fond of Noel, Mother," said Sylvia sweetly.

"I expect we all are," agreed Mrs Rastrick, looking with hopeful approval at her eldest daughter.

Ellen left the room, feeling beyond words altogether. Leonard actually married for money to Miss Stanger and both tied now when they had not planned to be! All her fault! Well, it was, for she had acted on Peter's suggestion, hadn't she? This was dreadful. She could not even share her deed with Libby, or make any reference to it. The marriage itself was supposed to remain a family secret, but when Ellen attended an emergency Clarion meeting called to pull together a subscription for the stricken Peter, ailing Stanley and potentially damaged John Henderson, all unable to work for the present, she found herself confiding in Albert. Since he belonged to her class peer group, she felt instinctively she could trust him with some part of the news at least. Peter was still unconscious in the infirmary, Stanley was too ill to attend and John was lying injured at home, unable to come. Ellen thought of something she could at least try to make amends with by telling someone of it. She pulled Albert aside.

"Albert – I was there at the fire with Leonard."

He regarded her sympathetically.

"Were you? Poor Ellen, how frightening for you."

"I heard what the doctor said about everyone. It isn't just Peter and John. Stanley isn't here because, well, because he has tuberculosis. The doctor asked him if he knew."

"Poor fellow, poor fellow, indeed!" said Albert with sincere compassion. "He coughed dreadfully on our last ride out, didn't he? I am not wholly surprised. We must see if we can do something for him too."

"I knew you would think so. The strangest things have been happening. Leonard has married Miss Stanger in secret."

"Your brother? Rastrick's heir becomes Stanger's, then." A momentary look came over his dark eyes which she could not read, then his expression returned to its customary candid warmth. "Well, he has made his own bed, Ellen. Let him lie in it. You doubt he will be happy?"

"I know he will not and it is all my fault! Well, partly."

"What do you mean?"

"Oh, nothing at all," she said, distraught at her near

confession.

"My dear young Ellen, what could *you* have done to affect his decision?"

"They were already engaged but it was not, I think, intended by either that they would go through with it. And I was told to speak to nobody about it!"

"I promise to tell nobody else, then. And since they *have* married," he answered with a smile to ease her conscience, "then they must have intended it after all. Now, let us speak to our friends here and drum up a good subscription. Noel is not here again but we will see him next week at his party and I will make certain sure to dun him for his contribution then. I am quite sure he will be generous with it."

"So am I!" declared Ellen of her favourite.

She spoke with such girlish enthusiasm that Albert laughed. Jane Ellison looked around at them with curious envy, wishing she were speaking to him instead of Eustace Horsfall, who was trying to persuade her to visit the school again. The evening was a success in terms of raising funds for the men. People spoke in turn with impassioned feeling about the deadly situations which volunteer firemen found themselves in and how dangerous the mills were, flammable death traps where workers were always at risk. This took up everybody's attention for the rest of the night.

***

Jane knocked once more at the almshouse door, feeling shameless, forward and also compelled to go. Albert opened the door in some surprise.

"Why, Jane!" he exclaimed. "You are come early for your picture, you know?"

"I have the date wrong?" she exclaimed, the colour rising in her cheeks at her pretence for arriving at his door.

She knew he would be there, for she had heard him speak at the Clarion meeting of what days he intended to be at his studio the following week. A couple who were newly weds and had recently joined the Clarion Club wanted to have their picture taken. They had selected one day and so Jane had made sure to arrive on another.

"A full week wrong – for I do not have it glazed for you yet in its frame, but you may come in to see it as it is, if you wish. I would not wish you to go away again disappointed."

Jane dropped her eyes, although there was nothing in his other than a hint of flattered complacency to suggest that he meant any more by what he said. When she went in he offered her a glass of sweet sherry wine in a silver goblet like a tiny chalice, in keeping with the medieval-looking props all about the photographic studio. It was like being inside a Pre-Raphaelite painting, Jane thought. He showed her the portrait, the serenity of her face belying how she had felt about her photographer, both at the time and now, but if she thought her desire was not visible to Albert she was wrong.

"It does not do you justice of course," he said, giving her a tender look.

"You flatter me," she answered, blushing further.

"No, I do not. Jane. Let us be open with one another. Do not be afraid of your pure, honest feeling. Our bodies are free to speak of what our minds are taught we cannot share, you know. But don't believe it. We *can* seek liberty in our lives. Haven't you felt this already, as a Clarionette?"

"And is that how you live, Albert? Freely?" she asked, thinking again of seeing him with those two women and the rumours about them all.

"It is how anyone may live, if they have the courage to act as they wish to and be free together. Will you have that courage, Jane? Or do you prefer to stamp it down and live doing good with men like Eustace, admirable fellow that he is?"

He spoke teasingly and without coming close but he had touched a nerve very accurately. Jane put down her glass, impulsively crying, "I would never wish to be with Eustace!"

Poor Eustace was standing in, at that moment, as the embodiment of stifled convention between them.

"Then be free," said Albert, coming across to her now.

The longed-for caresses were felt so naturally between them, gently managed at first by Albert so as not to alarm her untried sensations, that Jane really felt a belief in the freedom of it all which he promised her. She threw herself without caution into complete abandonment with him. They remained in long embrace afterwards, until Albert softly disentangled himself and said it was time for her to leave or she would surely risk being missed at home.

"Do we belong to each other now, Albert?" she asked, reluctant to let his touch loose from her, so that he laughed a little.

"Belong? Better than that, Jane, we are free together," he said and although he kissed her, he also left her wondering what he meant, but she felt unable to ask.

"Yes," she said anyway, wanting to please him by seeming to understand.

"Do not fear," he assured her. "You may trust me to have made sure there will be no consequence for you. I would never put you in danger of your woman's body betraying that free spirit by making you with child."

Jane had not even considered such a thing at all and the start of guilt from her upbringing brought her hastily to herself, so that she gathered up her clothes in a confusion. He stopped her embarrassment by helping her to dress himself, gently gathering in the ribbons of her stays to tie them and kissing the back of her neck at the nape as he did so. It was only after leaving that she realised he had made no promise of a repeat meeting between them. He had spoken as if they both understood they had made a choice at that moment and he respected her independence in that, as he knew she respected his. She had turned up at his door and he had let her in. The decision to do it had been hers alone.

Even as this reality sank in, an infatuated fixation on Albert began in Jane. Days passed with her hoping, against all reason, for some token from him, a note or a call paid to the house even – some sign at least, but none came. She felt a heart-wringing jealousy of the two women, Hannah and Sarah, who were said to be his lovers. Those rough mill women, she thought, who could surely not know love as she did! She could scarcely credit, in spite of the Clarion Club's ideals, Albert's association with them. Then, suddenly, she thought she understood. Of course! Albert knew she would come to see him again and had felt no need of saying it! The next time she saw him would be when she went to collect her framed picture, on the actual arranged date. When she did finally come to the studio door again, it was with such eager anticipation that she had barely slept, the image of him almost unreal in her mind, although she had thought of him constantly. She was proud of herself for resisting sending any note to Albert and letting down the notion of mutual freedom he had respected her for embracing with him.

"Ah, Miss Ellison!" he greeted her with rather loud formality, "Do come in. I have a sitter but it is no trouble at all for you to collect your picture."

Jane was full of abashed confusion and visible distress as she pulled herself together so unexpectedly from what she had anticipated. She entered the studio to find a mutton-chop-whiskered gentleman sitting stiffly in a chair attempting to maintain his pose.

"Do relax a moment, sir and we will resume shortly. Miss Ellison, have you met the vicar of St Jude's previously, the Reverend Victor Craddock? Miss Ellison's father is a clergyman too, sir."

The man stood up to bow and said with a smile, "Miss Ellison and I are already acquainted, Mr Dewhirst. How is your father, Miss Ellison?"

"He is well, thank you, Reverend Craddock," Jane managed to reply, feeling blanched in the face and lip and turning beseeching eyes to Albert as he produced a parcel for her.

"Now, I have it wrapped ready as you have already seen it," he said, with no private message in his civil expression. "I am sure your father will be delighted to have your image as his gift, Miss Ellison."

Jane realised, with utter shock, that she was being most courteously but firmly dismissed as he showed her to the door, very much in earshot of the gentleman within, who had resumed his seat in the studio.

"Albert," she murmured urgently when they reached the privacy of the doorstep.

"Well, Jane? We cannot speak now, you know."

"No. I see that."

"I knew you would. Just as I knew you would see liberty when I opened your eyes to it. It is a fine thing, Jane."

He gave her a smile and look of such warmth that her heart melted. She smiled back in spite of her dismay as he closed the door, retreating, only grateful to think that she had not given herself away so much as to lose his good opinion of her as a truly free woman. Well, she told herself, then she would be one and hold her dignity and her hour until she could meet with him on that basis again. She had not a doubt, after that look he had given her, that she would, and it was enough to buoy up her romantic feelings with some kind of certainty.

***

Libby was absent from the house during these events. She had been allowed to nurse her married sister, who was lying in after a difficult birth, but was now back. Ellen had both missed her and was glad she had not been present because she would have been afraid of confessing to Libby what had happened if she had been pressed to do so. Visitors were not being encouraged in general, to avoid the news of Leonard's marriage becoming widely known as a surprise in the neighbourhood. Mrs Butterworth and Kenneth were met with polite fictions that the household was afflicted with heavy seasonal colds which they did not wish to pass on.

Peering invisibly out of the draped lace net curtains round the window, Sylvia remarked to Ellen, as the callers went away again, "There they go! Poor Kenneth looked quite downcast when Libby refused them entry. Mother was glad to have pretty Libby away from Leonard, you know. My guess is, though, that she would have much preferred to be worrying about that distraction than seeing her beloved boy married off to Carrie Stanger!"

"Libby and Leonard?" exclaimed Ellen in unwary surprise. "But Libby has always liked Albert Dewhirst!"

"I was not being serious, Ellen. Albert Dewhirst? Wherever did she get that notion from?" Sylvia gave her merry, contemptuous laugh. "What fantasy gossips you and that maid are together."

Ellen coloured guiltily but said nothing, it being better that Sylvia thought this was all that lay behind their talk and changed the subject, saying, "Anyway, Miss Stanger,

I mean, Carrie, has been very good to the injured men, paying for their care. I am visiting them with her later at the infirmary."

"How strange to think of her as the second Mrs Rastrick. Even *you* cannot get your tongue around it, Ellen. Well, I will not be joining you. I have a dressmaker's fitting for the gown I am to wear to Noel's party."

Sylvia drifted off about her own affairs, leaving Ellen to her thoughts, which followed their own anxious circles over and over again at present, until she was forced into practical action of some sort in order to feel that any kind of atonement were being made. She now had free access to her brother's bicycle and before the afternoon visit to the infirmary with her new sister-in-law, she cycled down to the stonemasons' yard where John and Cyril worked, to see how the sculptor fared. She knew that John Henderson, at least, had been released now from hospital, only returning to have his bandaged hands dressed. She felt a guilty criminal indeed as she was welcomed into where John sat watching Cyril work at a gravestone. John's own piece was draped over like a shameful secret which he could not stand to look at, as she realised by his distressed look across at it when she asked how he did.

"It'll be a while yet before I can work, Ellen, but I'm doing better than poor Peter, still lying in his bed and not come to himself yet in the infirmary hospital."

"John here is doing very well, Ellen. I fed him like a baby, didn't I, John?" teased Cyril.

John gave a humorous grimace. "Aye, but I can hold a knife and fork again any road, so at least I'm off your dratted soup."

"I have brought some of our seed cake," said Ellen, producing a carefully folded linen napkin from the bag she had tied around her waist before setting off. "I thought you might like it."

"That I will. Bit of home baking never goes amiss," said John, smiling kindly.

"Thank you, Ellen," said Cyril. "I'll give it him with his tea before I get off myself."

"I didn't know you lived here alone, John?" said Ellen next, surprised, since most of the working men seemed to have families whom they still lived with, and he had spoken to her of his.

"I do. I send money along home to the rest up in Queensbury for Mother to manage but there's others at home old enough for work these last few years. Means I can stretch my wings a bit as a sculptor, not so tied to being a stonemason. Or – I believed I could."

"Oh, John!" she exclaimed. "Is that another statue?" For she had seen his look again at the draped plinth, an angry and frustrated look which he tried to suppress.

"It was. Is. Will be. Look, if you please to."

Ellen glanced at his expression to see if he really wanted her to look and thought that he did, as he nodded to her with a kind of grim encouragement. He was trying to repress fear and sorrow that his injuries might cost him his talent, never mind his labour, and she could see that the first was the dearer of the two things to him. Biting her lip with her own guilty emotion, she went to lift the cloth and saw the almost completed statue of a graceful figure with a beautiful face, a face whose features were an idealisation of one she knew well.

"Sylvia!" she said in involuntary exclamation.

"Nay, 'tis a nymph with no name. She is to stand in Noel's garden in a rose arbour."

"But – it is Sylvia."

"It's a fancy," John said roughly. "That's all. See, there's a stone angel memorial I began there with the same looks."

Ellen looked and saw that there was. She wondered that John did not see himself how her sister's face was the inspiration of both images.

"Noel commissioned it," said Cyril of the statue, glancing at him to be less harshly spoken.

"If it is ever finished," said John, still speaking more bitterly than usual, his emotional nerves as exposed as the physical ones in his damaged hands. "The angel's for our stock. Or will be. We carve memorials for folk to pick from."

Ellen's eyes filled with ready sympathetic tears, so that both men hastened to comfort her. This made her feel worse than ever and she made to leave, explaining that she was to visit the infirmary that afternoon.

"I am going with Carrie Stanger." Another lie by omission touching her lips, as she was not to tell anyone of the marriage yet.

She thought guiltily of how she had blurted it all out to Albert at the Clarion meeting, but he *had* agreed to be sworn to secrecy on the subject.

"A good woman – she acts as she speaks," said John approvingly, and with those words, they parted again for the present.

Ellen felt terrible about what had befallen John and at seeing how crestfallen his usually confident manner was. When Carrie (née Stanger and now Rastrick) appeared with her carriage to pick Ellen up to go to the infirmary, neither Mrs Rastrick nor Sylvia were present, or if either of them were, they remained out of sight – perhaps partly because nobody quite knew how to address their new relative. Carrie resolved this herself by shaking hands and greeting Ellen directly.

"Thank heavens that we may simply be Carrie and Ellen together now, without Miss Rastrick this and Miss Stanger that, although of course, as Clarionettes, we already are on those better terms. I think that will continue to be another of our secrets, though," she said, her hardy face as full of vigorous expression as ever. "Like your brother's marriage to me. Father has played us both false, I fear, by rallying tremendously now that he has me wed so a man may run the family affairs going forward." She spoke with fond humour, her real affection for her father showing through her joking tone. "Leonard gets on very well with his fate and is beginning to enjoy himself, for I leave him quite to it with my father and get about my own business, as I promised. Which reminds me, after this visit, Ellen, I must ask you to carry out distributing monies to the men's families – Peter and Stanley's, that is. And they must of course think all comes from the collection made, not from my father's purse. We must give them that dignity as fellow Clarion comrades. I am speaking at a meeting in Manchester and my dear friend, Fiona O'Brien, is expecting me for the night. I have a steam train to catch later on."

She cracked the reins with as much force as Leonard would have done and steered at pace through the traffic to reach the infirmary, leaving Ellen impressed and feeling both invigorated and comforted by her company. Ellen sensed in Carrie a strength of character which would never lure *her* into doing something so much against her better judgement as Ellen had done. She reminded herself that she was not the instigator and they were to see *him* soon enough. Her feelings about Peter vacillated and were at present hostile rather than friendly after her visit to the sculptor, John Henderson. The blame was not hers alone. She remembered something John had said to her himself on the day they had been out cycling up to Beacon Hill, when she had talked of feeling she had done nothing in life of use yet and he had said, "Whether it's nothing, a good thing or a bad thing, there's no point rolling in the mud about it. Just make your mind up to move on with what you *can* do. That's why we're Clarionettes, Ellen!" as they slogged up the last stretch to the top view.

It was good enough advice to apply to herself today, she thought. How different that day had been, and the one at Hipperholme's Sunny Vale Gardens! There would be others like it again, she thought, suddenly feeling a whole lot more sanguine in Carrie's solid company. Nobody need ever know about the motives that had gone so wrong. To ease her own conscience would bring even more destruction down and Peter might never even come round. As if these thoughts were enough to complicate matters in themselves, she and Carrie found Peter Lumb was conscious, awake and coming back to himself. When he saw Ellen, a puzzled and wary frown appeared as he stared at her.

"Ellen Rastrick," he said flatly. "What brings *you* 'ere?"

Ellen flinched slightly. Uncertain as she was about what he might say, she had not expected any rude rebuff, nor to have her name spoken as if she were the very last person he wished to see, although immediately, she could imagine that she would be. Did he think she had given things away? Or worse, did he not remember clearly and think she and not he was the author of disaster at Stanger's Mill? Uneasy sensations coursed through her as she left Carrie to do the talking.

"I am glad to find you awake at last, Peter. You, Stanley and John were all harmed in the fire you fought so bravely at my father's mill. Ellen has come with me from the Clarion Club, for a subscription has been raised to support the families in need while their working man is out of action. I hope it will reassure you to know it."

Here, Carrie reached to shake his hand cordially, while

Peter fixed Ellen, beside her, with a defiant and demanding stare. All at once, she understood that he did remember, and fully, that they had acted together. His look was also accusing.

"Aye, we risked our very lives to save that mill from burning down. Did it?" he asked bluntly.

Ellen thought that, given what had happened, he perhaps wished, with rancour, that it had.

"The chimney fell," Ellen blurted out. "And John Henderson will most likely never sculpt again because he stayed on top to save *you*r life."

She sent waves of blame back from her eyes to his and he settled back on the pillow with a bitter smile.

"Always the poor workers who get harmed. Always us. Never the owners, is it? Oh, no, never them as already has it all."

"Now, Peter, you must not distress yourself on anybody's behalf," Carrie reassured him. "All the men's welfare will be maintained and any who are not able to return to what they did, we will support to find other work through the Clarion Club. Independence for all in every sphere. That's our aim."

"That's *your* aim, mebbe," he retorted, with tired hostility.

Ellen took this personally at once as some kind of accusation against her own motives. She felt that she positively blazed with guilty dread and hated him for it. *He* had made her share the responsibility for this! He, who had laid the plan and set the fire! Horror-struck, she was silenced again by her culpability. Just then, Stanley came up and Carrie greeted him warmly, saying, next to both men, "We don't know how the fire started but it is made safe now. And when rebuilding is done, the newest measures against fire and accident will be put into its construction."

"That's something, then," Peter said grudgingly, and, of course, Carrie took it that he meant it as it sounded, that the sacrifice he and his fellows had made of themselves when battling the blaze would benefit future workers in the mill.

"It is," she said, nodding, "and so some good will come of it, as you say. Fix on that thought as you recover, Peter. Now, Stanley, you are looking much better, I think."

"Yes, thank you, Miss Stanger – the food is good for building strength back and there is fresh air and exercise to be had in the grounds here. I feel I'm picking up just grand."

"Good," she said, shaking his hand too, as Ellen did in turn, hoping that the improvement was a hope for his recovery from the dreaded killer disease.

Not all died of it and Stanley was a strongly made young man who had survived hardship into adulthood already. They had the addresses now for both families and Ellen was to go to them, in the company of Eustace, apparently, who Carrie said had offered to go with her and would be waiting outside for them now.

When they made to leave, Peter Lumb called out in his agitated, aggressive way, "Tell John Henderson I'm sorry for it. Ah'd never 'ave asked him to do it! I were unconscious, weren't I?"

It was as if he meant to exonerate himself from John's predicament as a result of helping him, Ellen thought, outraged by it. Closing his eyes, Peter fell back on the bed.

"He's not quite himself yet," said Stanley apologetically as he walked them to the door.

Ellen looked up at him. She was full of angry panic and only just prevented herself from saying that, on the contrary, she could assure them all that Peter was very much himself, the essence of himself in fact, so single-minded that he lost sight of all good feeling! How could he speak so about John, who had acted with such true generosity and courage? As if he understood something of what she felt, Stanley explained, "He's had things hard always, you know, Peter. And he takes things hard too. It might not have sounded like it but he's blaming himself now that he knows about John's hands. He meant that if he weren't unconscious, he'd 'a held John off from coming after him and getting hurt."

Ellen could do no more than nod and swallow her words back, bidding him goodbye and being hurried out by Carrie to meet Eustace, ready to go up to the men's houses with the money for their families. Carrie dropped them off in the town centre and hastened away herself to get ready for her own later journey.

"I brought some copies of the *Clarion* to give out," said Eustace. "On our way."

It was typical of his conscientious nature that he had thought they ought to make the most of the opportunity. Ellen felt grateful to be with somebody whose motives were what they said they were and did not bombard you with what sounded like simple truths, ones which you surely already agreed with and therefore should act on. She continued to be alarmed by how easily she had been persuaded into action by Peter, as much as by the outcomes of what they had done.

"I wonder if you ever see anything of Jane Ellison?" Eustace asked diffidently. "I had hoped she might come to the orphanage school again because she was a great help, but it seems her time is much taken up with parish work for her father."

"No," she answered. "We have never seen much of one another. But we will all meet at Noel's party next, won't we? For his statue unveiling!" She brightened and laughed at the thought, adding, "The famous statue."

"Statue?" said Eustace, sounding puzzled. "Is it another fund-raising party?"

"Whilst there, Albert Dewhirst will ask Noel to contribute to the funds for the firemen, certainly. He said he would to me."

"I – I do not think I have been invited," hesitated Eustace.

"But yes, you have! We are all invited, all the Clarionettes."

"Perhaps I did not realise. When is it to be, exactly?"

"I think in a couple of weeks' time and it is to be on a Saturday, when the workers will have the afternoon off. He is making it a tea-party extravaganza, as he calls it. Everything Noel does is an extravaganza, isn't it?"

"Yes," he agreed mildly. "I suppose that it is."

"I think it was very kind of him to make sure he picked a day when the mill workers would not be working, now that people can have Saturday afternoons off. It is only poor Libby who will be on duty at home while we are out. So far, we have not found a reason to ask that she be there, for Mother and Sylvia will be, so I will not need a chaperone and it is not her day off. If she turned up there unexpectedly, Mother would not allow it and her situation would be at risk."

"That is a difficulty," he agreed, without suggesting any solution to it.

Eustace did not especially like Libby, whom he suspected of finding him laughable and plain. Eustace was just as attuned as Ellen was to being found wanting by those more gifted with personal attractions. He was rather pleased Libby would not be there, if he were going to be. Choosing a spot on Commercial Street busy with passers-by, they gave out their papers to those who would take one and then walked out to the poor area up from

Dean Clough Mills where Stanley and Peter's families lived. For Ellen, although she had become more used to the smells of ordinary people who did not have access to personal hygiene and fresh linens as she did, going into the confines of the crowded back-to-back terraces, so poky, dark and ill-maintained, was difficult.

There was a smell of waste water from drains and sewage from the communal closet outside in the street. Inside it was that of mouldy damp, of unaired shared beds, of the wrinkles of old sweat in clothing still having to be worn. Grease, grime and grot hung in every corner of worn-out brick and mouldy plaster, however often floors were swept and the few pots washed clean. It was not the fault of the people living there, it was the poor conditions they lived in and the poor quality of the lives they had to live in them, however hard they had to work to afford it.

They were all the conditions which Ellen had heard spoken of with heated passion at the Clarion Club meetings, sometimes by the men and women she cycled with. The ardent audience applauded, crying 'Aye!' to those exposing the truth about things. What struck Ellen most, coming from her own big house so crammed with commodities of all kinds, was how very empty of all but people these insufficient dwellings were. It made her feel indignant and helpless. Also, she shrank from this poverty and, truth be told, from the people themselves. She found she could not help it, for all she spoke to the working-class Clarionettes of her walk of life being as much happenstance as theirs was.

But here, luckily, Eustace came into his own. His work at the orphanage made him completely adept at making a straightforward connection. He was down to earth, business-like about it. One mother invited them in, the other guarded the door with something of Peter's own antagonism. Eustace spoke to each of them regardless with the same polite respect, his awkward stutter-spitting not in evidence since he was quite at ease in all this. Where he and Ellen were invited in, they went in and exchanged some brief civilities without embarrassing the householder by looking round or expecting to sit down, then left again. Where they were not, Eustace handled the situation deftly at the door. Ellen stayed quiet and gratefully followed his lead.

"Good afternoon, madam," Eustace began, as their knocking on at doors was greeted with a look from each mother in turn which as much as said, 'What do you want?'

The women's faces showed they had a lot to deal with in life and that its surprises could only be dealt with day to day and one thing at a time. Was this visit a threat such as a debt being called in, a rental hike, or interference from some parish authority who had a mind to remove a widow's surplus children now the working son was out of action? Who had sent them and why? All this and more went unsaid as they warily answered the door to these well-dressed callers. Ellen felt self-consciously ashamed of herself, a privileged intruder in a world where she could almost be looked down upon herself for not knowing the half of it. It made her understand something of Peter's attitude. Neither mother said anything at first, just waiting for Eustace to explain himself, which he did with admirable aplomb.

"We have come from the Clarion Club with your son's subscription collection for the family while he is indisposed. Oh, but I do apologise, I see you did not expect us?" he frowned hesitantly. "Then there has been some miscommunication. You know, of course, that your son is a member of our club?"

Peter's mother said shortly, "My son's business is his

own", (no blame attaching to me for any of it being the implication) and Stanley's just shook her head noncommittally. Eustace pretended that advance notice of their arrival with moneys due to the families should have been given, and apologised for taking them by surprise.

"We are a mutual group and we subscribe together, so that if ill befalls one we all put to and cover any family needs as best we can. We are all friends and know each other from meetings and our cycling excursions. Your son is a great pal of ours," he repeated to each.

Both looked relieved, proud to hear it and astonished all at once in their different ways. Ellen and Eustace did not look very likely friends for either of their millworker sons. At this point, Eustace made to hand over the package of money notes and coins, eagerly accepted out of need and because pride now allowed it. This was not charity, although they would have had to accept that, and gratefully too, if it had been. Here, Stanley's mother invited them to step inside briefly so the transaction would not be visible to equally needy, inquisitive neighbours. Peter's simply took it, with that air of angry entitlement that Peter had himself, going swiftly inside with a nod and closing the door again in their faces. This abrupt dismissal was their second call and they were able to leave after that, much to Ellen's relief, as Eustace continued to say, "Good afternoon, Mrs Lumb. A pleasure to meet you", just as politely as he had done to the more receptive Mrs Jagger.

Both women had reached a point in life where, due to their age and hardships, they looked more masculine in the face than feminine. Mrs Jagger was stout from bearing many children whilst Mrs Lumb was dwindled by it. Ellen's mother was probably the same age but looked years younger. She had not lost her softness of feature, or so many of her teeth.

When they left Ellen said, "Eustace, you spoke so well to them. I found it impossible to find the words for anything!"

"Oh, thank you but it is nothing, only seeing all people as being deserving of every courtesy. I am a teacher, you know, so more used to talking to strangers, that is all."

Ellen realised that there was a very admirable principle behind this simple statement and that the difference between Eustace and others of the Clarionettes was that his allegiance was selfless and genuine. His ideals were more widely generous, like John Henderson's, than those who, like her, had the vaguest notions of a fairer world and were looking for some freedom for themselves. Thought of John made her exclaim, "Oh, Eustace, what of John? He was hurt too."

"John will not have it. He said he would soon be working again and the money should go to those with dependent families."

"I hope he will, then."

"He and Cyril Rastrick have a business together, don't forget. Cyril and John are both bachelors and I am sure Cyril will keep all the work going until he can."

"Yes. And Noel has two statues commissioned from John. One is completed, of course, but the other is not finished."

"I think John is the kind of man who will find his support in being determined he must get back into his own stride and trade and that will also be his best medicine. We can only try to keep a quiet eye on things,"

"*I* will!" declared Ellen. "He once told me I could go to the studio to watch them work and practise learning to draw the designs if I wished. I will do it! And perhaps I can be of help to both of them. I am no artist but I learned calligraphy and copperplate well enough."

"A fine notion, Ellen, and quite in keeping to offer

that, one Clarionette to another. He cannot object if you present it to him on that basis," said Eustace with a kindly smile.

"Thank you, Eustace. Well thought of."

"Yes, but it would be better he did not think it discussed at all, I imagine," Eustace went on. "Would you be prepared to consider reading with my orphans too, Ellen? You might find it helped you get used to the people you wish to work alongside in our organisation."

"Yes!" Ellen agreed at once. "I will be happy to."

"That is kind. When would you like to come?"

Ellen considered what engagements she was required for with her mother or sister and suggested the following Tuesday morning, which was happily agreed between them. She felt better in herself when they parted, as if she *had* tried to stop rolling in the mud about what had already happened, as John would have put it. Peter, she thought now, was perhaps simply afraid, and he was still too helpless in hospital to be running away from any arrest for arson. It was the first time she had thought of that word in connection with the fire and it made her shiver as she sat, alone now, in a cab taking her back from the town centre to her home in Saville Park.

Of course, that night was the one when there was a full report of events in the *Halifax Evening Courier*. Speculation was rife as to how the blaze had begun. The old-fashioned condition of the mill and the way things were stored in it, together with some chance spark that had probably smouldered unseen from the day when the mill had last been running, was thought to be the cause. Once more local fireman, Peter Lumb, who had been so heroically present at the Bradbury Flour Mill blaze, had been involved and fought bravely with his fellows. He was currently in hospital as a result in the infirmary. The reporter wished him and his fellow volunteer firemen well and concluded that another sad accident, fortunately without loss of life, showed how much safety measures were needed in the valley's many mills and factories.

After her father had read it all out to them over dinner and said, "You see, Mary, how needful it is for Leonard to improve affairs at Stanger's?" Ellen managed to get hold of the paper as her mother was prompted into another outburst about how appalling it all was about Leonard having married 'that dreadful woman.

Ellen took the paper to her room and decided on two things. She would visit Peter again by herself to tell him there was no risk of them being found out, and she would visit John and Cyril's workshop the very next afternoon. She would see Peter in the morning, then on to the studio. Her mother and father were out for the day, journeying to Leeds for Mrs Rastrick to buy a more in vogue hat and to dine out, by way of some recompense to her outraged feelings.

"What's been going on, Ellen?" Libby asked later, sensing that she was not as abreast of events as she was used to being and that Ellen, for once, had not told her everything.

"Only what you know of. Poor John injured. Poor Stanley ill. Peter in hospital."

"Not poor Peter then," she commented, brushing out Ellen's hair, which was getting past its greasy phase and now had a more silken sheen to it after that attention. She saw in the mirror that her skin was better too after cycling about in the fresh air, without that sallow, blemished look she so detested.

"No. Not poor Peter," agreed Ellen, and they smiled at one another in the mirror, having commented together in the past about *his* spiky and abrupt behaviour. "I wish you weren't going to miss the party on Saturday at Noel Ogden's, Libby. It is very unfair when you are as much a

Clarionette as anybody!"

"I know, I'm sorry to miss it too," answered Libby lightly. "I want to come to the next meeting though. I would have liked to hear Miss Stanger. She's another secret Clarionette, isn't she?"

Ellen nodded and said, "Yes, just like us, Libby!"

They smiled as confederates and then Libby hooted at the idea of young Mr Leonard being married to strange Miss Stanger, as was.

"We used to have a bit of a laugh, me and him," she said reminiscently but not in any tone of real regret, more as if he were a harum-scarum to be amused by, which, Ellen supposed, he had been really, so far in life. It was hard to imagine her lively young brother already tied to business responsibilities of his own, and married to gain them!

***

Mr and Mrs Rastrick had set off after breakfast and Sylvia had been called for by Kenneth and Mrs Butterworth to go for a drive in their carriage to visit some other neighbours. Having nothing else planned, she agreed. Ellen kept out of sight, just in case Kenneth invited her along too out of kindness. She did feel a little guilty because she still had his book and really ought to have taken the opportunity to return it but she was anxious not to be diverted from her own day's intentions. Putting the newspaper in her bag and tying it round her waist, she had a cape around her shoulders with a hood attached since it looked and felt very much like rain. The hills that circled Halifax town centre were closeted today under a lid of grey cloud as she cycled along to the Royal Infirmary first.

It was a new set of buildings in its own grounds, only recently opened on the same day, 25th July, as the new covered market, by the Duke and Duchess of York. It replaced the old Huddersfield Road Infirmary, which had been overwhelmed by local need. The new infirmary had been founded by many of the town's benefactors for public good, the Crossleys, owners of Stanley's carpet mill, being some of its key subscribers. She found her way to the ward Peter lay in and found him staring at the ceiling, as if his furious gaze might break through it and lift him out of his frustrated incarceration there.

"Peter!" she said excitedly, going to him as he raised himself on his elbows, surprised to see her.

"Ellen!" He sounded and looked, in contrast to yesterday, pleased and puzzled by her appearance. "I didn't expect you to come back."

"Look – I have brought the paper to show you." She looked around hastily but there was nobody listening to them, no nurse on duty and other men asleep in their hospital beds. "Are you able to read it?"

"What do *you* think?" he said, with a return to amused truculence.

"I meant were your eyes recovered enough to see properly, not that you couldn't read, Peter!"

"I know that, lass. I were teasing you. I do sometimes, you know. Is it – good news, for us, like?"

"Yes!" said Ellen, opening it at the folded page she had made ready to show him.

Peter read it eagerly and then gave a sighing smile of satisfaction at Ellen, nodding. He looked for once as youthful as his years, tension sloughed briefly, and what she read in his eyes now was alliance and expectation.

"I told you we were in it together, Ellen."

"But yesterday you were so hostile—" she whispered accusingly.

"I'm sorry. I thought, when I saw you with Miss Stanger, that you might have ducked it, slung the muck my way, being as how that'd be easy for you. I misjudged you, lass. You're worth knowing, Ellen Rastrick."

Ellen realised that this was high praise indeed coming from Peter and she could not help, for all her misgivings about him, feeling pleased to have passed some test. She also realised, however, that instead of this drawing a line under things as she had expected, or rather hoped, he saw her as having, after dipping her toe into dangerous waters, taken the plunge altogether. Well, she only had to say 'no', that's all she had to say, if anything further came up from him! Meanwhile, she would keep him on an even keel and out of harm's way, or out of the way of causing any more of it, if she could. If he thought this danger buried and himself safe, he might release her from any further obligations to prove herself true to her ideals. Just say 'no', she told herself again, if he pushes you.

"How are you?" she asked.

"Fit to be tied. It's driving me crazy, Ellen, just lying here now I'm awake!"

"I think you will be let go soon, Peter. You look well enough now. Why don't we go to Sunny Vale Gardens again when you do, have a row on the boating lake and feed the ducks? It will help you to convalesce."

She said this on impulse as a way of keeping him distracted from angry actions, scarcely expecting him to agree, but again, Peter looked pleasantly surprised.

"Why don't we?" he agreed. "It's a kind thought, Miss Clarionette. It were a good day out that, weren't it? All of us together?" He smiled about it more pleasantly than usual. "It'd be nice to do it again. Even if there is just us two next time."

She felt more relaxed at finding her offer was received in the spirit of their mutual membership of the Clarion Club and not misinterpreted, which would have been awful! Worse even than John Henderson's accidental suggestion that she might have favoured him. She would be seeing Noel Ogden at his party on Saturday and, for that pleasure, she simply could not wait. Feeling that relations between herself and Peter had been made as healthy as they could be and that she had settled his restless spirit down a little, she said, "Eustace and I took the money to your mother, Peter, and Mrs Jagger. Where is Stanley, by the way?"

"Out in the grounds for the air," he answered abruptly at hearing that news, his face darkening again. "So, you saw my 'ouse, did you?" he said, with a defensive sneer in his tone.

"No," said Ellen. "We knocked at the door and gave your mother the money, then went away again. We didn't want to be in anybody's way, you know."

She smiled at him, as if what she had found there had been the most natural thing in the world for her to see and no more remarkable than one of her usual visits to somebody in her own circle. Peter's brow cleared again and she thought, gratefully, that she had learned something from Eustace that day and managed to express herself just as he said was needed, that everybody should be spoken of and to with equal courtesy.

"Ta, then," Peter said with as much brevity as possible and there that subject was left.

"Would you like to keep the paper, Peter?"

"Nay, you keep it for us both, Ellen. Safe like." He made it sound as if the paper itself and the false conclusion in the article was some further secret contract between them. At this, her heart sank slightly again about the implications of keeping silence between the two of them and yet, what else could they do, in truth? She got up to go and he said, quite cheerfully for Peter, "I'm looking forward to that rowing-boat, Ellen, lass!" as she left him in the ward looking a bit less restive than when she had arrived.

It will be all right, she reassured herself, cycling off to go to her next destination at the stonemasons' yard. It has to be.

She wheeled her bicycle into the yard listening out for sounds of activity and called into the studio with a hesitant "Hello", before going in, hearing the sound of chisel and hammer ringing out. Cyril was working but she could not see John. Cyril looked round at her and stopped what he was doing.

"Hello, Ellen?" he said, a slightly puzzled query in his tone.

"Hello, Cyril," she said brightly. "How is John? I have just come from the hospital and Peter and Stanley are recovering well. I wanted to come and…well, to help." Here she trailed off for a moment before braving it, saying, "Do you remember, when I fell off my bike, John said I could come and learn to draw, or to sculpt even? Well, I can't do that, of course, but I thought that perhaps I could help with anything that's needed? I don't know, writing out, or copying, for your work, that John can't do just now and might save you time? I am good at calligraphy, if not drawing."

"Now that's a thought!" said Cyril. "Would you like to?"

"Very much! If you will let me try."

"Well now. There's a book of lithographs over there and – here, let me show you." Putting down his tools he came over, brushing stone dust off his apron. "Do you see these lettering designs? Do you think you can copy out the 'A' if I rule the page for you to size? Then I would like a tracing of this standing angel figure. That doesn't have to be to scale."

"I will try, Cyril."

"This will save me time, certainly. John's resting in the back – he has to take laudanum relief sometimes and that lets him sleep a while. He'll wake and join us soon. I think you'll find him more cheerful. He had his dressings changed and the hands aren't infected. He'll soon be able to begin exercises for the fingers and I don't think the doctor gave him false hope that some return of feeling and ability will begin soon." He looked at Ellen's transparent face and said, "Is there something else, Ellen, that you'd like to tell me of? What did Peter say to you today?"

"Oh, no! Nothing at all!" she hastened to say, blushing furiously. "Peter? Why, nothing! You know Peter."

"I do know Peter. Which is why I asked," he said, still studying her with considerate concern. "I cannot imagine him saying *nothing*," he added ironically, making her smile a little.

"Well, he complained greatly of being stuck in the hospital. I said I'd go boating with him at Sunny Vale when he was better, to cheer him up."

"Hmm. Peter's good at putting people under obligation to him. Don't let him push you around, Ellen."

"Oh, no, of course not," said Ellen unconvincingly.

"All right," said Cyril with a smile. Seeing her discomfited, he backed off for the present. She began carefully transcribing the decorative letter 'A' on to the paper Cyril had prepared. He pronounced it good and then said, with a mischievous grin, "Now, how are you with writing epitaphs? We can always do with some inspiration there. Noel writes some very rude ones!"

"I'll bet he does!" said Ellen and so it was that when John reappeared, woken by it and wondering what all the laughter was about, that he found Ellen and Cyril giggling to the point of tears and vying with one another to come up with the most mawkishly bad taste verses they could think of themselves.

"I hope you haven't been reciting Noel's limericks to

Ellen's tender ears," said John, smiling at the scene of helpless laughter. "They're highly scurrilous and not at all suitable."

"Oh, no, never that! We're just making our own epitaphs up. Ellen's worse than we are! Who knew such a naughty sense of humour was inside there," said Cyril, tapping the side of Ellen's head with one finger. "Go on, show him!"

They had been writing down their efforts, then sharing them with one another, aiming for increasing levels of ludicrous bathos. Ellen hesitated, then Cyril snatched her scrap of paper away and gave it to John, who read it out slowly and with a very disapproving face.

"*Here lies baby Abigail*

"*Who, truth be told, got very pale.*

"*Her chubby fists now hold a harp,*

"*No longer gasping, like a carp.*"

A short silence followed as he looked at Ellen with calm severity. She looked down, awkward and shamefaced.

"Priceless!" he said, bursting into hearty laughter himself.

"Oh, John! I thought you were thinking it was just dreadful of me!" exclaimed Ellen, laughing again in relief.

"I do," he said. "It's scandalous, that's what it is! Let's see yours then, Cyril."

"All right, but Ellen's was the best. Here."

Again, John read it aloud.

"*The water of life*

"*Has cost me mine.*

"*Beware, dear friends,*

"*Of brandy wine.*

"*Pass by the tavern's merry door*

"*Lest heaven opens its portals more.*

"Terrible rhyming. And the wrong liquor, Cyril. The water of life's whisky."

"Poetic licence, John. Are you rested?"

"I am, thank you."

"Ellen has come to do some work for us but I distracted her. See, she's started drawing out my gothic lettering for me from the book template, only then we went on to epitaphs."

Here, he and Ellen caught each other's eye and fell into giggling again, completely overtaken by it. John looked at the lettering.

"This is very good, Ellen."

"I will trace the angel next. I thought I might come to do what little I could to save time with things. I hope you do not mind it, John? You said I might come and learn to draw here and I might not be so in the way if I do it while you are recovering?"

It was nicely put and saved everybody's face.

"You are welcome to do it, Ellen. As I said, anybody can learn to draw if they put their minds to it. I'm happy to show you a few things, explain techniques."

"Thank you, John. I would like that!" said Ellen. "I will come as often as I am able. Oh, and I am going to read to the orphans too, at Crossley and Porter's School."

"You are? Eustace twisted your arm then, did he?"

"No, he did not at all, you know. He came with me to give the money to Stanley and Peter's mothers from the Clarion Club. He was so good with them and kind. He made it seem quite the natural thing to happen, so that they were happy to take the money in the end. I think they wondered what we wanted to begin with."

"*You* took it, Ellen?"

"Yes." Of course, she had offered because it was part of what she felt she had to do, being responsible for the situation in the first place. "I did not mind in the least."

(She had, of course because it had felt a very uncomfortable experience.) "I said I would like to do more and Eustace suggested I might come to read with the orphans."

John responded warmly, "I don't know about you, Cyril, but I'm very impressed indeed with Ellen. She's proving to be more of a Clarionette than any of us! Good for you, Ellen. Never say you don't know what to do with yourself again because, you see, you do. It's just as we were discussing up there on Beacon Hill. If we find our way forward together, you find your own way too."

"Thank you," Ellen said with modest pleasure, feeling quite glowing amid all this approval and beginning to forgive herself, if only slightly, for what could never be admitted to anybody else.

After this, under John's guidance, she carefully traced the angel design and then tried to draw it herself because he said her fingers and mind would remember what to do now she had tried it once. The resulting effort, although the tracing was fine, reduced them all to helpless laughter again. When she pronounced it done and John came over to look, having left her to complete it without him breathing over her shoulder to put her off, as he put it, he regarded the drawing with some effort at self-control.

"Well. It's not perfect but…it's a start," he said.

"It's ridiculous!" exclaimed Ellen, both of them unable to help laughing and, once started, none of them could stop, Cyril hooting at the sight of it too.

"I love it! I'm going to put Noel's face on top of that very drawing and give it to him at his party!" he exclaimed. "And have his head exactly that size."

The angel was so out of proportion that it had two enormous hands and feet, the thick neck of a steeplejack and the face of a pinheaded demon. The wings were the only real success, swooping out in scalloped lines to mimic feathers and stretched wide. It appeared to be wearing a dress, in the shape of a triangle, that for some reason stopped about the knees of its matchstick-thin legs above the huge feet.

"I will do better next time. I promise you," said Ellen, wiping her eyes.

"Of course, you will. What fun, though!" laughed Cyril, and John agreed.

"I'm so glad you came, Ellen. You've brightened up my day no end," he said, shaking hands with her, while Cyril gave her a light hug, so that when she left for home again, it was with a happier heart than she had had for quite some time.

Chapter Six

Leonard, late one late evening, walked through from his room to Carrie's, where he found her at her dressing-table with her hair down, plaiting it for the night. She usually wore it pulled back in a coiled bun right away from her face, an unflattering look but done so that it did not annoy her, unsoftened by the dressed curls in front which most other ladies preferred.

"Why, Leonard!" she exclaimed, surprised, for they had separate bedrooms by prior agreement but which her father and the household need not assume meant that they remained apart in, there being a connecting door.

"Can I come in?" he asked, smiling and walking over to her. "I haven't seen you with your hair down before."

It was a chestnut mane with a vigorous-looking spring in it, rather like Carrie herself.

"I should like to cut it off and have done with it," she said with an exasperated frown. "I did once when I was about twelve. Father was beside himself, so I had to grow it again."

"Oh no, don't," he said. "It's rather lovely. We haven't had much time to talk together, Carrie, since our hasty wedding day. You've been so busy in Manchester, and I've been with your father agreeing repairs at the mill. I wanted to say how much I admired the way you dealt with the fire – your self-control and then your kindness and generosity towards those men. And I hear that you and Ellen visited them together at the hospital? Ellen has written to me and I believe she is very glad of her new sister-in-law."

Carrie made a quiet, harrumphing noise, self-disparaging but pleased.

"Then I am glad too," she said, continuing with her plaiting.

Leonard put his hand on her shoulder tentatively and smiled at her in the mirror. At once catching his intention she said, "Oh no, Leonard. We both understand each other that this is a 'mariage blanc'. There is no need at all."

He withdrew his hand looking a little disconsolate, for it had not been likely that, of the two of them, *he* would be the one to find himself rejected. Although it had been clear between them that they would live their own lives and he was under no obligation whatsoever, Leonard's admiration of her had made him begin to warm to Carrie personally. He respected her resolve and was piqued by her evident independence. He now realised her underlying sophistication and envied the satisfying world she seemed to have with her women friends in Manchester, which was so full of activity and purpose.

"But – Carrie?" he said questioningly.

She put down her hairbrush and turned to him kindly, putting her own hand over the one still on her shoulder and patting it.

"Len," she said. "I could never risk childbirth at my age and there is still a chance of it. I have far too much to do in life to die before I have done it, and I would make an execrable parent. I have no patience for children. *You* are too young to want them, in my opinion." She smiled and he smiled in return, possibly with a little relief as well as rueful disappointment. "You may do as you please and with whom you please, with discretion naturally. Father may have rallied but his illness is underlying. I will not tie you to me for years to come. I promised you that and I will keep to it."

"Perhaps I would not mind that as much as you think," he said. "Now that I know what a remarkable person you are."

Carrie laughed.

"Let us be happy as we are for the present, then, Len. That is all anyone can ever plan for in this life, while hoping to do what we can."

"What a sound, practical girl you are," he said.

"*Girl*! Good heavens, Leonard! If you do wish for children in future years, you may have them by amicable separation from me. As I said, we will annul the marriage. Oh, I do not say it in any anticipation that you certainly will. I merely tell you that you will be free to do as you please during our marriage and afterwards, as will I be, just as we agreed."

"I thought that now – now that we are closer – perhaps that might include the two of us as well?"

"No, Leonard. I have told you of my reasons. Your person is a very pleasing one, I am not denying that."

"Thank you," said Leonard, who had surprised himself by beginning to find his wife physically attractive as well as admiring her character.

"I know," said Carrie, thinking of a way of providing him with more female company which would innocently divert him. "Why don't you invite Ellen to come and stay with us? I am sure you would enjoy it and so might she." She stood up, put her hands on his shoulders and kissed him lightly on both cheeks. "Goodnight now, Leonard. I will see you in the morning. Sleep well," she said, and so dismissed him.

Leonard retreated to his own bedroom again and examined his feelings, regarding his lively good looks in his own dress mirror. He was not used to having his appeal resisted and, accustomed to seeing the arrangement between them from his own viewpoint, which was that Carrie could never imagine him to have any bodily interest in *her*, he found himself surprised that it was she who really did not wish for any intimacy with him instead. In spite of himself, he found he wanted to impress her enough to find him attractive in return. Since he had wholeheartedly agreed to every aspect of her proposal when she made it, however, he had no grounds for feeling aggrieved at all. And he wasn't – he was, if anything, more gradually intrigued by Carrie than ever. He smiled at his reflection.

"Well, that's one in the eye for you, my boy. Who'd have thought it?"

He *would* invite Ellen to stay some time soon, he decided, because he missed his youngest sister very much indeed. Once again, Carrie had made the right suggestion to him.

***

There were a couple more Clarion Club meetings arranged due to the activity of distributing the papers and collecting subscription moneys to keep the families of the injured firemen going. New members were joining and there was a sense of excitement, the feeling that something fresh really was stirring. It drew in more people, who came to it with their own reasons for wanting to impress in this new goldfish bowl of activity. Among them was Felix Sykes, the new curate at St Jude's, whose vicar Jane had met at Albert's studio. His arrival was sending a few ripples through the Clarionettes. He took a forensic approach to dissecting their observations, like a scientist pulling the wings off butterflies to see if they could grow new and better ones, opinions which he might deign to listen to. He was almost as scathing a character as Peter Lumb, in the way that people who pride themselves in not suffering fools gladly like to be. Peter Lumb himself, being out of hospital now for some days and recovered but still not in work, had attended the meetings and met him too. His view of Felix Sykes, when Ellen asked him later what he thought of this particular newcomer, was succinct.

"Arrogant sod." The rough tone and colourful language, while shocking, made Ellen, who was rowing them both, as promised, in a boat at Sunny Vale Gardens at the time, laugh out loud.

"Peter!" she exclaimed.

"Well, it's obvious that he is, in't it?" he said with a bit of a grin. "Here, let me row for a bit. I'm strong enough for a turn now. I've picked up again after all that cycling," he added because in spite of insisting he was quite able for it, the strenuous ride up the hills to get there had been stop and start for some of the way, pausing for rests.

Ellen gladly gave him the oars and trailed her hands in the water to cool them, watching the surface dimple as a slight, warm breeze passed through. It was a humid, overcast sort of day and there was a heaviness in the air. At the last meeting, Felix Sykes had been involving her in a discussion about the need for more free public libraries (something which had been a topic of debate at the meeting) and what kind of literature they ought to provide for people's edification. Being a curate, he felt some censorship would be required for the great unwashed. It was too big a subject for Ellen, who was struggling to answer when Peter, who had been looking on, came to Ellen's rescue.

"Nah then, Ellen, lass. When's tha tekkin' me boating, like tha said thee would in't hospital?" he asked as broadly as he could manage, to offend Felix's ears if possible.

In her gratitude, she had offered to do so as soon as possible and so here they were together. Peter's light hair was caught in a brief gleam of sunshine, lifted by the air into straight little feathers and he looked nicer than usual, being relaxed. He had been nicer than usual too, in Ellen's company today.

"I suppose he's interesting," she said tentatively, of Felix Sykes.

"He'd like to be," said Peter darkly. "Not the same thing. Don't be fooled by the like of '*im*, Nell. You're better than that."

Ellen realised two things at once. He had used her brother's diminutive for her name, an affectionate term, and he was laying some private, unspoken claim to her interest himself. She looked up at him because his downright certainty and way of being with her made her feel some kind of pull back, not just the confusion she had felt since he persuaded her to help in setting the fire at Stanger's Mill. She smiled and he smiled in return. For once, it felt quite natural between them to be friends.

"Let's go and have tea and a bun after this from the café, Peter?" suggested Ellen.

"All right, Miss. Your wish is my command," he answered with ironic gallantry.

They carried on around the Alexandra Boating Lake for a little while more and were sitting under the bandstand with their refreshments when the threatening thunderstorm briefly broke. They smiled at those people caught out in it who were shrieking and running for shelter.

"My mother calls downpours like this 'rain coming down like stair-rods'," said Ellen, as a crash of thunder broke overhead. "Funny sort of saying, isn't it?"

"You aren't scared of it, are you, the storm?" commented Peter, impressed.

"Oh, no! I love thunder."

"Come on, then, lass. Let's get out in it where we can see the lightning."

He grabbed her hand and pulled her out into the rain, both of them scrambling out and up a hillock as others were rushing under the cover of the bandstand. He pulled her up behind him and they landed at the top under some trees, panting and soaked in warm rain, to watch the lightning zipping across the higher hillsides surrounding them.

"We're not on't high ground, so we should be all reet," said Peter.

"Come away from these trees though," said Ellen, pulling at his hand in turn to drag him to a safer spot.

"Sheet lightning. It's forked as is dangerous," said Peter, resisting. "We're safe here." Realising she still held his hand, she let go and he looked at her with an understanding half-smile at her sudden embarrassment but didn't speak of it. "Look over there!" he said. "Spectacular, that is!"

The storm was brief, intense and dramatic, the noise of the thunder echoing in the bowl of hills, the silent flashes of electricity charging the air with the smell of it. Ellen laughed.

"It's amazing!"

"This is living, this is," said Peter. "Right in't middle of all that!"

Awed by it, they looked at one another, their faces very close to. With fat summer rain pattering into the trees above them, Ellen experienced her first kiss. His lips, momentarily on hers, were soft and warm. Then it was over, leaving her astonished that it had happened at all.

"Peter!" she exclaimed.

"What?" he said, mock-shocked. "We'd better go back dahn before you take even more advantage of me. I've got me reputation to think of, you know."

It made her laugh, something she rarely associated with Peter Lumb and any awkwardness vanished. Peter, like the storm, was all short, sharp shocks, it seemed. It had come out of the excitement of the storm itself, and like that, the moment had passed. She felt it was as quixotic and isolated a moment as when they had set the fire together. They ran back down, wet but not cold since the day was so mild still and set off to cycle back, the ride keeping them warm too. They freewheeled down to Stump Cross and struggled up the incline past Shibden Park, then down the steep hill again to North Bridge. Once across there, they parted ways.

"Raight," said Peter, smiling and holding out his hand to shake hers. "I enjoyed all that. I'll sithee, Ellen, lass."

"Sithee, Peter, lad," Ellen responded in kind, making him laugh. "I enjoyed it too."

Satisfied, Peter nodded, waved at her cheerfully and wheeled off in the other direction, as she made for home herself to change out of her spoiled clothes before her mother spotted her. Libby, though, rung for to assist with wet things and wet hair, did see the wreckage and said curiously, "What have *you* been up to, Ellen? Owt or nowt?"

"Nowt," answered Ellen, Peter-like, so that Libby laughed.

"Oh, nowt, was it? Or maybe it was owt," she teased.

"Mebbe," answered Ellen, "Ask me no questions..."

"...And you'll tell me no lies. I see," said Libby, smiling and going away again with the soiled dress to sponge down.

Little did she know, thought Ellen, recalling, with a frisson of wonder, her lightning kiss with Peter, as she would always think of it, and the equally bright flash of sensation she had felt in that moment.

***

Jane's lot had been drawn to go out with Hannah Robertshaw to deliver the *Clarion* and their agreed day came round on Saturday afternoon, when the mill was closed. Sarah was matched with Noel, who had not committed himself to any occasion for it as yet, since it was rather more mundane an activity than he cared for. Jane had hoped to be matched with Albert, of course, but he and Cyril had come out as a pair. Given that Hannah would be working that day in the morning, Jane had said that she would come to Hannah's home as that was on the way into town, Jane herself having to cycle down from the vicarage at Queen's Road.

"I'll bring the papers," she said. "That will save you time, Hannah."

"Aye. And give you a gander at *us*," remarked Hannah, sounding amused. "That's what it's really abaht, in't it?"

"Why would I wish for that?" asked Jane stiffly, all starchy vicar's daughter, suddenly anxious lest her tryst with Albert be known to his mill women, or even, heaven forbid, laughed at between them all, an unbearable thought!

"Because everybody does," said Hannah, who had a broad, handsome face and serenely ripe curves.

She looked across at dark, tricky Sarah, who caught her eye and smiled back in that secret way they had together.

"I don't know what you mean," retorted Jane.

"Oh aye, you do," said Sarah, hand on slender hip, in her case being on the more girlish side in figure. "Don't be pretending."

"Peter and Stanley have already come calling. Be Eustace next," said Hannah.

"Or that Libby," said Sarah, at which they laughed together again, a comfortable joint force.

"Come if you like, then. You won't find Albert in, though," said Hannah carelessly, turning aside. "If that's what you're hoping."

"I wasn't," returned Jane smartly.

"Oh, aye?" said Sarah laconically, raising a knowing eyebrow and turning aside with Hannah too.

Jane had felt hot and cold all over. Where did she stand here? Did they know about her, or was it just that they knew all the Clarionettes had a prurient curiosity about their set-up with Albert – whether intrigued, attracted, or repelled by it? She had looked around for Albert but he had not been within hearing. In fact, he had not been near her at all during that meeting and, whilst not seeming to avoid her in any way, remained at a tantalising distance from her the whole evening. At least, due to that, he had not known of her intention to come to the house. She felt just as ambivalent now that she had arrived there, at that little enclave where the squat old cottage was, its very roof slabs of heavy stone seeming to press down on the private life within. *Did* the mill women share what she had done with Albert? No! What *she* had experienced with him, that joining of their inner selves, was beyond any coarse interaction either of them might have known, Jane was sure of that! She knocked on the door and Hannah opened it.

"All reet?" she said to Jane, looking her over slowly and making it clear she was still under no illusion as to why Jane had chosen to call to the cottage.

"I've got the papers," said Jane.

"I'll be right out then," said Hannah, going back in.

She deliberately left the door wide open to Jane's curiosity as she went to fetch whatever else she needed. Jane caught glimpses of some of those photographs on the walls of the hall although, uninvited, she dared not transgress by stepping across the threshold. She looked from one side of the walls to the other, full of images, all of these women in different poses and partial costumes, or perhaps without any at all. It was dark in there, only the light from outside picking out the shapes on silvery plates, from which soft flesh seemed to gleam. She licked her dry lips, feeling hot all over again and remembering the feeling of it all, of Albert touching her, becoming part of her and then separate once more. After a few moments, Hannah reappeared and looked at her again. Jane knew that she had been caught out, as expected, looking at the photographs, trying to see in and wanting to know something more of what went on it that cottage with Albert.

"Are you ready now, then?" asked Hannah with a half-smile, as if they both knew she had given Jane time for the good long look she wanted.

Jane flushed again because little did Hannah know, or did she, the reason for her interest? It left her quite unable to chat to Hannah as she had intended, to find more out by pretending companionable interest in her life, one Clarionette to another. Jane seemed incapable of doing anything more than exchanging safe banalities as they went about their business of giving out the papers by the Borough Market, each in a different doorway. Hannah, just like Albert, was quite capably keeping her distance and Jane, who had felt so superior to her and to Sarah, was no longer so sure of herself there, either. The papers given out, they parted scarcely more friendly than when they had met and yet, on the surface, all was quite civil between two people who knew each other as acquaintances, happening to share some aims and interests as members of the Clarion Club. Jane, though, burned with a new resentment. She would take him away from them, oh, yes, she would, she thought unclearly. Somehow, she would do it. Albert should be with Jane because who else could love him as she would? Certainly not they!

Back in her room, she found herself consumed by this jealous sense of entitlement. If she told him, as fully and passionately as she could, that he would only find true freedom with her, using his own precious word to express *her* feelings, surely he would see it and come to her alone? Jane wrote Albert a long and ardent letter, fluent with her certainty that now they had found one another, nobody else mattered. Before she could repent of it or think again, she had sealed it and run out to the post, sending it to him at the cottage itself, not even caring if somebody else read it too, or first. Perhaps she even hoped they might do and that her letter would explode the relationship between the three of them there. Coming back in, she was so flushed and out of breath that her father, coming to look for her to hear his draft sermon for Sunday, asked her if she found herself quite well.

"Your cheek is quite hectic, my dear and you are usually so pale!" he remarked.

"I have been out cycling, Father, that is all, to be faster in posting round your tracts," she fibbed.

"That is not a high-speed activity as a rule, Jane. I would advise you to take it more steadily next time, or you will quite wear yourself out. I don't think the Lord demands exhaustion of you with the task. Now, sit down and listen to this. You know how I value your opinion."

Jane scarcely heard a word, naturally, of her father's carefully crafted ponderings on some chapter of the New Testament. To conceal this, she praised it so highly that he looked slightly suspicious that she was poking fun at him.

"I doubt it to be quite so inspiring as all *that*, my dear child, but you are very kind to say so, all the same. Now – the vicar of St Jude's brings his new curate to tea today. I would like you to preside if you are not off again on your bicycle. Really, these modern ways of getting about are quite confounding. But you *will* do it!"

"Yes, Father, I will," said Jane with a smile, although

her heart rather sank at the idea of the formidable Felix Sykes appearing which, in the company of the vicar of St Jude's, he duly did a short while later.

Over tea, Reverend Craddock said, "I met your daughter at the studio, Reverend Ellison. She came to have that portrait taken which I see on the table there, as I was sitting for mine. I am engaged to a lady in Leeds and she insists that an exchange of photographic portraits is quite necessary. A most uncomfortable business I found it too, sitting still for all that time. Did not you, Miss Ellison?"

"Oh, certainly. But I bore it, to give my picture to Father for his birthday."

"It is very nice to have, my dear, although, of course, I see the real you every day," said her father mildly.

"But the photograph will remind you of how I look now, when I do not in years to come, or when I am no longer living with you here," she added rather dramatically, being in a heightened state of sensibility altogether and leaving the suggestion that she might not be living on this earth either hanging in the air.

"Oh! I am not at all sure I don't find that idea rather alarming and sad. To be frozen in time forever and yet for you not to be real after all!" exclaimed her father, moved in return by her tone.

There was a profound melancholy in this which struck everyone into momentary silence. Felix Sykes said, "I think that is a very deep notion, sir," which was certainly praise from him.

The conversation turned on to a more philosophical debate about the ephemeral nature of life and what morals could be drawn from it by clergymen to pass on to their flock. Jane stopped listening and thought about Albert opening her letter and reading it. What would he do and say when he wrote back or next saw her, what sign would he make that he understood? She was sure that he must do. That evening passed, the morning, afternoon and evening of the next, and the one after it too with no reply from Albert, however. Perhaps he would simply call at the house?

She haunted the vicarage windows to no avail, barely leaving the building in case she missed him, sure he would come to her. As the days passed, though, there was still no word from Albert and he did not, of course, call at the vicarage. Jane's feelings about her action fluctuated from wild panic that she would be exposed in revenge by those mill women and her reputation ruined, to fear that Albert hated her for trying to force him into responding to her needful love when he had been so expressly clear that liberty was his principle. Worse still, to abject misery that it was the mill women he loved and it would never be her. Flashes of anger and rejected despair passed through her too when, for all that she longed for the idealised Albert she had created in her mind, she hated the real Albert for acting exactly as he had said he would. His words, spoken lightly then and which she had not protested at in any way, passed constantly through her mind, when he had broken their embrace and she had tried to cling to him.

"We are free together."

"Yes," she had agreed and been praised by him later for 'understanding it'.

Her letter went back on that adult sophistication, didn't it? She must make amends in order to be able to see him again, 'freely', as he insisted, if only she could be with him bodily again. The recollection of it all tormented her so that, by the time it came to the day of Noel Ogden's party, she told herself she was quite resolute. She would approach Albert calmly and as if she assumed all was quite agreed between them already. She would say her letter had been a part of exploring freedom together and not a rejection of it. She would turn things around between them again because that connection had been so very strong that, surely, Albert must feel it too? Yes, she told herself, that would be what she would do.

Jane dressed herself as finely as she could and did her hazelnut brown hair into braided coils about her head, aiming to appear as a mature woman in command of herself. Her face was pale and composed as she took the hansom cab she had hired to travel there. She had told her father, truthfully, that she would be meeting Ellen and Sylvia Rastrick at a social gathering and would be back in the evening. Being an only child, she was afforded more freedom than many young ladies and she was over twenty-one now, so that if she assured her father she was in the company of young ladies, he did not trouble himself overmuch as to her activities. She had, after all, never given him any cause for concern and he was always busy, being a conscientious vicar with many sick parishioners to visit and comfort if he could.

***

Noel's terraced garden was strung with paper lanterns in gaudy colours. You could see them, like exotic flowers, on the approach of the curving driveway up from the road. The house was full of people, going up and down the sweeping staircase with its curving banisters, passing in and out of his various grand rooms with tall windows flung open on to his grounds, or standing on stone balconies to admire the view outside them. There were glinting champagne flutes laid out ready on a silver tray in the hallway, where a white cloth was draped over the statue of Alexander the Great, ready for the flourish of Noel's great unveiling of it. Ellen and Sylvia arrived together. Their mother had wanted to join them but Sylvia had pointed out that she was old enough to chaperone Ellen, as was Ellen to chaperone her. Mrs Rastrick made some remark about not wishing to be in the way of things, whatever that meant. Ellen was only glad she did not have to worry about being discovered by her mother as knowing those Clarion Club members who would be deemed highly unsuitable.

Sylvia was in a dress of pearl pale shot silk. A gauzy puff of lace frothed up around the top of her bodice, barely concealing her cleavage. Her waist looked small and her feet were in glacé kid shoes. Her hair was high-crowned, crystalline beads threaded through it, with curls falling tenderly across her brow. She looked like a fairy-tale in the making.

"You wait till you see your sister," Libby had told Ellen earlier. "There's something in the offing there all right."

"What do you mean?" Ellen had asked, not having seen any of these preparations.

"You'll see," said Libby, looking critically at Ellen. "That dress isn't new, is it? You should have gone shopping in Leeds with your mother as well."

"It's my best one and it fits me and suits me, doesn't it? You always say it makes the best of me, Libby. Besides, I'm not interested in dresses really," said Ellen, who thought hers looked well enough, or had done, until she saw Sylvia and rather gasped at the sight.

"Sylvia! Why are you in such extravagant things?" she asked.

"Oh," said Sylvia indifferently, "Noel wishes me to sing duets with him at his party and insisted I must be fancy. You know what a show-off he is."

"Yes. I expect he will be fancier himself, though," observed Ellen with an indulgent smile.

When they arrived, Noel greeted them enthusiastically and swept Sylvia off to his grand piano in another room, to go through what pieces they would sing, he said. They came back out shortly afterwards. John and Cyril arrived and Ellen laughed out loud as Cyril made a great show of presenting her drawing to Noel, having attracted the interest of everybody nearby, fortunately not including Sylvia, who had been drawn into other company looking round the house.

"Here is the design for your companion piece to your statue of yourself as Alexander the Great," he announced, passing him a rolled-up scroll of paper. "I have taken the greatest trouble with drawing it, and John is sure his hands will soon be recovered enough to begin carving it."

Noel looked flattered and delighted. He was dressed in his Oberon outfit and seemed even larger than life than he usually did.

"Really?" he cried. "And what am I to be?"

"Why, the Archangel Gabriel, Noel, the crème de la crème of heavenly beauties."

Noel chuckled appreciatively and unrolled the drawing. There was a moment when his reaction was undecided. He looked chagrined and wounded for an instant, which made Ellen cry out anxiously, "Oh! It was not intended as a cruel joke, Noel. I drew it, but it was only to try and copy a design for Cyril while John cannot do it. It was not meant for anything but that!"

Noel looked at her and back at the drawing and then, as Cyril and John had done before him, fell into helpless laughter at its buffoonish grotesquery.

"Good heavens, Ellen! I fear that art is not your forte," he said at last. "I blame Cyril entirely for this outrage and not you at all." He exchanged an impish look with Cyril and everybody laughed again. "It is, however, so unique, that I think I will keep it and have it framed as a warning to my vanity."

"An excellent idea," said Cyril.

Other guests arrived, among them Albert, looking dapper in a dark suit and snow-white shirt and silk cravat, both of which set off his looks very well. He was highly amused by the drawing, which had become quite a talking point. Hannah and Sarah were arm in arm but not obtrusively with him, since this was such a mixed occasion. Jane watched from afar, admiring but unseen as yet by Albert, who was in very good spirits with everyone. Ellen saw her and how she stood aside, but then noticing that Eustace had hesitantly appeared, concluded that Jane was keeping out of his way. Ellen, since she was responsible for his presence, greeted him with a wave and he came over.

"I am looking forward to introducing you to the orphans, Ellen," Eustace said pleasantly. "I hope you still plan to come?"

"Certainly, I do!" she promised. "Look, we all have to go in to listen to my sister and Noel singing now!" she added, disparagingly.

In the crowd of many people, she had not seen Peter and Stanley until everybody was in the room and the lieder had begun, Sylvia playing and Noel standing by her, singing with her and turning the pages. Peter had not seen Ellen, either, but she was struck by his reaction to the music, completely concentrated and looking entranced by it, as if it opened the gates to another realm for him. He stood quite still. Jane saw Albert standing further to the back and drifting out to the balcony view, not being especially interested in the singing. She slid around the edge of the group so that she could slip in there unobtrusively beside him.

"Albert," she said softly, conscious of entreaty in her voice but unable to help it.

He turned, to her relief, with a smile.

"Jane," he said politely, glancing cautiously around

the room behind them. “How do you do?”

“I don’t care about people seeing us speaking alone!” she answered, stung by seeing him check and also take a step aside because she was too intimately close by for propriety.

“Well, you ought to for your own sake,” he said, adding with a tease, “in public at least. The whole neighbourhood is here! Let us pretend we admire the outlook.”

“I’m – I wanted to say I was sorry about – writing to you,” she murmured hesitantly, turning with him to look out of the window and dropping her voice low as requested.

“Not writing to me, did you say?” he asked, mishearing. He smiled at her when, clutching gladly at the reprieve this offered, she nodded. “We have no need of letters, you and I, Jane. We understand one another, do we not?”

“Yes,” she agreed, swallowing all the things which she really wanted to say and only glad that he seemed to still believe her ‘free’, that odd word he bandied about so often. It was as sticky as flypaper, catching all her tender feelings and leaving them stuck on it, immobilised. “Kiss me,” she said impulsively, “here behind the curtain while nobody looks!”

He smiled again at that. Thinking them unobserved in the embrasure when he had scanned the room, where most people had their backs to them while listening to Noel and Sylvia perform, he did so.

“See how wild you are, Jane?” he joked, moving swiftly back again. “I knew I would be letting a cat out of the bag that afternoon.”

She smiled up at him, feeling exonerated and liberated from all the angst of her past days. Perhaps her rash letter had never arrived! Maybe nobody had seen it at all! She imagined it wandering the world to be read eventually by some random stranger envying whoever those words of love were addressed to, as surely they must. She had written in haste and repented at leisure – it may be that she had put the wrong address on it altogether in her upset at the time? Now, she could only hope so. Albert did not love her, no, but he thought there was something between them, certainly, something unique to them, didn't he? That was not spoiled! Happier, she allowed him to bow and walk away from her back into the music room. A moment or two later, she followed on too and applauded the singers with everybody else.

What she had left out of account was that the singers were facing that end of the room and Noel was tall enough to look across the heads of the audience and see Jane and Albert together. Mingling with the guests, he leaned down and breathed into Jane's ear, with what sounded like kind reproach, "Oh, Jane, you have not become entangled, have you? He has his ménage a trois, you know, and there is a strong mix there already. Add yourself to the brew at your peril, my dear. Now, excuse me, I have an announcement to make."

He swept to the front of the room again and asked everyone to walk through with him into the next chamber. There, two chairs, his Oberon throne chair and another, in which Sylvia sat, were placed. Noel went across and sat next to her, raising her hand to his lips and announcing in rich and theatrical tones.

"May I present my very own Titania, who has this day agreed to become queen to my king and will join me one day soon as my wife here in this, my enchanted palace!"

They both rose, Sylvia now with a garland of white roses on her head to match the ones he wore himself. They turned to one another, her hands raised in his, and kissed delicately, then turned back to the crowd of guests,

Sylvia calm and beautiful, Noel resplendent and beaming with happy complaisance. Ellen was standing with John and Cyril and heard Cyril exclaim with some vehemence, "Oberon! I could stab him like Banquo and he can be a ghost at his own feast!"

"You expected it," John said, low and restraining. "You knew he would one day."

Ellen risked a startled glance at Cyril, who was glaring at Noel as if he would like to hit him and embrace him at the same time. What an odd friendship it was, she thought, and so fierce somehow. But then, many of the Clarionettes had odd friendships together, didn't they? It was one of the fascinating things about them.

"He doesn't mean it," she said. "He *can't* mean it! Sylvia can't mean it! They don't love each other."

"No, Ellen, but they don't need to. Do they?" said Cyril bitterly and stormed off, his boots clattering noisily on the floor. A few of Noel's society neighbour guests turned to look, puzzled, as they had no idea who he was anyway.

"And now," announced Noel, master of all ceremonies for the day, "let us unveil my statue and drink champagne. A toast to each occasion!"

"Trust you to think your statue is as important as your engagement!" called out Albert, laughing, which broke the ice so that other ripples of laughter eddied around the room and, mostly in good humour, the guests followed out to the chequerboard hallway to drink the champagne now being poured out to toast the happy couple. Noel whipped the cloth off his statue with a flourish but Ellen, looking around for him, could not see Cyril, who had laughed so merrily earlier over his joke with Noel about her drawing.

"I hope you do not mind it too much, Ellen," said John to her of the engagement announcement.

"Oh, no. I do not mind for myself at all," she answered, surprising herself by finding that she meant it and that, although pained, she was not as wounded as she expected to be.

"I am glad of it. Them things are best grown out of."

"I'm not a child, John!" she objected.

"No," he agreed. "I'd better go and make sure Cyril isn't looking for a hammer to smash my statue up with. I wouldn't put it past him right now."

"Why is he so angry about it?" asked Ellen. "I am sure they will still be great friends if they want to be. Sylvia will not mind it. Well, I don't think she will, although she can be a terrific snob. Sylvia would never be a Clarionette! She won't let Noel be one for long, you know, once she finds out."

"If *she* does not mind, Cyril will. It changes things, you see. Socially. You know," he added, rather confusingly to Ellen.

She sensed, without understanding it, that this was not really what he meant. He left her to go and find Cyril and next, Peter appeared to speak to her.

"There you are!" he said bluntly, as if she had been avoiding him.

"Yes, here I am," she agreed, knowing him better now and not taking this tone at face value.

"Did you know?"

"No. I didn't."

"Reet. I didn't think you would," he said, studying her rather as John had done.

"It's all right," she said.

"Is it? Oh. Good. I should hope so too," he added in his dry, laconic way, so that she blushed, knowing he referred to their kiss together in the storm.

Hastily, she changed the subject, saying, "Peter – I didn't know you loved music so much. I saw how you listened to the singing."

"Aye – it's when those notes give you the shivers and goosebumps up your arms. It's the oddest feeling, like it's running through you some'ow."

"Should you like to go to a concert? We often do, at the Halifax Theatre."

"I'd love it! I've never bin there. Can't afford it. I'm working again soon, though. Stanley's got me in at Crossley Carpets for a couple of weeks. Talked me round in't end."

"If you didn't mind, I'd be happy to get some tickets. Mother's always got programmes for things."

"Thank you, Nell. That'd be grand."

"Tchaikovsky and Beethoven," she said. "That's the music for *you*, Peter. Romantic rebels and revolutionaries. I'll see when there's a concert with some of their music being played by the orchestra."

He smiled slightly, appreciative of the insight and rather flattered.

"Ah can see why you'd say *that*," he said roundly. "And I can't deny it."

"That's settled, then."

"Aye," he agreed. "It'd be a good thing to do, you know, to get the Clarion Club subscriptions going so more folk can get to hear the music. There's plenty of it about here, a good place for it. But most can't afford to go."

His face lit up with the inspiration.

"A wonderful idea, Peter! Let's suggest it at the next meeting."

"After t' concert though, like," he added, with a touch of his usual truculence, not wanting to lose the opportunity she offered, or have it diluted with others present in their company.

"After the concert, yes," she agreed. She sighed. "I

suppose I must go and congratulate my sister. Although I think it very rude of her not to have told me."

"Well, he hadn't asked her yet, had he?" Peter pointed out prosaically, making her laugh.

"No. I suppose not," she said.

Sylvia herself was being fêted by many guests and had not noticed her sister talking to a person of lesser status, although she was being particularly gracious herself to John Henderson, when he forced himself to go and congratulate her too. Ellen was pleased to see that Sylvia, who knew when she was admired, looked a little put out by how unmoved John's expression was throughout. Ellen knew how he had felt about her sister after his unguarded outburst in the studio that day and she was pleased to see his dignity so intact. Perhaps his words about things being best grown out of had partially included himself? Ellen went over to speak to Sylvia, and Noel joined them. In all the crowd she lost Peter, although she looked round for him to say goodbye when Sylvia gathered her up, wanting to leave to make the announcement at home that she and Noel were to be engaged to be married. Noel would join them later on, he said, when he had seen all his guests out, moving off again among the excited chatter of the visitors.

"That should cheer our mother up no end after Len," remarked Sylvia callously, gathering up her ethereal skirts to climb into the carriage.

"Did he ask Father's permission?" enquired Ellen.

"He did, although he did not need to, for I am over twenty-one and, anyway, he would hardly be likely to object to Noel Ogden's suit, would he? The Rastrick empire won't just be bobbins and worsted now, will it?"

"No. I suppose not," Ellen agreed, getting in beside her and wondering, as they left, if John had found Cyril and if Cyril had calmed down. "Sylvia – I heard what

Albert said to you, you know. What will you do?"

"What did you hear?"

Ellen had been near enough to hear Albert's words as he had bent over Sylvia's hand to congratulate her too.

"Why settle for Noel, when you could have me?" he had said with a flirtatious look, secretive and daring.

Sylvia had just smiled but she had looked back in the same way, Ellen saw.

"He said to marry him instead!" said Ellen now, indignantly.

"Hah, *Albert*! Not in so many words, he didn't. Besides, I can hardly throw my fiancé away for a new one on the same afternoon I become betrothed to him, can I, Ellen? I am sure *you* would prefer me to, though?"

"I don't care what you do, or Noel, or Albert. They are flighty people, with no substance to what they say."

"Oh, are they now? You've changed your tune."

"Perhaps I have. I know why Albert said it to you, anyway. At the time, when I told him about Leonard marrying Carrie Stanger, I couldn't see why he looked so suddenly thoughtful. Now I do. He knows Len will have no heir for Stangers with Carrie, while he could have one with you and gamble on inheriting there if he will not from his own father, not being the oldest."

"He might. It's a world people die young in. Who is to say he won't outlive his brother, Maurice? You are jumping to some very big conclusions, Ellen."

"Perhaps. But Albert has a certain reputation, you know, and I know all about how he lives."

"How he lives? What do you mean?"

"Did you see two women there today, arm in arm together most of the time? One very quick featured, the other with a voluptuous figure?"

"No. Why? Who are they? I saw Jane Ellison, the vicar's daughter, making eyes at him but that's all I noticed. I had Noel to contend with and he sucks all the attention out of you onto himself. Anyway, when were *you* talking to Albert Dewhirst?"

"Never mind," said Ellen curtly in answer to both questions, thinking better of blurting out what she knew of Hannah and Sarah's set-up with Albert and of giving herself away as a member of the Clarion Club.

It was a radical environment which her parents would be dead set against if they knew of where she really went on her bicycle. Things were bound to come out eventually, though, she thought, sighing to herself. If Noel was engaged to Sylvia, he would never keep his counsel about it with her parents in the end. She would have to speak to him, she decided and swear him to secrecy on her behalf because she needed that society very much.

"Oh, never mind. I've got other fish to fry than listening to you making up stories about other people. You always have done, Ellen. The real world's never quite enough for you, is it? I will deal with Albert if need be but he has had no encouragement."

"In looks, he has. That's what *you* trade in, Sylvia, since we're being so honest in our opinions of one another," returned Ellen smartly. "What about poor Kenneth Butterworth?"

"My faithful hound? He has not worked up to speaking in case his mother does not like it and so he has missed his opportunity, hasn't he?"

"You know what I think? The real reason you accepted Noel is exactly what you said when we first got in the carriage. You can't bear it that Len got married first, even if it was for all the wrong reasons! You want to make sure you have a big, shiny occasion and that that's what everybody will remember. Just because *you* want to marry money too!"

Sylvia looked at her under her long eyelashes.

"*Do* I?" she drawled, with a superior half-smile which said that at least *she* had the choice to do it – that is, to marry at all, being the implication of her reply.

"Well, I wish you joy of it!" declared Ellen, bouncing back crossly against the seat of the carriage. Neither spoke again until they arrived home, when Sylvia swept in to make her announcement and begin her reign as the supreme achiever of the family, one who was advancing its prospects to the height of their expectations of her.

As predicted, Mrs Rastrick was full of such sheer delight that it was quite unbearable. Ellen went upstairs to get out of the way of it all and dug out the concert programmes that were coming up. She found one which would have exactly the kind of recital she had in mind for Peter to enjoy and decided there and then that she would purchase the tickets for it. She wrote a note enclosing payment, and rang the bell for Libby to go to the post with it for her, after she had told her all about the party and Noel's proposal to Sylvia.

"I'm pleased it doesn't distress you, Ellen," Libby said. "I thought it would when it came to it, as it was bound to do, you know."

"It doesn't. John Henderson said that to me too, Libby."

Libby smiled and a dimple appeared in her creamy cheek.

"Aye, he would. He's a good fellow, that. I like him. We talked at the last meeting and his hands are getting much better, he thinks."

"I go to help out at the studio, you know, Libby," said Ellen, laying claim to more intimate acquaintance than Libby could have.

"Aye, lass. I know you do," answered Libby. "Give me that note to post, then, if you want me to go. Your mother and Sylvia will be wanting me any minute."

Ellen gave it to her and thought that she didn't remember telling Libby she went to the studio, but perhaps she had? Or maybe John had told her about it. It was hard to remember nowadays who had said what to whom in their little circle, since she had to keep it so discreet in the household herself. It suddenly occurred to her that Libby might be walking out with John on her second Sunday and that, if she were, Ellen wasn't at all sure how she felt about it. No. Surely not? Libby was another one who, if not actually under his spell, was more susceptible to Albert's charms than John's more down-to-earth ones. She wouldn't be walking out with John, would she? And for all she said about his hands, Libby would want an able-bodied man to partner her because being able to earn a livelihood, or have an income of his own, like Albert, would be a priority for self-preservation in the world.

Ellen found she was comforting herself with that thought and then wondered why because now, she herself was increasingly tied to Peter, wasn't she, even though she had not looked for or expected it? She tried to imagine kissing John in a lightning storm and couldn't, which, she thought, put paid to any confusion about *him* in her mind, didn't it? Ellen sighed and wondered how a person was supposed to know if they were falling in love with somebody or not. It was a matter which seemed far more clear cut in books, as was whether you were attracted to someone or not. In her case, if she was, it didn't seem to be all the time, did it? So perhaps she just wasn't? Or was she? Did she know what that felt like or was she imagining it? Had she been kept in too much ignorance to have any real idea of it? She could tell that she and Jane Ellison were far more naïve than the working-class women in the Clarionettes Club. They knew how to talk to men by instinct and seemed quite relaxed about it. It was quite clear when they were flirting together or not, whereas Ellen didn't have a clue about where to start. She sighed to herself, pondering about it.

Noel arrived and so she had to come downstairs. He had timed it to appear just after Mr Rastrick senior arrived home from the factory and had heard the news from his wife and daughter, so that Noel could be fully congratulated in full in the first fine careless rapture of their delight in him. For all that Ellen saw what a shameless showboater he was, she still felt a pang that he had chosen Sylvia and never known that Ellen herself had admired him. He said to her later in the evening, in a private, joking aside, after more drinks and toasts, and showing more than ever that he had never really noticed her…

"You are far too sensible, Ellen, to have ever looked at me. I resigned myself to our being comrades as Clarionettes long ago. So, I had to turn to Sylvia."

"I certainly am," she said rather defensively. "And just as well. Do you know that Cyril is most upset?"

"Cyril? Oh, never mind him. He always comes round," said Noel with careless elan, which was, thought Ellen, just typical of him and she had to smile in spite of herself.

"You will keep it secret about me being a Clarionette, won't you, Noel?"

"Certainly, for I wish to continue as one too. They wouldn't approve of us, would they?" he added satirically.

"No, they wouldn't," she agreed and then they were called back into the family circle because Noel was now staying for dinner.

He entertained everybody with many laughing tales which kept them amused for the rest of his visit. He had produced a beautiful engagement ring for Sylvia, which she wore to great effect on her slender white fingers as she played the piano when, inevitably, they both sang a duet for the family after the meal.

***

Ellen wrote a letter that very same evening to her brother, Leonard, telling him about this, to her, still astonishing turn of events, that Noel Ogden had become engaged to be married to Sylvia. She even said that she was quite certain it would never have happened if Len and Carrie had not got married and made Sylvia feel she should make haste to go one better. *Mother is quite beside herself*, she wrote. *Of course, Sylvia is just as she always is, since nothing ever seems to excite her. I must say, though, that she was rather unpleasant to me this afternoon. It will be quite horrid being stuck here while all that wedding flummery starts up, and Noel isn't nearly such good company as I have found him to be before*. This precipitated an early note in return inviting Ellen to come and stay soon with Leonard and Carrie, which she was glad to accept.

Ellen's next social outing, though, was one she had arranged herself, the concert she had invited Peter to at the Halifax Theatre. He paid absolutely rapt attention, leaning forward in his seat throughout the entire performance of Beethoven's ninth symphony.

"Now *that* were something!" he said to Ellen as it finished, lost for any other words in his wonder at the music surging through the concert hall, magnificent and transporting.

Ellen had taken seats in the middle of the stalls but knew she might risk being seen even so. Her courage for flouting convention was rising, though, the more time she spent with the Clarion Club and its activities. As she and Peter were leaving, she was sure she saw Mrs

Butterworth craning round at her in the crowd departing. Sure enough, moments later, Kenneth's kindly and, at present, enquiring face, appeared before her, courteously bidding her a good evening. In evening dress, he wore a brushed top hat and carried gloves, in great contrast with Peter's best clothing, she was at once uncomfortably aware.

"I do hope you enjoyed the concert, Ellen," Kenneth said, smiling at her and, naturally, she had to stop and greet him.

"Very much," she said, as her companion did his best to fall unobtrusively back into the crowd but, of course, he had been noticed.

"And behind you, I think this is one of the gallant firemen we saw doing their drill that day on Albert Promenade rocks? I am pleased to meet you again, sir," said Kenneth, gently civil.

"All reet?" returned Peter with his bittersweet hostility, in which Ellen felt she now recognised a gruff shyness too.

Peter sighed and shifted about impatiently, not wanting the banalities of some dull conversation to break the heightened feelings still with him after the concert.

"Let me see you home, Miss Rastrick," said Kenneth, speaking with killing politeness in the face of this uncouth presence. "Mother is here and our carriage is just outside. When she pointed you out in the stalls I told her you seemed to have come alone and so she insisted I came to collect you."

Ellen cast a desperate and apologetic look at Peter, who nodded at her to leave and said abruptly, "I'll say goodnight, then", cramming his own cap back on and pushing his way off out through the mainly well-dressed concert goers before she could answer. Halifax being a place where classical music was loved, not all the audience was middle class and so he did not stand out entirely from the crowd as he made his solitary way to the exit.

"I thought it was best," said Kenneth with neutral courtesy. "You know what Mother is like."

"Yes," said Ellen, trying to sound more gracious than she felt and resentfully giving in. "I do. Thank you, Kenneth."

Once again, her feelings towards Peter were confused by her sense of guilt, this time about him being in receipt of a social snub from Kenneth to keep their association from been known of, even though it was quite agreed among all the Clarionettes that the 'ladies' among them would have to remain members in secret in order to continue belonging to the club. But, in spite of that caution, before they reached the carriage Kenneth said lightly, "What an odd coincidence. Or is there more to your knowing those men whom we met than you said at the time, Ellen? And to your cycling excursions? It seems everybody is doing all sorts of things I know nothing of. Your sister's engagement announcement came as quite a surprise to me. What a dull fellow I must seem."

"Oh, no!" protested Ellen. "You are the nicest of people and I would have been quite lost without your books and our discussions about them! You are far too good for Sylvia, you know, Kenneth."

"Thank you, Ellen. It is very kind of you to say so."

On impulse, she said, "I have wanted to tell you before and to ask you to join us. Kenneth, I belong to a cycling club and so does Peter Lumb, who you saw at the concert just then. We are all members together, do you see? We go out cycling and there are both men and women from all parts of our society here amongst us. It is a great thing, and all about doing good for people." Here, she glossed over the more radical aspect of the Clarion Club saying,

"I have been to read with the orphans at Crossley and Porter's School after meeting one of the teachers there, who asked for volunteers. Should you like to do that, Kenneth?"

"Oh, I see. One of your charitable ventures, Ellen," replied Kenneth, his brow clearing of the puzzled frown he had worn before. "Well, I am not sure that reading to orphans is quite my bent but the cycling must be pleasant. I will consider it. Thank you for asking me. But…were only the two of you from that club present as music lovers in the hall here?"

"No, they weren't," said a new voice, a deep one belonging to John Henderson. Cyril was beside him and both of them now came up too. "A few of us are here, ladies too. We enjoy music as well as cycling in our group, sir." For all that they had come so unexpectedly to her social rescue (and if there were other ladies present from the Clarion Club, Ellen hadn't seen them) she now found herself blushing furiously because John must have seen her out alone with Peter as well, like a courting couple! "Since you'll be seen safe home now by Mr Butterworth, we'll say goodnight too, Miss Rastrick," John finished politely.

"Mr Henderson!" exclaimed Kenneth. "I have heard of your recent exploits and, I had been about to say, those of Mr Lumb too, but he left before I had the opportunity."

"Oh. No more of that," said John with dismissive good cheer.

He and Cyril made polite little head bows, said goodnight and left too, so that Ellen and Kenneth followed after.

"Don't tell your mother, pray!" hissed Ellen urgently. "There is no harm in what I do."

"I would never dream of it," he assured her, as they reached the carriage in which his mother, all agog, was waiting. “The cause of good works is worthy, I am sure, and the whole world may listen to Beethoven, I suppose. But you must take more care about being out and about alone in public, I think, Ellen. Even if others you know from this club are to be present they are not, well, not your natural companions. Are they?”

“Oh, Kenneth, how stuffy of you,” said Ellen. “It is a respectable concert I have come to and I *am* surrounded by my peers anyway. *You* are here, are you not?” she tried to laugh at him.

Greeting Mrs Butterworth with her best smile, she asked how she had enjoyed the concert. Ellen explained her solitary attendance as being because nobody else in her family could join her, but she adored Beethoven and so had come alone. Knowing that she would be in the polite company of many of their neighbours her mother had permitted it, she added, ramming the point she had made to Kenneth home.

“I do not think you should be clattering about in hansom cabs at night alone, even so, Ellen,” reproved Mrs Butterworth. “Had I a daughter, she would not be.”

“Yes. Mother is distracted by Sylvia’s wedding, or I am sure she would have objected more strongly,” said Ellen, with a disarming smile.

This had the desired effect, for Mrs Butterworth was immediately launched on the topic of the forthcoming nuptials with Noel Ogden. Ellen could not help feeling that there was some relief in her interest – relief that she would not yet lose her bachelor son to marriage and not, now, to the cool-featured Sylvia, whom she would not be able to dominate. Whatever Kenneth’s own feelings on the matter were, he kept them to himself as his mother chattered tactlessly on.

Chapter Seven

Jane found herself going out for bicycle rides down into the bottom of the town and circling that witches' stone cottage, as it had begun to figure in her mind, distorted into something which imprisoned her own lover there. They had no right to him now. She knew that nobody was there when she went because it was during the mill's working hours. Doing this fed her inner obsession with Albert, from whom she still waited to hear. If only those two women were not there to steal him away from her! This gradually translated into imagining how to ensure that they were not. She had no affinity with them as people, not even in the Clarion Club, which she had joined to escape the confines of the vicarage and seek the male company which she was denied. Now that she had found Albert, she must make it possible for him to escape his trap with these inferior mill women. They should simply be got rid of if they would not listen to her, like the vermin at the vicarage, of which, it being a large and draughty building, there were always plenty to be dealt with. She was so far down the dark rabbit hole in her head that it made her irrational enough to begin playing out the fantasy she had in mind.

Jane made the bread for the household and on this particular day she made a special loaf, the flour liberally laced with arsenic powder from the lethal poison bottle kept in the cellar to add to bait. Wrapping it in a white cloth, still warm from the oven, she put it in her bicycle basket and cycled down to the cottage on Saturday afternoon. What if Albert were there? She would not give it to them if he was but she believed, from something that she had heard him say before, that on most weekends he was expected to be at the family home dining with them. Would she do it? She did not know. Not if they listened to what she had to say, she reasoned unclearly. It did not even seem real to be thinking and acting like this, as if she were Jane in a dream and under some irresistible compulsion. It was only wicked in thought as yet, she told herself. Once more she knocked on the cottage door and, this time, it was Sarah who answered it.

"Jane Ellison," she said, not sounding very surprised. "So, you got up the courage to call, did you? We heard you'd been hanging around."

"Can I come in?" asked Jane with a smile which was difficult to force, feeling the strain of her intention even though it had not become real yet. "Is it just you and Hannah at home?"

"Aye. If tha wanted to catch Albert, tha's come on't wrong day," said Sarah, speaking more broadly now that her ire was roused and not smiling back.

She opened the door, however. Jane brought the loaf out of her basket and took it in with her. She followed Sarah down that hall full of those soft-limbed photographs, loose hair tumbling about, breasts bared beneath. One she saw was an overtly sexual pose, with Hannah standing, one leg stepping forward into a tin tub to bathe, with only her long hair falling forward to cover her modesty. Jane drew a sharp breath at the sight of it, stabbed by jealousy and distaste at the intimacy it seemed to display between subject and photographer. Sarah called for Hannah.

"'T vicar's daughter's 'ere, Hannah!" and she led Jane into the kitchen which doubled as a sitting room.

Hannah appeared too and they stood with folded arms looking at her. Jane put the loaf down on the table.

"I – I brought you some bread," she said. "I made it this morning so it's nice and fresh."

They looked at it and her, then one another.

"I'll make some tea," said Sarah flatly, putting the

kettle on a small iron range, already lit to heat hot water in the back boiler so they could wash the morning's grime off, finished at the dye works for the day.

Three cups were laid out on the table and the teapot in the centre, looking comfortably at home there next to the poisoned bread, which looked cottage cosy too in its snowy linen cloth. Hannah unwrapped it and handed the napkin back to Jane.

"You'll be wanting that back," she said and Jane quickly took it, belatedly noticing her own monogram, for she embroidered all the household linen herself and marked it for the laundry. It made her heart bump to think she could have given herself away by it.

"We know why you're here," said Sarah, looking at her after a silence in which they had begun sipping their tea, waiting for Jane to speak further.

"Oh?" she answered, finding herself tongue-tied now that she *was* here because, face to face with them, their reality as people and in their situation was too strong for her to speak of herself and Albert to them. In fact, they saved her the trouble.

"You can thank us that he hasn't run a mile from you. We burned that letter. Do you know nowt about men? If you want him, have him while it's good but see it for what it is," Sarah told her baldly.

Jane's face burned with appalled shame.

"You read it," she whispered, tears springing to her eyes.

"Aye, we can read, tha knows! Don't tekk on, lass. Tha's new to it all and brought up soft on love. We know what Albert is and what he wants of us. We've got ourselves to take care of one another. Now – think on. Think of yourself, not always of him," said Hannah.

"Albert will go his own way in't end. He'll have to. That's how it is. Clarion Club or no Clarion Club, we are not equal. *You* don't think *we* are, do you? It's built in, see?" added Sarah.

Jane bowed her head, mortified and increasingly aghast at what she had intended to do when she came here. It seemed so mad a thing that if she hadn't known she had done it, she could scarcely believe now that she, of all people, had put arsenic in a loaf of bread!

"He's coming for his tea later on before he goes home," said Hannah. "We'll give him some of your bread with honey on it. You'd like that, wouldn't you? We won't tell him, like, don't worry."

Jane felt the shock of apprehension drain her face. Without hesitating, she did what she had just decided on already, lifting her full cup of sweet tea and letting it slip, so that it drenched the loaf and ruined it.

"Oh, I'm so sorry!" she exclaimed. "How dreadfully clumsy of me! Now I have spoiled my gift." She picked it up immediately and said, "I will go now and throw this away. I know I have made a great fool of myself." Taking a sobbing breath she cried out, "I'm sorry! I'm so sorry!" with such feeling that the two women stared.

Jane rushed from the cottage. She thrust the soggy bread into her basket again and rode away on her bike with her hands shaking violently until she had disposed of it in a midden on the road well away from the cottages, now hoping that it would not even be fatal to a rat.

Barely able to credit what she had almost obsessed herself into doing, potentially murdering not just Albert's lovers but Albert himself, Jane felt some perspective shift back into focus. Yet her peace of mind was so lost that she still could not recover herself as she had been before Albert knew her physically and, as she firmly believed, changed her and himself forever.

***

Embarrassed after the concert, Ellen avoided the

stonemasons' workshop for a while, her time taken up with other people – in snatched, clandestine cycle outings and debates with Peter, occasionally reading with Eustace's orphans, or being busy with social activities in her home. Kenneth had begun to pay quiet attention to Ellen now that Sylvia was engaged, calling at the house and taking her out for walks or carriage rides, suggesting they might see an exhibition of art or interesting museum artefacts. She appreciated all this for taking her out of the atmosphere which was so absorbed with Sylvia's wedding plans, as there was certainly a foundation of friendship between them. Libby teased Ellen about it but it was too smooth a transition from Sylvia for Ellen herself to think he had intentions in any other way. His manner towards her was as it had always been, so she had no self-consciousness with him about that.

Peter, difficult and unpredictable but always open, had become her weathervane, the distorted barometer set at stormy against which others were measured. She began to lose sight of his irresponsibility and the way he could act on impulse. The damaging chip on his shoulder at being frustrated by his lot in life was starting to seem less begrudging than entirely justified to her. She did not tell Kenneth, when it came to it, when the next Clarion Club cycle ride was to take place because he had tried, in his quiet way, to separate her from it at the concert. She was sure that he would find some occasion or outing which she would not be able to refuse in order to stop her from joining in with it if she told him when it was to be. Kenneth was, at bottom, too respectable for the Clarion Cycling Club, she realised, something which he clearly thought Ellen ought also to be. And this was quite apart from its radical aspect, which he knew nothing of so far! Ellen had no intention of falling in line with him on that, and she had time to attend this next cycle outing before her visit to Leonard and Carrie was due.

All the firemen were now recovered enough to join the group apart from John who, although back to trying to do some work, could not risk further strain or damage to his hands by cycling yet. Cyril, however, *was* there and he said, "Ellen! We have missed you at the workshop lately?"

"I am sorry," she answered. "There has been so much happening. I am much called on socially at home at present with the wedding planning and then, I read often with Eustace's orphans at the school, you know. I did not think I would be as needed to help out now that John is improving so quickly in his skills?"

"But, Ellen," he laughed. "Your artwork is beyond compare!"

"Oh, yes, I am sure," she answered with a laugh, just glad that he hadn't mentioned the night of the concert.

Today, they were heading out to the moors beyond Illingworth. Peter and Stanley were to join them there from where they lived. Noel Ogden had come and now he and Cyril were deeply involved in conversation from the start of his arrival, late, as usual, and for whom they had had to wait. A magnificent spread of moorland stretched before them, with the widest of views on either side under cloud-filtered sunshine. Once more, Libby and Albert had drifted ahead to ride together, with Hannah and Sarah further back. Ellen was beside Jane and noticed the strained look on her face, although she could not draw the other young woman into conversation. When Peter and Stanley joined them, Ellen fell back in beside them and Eustace came up by Jane in the front. When they had all halted on the moors and dismounted to admire the view, Noel made one of his announcements.

"Do you remember when we stopped on Albert Promenade and I said I wanted to purchase Wainhouse

Tower? Well – now I have done it!"

"What?" exclaimed Peter, instantly outraged. "Tha's bought a great stone toy for thissen? You could have done some good wi' that money! Built some decent houses for folk or summat."

"I can still do that if I wish, Peter, *and* have Wainhouse Tower too," pointed out Noel, which did not exactly endear him further. "I have bought it as a gift for my future wife. We will have picnics up there with our children," he said fancifully.

"Good God!" exclaimed Cyril, sounding disgusted, while Ellen burst out laughing at the idea of Noel and Sylvia having some brood nesting at the top of Wainhouse Tower along with the pigeons which inhabited it.

"Meanwhile," Noel beamed at everyone, "the Clarion Club will enjoy its spectacular views first. I vote we all go up it at the earliest opportunity. I will receive my paperwork for it soon and, of course, the keys!"

It was perhaps this that made things more volatile that afternoon. Peter, Eustace, Stanley and Ellen were strolling about together in a group, all noticing how Jane Ellison was fixated upon Albert and Libby flirting, while Hannah and Sarah, arm in arm as they nearly always were, looked on inscrutably from a slight distance. Jane seemed to avoid them all and be quite unable to speak to anybody.

"That un's going t'wrong road," said Peter, nodding across at Jane's darkly possessive looks towards Albert. "I reckon we warned the wrong one off him, Eustace. Libby's just messing but her – I reckon he's done some damage already."

"To *Jane*?" exclaimed Eustace, horrified at the notion. "Oh, no, that cannot be allowed. Not to somebody like Jane. Why, it would destroy her! I am going to speak to him."

"Let's both do it," said Peter, marching over to Albert and, at the sight of him and Eustace, Libby moved aside and came away back towards Ellen.

Albert turned a careless smile towards both the men. Whatever it was that Eustace said to him, it only drew a casual and dismissive laugh because, of course, really, he despised earnest Eustace. Peter's method of speaking to Albert (taking violent exception to Albert's suggestion that people should mind their own business) was to punch him squarely on his hitherto perfect nose. Albert's fine eyes began to blacken as the nose spluttered with blood. Everyone rushed across to intervene and Ellen was not alone in hearing Peter's words.

"We *are* all each other's business. That's why we're in the Clarion Club together. You're not playing fair with any of them lasses, Albert, and you know it. Yon vicar's daughter's tekkin' bad ways. Can't you see what you're doing?"

"You are courting disaster, Albert," cautioned Eustace, handing him a copious handkerchief to pinch on his battered nose.

"Albert! No! What have you done to him?" Jane exclaimed.

She tried to go to him but Noel smoothly intercepted her for her own sake, blocking the way and saying loudly, "Why, Albert, you poor, unfortunate fellow! Allow me to escort you home before you exsanguinate all over Ovenden Moor, which would be quite frightful for one and all to witness!"

Albert was too shocked to do more than allow himself to be led away by Noel and Cyril, while Hannah and Sarah, after surveying everybody in their dispassionate way together, followed on their own bicycles. Noel and Cyril accompanied Albert back down the hill, leaving the rest of the Clarionettes behind. Ellen and Libby looked at the mutely humiliated Jane, who had caught something of why Albert had received a punch on the nose.

"Invite her to your house, Ellen," Libby muttered. "She needs a friend, I think and she won't count me as one."

"Jane!" said Ellen immediately, feeling the woman's obvious pain. "Won't you come back to my house with me for a while? I think all that has distressed you."

"Good lass," said Peter. "Take her there. Look after her a bit, won't you?"

"I will. Eustace, won't you come with us part of the way?"

"I would be glad to escort you," he agreed. "I do not think it was necessary to strike him, Peter," he added, but without much condemnation.

"Aye. It were," said Peter and nobody made any further comment about that. "But I'll shake hands wi' 'im next time we meet. If he behaves hissen, like," he added wryly, for the Clarionettes, while not pacifists, aspired to a brotherly love amongst themselves ideally.

The three women and Eustace set off next, leaving Peter and Stanley waving at them from the heather and saying they would follow on down soon, for it was more discreet that way in terms of Peter's friendship with Ellen, and besides, the two men could enjoy their outing for longer, since they did not live so far away. Jane's head buzzed with confusion. Albert had barely spoken to her again, had made her hate him when she had been longing so much to see him! She had felt rejection constricting her body physically, so anguished was she by being effectively ignored. Why, when he had not known of her letter? Why, when they had snatched a stolen kiss behind the curtains on the balcony at Noel's party and he had promised other days together? Why, when she had held back, had done nothing but wait, abiding by his rules? An unwelcome clarity came to her that his rules simply meant that he could please himself, living like a bohemian when he chose to in one of his two worlds, or slough that off and don his evening suit to be a rich gentleman again, unreachable by the rules of etiquette and respectability. Certainly not by Jane, a humble vicar's daughter.

Eustace parted ways with them at the bottom of the town. Jane now followed Ellen and Libby (whom she resented because Albert flirted with her on the cycle rides) reaching the Saville Park villa in a kind of daze.

"Mother is out with Sylvia courting future wedding guests with calls, so we are quite safe for the present from their company," Ellen assured Jane. "Do come inside and rest a little with me. It has been a long ride and an eventful afternoon for everybody."

Libby discreetly left them and said she would have tea made and sent up.

"Jane," said Ellen gently when they were alone. "Have you fallen in love with Albert? Is that what Peter and Eustace meant? I know what it is to love and not have it returned. I loved Noel, you know. Well. I thought I did. Until he asked Sylvia to marry him and by that time, you see, I had already begun to see him differently, so it did not pain me as much."

"Everybody knows!" groaned Jane, still much distressed.

"Everybody knew I loved Noel and I never thought they did. I expect you did too, Jane." Jane acknowledged it with a sniff and a nod. "So, you see, it is no shame to you. Albert is an atrocious flirt and I am very glad that Peter thumped him on the nose."

Jane half laughed, her breath less ragged now.

"So am I," she admitted, recovering.

Libby brought in the tea tray and, seeing a different tea set, silver this time, with an elegantly turned spout and handle on the teapot, Jane thought of her deranged attempt to deliver a poisoned loaf to Hannah and Sarah. "Sometimes I feel I am running quite mad!" she said.

"Sometimes I do, too," said Ellen. "Living the way we have to, when the menfolk can please themselves, it's hardly surprising that we do, is it? But, you know, Jane, I had rather be us and suffer for loving a person than be my brother, Len, or Noel, or Sylvia. Marrying somebody they do not love at all for money and position because they think they need to!"

Jane began to recover. Not all was known. Even Hannah and Sarah had not said they knew the full truth – that Albert had already lain with her. Her letter had been couched in terms of high-flown sentiment and what might be guessed at had not been stated. Only she and Albert knew the full truth. There and then, she decided never to speak of it. What Ellen said was right, she knew. Already, in the cold light of this day, her delusional passion, so hotly possessive, was beginning to recede while she was in other company, relieving her overwrought state. Ellen poured her some tea and, while Jane began to drink it, continued with, "Let us be better friends, Jane. We are here together to support one another as Clarionettes, are we not?"

Jane nodded and thought of how Albert's mill women had spoken to her too.

"I would like that," she said. "Thank you, Ellen."

Not long after this, Kenneth Butterworth called in by chance. Ellen thought it an excellent opportunity to introduce him to Jane, so that she might have acquaintance with a kinder man than Albert Dewhirst, and also so that Kenneth might turn his considerate attention elsewhere too, with any luck. They exchanged pleasantries in a reasonable way and Kenneth discovered he knew Jane's father, this meeting reminding him that it had been far too long since they had spoken and that he would like to pay a call to see him. When everybody left later in the afternoon, Ellen was hopeful that things might have gone rather well after all. Libby came in to clear the tea things away.

"She thought you were in love with Albert too, you know, I think," Ellen told her. "For a while, I did too. But I do not think you are, Libby, are you?"

"Nay," laughed Libby. "That I'm not, easy on the eye though he might be. I'm not that daft, Ellen."

They could not speak any further, as Sylvia and Mrs Rastrick now returned and so the subject was left there for the present. Ellen congratulated herself that Libby had been so taken up with flirting with Albert that she had missed again any interest between Ellen and Peter Lumb, which was all to the good too. She thought, a little guiltily, of John, who had missed out on their cycling club trip, and of how Cyril had reproached her for failing to go to the workshop. She decided that she would go to the studio tomorrow after all, perhaps in the morning, if she were allowed to have the time to herself by her mother and Sylvia.

***

Ellen glided into the workshop yard on her bike the following morning in a light drizzle, her hair caught up with droplets like a cobweb covered in dew when she arrived. John and Cyril were both there and at work, the sound of two sets of hammers and chisels, one more haltingly deployed, ringing out through the workshop as she came in.

"Ellen!" exclaimed John, breaking off and turning round. "I am pleased to see you. Here, let me take your coat – it's damp, is it raining?"

"Only a bit of a shower. I am glad to see you too, John. We missed you yesterday on our ramble."

"Fireworks, I believe!" John laughed. "Cyril tells me Peter Lumb punched Albert Dewhirst on the nose!"

"He did," agreed Ellen, "and Cyril reminded me that it was too long since I came to see you both in here. I am sorry – things just seem to have been very busy!"

John and Cyril looked at one another and John said, with reference to the concert evening, "Be careful of Peter, Ellen. He's a brave lad but he's a reckless hothead. He's a daredevil fireman, and sometimes that's good and sometimes it goes wrong. I'm not blaming him for it. It's how he is. I doubt he'll make easy company for you."

"I know," she answered, aware herself, of course, of just how generous it was of the unwitting John *not* to blame Peter for it. "I think lots of things make him angry. He hit Albert because of – well, the women in our group. But also, I think because he got laid off again from the dye works. He's like that."

"So long as you see it, Ellen," said Cyril. "You're the gentle sort. Don't let him put you under pressure. He'll know that he can."

This all brought very uncomfortable recollections and sensations about the mill fire back to Ellen. She hastened to reassure them and then change the subject away from Peter.

"We are friends, that's all. We are all friends, aren't we, in the Clarion Club? He has good qualities too. He likes music, I found, and so he came with me to the concert. Oh – I took Jane home with me yesterday, Cyril, to look after her a little bit. I should like to be better friends with her and I think we will be."

"That's good, Ellen," Cyril approved and said (as John nodded his own approval at her), "Albert's the real thing, you know. He believes in the bohemian life."

"I'm not so sure about that," said Ellen. "Do you remember Noel's statue party, when he announced his sudden engagement to Sylvia?"

"I'm hardly likely to forget it!" exclaimed Cyril, his face flushing pink.

"I heard Albert say to Sylvia 'why settle for Noel when you could have me?' Nobody else heard him but I did, I was right beside them. I haven't told anybody else, except I told Albert I'd heard him say it."

Cyril's alert face responded with a mixture of emotions, hope mixed with irritation being the main ones.

"Why would he say that except to torment?" he asked. "He likes to seem the prize, doesn't he, Albert? I saw no interest from Albert towards your sister before, beauty though she is."

"Well – because he is no more committed to the Clarionettes, really, than Noel is. And because – if he and Sylvia bore children – they would inherit my family's money in the end and Stanger's too. Len and Carrie will not have any heirs together. But I shouldn't gossip about any of them, I suppose."

"Perhaps not but I am glad you did," said Cyril thoughtfully. "I don't think Noel will go through with it anyway," he added.

"You mean you hope he doesn't," scoffed John. "Don't you go living in other people's fools' paradises either, Cyril. You know better. You've let him get the upper hand. And you said you never would."

"I know I did." Cyril bit his lip thoughtfully, his fair skin colouring and paling with his feelings as they came and went. "Do you know, I forgot to tell you, John, he's actually bought Wainhouse Tower after all! He told us yesterday."

"Has he?" John shook his head in bewilderment. "What a strange creature he is. All quixotic decisions for showing off. I don't know why you both seem to adore him so."

"It's because he's different, John, and I don't adore him," Ellen defended herself. "Not in the least."

"Oh – not in the least, eh, now, is it?" smiled John. "Well, that's one less rival for his affections for you to worry about, Cyril."

"They're all welcome to him!" declared Cyril, sounding aggrieved. "The man is impossible!"

"I'd agree with you there," said John, laughing. "Now, Ellen, let's get you to work for us. Can you copy some curlicues? Traced and then inked out bigger if Cyril rules the lines for you? My fingers aren't up to that yet."

He wore leather half-gloves strapped round his hands to support them, the fingers, shiny with healed scar tissue, moveable only up to a point as yet.

"Your hands are getting so much better, John!" she said, pleased to see it.

"Getting there," he said, adding, "I'm determined to get my dexterity back as fully as before. I'll have to stand down as volunteer fireman now, though. I can't risk my future on that any more."

"No, indeed, you must not!" agreed Ellen. "I saw it all and – I wish none of you did again."

"Well, we're drilling again soon," said Cyril. "Got a new man stepping in. Can't leave the town to burn down and all the mills with it, can we?"

"Health and safety in the workplace is what we should be pushing all the time through the Clarion Club meetings, you know. Accidents to people, fires, dangerous substances everywhere. It's one thing we *can* try to make a difference about, Peter says," said Ellen. "He says we have to keep it in the front of people's minds, especially the mill owners."

"Oh? That's what *Peter* says, is it?" said John

satirically. “Sounds like he’s got one mill owner’s daughter’s ear about it any road.”

“Well, yes. He has. About that. In fact, I mean to speak to Len about it all, and Father too. I’m going to stay with Len and Carrie at Heatherfield very soon, you know.”

“Are you? You’ll enjoy seeing them but we shall miss you here. It’s down Ryburn Valley, Rishworth way, isn’t it?”

“That’s right,” agreed Ellen, enjoying being told that she would be missed.

“And how was Libby yesterday?” asked John, very casually.

Ellen frowned a little.

“She was flirting outrageously with Albert Dewhirst, if you really want to know,” she said.

John just laughed.

“She likes to get him going, doesn’t she? It’s a pity he’s too vain to realise she were only winding him up a bit,” he remarked, grinning, pointing out the page he wanted Ellen to copy while Cyril ruled out the paper for her and marked some size dots as a guide. “He’ll not be a pretty sight himself for a while anyway, will he? Not after Peter’s handiwork. Serves him right, I suppose. Not that I’m condoning a thump in the fizzog.”

“I didn’t know you and Libby were particular friends, John?” remarked Ellen, equally casually and looking down at the scrollwork design rather than him.

“Like you said,” replied John, “we’re all friends in the Clarion Club, aren’t we?” And with that, Ellen had to be content.

She looked at Cyril from time to time as she traced out the design carefully, liking the thick black line the soft, artist’s pencil made. She thought of how he sparred with Noel and thought it was a good job somebody tried to keep Noel a bit in line, even if Cyril did seem so very put out about Noel becoming engaged to Sylvia. Perhaps it was because, having become such unlikely but very great friends at some point, he felt Noel was letting himself down by becoming engaged as impulsively as he seemed to do everything else, especially to someone like Sylvia. Sylvia was as distant as Iceland and shared none of Noel's spontaneity and joie de vivre. Well, people did say opposites attract, didn't they? Which made her think of Peter and herself. Were they attracted, or were they, at bottom, just friends and comrades? Ellen found that she was not very sure. They had met several times since the lightning kiss but it had not been repeated yet, just somehow understood between them as a shared moment which brought them a little closer.

***

A few days later, Albert himself, with a plaster over the bridge of his nose and his full dark eyes still bruised but looking as attractive as ever, called at the Rastricks. Now, this was a highly unusual thing in itself. Even more unusually, Jane Ellison was on his arm.

"Good afternoon, Ellen," Albert greeted her. "Here are Jane and I come to see you. I hope it is convenient."

"Oh! Yes!" she answered, taken by surprise as they were shown in. "How are you, Albert?"

"Reminded of my manners," he said, rather ruefully. "I will not be slighting of Eustace in future while Peter is by. I think they both misunderstand me, which is hard on a fellow," he added, with his boyish white grin. "Now, Jane, here, is really very good friends with me, aren't you, Jane, and I hope you are too, Ellen?"

Jane looked rather glowing to be beside Albert and she gave Ellen a look of shy delight which also begged discretion about her former confidences and distress. She meant to retain her composure, which Ellen was pleased to see.

"Of course," Ellen answered, waiting to hear the reason for their visit and ringing the bell for tea.

It was Libby's second Sunday and so she was not on duty, the bell answered and afternoon tea delivered by Mr Rastrick's manservant, who doubled as butler when necessary. Albert, Ellen was pleased to see, looked fractionally disappointed not to see her maid.

"I called upon Jane at the vicarage, and we have taken a pleasant walk out, culminating at your door," said Albert.

Jane gave a little smile to herself, so that Ellen thought whatever they had discussed together on the way had pleased her. In fact, Albert had arrived at the vicarage quite unexpectedly. He had asked Jane to join him in a walk after coming in and exchanging a few deferentially courteous words with her father, who seemed pleased to find so eligible a gentleman as young Mr Dewhirst acquainted with his daughter. To Jane's surprised delight, they had gone straight to Albert's photographic studio and the second half of their walk had begun after a very different kind of interlude between them.

All Jane's fears were settled for the present, her romantic longing to see him relieved, even more so by Albert's still being with her now, on an ordinary social call among their own class. That was how easily her determination to keep herself calm and be more sensible about Albert had been swept away, her attachment to him on any terms ensured again, while, for his part, he merely continued as he had said he would do with things between them. Another dalliance together had been promised and now it had been enjoyed. Albert, if he really had felt he needed to do so, had made amends for what he believed others had wrongly interpreted when they had been on their cycling outing on Ovenden Moor.

When he had said to Jane afterwards, looking into her eyes lying next to her on the heap of cushions on the floor which he had cast down for them to lie on, "You see how well *we* understand one another, Jane", she had made no denial of it.

Once again she had simply answered "Yes, Albert", feeling just as powerless to question this fragile pact as before, lest she drive him away again.

"I was never ignoring you, Jane," he continued. "Merely being discreet among our peers. They are more judgemental than you might think. As Peter demonstrated. They do not understand it as we do."

"But you gave me no sign, Albert! No word."

"Our unity is not measured by calling cards," he said, smiling and kissing her again, brushing her heavy loose hair aside. "Is it?"

"No, Albert." Jane did not wish to let herself down in his eyes now by not being the free spirit he had cast her as, even though she knew perfectly well that she was not.

"Well, then," he said, as if that meant they were quite agreed. "Let us refresh ourselves, dress and go out together." And to that, of course, she consented with great pleasure.

Now that she was with him, the distorted and forlorn passion which had led her to make that poisonous loaf of bread seemed to be the act of somebody else altogether, somebody who lived in a dark world, not this sunny one to be experienced in Albert's actual presence. Rarely did you see Albert frown and he was always ready with an easy smile or a jest, wanting to enjoy life. The thought of what she had so nearly done, and to those two women who had never offered any harm to her – who had even, so strangely, supported her in their way – just now seemed quite unreal. She would force it from her thoughts forever, she told herself, and never go down that tortured road again. But this, of course, was while she was in Albert's lively company. It was a different story lying awake through the long nights alone at home, knowing him to be with them instead of her. Just now, seated decorously in Ellen's drawing room, Jane could have laughed out loud that nobody had any idea what she and Albert had been doing together shortly before. Mrs Rastrick and Sylvia soon joined them, returning from yet another excursion to the dressmakers, for a full new wardrobe seemed to be in demand already.

Exclamations were made about Albert's nose, which he deprecatingly explained away, with a mischievous look at Jane and Ellen, as the result of an amateur boxing spar he had been tempted into with a friend when he had failed to avoid a blow. Mrs Rastrick also knew Albert, of course, from the manufacturing circles of business people who dined together.

"The young ladies have involved me in a charity bazaar, Mrs Rastrick, and so here I am, bound and committed to its organisation."

"Really, Ellen, for someone so interested in clothes for the poor, I wish I could interest you in some for yourself. I can never encourage her to come with me and Sylvia to be measured for gowns!" commented an exasperated Mrs Rastrick.

"Thank you, Mother," said Ellen dryly. "But I am not interested in having more dresses. I have plenty already. Others do not."

"Oh, well – if you must, you must!" declared Mrs Rastrick, raising her hands as if to halt another unwelcome tirade from her daughter (and to be fair, Ellen had been more forthcoming of late at home with her views due to the Clarion Club and Peter's influence). "We are delighted to see you and to meet Miss, er—?"

"Ellison, Mother. Miss Jane Ellison. She is the

daughter of the Queen's Road ministry's vicar."

"Oh," said Mrs Rastrick, the small exclamation managing to show that Jane was not of their class, quite, nor of Albert's, since she measured that by financial status in the main.

Sylvia presented Albert with a demure, knowing smile, of course believing that his visit today was due to her. Ellen, remembering the words she had overheard him speak to her sister at Noel Ogden's statue party, could not find herself dismissing them so easily as John and Cyril had done. Perhaps Albert *was* here hoping the sight of him would remind Sylvia of his half proposal? If so, poor Jane and, also, how typical of him to bring another lady in his company to show that he was sought after. Jane, however, was quietly aglow and indifferent to these various implications, not being aware at all of Albert's having spoken to Sylvia on the day of her engagement. Albert was too subtle to reveal anything himself, of course.

"I think Miss Ellison and I should take our leave of you now. I am sure there is much to discuss about the forthcoming wedding. Once more, my congratulations, Miss Rastrick."

"Mr Dewhirst," responded Sylvia, with an elegant bow of her head.

"Oh, but you must take tea!" objected Mrs Rastrick.

"Thank you, Ma'am. But as you can see" – Albert politely indicated the silver tray and tea set – "Ellen has already refreshed us." He stood up and offered Jane his hand to rise from the couch, rather as if they were at a ball together, so gentlemanly and formal was the gesture.

"Come, Miss Ellison, we will say good afternoon and I am sure Ellen will rally us soon enough to the cause."

Ellen, unseen by her mother and sister, pulled a face at him for this teasing statement, which sailed very close to the wind of the reality of their acquaintanceship together, and Jane smiled a little conspiratorial smile at her too. Ellen rang the bell again and the manservant appeared to show them out.

"You will be sure to call again?" called Mrs Rastrick after Albert's departing figure and he called back his thanks for the invitation.

"Well, well..." said Sylvia, with an arch of her delicate brows. "How interesting of Mr Dewhirst to call."

"They came to see me, Sylvia," said Ellen.

"And remained until *I* returned, Ellen," Sylvia pointed out. This was between themselves as their mother was still fussing after the visitors, standing in the doorway and looking down the hall. "That tea was drunk long ago. The pot is stone cold."

Ellen tutted.

"We had charity business to discuss," she claimed.

"Quaint of him, if so," mocked disbelieving Sylvia. "I am going to put away my new gloves. I cannot believe how many pairs Noel insists upon for different occasions. My trousseau will be a positive caravan on our honeymoon!"

Excusing herself to their mother, she left the room and Ellen soon did the same, there being only so much triumphing she could endure at a sitting. Mrs Rastrick was quite as full of it as Sylvia at present, her disappointment about Leonard temporarily overcome.

Chapter Eight

Ellen thought she would be pleased to escape wedding fever at Saville Park when her visit to her brother and Carrie became due, although it seemed to Ellen that the bridegroom to be did not call to visit his affianced as often as might be expected, seeming to have thrown himself instead into even more lavish rebuilding work at his own house. There were also rehearsals afoot for his theatrical presentation, which seemed set to be more a series of tableaux where everybody could be dressed up to Noel's heart's content, or heart's desire (a phrase he liked to use for many things), rather than an actual performance. There were only certain speeches the participants were required to start learning. He made vague mentions of 'Michaelmas' as being his chosen date for the occasion. Sylvia, busy with that and her ever burgeoning wardrobe ready for the big day, to arrive symbolically on the first day of spring in March (when Noel poetically claimed the new year really began), did not seem piqued by any inattention. There was something unreal about the whole thing to Ellen's mind, a thought she had shared on her last visit to the stonemasons' yard, which had made Cyril strike all the harder at the letters he was chiselling out on a granite obelisk, becoming very pink in the face.

"Least said," suggested John, nodding towards him, and Ellen agreed, realising that Cyril was just as offended by it all as ever.

She dropped the subject, getting on with some gilding for John on a piece he had already done, his dexterity still not fully returned for finer brush work. Ellen had some news to share about another Clarionette, and she wondered if it had already been heard of.

"Did you know," she began innocently, "that Libby

has left us?"

"I'll be damned!" exclaimed John, sounding rather admiring and pausing in oiling whetstones and tools.

"You knew she was thinking of it, then, John?" perceived Ellen.

"She might have made mention," he said casually.

"She said she could not feel the same about working for our household when she was seeing me in meetings of the Clarion Club and on our cycling outings. Also, Mother complained she was becoming rather pert, so we were afraid we might get found out."

"Has she taken another position, then?" asked Cyril, looking up from his chipping.

"Yes, because it wasn't just that. Noel has insisted on hiring a French maid to dress Sylvia's hair and Libby said if she wasn't good enough to put curling papers in any more then she'd just as soon go and be a maid elsewhere."

"Where's she gone to, then?"

"Well, you might not like to hear it, John."

"Oh?"

"The Dewhirsts. Albert's mother has snaffled her right up because she has daughters coming out soon and wanted somebody presentable to be their lady's maid."

"You're right," said John shortly. "I don't like it."

"Albert's a Clarionette as well, isn't he? Why does she want to go there, if it's a problem for her that you're one, Ellen?" said Cyril.

"It won't be *his* hair she's asked to curl, will it?" said John drily. "Libby's wise to him, anyway, and it will be a good position for her otherwise. Any road, he's not there a lot, is he, with his little set-up?"

If this sounded like wishful thinking, nobody said so. Here, the urge to gossip got the better of Ellen.

"Albert came to our house with Jane Ellison the other

day. It was quite strange, I thought. But then I think, do you know, Cyril, that he came to catch Sylvia? She was out at first but I know Sylvia thought the same. She told me so."

John shook his head disgustedly.

"That fellow's playing so fast and loose that he'll catch himself coming back one day!"

"Peter's punch on the nose taught him nowt, then?" commented Cyril, brushing stone dust out of his carvings. "It should have!"

"Aye. Ah dare say..." said Ellen, imitating Peter broadly and dropping her voice, which made them both laugh. "All I'm saying is...that I wouldn't put it past Sylvia, either, to change her mind," she added in her normal voice.

"Neither would I," said John, who seemed to have got over his fascination with Ellen's older sister by now.

"I don't think Noel has the least idea, though," pondered Ellen suggestively.

"Well, he won't have, will he, unless he gets told. It wouldn't occur to Noel Ogden Esquire, would it, that anyone would throw him over?" commented Cyril, getting up and dusting his trousers down too. "I've not said owt to him so far. Hardly seen him."

Having planted the seed again that there was a way of putting a spoke in the wheel perhaps, if Cyril wished to do it, Ellen left. She liked Cyril and whatever was putting his nose out of joint about this engagement she, personally, would like to see Sylvia's delicate nostrils getting the same treatment by some means or another.

***

Ellen left to pay her visit shortly after this, Leonard arriving to collect her and a small trunk to stay for a couple of weeks, with intermittent calls back to Saville Park for dinner occasions planned to be shared between them all. Len's plan was that, if both Ellen and Leonard were returning there, it would make it easier for Carrie to be encouraged to join them too. It was a relief to be away from the house, Ellen felt, as they went along the tree-lined roadway, a mixed deciduous woodland climbing the hillsides making bosky corners and tunnels to go through,

"I hope Mr Stanger is more talkative than we found him on our first visit, Len!"

"Oh, that was just to put us in our places, Ellen. It is quite different now, I promise you. And you know Carrie better, don't you? She plans to spirit you off with her to Manchester sometimes."

"I should like that," said Ellen.

"So should I but *I* am not permitted to go along," said Leonard ruefully. "My wife is a most determined person."

Ellen laughed at that, which she could only agree with. She was warmly welcomed by Carrie, and Mr Stanger too was kindly enough in his greeting of her. He walked with a stick now, rather slowly and seemed to have failed from the Mr Stanger of old. Leonard retreated to their business discussions while Ellen got settled into the room which was to be hers for the stay. Carrie helped her unpack her trunk, there seeming to be little in the way of household servants here, only a cook and day servant, who did not live in. Carrie, it seemed, lived by her principles.

"You must do your own hair here, Ellen," she told her visitor and Ellen truthfully replied that it did not take much doing, which seemed to go down well.

The first week passed quietly enough and Ellen only had one uneasy moment, when Len took her along to show her the restoration and development work being done on the old mill building which she had helped to destroy. It included having far more windows for light and air, the separation of product from dangerous places such as the chimney (the foundations of which were being rebuilt as they watched on for a while), and serious planning for health and safety in the workplace. Carrie had been persuading both Leonard and her father that this was integral to the general welfare of both workforce and eventual profit, Ellen's brother told her, and it was being given careful consideration.

Conversations on that topic could get quite lively around the dinner table. Ellen could see that Len felt his wife's convictions carried weight and he backed her up in them where Mr Stanger demurred. A sticking point at present was that Carrie proposed there should be compensation for injury from the employer when workers had been harmed in the course of dealing with machines. She said it ought to be part of their contracted agreement and that it should not come at a price of contribution from the wage, as Len and Mr Stanger were eventually minded to suggest. Ellen joined in her further argument that a competitive wage for a better workforce was also a better wage, not a meaner one, especially if you were presenting your factory as new and forward looking. Here, the menfolk scoffed that this was mere womanly sentiment and not good business sense and there, having won some ground on the compensation front, Carrie and Ellen left it for now.

The advances that had been made and the advantages that might come out of the new Stanger's Mill almost persuaded Ellen that Peter had been right. Dreadful as their act had been, so destructive to the present conditions of the now laid-off mill workers, it might indeed have made an active contribution towards a nobler future, she now began to believe. Inspired by the feeling, she wrote to Peter in glowing terms about it. Going further, when Carrie invited her to Manchester, the private reason being to hear speakers about improving holiday entitlements for workers on the anniversary of the Peterloo Massacre (an occasion which would also be remembered on that day), she asked if she could invite Peter too. Carrie knew of him only as a fireman and member of the Clarion Club, of course, and was happy to agree. As far as Mr Stanger and Leonard were concerned, they were ostensibly only visiting Carrie's old schoolfriends over there and indulging in some lady's debating club activity for charitable benevolence. The arrangement that Peter would go too was kept between themselves. As they were dropped at the Halifax railway station and descended the steps to the platform, Ellen asked if Leonard really still had no idea about the political nature of his wife's involvements.

"Leonard knows what he chooses to know and stops short of what it would be inconvenient to him to be faced with. Which suits us both for the present," Carrie said.

Ellen had to agree that this sounded like Len. She had found it useful enough herself when asking to borrow his bicycle for her own excursions with the Clarion Club. If she had sometimes wondered if he knew more, as he might easily encounter Albert and Noel in the circles they generally moved in, he never said so or provoked any direct mention of it. Ellen had sent the money for Peter's ticket. He was to meet her the following day to hear the speeches at the Free Trade Hall and attend the rally in St Peter's Square.

Carrie was pleased Ellen would have somebody to be with her, as she herself would be involved apart with some of the occasion's arrangements, and she approved of a Clarionette companion, quite unwitting of his having been the Stanger's Mill saboteur. Ellen and Peter stood together looking up at the platform before the Town Hall from St Peter's Square. The speeches were stirring and the atmosphere very emotional. The outrage and tragedy that had happened there eighty years before was almost in living memory and certainly still very alive in that of the people present. Hearing of it all in such emotional circumstances, on the very site of the event, was deeply moving.

Peter, who had angry tears standing in his eyes by the end, exclaimed to Ellen, "All them folk, Ellen! Just trampled down like that! Heartless! Deliberate! You see? That's why we have to take the fight direct to *them*. They're armed and we're not. If they haven't got weapons, they've got power. We've got neither! We have to find ways to attack back. Now do you understand, Ellen? Why we set that fire? I think you do from what you wrote to me."

"I think I do, but, Carrie's already with us, isn't she, Peter? And she's full of the same feeling."

"Aye. I'll not deny it. I've heard her. But she's all for ideas 'n talk. It's action we need! The factory owners' machines are still rolling on full steam ahead, making money for them and to hell with the workers! Everywhere!"

"Not now at Stanger's it isn't, is it, Peter? Why don't we talk to Carrie? I believe that she and I could persuade Len to take you on as adviser on the new mill conditions they're working on. You could make real change then!"

"Eh? *Me*? *There*!" he exclaimed, genuinely taken aback, but Ellen was determined to walk him back into the lion's den and set him to do battle in the right place. When she and Carrie went to take the train back from Victoria station, Peter travelled with them and the next thing they knew, she and Peter were talking excitedly to Carrie, who was impressed by Peter's blunt fervour and the strength of his convictions. After some discussion of the day's speeches and the memorial occasion, Ellen introduced the subject in question.

"Peter worked in Bradbury's, that flour factory that burned down as well, Carrie. So he knows all about dangers in the mills. And I think a man would help persuade Len and your father much better on the idea of injury compensation."

"Aye – but a *working* man," put in Peter, in his defensively hostile way. "That won't be the same, will it?"

"It could be," considered Carrie, "if you were advisory foreman. Of course, we won't make a mention of the Clarion Club to either of them. Peter, come to the house on Wednesday. Ellen and I will have had a day to speak to Leonard and my father. I believe we are at a point where I may persuade my husband that to have a young, forward-thinking man at his elbow in devising the mill's practices could be a considerable advantage to him."

"All right. What time?" Peter asked, not quite able to be gracious with thanks to her even now, until Ellen gave him a dig in the ribs and he added, "I'd be glad to help out wi' it all. If I can."

"I'm sure you will," said Carrie, as direct as ever, smiling at him as the train pulled in. "Let us say eleven o'clock. I will have prepared the ground."

"But – how will you say I'm known of?"

"Why, by reputation, of course, Mr Lumb."

"How's that?" he asked, alert to danger.

"You are one of the hero firemen who tried to save our mill, are you not, Mr Lumb? That will impress them both quite sufficiently for a proper introduction from Ellen and myself, who visited you and your comrades in the hospital after the event. In my eyes, and I am sure in theirs, there is an obligation towards you from our family. Your expertise in the world of manufacture when you explain it will, I am sure, be welcome. We may say with absolute truth that we recently encountered you again together and you mentioned your situation to us. Ellen, we will go into town tomorrow on the pretext of gloves and that can be our little white lie about it. Now then, Peter, Len is always crying on about the need for fresh blood in Father's business and you may provide some. Come, Ellen – we must go up and not keep our driver waiting. He's getting on a bit and it's raining out there. I dare say the poor man will be glad to get out of it again."

Ellen gave Peter a conspiratorial smile. He smiled back at them both and said, rather more cordially than before, shaking hands with each of them in turn, "It's been grand. Thank you. I'll sithee on Wednesday, then."

He was still looking up at them from the platform when Ellen glanced back down as she and Carrie hurried up the stone steps with their portmanteaus. Lightly falling rain in the flares of the lights made a gas lamp halo round his capped head. She felt she knew that if they had been alone together then, he would have kissed her again. Once in the carriage, Carrie said, "Leave it to me, Ellen and step in if I give you a sign to do so. Oh, and if you and Peter are particular friends, I would maintain that discretion of yours about it."

She spoke factually, as was her habit and Ellen replied in kind, "Thank you, Carrie. I will", without clarifying anything as, really, Carrie had just about summed things up between herself and Peter without the need for it.

Ellen had been quite relieved to see Peter in Manchester. The seriousness of Carrie's friends at the house they had stayed in overnight, the earnest debates and talk of women's education and suffrage among pioneering spirits, unleavened by the social activity which was key to her participation in the Clarion Club, was on quite a different level from what she was used to. She felt they would see through her to some frivolous and apolitical core in an instant. Ellen was not political in their sense of it. She was an instinctive socialist, with no appetite for the intellectual discussions and battles among inner circle groups of activists over who should lead, who was right, who had the purer concept or the more real commitment. She was younger than the other women who had been there, granted, and they had, within those arenas, their own ambitions, but even so, she sensed she was not one of them.

Carrie's friend Fiona, their hostess, was fiercely committed to women training as doctors. She had not achieved it personally and was not young enough now to avail herself of any hard-won opportunities to train for it, but worked dispensing medicines on a voluntary basis at a children's hospital. Fiona was a busy, frustrated kind of woman, an energetic talker filled with ideas where Carrie was silent until she had something to say, when she was eloquent enough.

"She hasn't changed a jot since I was at school with her, Ellen," Carrie had said, smiling as she introduced them. "As lively as a young girl still about everything, as you will see." And as Ellen had seen, she was.

Fiona had strong eyebrows, a mass of frizzy hair compressed into a bun and a gesticulating, jerky manner which made her seem angrily forceful where she was really being enthusiastic. Like Carrie, her kindness was not visible on first acquaintance, but between the two of them a deep friendship clearly existed, one with strong foundations. When Ellen and her sister-in-law returned to Heatherfield – that big, sombre house which seemed to Ellen to have slipped down the hill to embed itself in the valley bottom because it was unable to cling on due to all the rain tippling down on it and dripping over it from the trees even now – Ellen told Leonard about Carrie's friends, and Fiona in particular. She thought lighter-hearted Len would be amused by it (although she left out the detail of quite how political it all was). Indeed, he *was* entertained and laughed although, in a sudden jealous pet which surprised her, he said, "At least *you* have been allowed the privilege of meeting these ladies, Ellen. Carrie keeps her friends quite apart from *me*!" and looked rather flushed and put out as he spoke.

"Why, Len!" exclaimed Ellen. "I expect she simply thinks you are not interested, being so busy with the mill business."

"Yes. Quite. And so I am," he hastened to say. "But I like to spend some time with my wife too, you know."

From this, Ellen realised that he had come to appreciate Carrie's qualities and that it was *she* who did not change things between them rather than Len creating the dynamic. Of course, Ellen did not know about the separate bedrooms signifying that they were not man and wife in the fullest sense of the relationship and, equally, she was vague on that aspect of life, being brought up with the prevailing decorum about such things. Now, meeting men among the Clarionettes was waking those physical sensibilities up in her, as it had done in Jane, but Ellen was still naïve about any carnal detail. Seeing only that he felt excluded in some way, Ellen said, "Why don't the three of us ride out on our bicycles after lunch? See – the rain is stopping and the sun may come out for us."

Len had left his bicycle at home for her use and bought himself a new one here. They had brought Ellen's with her precisely so they could enjoy the exercise. Her brother brightened with the suggestion as much as the weather soon did. Carrie was willing and, with Mr Stanger settled in his study with a book and a blanket over his knees, a small fire beside him, they rode out into an August afternoon from the dim gloom of the house, which always felt cool in the interior. This particular afternoon outing was something Ellen always remembered for, as they reached a rise, from across the valley, as magically as if belonging to a fairy-tale, a parade of hot air balloons travelled silently across. They seemed to have come from another realm, as if the gilded onion domes of Russian palaces had taken flight in some enchanted transformation to travel the world. They watched, fascinated, until the balloons passed over in a gaily coloured line.

"Now, *there's* a club I would like to join!" exclaimed Len. "Imagine doing that! Better than your cycling blue stockings, Ellen!"

"It's not all women, Len!" she was stung into replying. "And you know some of them, don't you – Albert and Noel? In fact, one of them means to call on you tomorrow. Not Albert or Noel – Peter Lumb."

"Call upon me? Why?"

"He is one of the firemen who so bravely tried to save the mill, Len," said Carrie. "Ellen and I visited the men in hospital and he was one of them. We met him by chance in town yesterday when we went in for our new gloves. I have invited him. He is in need of a position and has a great deal of interesting ideas for new factory methods."

"Has he, indeed?" exclaimed Len, impressed by his wife's foresight. "Then I will be interested to meet him and talk about them. I need a good man to lead the way for our workforce."

"Precisely as I knew you would think, Len," said Carrie, and they smiled at one another with a warmth which Ellen thought rather touching.

Len had not respected Carrie before he married her and perhaps not even when he did so, but he clearly did now and wanted to win her approval of him. Ellen thought that no bad thing for Leonard. Yet she also felt a little sad for him because he was so young, still starting out in his life when Carrie seemed so decided about her own world and his place in it already. Peter arrived on time and he and Leonard, after a brief exchange of greetings with the ladies, went to speak privately.

"I hope it goes well," said Ellen. "Peter can be a bit outspoken, you know, Carrie."

"He has passion, certainly," agreed Carrie. "I think what he needs is direction. Perhaps this will give it to him. At least for a while. He struck me as being a restless soul."

"Peter says his employers called him a malcontent when he tried to speak up for others."

"If he is angry and bitter, Ellen, that may bite deeper in him as he gets older, if he does not find a means of satisfying that energy. We shall see. But you should bear it in mind, my dear. You are at an impressionable age and ideals are very good at carrying a girl's feelings away."

She was busy writing a letter and glanced up as she spoke, but only for an instant, so that her words did not sound critical so much as dispassionately honest. Ellen was disconcerted by Carrie's penetrating insights and flustered by the direct reference to a socially impossible attraction between herself and someone like Peter. It being spoken of gave it a reality which panicked her at once.

"Carrie – I shall never marry and so you may spare yourself any concern on that account! And certainly not…" She tailed off before saying his name or saying, 'anyone like him', feeling once again that now familiar confusion of hers about those who were working-class people in the Clarion Club, Peter included.

It was a confusion which made her feel hotly unworthy of what she professed and yet, she still felt it. Carrie said no more on the subject and finished her letter, while Ellen silently composed herself.

"You may ring for our coffee, Ellen, if you do not

mind?" Carrie suggested after an interval. "I think it is time."

They drank it together, waiting for Peter and Leonard to emerge, which they eventually did, shaking hands.

"Well, Carrie and Ellen – you already know Mr Lumb, but let me introduce you to him as our new foreman manager," said Len. "He is able to begin and happy to take one of your father's cottages on the bend of the hill just along, Carrie, so that he does not have so far to come to his work. Shall we say, in a couple of weeks, to give you time to organise your move, Mr Lumb?"

"Aye. That'd be time enough," he said.

"I'll take you now to show you where it is – they are only small but we have a vacant one at present."

"All reet," agreed Peter, sounding gruff but pleased enough and standing on awkward ceremony as to his dignity throughout. "Mrs Rastrick, Miss Ellen Rastrick – I am pleased to see you again and thank you for recommending me."

"Not at all," replied Carrie.

Ellen, such formality from Peter feeling strange immediately in spite of her earlier thoughts, said on impulse, "Wait – I'll come with you!" and hurried off to get her wrap.

Already, Ellen was beginning to wonder if she had done the right thing by putting the unpredictably hectic Peter in the midst of the tranquil Stanger family pond that seemed to be doing well so far. In spite of Len being married to her, she continued to think of Carrie as Miss Stanger really since, with her independent ways, that was how she still carried herself in Ellen's view. Leonard and Peter were waiting for her on the front step with the wide, square front door open to the green hillside view running directly up. A dappled sunshine, instead of rain for once, was dropping upon them from the overhanging trees. It was a house that seemed to attract rain and the surrounding woods called up a morning mist even on dry days. Peter was taller than Leonard by a few inches, his profile, as their heads were turned to speak to one another, more angular as he glanced down at his new employer. Even from the back he looked all elbows somehow, ready to shove about. It amused Ellen to see it in his stance.

"Here I am!" she called out and they both smiled as she joined them, setting out for the road and the climb to the bend around which the small cottages were invisible until you reached them, tucked into the lee of the hill further up from Heatherfield. The hillside opposite the cottages was wooded and they would surely be dark inside most of the time but they looked sturdy, thick-walled and made to endure. Leonard produced a key and they went inside.

"This one is empty now, Peter. A few places hereabouts are, since the mill burned out. People had to find work elsewhere. Old Joshua Leyburn and his wife, who lived here, decided to retire and move away when the mill went down. I think their daughter took them in over Barkisland way."

Ellen glanced at Peter, biting her lip at this guilty responsibility and he looked a little stressed too but soon rallied.

"I'll make it all up to them," he declared. "They'll have a better workplace to come back to than the one they left, if they want it."

Ellen knew why he made that choice of words if Leonard, who answered lightly, did not.

"Yes. That's the ticket. Do you think it will suit you here?"

"Oh aye, of course," answered Peter.

"We will put a bed in for you, naturally, upstairs, and

perhaps a new table and chairs for your kitchen. I'm sure there were more things before..." Len frowned at the paucity of furnishings.

"Nay – they're grand as they are, them," Peter said, not being much of a one to notice that anyway. "And I can bring me own bed. I do have one, you know," he added, prickly.

"Very well," said Leonard. "But there's no need. Cumbersome piece to transport all this way."

Leonard and Ellen knew as well as Peter did that his bed was likely to be required by others in his family, being an expensive item, if he really did have one. It was rather more likely that he slept on a simple mattress on the floor.

"Well, then. I don't mind if you don't," conceded Peter, honour being satisfied by suggesting he could supply this himself.

There was not much comfort in the place, unfurnished apart from one wooden chair with a broken spell left in front of a small unlit fire with an oven to the side. A narrow window with a deep casement cast a little light, although most of it came from the cottage door left open behind them. Peter went upstairs and, after a cursory glance at the one room up there, he came back down the narrow, unrailed stair to say, "It's all reet, that is", by way of approval.

"Good," said Leonard. "Now, I need to get back, I am afraid. I have a business appointment in town to go to."

"Mr Lumb, should you like to walk up and see the Moor before we turn back ourselves?" suggested Ellen on impulse, knowing he would like it. "It's a fine view and just along the road here. We would only be a few moments behind you, Len?"

"Very well," Leonard agreed.

He made no demur, since she made out she would

scarcely be out of his chaperoning responsibility for more than five minutes and on the public highway anyway. Besides, he still saw her as rather a child and Peter was only a workman, a respectful employee being briefly shown around by the owner's sister. Shaking hands with Peter again, Leonard left them on the road outside the cottage.

"It's a lovely day but it's cold and dark in there, Peter," said Ellen.

"I'll not be in it much. Let's get on out of it, then, and see that moor tha's on abaht," he said.

A woman hurriedly came out next door to beat a rug, curious to see her new neighbour and exchange a few words.

"Tha's moving into Leyburns', then?" she asked.

"Aye – Peter Lumb," he answered. "Working at Stangers. Getting it going again, like."

"Dorrie Starkey. You'll be seeing our Norman there later on, then."

"Aye," he agreed.

Ellen smiled in the background and was nodded at too, for of course, everybody here knew who everybody was in the Stanger family without much need for being told about it and curious eyes had watched her and Len arriving with Peter.

"Miss Rastrick," said the woman, going back in with her peg rug, having beaten as much coal dust out of it as was possible against the wall as they spoke.

***

Peter and Ellen set off up the hill again. Further along, the road climbed up through Booth Wood to Rishworth Moor above the treeline. The highest tops were a pale bleakness of bleached grass with rock bones sticking out of it, as they were nearly all year round. Heather was in bloom where they stopped to look around, so Peter and

Ellen walked into the tussocky ground to cut some with Peter's pocket knife for Ellen to take back.

"You can breathe up 'ere," said Peter. "I wish Stan could be 'ere an' all. He's fair choked with coughing now."

"Poor Stanley," said Ellen. "Let me speak to Len! Would he come too?"

"Nay – he'll not leave his mother or Crossley Carpets – I think he feels he were born part of their looms, that lad," said Peter.

"He wouldn't like it if you wanted to burn that one down then," commented Ellen, touching on dangerous ground.

"You cheeky beggar, Ellen Rastrick!" Peter retorted with a laugh. "You played your part."

"I know. But – those empty cottages. Did we really do right, Peter?"

"I don't know," he admitted. "But it's done nah, in't it? And I'm grateful for all this today."

He turned to look at her, their arms full of the tough, coarse heather, and stooping slightly, he kissed her lightly on the lips, once. As at Sunny Vale, he took her by surprise with the gesture, over in an instant. This time, recently agitated too by Carrie's words about Peter, Ellen felt a confused panic about his brief kiss, while pleased and touched by it. As if sensing her thoughts, straightening up he said, "Why would someone like you admire that ninny-headed Noel Ogden, Ellen? I know you did. Mebbe you still do. I hope his being engaged to your sister does not wound you too badly."

"No," she said shortly, offended by his reference to Noel and that he slighted him.

Although Peter had kissed her again and she liked it, she also felt conflicted, compromised by what he had made her do alongside of him that day at Stanger's Mill.

There was a complex assumption of their being tied together by it which she felt helpless about and he seemed so sure of. They looked around at the view again, the sun warm on their cheeks.

"Folk say I'm all hedgehog, me, always have me prickles aht. I know I do, but they're not inside of me, Ellen. You've been a good lass to me and I'll not forget that," Peter said after a moment.

She smiled up at him at this, wondering if he would kiss her again but, just like the lightning kiss, he did not. Ellen felt then that, just as before, this was more about thanking her as his comrade and friend than kissing her as a sweetheart. She wasn't sure how she felt about that, either.

"Come on, then, let's get this back and you can put some in a jar for t' table, Ellen. I'll take some back to me mam for hers. See if she likes it," he said.

"I'm sure she will," Ellen agreed and they went back down to Heatherfield, where Peter bade her goodbye, heading off on his bicycle with sprigs of heather sicking spryly out of either side of his jacket pockets, a comical sight which made her smile as she watched him go.

"Carrie – look, I have brought us some heather!" she cried on her return and they busied themselves with finding glass vases to cram the tough stalks into, the tiny flower heads a vibrant violet against the green hillside beyond the dining room table.

"You went up to the Moor? We should take a picnic there one day while you are here and the weather is good. I am sure Father would enjoy that. It's put colour in your cheeks, Ellen."

Ellen smiled, thinking of Peter's brief kiss and what it might mean. No doubt she would ponder about it while he forgot it altogether, she thought, and what would be the point in that? She would be gone back home before

Peter arrived to live in the cottage in any case, though, for her visit was nearly over.

***

Noel Ogden had planned a picnic to be eaten at the foot of Wainhouse Tower, before which all the Clarionettes would climb to the top to enjoy the two bottles of champagne he had had taken up there to toast his new ownership of the view from there. He was already waiting there for them with his picnic brought over by cart from his house, left ready in baskets for them to help themselves.

"Here we all are, you see!" Noel called as they cycled along to him and dismounted. "I would have brought my butler to serve us but I thought you would disapprove since we are here as the Clarion Club."

Cyril said, "It's not all I disapprove of, Noel." But Noel ignored him.

"Come, everyone – our champagne won't exactly be getting warm up there but I do so long for you all to see from the top – it is magnificent!"

"We are not all here yet, Noel," said Ellen, looking around.

John and Libby now rode down the cobbles of Wainhouse Road together and walked their bicycles alongside to the group.

"Libby!" called Ellen. "It seems so strange not to be arriving with you!"

Libby came to give her a hug, quite as a friend, and said, "I've missed you too, Ellen." Which Ellen found touching.

"You came with John," she said, surprised.

"Aye, I did," replied Libby. "And you came with Peter Lumb."

"No, we met along the way here."

"Mebbe we did an' all," quipped Libby in return, but

there was something in her manner which belied that.

Hannah and Sarah were strolling arm in arm while Albert joked with Noel, glancing across curiously at Libby and John. Ellen thought that it rather served Albert right not to have all the attention his way. She looked around and said, "We can't go up yet – where is Jane Ellison? And what about Stanley?"

"Stan's too poorly to come, Ellen, I'm sorry to say," said Peter. "I don't know about the others."

Jane approached on foot just then, coming through the graveyard gates on the other side.

"Here I am!" she greeted them, hearing Ellen's words called across the gathering. "I walked here today."

Eustace hurried to meet her.

"I have not seen you for a long time, Jane!" he exclaimed. "I hope I find you well?"

"Very well, thank you!" she answered in a defiant kind of voice which almost seemed intended for other ears, but nobody else turned to her and Albert seemed very busy laughing his hat off with Noel.

Noel now made great ceremony with the key to the wooden door of the tower, which was sunk into a small gothic archway of stone. Circular steps showed leading up once he opened it to the daylight.

"Will you walk into my parlour, said the spider to the fly," remarked Cyril.

"Did you speak, changeling boy?" asked Noel sweetly.

Cyril scowled at him and folded his arms.

"Don't call me that," he said, looking provoked.

"It is our old nickname."

"*Our!*" scoffed Cyril. "There's nobbut *thee* talks like that."

"Come, everyone!" called Noel, ignoring Cyril and gesturing them all inside with a grand wave of his arm.

"Now, at the top, when you arrive there, you will see that this *is* a midsummer dream – the whole valley below you and on a clear day, which it is, you can see all the way to Blackpool and the sea, so they say."

"Oh, aye?" said Peter with his dour humour. "Let's crack on, then, shall we? I could get a taste for thy mucky champagne, Noel. I quite liked it when we had it for John's statue."

"Excellent! You can only go up one at a time," Noel explained.

"Unlink, ladies!" Albert said to Hannah and Sarah. "Onward, then! Lead the way, Noel, there's a good fellow."

"Gladly!" cried Noel, stepping inside like a knight on a mission.

He was wearing a silver-grey silk suit and a white waistcoat, which gave him a look of shining splendour, Ellen thought. He was soon lost in the gloom of the turns of the stairs, which were splattered with pigeon droppings. Arrow-slit-like openings illuminated the way and gave glimpses of treetops receding below them as their legs began to ache with the climb. Chatter had stopped with the labour of ascending.

"How much further is it, man?" asked Albert with a groan.

"His legs are weak from lack of standing up all day in't mill," said Hannah.

"Aye, you can tell the man who dun't work at machines all day," criticised Sarah. "And he does a fair bit of lying about too, does Albert."

Her words echoed up the stairwell, giving them an undertone of suggestiveness which might or might not have been present.

"Sarah!" said Albert, sounding mock-injured.

"Keep up!" called Noel. "Nearly there! Four hundred

and three steps in all!"

Eventually, the gloom gave way and they emerged onto a fine stone balustrade at the bottom of the ornate lantern top, two hundred and fifty feet and more up from the ground. There was space for them to walk round it and admire the view from the different sides, gasping with lack of breath and at the unexpected splendour and reach of the vista. If they could not actually see the sea, they felt as if they could.

"By 'eck, you can see to t'ends of the earth up 'ere!" exclaimed Peter, who was moved by the spectacle's grandeur rather as he had been by the music at the concert and, in a different way, as he had been by the words of the speeches at the Peterloo memorial.

Ellen felt that he had an instinctively deep reaction to things, another sign of hidden talents that could have been nurtured in other directions earlier in life, given the opportunity.

"Look at this stonework!" cried John, equally enthusiastic and admiring the talent of the sculptor who had carved out the pieces. Albert arrived at Jane's side, looking out with her.

"Now, this is as fine a place as we could have to be side by side, Jane, is it not?" he murmured and she smiled in delight, the strain leaving her face at being given this private message.

"It is," she agreed in a low, soft voice, saying no more but her words full of such feeling that he could not have missed it.

Ellen, who was on their other side, certainly did not, but her attention was distracted by Noel, grandiloquent as ever and opening champagne to toast the view.

"My friends, dear friends, companions and Clarionettes – I give you – The Wainhouse Tower!"

"The Wainhouse Tower!" they all cried, dutifully

raising their glasses.

The Clarionettes continued to admire the view, breezes crossing their faces, the champagne beginning to buzz in their blood. Ellen walked round again and came across Cyril and Noel together, standing very close.

"It changes nothing," she thought she heard Noel say in impatient remonstrance and then Cyril spoke.

"How can you do it, Noel, when…"

"Hush, man," said Noel.

"I cannot bear it!" exclaimed Cyril, dashing his glass accidentally against the balustrade so that they were both showered with crystal sprinkles, tiny shards glittering on Noel's white waistcoat.

He jarred bodily against Noel at the same time and if the balustrade had not been above waist height, disaster might have struck. Cyril reached out instinctively to grab Noel's hand and pull him forward. Noel held on for a moment longer than necessary and Cyril let go abruptly.

"You're all right," he muttered savagely and moved aside as he saw Ellen trying to get out of sight but with nowhere to go. "I wish your sister and Albert *would* do more than flirt," he said to her.

Noel only laughed to hear it, putting paid to any idea that this would cause him the slightest concern.

"Good God, what are you playing at there?" exclaimed John, coming round the other side at the commotion.

"Nothing whatsoever. Cyril broke his glass, that is all. The wind will blow it all quite clean away!" said Noel. "Now – let us go down for our picnic."

"Will your *fiancée* be joining us?" asked Cyril.

"Of course not, dear heart, she is not a Clarionette, is she?" answered Noel, pulling out a lace-edged handkerchief to brush the crumbs of glass from his frontage, which sparkled on it like spangles.

Ellen heard them, and probably John did too, but they

said nothing as Noel marshalled his party again to return to ground level, saying they could always come back up to admire the view once more after eating. Descending more easily than they had gone up, but finding it dizzying round the constant turns, they finally emerged again back at ground level to enjoy spreading out the lavish provisions which had been delivered for their picnic revel. Jane came bridally out of the arched doorway with Albert talking to her, having lost the pallor with which she had arrived, infused once more with the inner glow which she had worn when he brought her to visit Ellen.

"Did you strike Albert because of Jane before, Peter?" Ellen asked him privately, remembering how Peter had lashed out on the moorland cycle ride.

"Mebbe – but more because Albert's Albert, in't he?" said Peter, encapsulating in one the maddening nature of that young man's cocksure charm. "Even if he did give me a bit of an 'and for a bit."

"Do you like Jane?" Ellen pursued, struck by the idea for the first time.

"Well enough, but nay, not like *tha* means," answered Peter becoming broader in accent, possibly from embarrassment at being put on an emotional spot. "Either we're comrades or we're just men and women laiking abaht. I know which I want it to be." Ellen was not sure if she were relieved or disappointed by this statement. "Which isn't to say…" Peter was just adding hastily when Albert himself swanned over with his hand stuck out to shake his.

"No hard feelings, Peter? I don't want another bop on the nose."

"Aye, well…"

"I know, I asked for it." He favoured Peter with his disarming smile and said, "I am so sorry you got laid off again. I tried my best with the old man…"

"Ah dare say," said Peter, in that way he had of sounding both flat and disbelieving at the same time, so that it was impossible to be sure of his real feeling about it. "I'm sorted any road. Ellen here – she's got me took on at Stanger's. Advisory foreman, like, to her brother. I start soon, not that they're near opening up again yet."

"Well done, Ellen," said Albert, sounding impressed. "Foreman too!"

"I only accepted as it means I'm sorting out better working conditions," Peter hastened to point out.

"It sounds an excellent opportunity by anybody's reckoning!" said Eustace, coming up to them too and offering his own hand to Albert. "Let's all shake on friendship again, since we were all party to the blow up."

"Gladly, Eustace!" agreed Albert. "Come and talk to Jane with me. I have her sitting over here with Hannah and Sarah, do you see?"

"Nicely done," said Peter drily, watching Eustace go over and put an end to whatever private circle Jane might have thought she was being drawn into.

A faint shadow crossed her face again but soon all eyes were back on Noel making great play of cutting up a ham and joint of boiled beef, to hand out with bread and salad. Cyril and John were seated by Ellen and Peter.

"Look at him," said Cyril trenchantly.

"Never mind him," warned John. "Look to yourself, Cyril."

"I know," said Cyril, a shadow crossing his own face.

Libby came brightly over from laughing with Albert and his party and sat with casual ease by John and between him and Ellen, so that Ellen had to shuffle aside closer to Peter.

"How are you liking it at Albert's, then?" asked Ellen rather pointedly.

"I am *not* at Albert's," answered Libby. "I'm serving

Albert's mother and his sisters, which is quite another thing. I do miss you though, dafty. And all our nattering."

"I suppose they've got better hair," said Ellen.

"Well, it stays in curl," retorted Libby, laughing and shaking her own, which made John laugh and twirl one lock round his still half-gloved fingers playfully.

"You could make machine springs with them!" he said.

"Charming!" responded Libby.

It was the kind of teasing which suggested they were quite at ease with one another, at a tender stage of courtship. A flush of jealousy passed through Ellen. So, she had been right, then! And he had told her nothing of it, despite her being such good friends with him and Cyril at the stonemasons' workshop!

"John has carved a stone angel which looks just like my sister, Sylvia, you know, Libby," she said meanly. "Come and see it. It's in this graveyard just above now. If Sylvia saw it, she'd have a fit. It's one thing to look like an angel and quite another to be carved into a dead one, isn't it?"

In spite of herself, although she had meant to annoy Libby with this, she could not help the impulse to jointly mock Sylvia because that had been a bond between them for such a long time. Libby had used to say that Ellen's older sister was all silver plate that would soon tarnish and wear, whilst Ellen was pure silver that just needed a bit of polishing 'to shine up proper'. Ellen missed that. Ellen and Libby got up together to stroll through the iron gates and up the pathway of the graveyard which, like everything here, ran up and down hillsides. Ellen led Libby to a new white marble monument, not yet lichened by damp or blackened by soot. Looking at it again, she admired the delicate, goddess-like beauty John had given to the angel's graceful head, the inhuman coolness of her blank gaze capturing something of Sylvia too, classically anonymous though the statue was in style. A drapery about the angel's head fell back in soft folds to the arching wings half-open above her shoulders.

"She looks ready to fly up to t' top of Wainhouse Tower," said Libby. "And it is right like your sister, Sylvia, Ellen. In a way – if you want to think so."

This made Ellen look at Libby again, who was smiling, and now she saw Libby in the curve of the angel's mouth and the rounds of her cheekbones, the tilt of her eye corners.

"Why!" she exclaimed. "You modelled for John too, before he'd finished it."

"That I did. He weren't happy wi' it before. Besides, I told him she looked a right misery, and if it were made to look like Sylvia Rastrick, no wonder, either."

Ellen laughed, in spite of the jealous feelings running through her like a cold sweat. Not only did she miss Libby, but Libby was taking her place visiting at the studio with John and Cyril, which she had thought only she went to!

"You are all busy without me!" she burst out, resenting it at various levels.

Libby put her arm round Ellen's still narrow shoulders and gave her a half-hug, perceiving some of the reasons for this.

"Nay. I know you've been helping and learning down at the studio. That's good in't it? But you see, John's steady and he's ready for settling, you know. So am I. We're in our twenties and you're still a lass getting going."

"But, Libby!" Ellen protested at this practical summary of matters.

"I don't want to be a maidservant all me life, Ellen. I didn't just join the Clarion Club to get out wi' thee, did I?"

"No. I know. I've heard you speak at meetings sometimes."

"Well, then."

"But – his hands! He cannot work the same…"

"They're nearly mended and nowt's stopping him, is it?"

"No."

"I'll have my own home, Ellen, instead of living in other people's. And that's my start. With a man like John, it won't be the end of it if I want to work too. At summat *I* want to do."

"I didn't realise you hated being my maid so much, Libby!" said Ellen, her lip now trembling slightly.

"I didn't hate being *your* maid, Ellen. I hate having to *be* a maid. There's a world of difference in it. Besides, you and I are Clarionettes and friends outside of all that. Always will be, if you want it."

Ellen nodded.

"I do," she said and Libby gave her shoulder another squeeze before dropping her arm again. But Ellen wasn't satisfied yet. "What about Albert? When you went to work there, I thought, I mean, he's always flirted with you!" she burst out, full of implications. "And you were talking and laughing with him down there."

"Well, he tried it on, like, naturally. But I soon put him straight. I said, 'Flirting a bit outside were one thing. But not here in your mother's 'ouse and not wi' me. You've them other two I know about to think of. And I'm walking out with John Henderson.'"

"And he left it at that?"

Libby grinned. "Oh, he invited me down to that photographic studio of his. I said I'd come with John for a picture card of us in our Sunday best."

"And did you?"

"Aye, we did. And afterwards, Albert did leave it at that. Besides, he dun't stay nights at the family home often. We both know why, don't we? Family think he has a bachelor apartment in town."

"Maybe he does."

"Mebbe. I wouldn't put much past Albert. But he needs me to keep his secret about Hannah and Sarah from his parents, dun't he? He were proper shocked to find me answering t' door at his mother's, I can tell you. I said I wouldn't say owt if he didn't, and not about t' Clarion Club, either. I don't want that coming out or I'd lose me place before I was ready."

"Do you think Albert does believe in what the Clarion Club stands for?" Ellen asked next.

Libby considered for a moment.

"I think he's feeling his way with it. Like t'rest of us. It's a new thing. Besides, them two women, Hannah and Sarah…there's respect for 'em in 'im after his fashion. And he dun't keep 'em as such, they're working. Free, I suppose, in a way. Not that it'd do for me, like. Not one bit. Don't you worry about that!"

"Free…" pondered Ellen, picking up on that word. "People say that a lot about things in the Clarion Club don't they? I wonder what it really means sometimes. Anyway, I'm glad he's behaving himself with you, Libby."

"He'd get a right good slap from me if he didn't," Libby retorted. "Come on, let's get back before we miss the cake!"

"Oh no! I'm not missing cake!" Ellen answered, her teenage years resurfacing as she made to race back first, regardless of the possible impropriety of running in a graveyard, with none but the dead and the Sylvia/Libby stone angel to see her. They arrived back laughing and breathless just in time for slices of the iced fruitcake, which Noel was now cutting with his usual panache.

"Good God, man, you're slicing at it like a dragoon at an enemy!" exclaimed Albert.

"Yes, you're supposed to cut a cake, not slaughter it," said Cyril.

"Come and help me then, Cyril," said Noel and Cyril did, guiding Noel's hand with his on top of it with humorous force.

"Like that, and the next slice here…"

Rather as Jane and Albert had emerged, wedding like, from the tower's doorway, there was something of cutting the bridal cake together in Cyril and Noel's posture, it seemed to Ellen. Perhaps this struck her because she and Libby had just been talking about weddings? All of a sudden, Ellen realised it. Cyril loved Noel, rather as she thought she had done, and Noel was playing with him about it while acting as if it were a secret between them. Could there be such a thing between two men? Ellen had never thought of it before and yet the evidence was plain before her now that she perceived it. Cyril's distress, his words to Noel on top of the tower, his anger about Noel's engagement – he was a favourite displaced. Kings had favourites, didn't they? She knew that from her history books and Noel certainly fancied himself as a king of sorts. Poor Cyril! And yet, just now, he looked happy enough in the moment, rather as Jane did when Albert paid her attention.

She glanced at Peter, who was glowering across at the scene in sudden disgust at all this decadence and burst out unexpectedly, "What are we all messing abaht at? Climbing up private towers. Drinking champagne, eating cake, sitting on table cloths on the grass! We set out to *do* summat, here! I'm off! I'm going to see Stanley, like I should 'ave bin doing instead of this. There's things need tekkin' care of."

"Oh," said Ellen, taken aback by his angry remarks and saying, "Should I come too? We could take some of the food…"

"No! Stay where you want to be!" he flashed back and getting up, stormed off to his bicycle without a backward glance at any of them, riding away fast.

Ellen felt ashamed of him and for him, finding herself blushing, while at the same time realising that there was some truth in his boorish outburst. They had not set out to be pleasure-seekers and hangers-on of Noel Ogden. He had made himself one of their party and gradually was turning their outings into something else. Only, was he? This was something special he had invited them to, had gone to the trouble of organising, show-off about it that he was, and of owning Wainhouse Tower on one of his whims, but Peter's reaction was unfair. To switch like this when he had been enjoying himself as much as the rest of them made her think him a hypocrite.

"I can't believe Peter's being so rude!" she exclaimed. "He loved it up on the tower and he was laughing about having champagne."

"Nay," said John, who knew Peter of old, of course, as one of the firemen. "It's just that he's bethought himself and he feels all wrong for being part of it. But he can't help being young and wanting to enjoy himself too, can he? He feels guilty about Stanley and coming when the lad's so badly. That's all. They're the best of mates, you know. Stan's quiet where Peter's loud. He were better with his influence, I think."

"Is Stanley so very ill?" asked Ellen, troubled now. "I thought he looked much better the last time I saw him."

John just shook his head.

"No. I'm afraid not, Ellen. That fire at the mill and the smoke he took in? He was already struck with the consumption and all that…well…I'm afraid it's very serious now."

A surge of full horror washed over Ellen. No wonder Peter felt so guilty! And so was she. First John's hands crippled and now Stanley perhaps dying, no, certainly dying.

"That fire…" she whispered, feeling her face and whole body flush deeply with the tears coming.

"Nay, don't upset yourself, Ellen. It wasn't your fault. Or Peter's."

"But it was," she barely murmured.

"What?" said John, who *was* slightly deaf as she had thought before and hadn't caught her words.

"Nothing," she said hastily, dashing the water from her eyes. "I'm just – I didn't know."

Looking up, she found other eyes resting on her, those of people who perhaps had heard, or heard something. Eustace was looking at her with pained concern, Hannah and Sarah had paused in their nearby strolling and Libby asked, "John, what have you been saying to Ellen? She's all upset!"

"Nothing. It's only that Peter's gone off in one of his strops."

"Bad lad! And after you being so kind as to set him up in a job, Ellen," said Hannah. "Albert told us before."

"It's not that. It's just that I didn't know Stanley was so ill."

"Ellen – let us go and visit him and his mother again," suggested Eustace. "I am sure his situation calls for another subscription from us all to aid the family."

"Yes, very well. I mean, that is a good idea, Eustace," said Ellen.

"You are coming to the school on Tuesday morning to read with the children, I hope?"

"I will be, of course. I like to do it," said Ellen, who had just resumed her weekly volunteering with him at the orphanage school.

“Then, let us go after that? Weather permitting. It is quite a way.”

“Not if we bicycle.”

“True, not so far then.”

Ellen hoped that *he* had not heard what she had said to John, that nobody had. She had not had any intention of letting *that* slip out at all. But as the picnic concluded and they made a last climb up to the top of the Wainhouse Tower, when nobody said anything or looked at her strangely, she began to be sure that they had not. She really had to be more careful! At the top again, she remembered how touchingly open Peter had been, so enthusiastic in his reactions to the view before them. Ellen wished he could always be like that instead of turning so suddenly to aggressive anger, although no doubt both strengths of feeling came from the same temperament. His reactions burst through too suddenly to be denied or restrained in time. She was sure that, on occasion, he regretted it. Besides, today’s turn around she could understand. It was because he felt so guilty himself that he had set a fire that had injured his dearest friends so grievously. John had recovered where Stanley would not. But John had said Stanley was ill already. Surely, it could not *all* be their fault, could it?

Albert left with Hannah and Sarah, all cycling out in their trio, with Jane, who had arrived on foot, watching after them. Noel and Cyril were packing up the picnic together and it looked as if the two of them meant to travel back to Noel’s house in his cart to return their leavings. Shortly, they did. Peter was already gone and John and Libby were the next to depart.

On impulse, Ellen turned to Eustace, both of them noting Jane’s now drooping expression and she said, “Eustace – I know what you think of Albert’s toying with

Jane's feelings. Would you think it right of me if I told her something I know? I heard him distinctly say to my sister, 'Why settle for Noel when you could have me?' and he meant in marriage. He was not joking, although Sylvia passed it off as such and he did not seem to care. It means he is not serious at all, and it might save Jane pain to know it."

"I agree with you," said Eustace. "I think her a fine young woman and one who deserves to be saved from any further distress. She is alone over there, look, and I will leave so you may speak to her discreetly. I agree that you should do it."

"Then I will."

Ellen went over to Jane as Eustace called over his farewells and said he would see Ellen on Tuesday at the school.

"Jane – may I speak with you? I know you were unhappy the day I brought you to my house and the cause of it. I want to spare you any further pain on Albert Dewhirst's account. He is a flirt, Jane. And only that. Quite apart from…" (Hannah and Sarah, she did not need to say) "I must tell you that I heard him ask my sister to marry him in preference to Noel Ogden. If she had accepted, then what?"

Jane's eyes widened and she paled, if that were possible, a little more, from shock.

"No, that cannot be true," she said in a low voice, which trembled slightly with the effort of restraining her feelings.

"It is true, Jane. *I*, at least, would not lie to you about it. I do not wish to distress you but – when you are with Albert, it is as if the sun comes out for you and when he leaves with Hannah and Sarah, as if it never will again. That is no good for you."

Jane bit her lip and looked down, her arms folded

tight.

"I know it," she said finally.

"Then you do believe me?"

"I do. I must go now!" And Jane hastened off without any further goodbye, back up the graveyard lane to the cobbled path leading down to her walk home, along King Cross.

Ellen did not pursue her, seeing that she was shocked and grieved by the news, but hopefully Jane would recover from it on her walk home and begin to see the reality of Albert, whatever that reality was. Ellen saw no villainy in him, just a selfish devil-may-care outlook that he could afford to have, dressed up with his bohemian notions that he felt allied him with the Clarion Club. Neither Ellen nor Eustace suspected the truth. Eustace had a very strong sense of right and wrong guided, not just by principles of decency, but by his kindness. Like Ellen, he had not seen through to the darker love possessing Jane, only that she had been misled by casual attention into a fictitious attachment which seemed unrequited. Neither Ellen nor Eustace were sexually experienced, nor had the slightest idea that Jane now was so, and that she had been tumbled into very deep emotional waters because of it.

Jane was consumed by her feelings, alternately elated (when she had been with Albert at the studio, or indeed in any way at all) and then thrown into a neurotic anxiety that she would never see him again. She fretted that in order to do so she must at all costs keep up the façade of belief in personal liberty which she had colluded in sharing with him as her lover. She had clear joy when they were together but when they were separated it was as if it had never really been and was just some fever dream of hers alone.

Jane's physical passion for Albert, conflated with her

deeply romantic nature, had combined into an infatuation which tortured her more with each absence from him and lack of word from him in between. Now and again, Albert would dash off a coded note of assignation, referring to passing his regards on to her father, whom he would hope to call upon on such and such a date. These she treasured and poured over pointlessly for hidden depths like Shakespearean sonnets. Ellen's words were a punishing blow which left her reeling and, arriving home to find herself alone with her father out on parish business, Jane cast herself weeping on her bed and lost herself in it altogether.

***

Kenneth Butterworth called to visit with the Rastricks the next day on Sunday afternoon. He had not often done so since the announcement of Sylvia's engagement to Noel, but he kept up his discussions with Ellen about books intermittently. He now proposed that they both go into town one day in the next few weeks to buy some more volumes together at the antiquarian bookshop in Bull Green. It sold both new and second-hand books. Purchases and orders were discussed in hushed tones at a small, desk-like counter, from which paper parcels tied with string were handed out as reverently as gifts of gold, frankincense and myrrh. They would be getting new stock in soon, Kenneth told her he had learned. Ellen was quick to accept the invitation. She loved to browse in there and there were few in her household or among her acquaintances who cared for it.

She asked, Jane still being much on her mind since the day before, "Kenneth, did you ever go to see Jane Ellison, I wonder, after you met her here that day?" she asked. "You meant to call upon her father, I believe?"

"I did, yes, but not for some few weeks now. Jane, it seems, is a reader of Byron and the Brontës and is all for gothic romance. I find those writings rather overwrought. The last time I called, a rather fearsome curate was visiting and made a great challenge out of our talk of literature. It was quite uncomfortable altogether and I confess, I have not visited since then."

"Really? Was his name Felix Sykes?"

"It was, you have met him too?"

"Briefly," said Ellen, passing quickly over it since it had been at a Clarion Club meeting but, of course, with Felix being a clergyman, it was likely that he would be involved in Jane's father's church-related society. "I found him fearsome as well. You think him interested in Jane Ellison?"

"It may be so. Or simply that he feels he has already made his presence felt in the vicarage there and mine was unwelcome to him. Some men are like that. All other company is competition for attention."

This was food for thought to Ellen, although she could hardly see Jane transferring her attentions from the handsome form of congenial Albert to a man such as Felix Sykes. It was a less likely prospect, even, than thinking Jane might come to appreciate Kenneth's virtues, for he had many, Ellen knew. She had not discerned either, when she had asked, any especial interest in Jane herself from Kenneth, which was rather disappointing, but perhaps she would not give up quite yet if the opportunity arose to put them together again.

"Tell me, have you discovered Thackeray and *Vanity Fair*, Ellen?" asked Kenneth, moving the conversation back to books.

"No, I haven't."

"Then let us seek it out next week. It suits my appetite for satire, although *you* may well find it shocking, Ellen," he teased.

"I will not!" declared Ellen stoutly, at which he

laughed.

"We shall see," he said. "Now, let me read you an extract of something quite extraordinary, *The Time Machine*, by H. G. Wells, published only last year and a real sensation. I will lend it to you now if you like it? It is quite visionary, and alarming too. I am seeking to place an order for his latest novel, *The Island of Dr Moreau* when we visit the shop. I am interested by the theories of Charles Darwin and that book explores some of the themes, I understand."

Ellen settled down to listen and was soon enthralled. When he stopped, she said, "Oh, yes, please, Kenneth. Do lend it to me! I will not be able to put it down, I am sure! I have never heard anything like it!"

Smiling, he handed the book across to her to enjoy later. As with anyone, a smile lit up his rather plain face to show the personality behind it and Ellen really could not see, when it came to it, what Jane might find to object about in him at all. She would do her best, she decided, to steer them together again. Here, Kenneth's thoughts turned to his own preference.

"How is your sister, Sylvia, Ellen? I do not find her or your mother at home with you today?"

"She is well, thank you. Sylvia and my mother are much taken up with weekend visiting at present. It seems her engagement to Noel has made her very desirable company."

Kenneth laughed gently.

"Or Mr Ogden's extremely affluent position has done so?" he suggested, with some bite.

"I would not doubt it. But think yourself lucky to be spared it, Kenneth, as do I. All that false pleasantry, when it is only about showing you are better than everyone else. How I detest it!"

Kenneth laughed again, this time more openly.

"Yes, it is really not very much to your liking, is it, social chit-chat? At least you have me to come and talk to you about books instead, Ellen."

"Indeed I do and I am very glad of it, Kenneth," she answered honestly.

"As am I," he agreed. "As am I. It is not everyone who enjoys that, either, is it?"

"I suppose not. Shall we have tea? I am sure cook was baking scones when I went down to see what nice things might be about earlier. She shooed me out but I am quite sure they will be done now, and nice and warm too."

"Delicious, thank you, yes," said Kenneth, settling back again as Ellen rang the bell. "Will Mr Rastrick be joining us?"

"He will for scones and tea, if not to hear us talking about books!" said Ellen. "I will go and get him now from his ledgers in the study."

Kenneth was so old an acquaintance in the family that Mr Rastrick had been quite content to leave them to their talk and reading aloud together for a short time while he continued with his work – not being, apart from the newspaper, much of a man for reading himself.

He came back into the room with Ellen, saying, "Well now you are done with all that, we may have some proper conversation, Kenneth. You're a stocks and shares man. What do you think of the new investment opportunities?"

He waved a paper list he had drawn up to ponder over, and he and Kenneth turned to monetary issues while Ellen conducted daughterly hostess duties. It amused her to see herself and Kenneth withdraw behind the behaviour expected of them, and once more she wondered if he might be amenable to the Clarion Club's ideals. She was still unsure, for she had never heard him express a single radical opinion in any context and he conducted himself conventionally in every other way too.

Still, there was a lot more in his character than wanting to make money with which to buy better status in the area, which was also a lot more than could be said for most of the manufacturing families whom she knew.

Chapter Nine

Ellen toiled up the road beside the Moor to the Crossley and Porter Orphan Home and School on Len's bike. It seemed built to house far grander residents than the county orphans being educated there for apprenticeships. Completed in the style of James the First, the building was large, expensive and ornate, combining Italianate and Jacobean influences. A domed clock tower struck the hours, visible all the way down the Moor. She found Eustace Horsfall with some of the children, playing a game of rounders with a bat and ball in the grounds. He was quite as enthusiastic as they were, his badly pocked face flushed healthy pink as he ran round gamely, with them ferociously trying to knock him out.

"Sir! Keep running, sir!" those on his team encouraged whilst, when he was caught out, the opponents jeered and catcalled, respect for their teacher forgotten since they were back in street game territory. Winded, he stooped over with hands on knees, gasping and laughing, then caught sight of Ellen.

"Miss Rastrick! You arrive in time to see me defeated!" he called across.

Ellen applauded him, as did the children, who were clearly fond of him she saw, and she called back, "A brave effort, Mr Horsfall!"

Break time over, the children filed back inside with them and Ellen was set to do some reading with a more infant class because the older ones were still far too unruly for her to deal with. A class of children, especially abandoned ones like these, could be a predatory group. Soon sensing weakness in any teacher, mockery and disrespect were likely to erode control. The younger ones were restive but not hostile. As always, most had their heads shaved to control lice and some were painted with iodine for ringworm, giving them a primitive, untamed look anyway. Although she did not shy away from them as Jane had done, or feel revulsion, Ellen felt no great affinity either with these roughly spoken youngsters. They were too different from her, although she pitied them, certainly, for their situation as orphans. Eustace shared the organisational opinion that they should be grateful to be housed and educated enough to work, although for the brighter ones, he did cherish better ambitions than a factory or servant's life. He thought of them perhaps teaching, like himself, one day, and Ellen felt much the same about them. After her session was over, Eustace came to collect Ellen.

"I have been allowed leave to visit a sick friend this afternoon, Ellen, for I am due some hours of personal liberty which I have not taken, covering for others instead," he told her. "So I am quite free if you still wish to go? I will go by myself if you do not, please don't feel you must."

"That's kind, Eustace but I do want to go. We all like Stan, don't we, and it seems so very cruel."

"Yes," he agreed. "There has not been time to do another collection but let us offer our support and assure the family that we will make one. If Stanley is so ill now, I doubt he will be working."

Ellen nodded and they set off down into the town and then out to the poor back-to-backs they had visited before. Mrs Jagger knew them at once, of course, when she opened the door.

"Mrs Jagger, we have come to ask after Stanley. Peter Lumb told us how ill he has been."

"Aye, he's been a good lad to our Stan, has Peter. He sits up with him at nights so I can sleep. I'll miss him when he goes to Stanger's."

"Stanley will too," said Ellen.

Mrs Jagger shook her head.

"Stanley won't be here to miss him. It won't be long now. Ah've seen it before."

"Oh, no!" cried Ellen.

"We will bring more funds, Mrs Jagger – only – the news came unexpectedly to us before our next meeting."

"Thank you," she said, but here she was interrupted by Stanley's voice.

"Who is it, Mam?" He appeared at the door, standing but very changed. It was a shock to see him like this, as if an old man's face and skin had been draped over his strong young man's body, now yellowish and wasted. "Ellen and Eustace! How kind of you to visit." His voice was hoarse and weak and he strained not to cough, a handkerchief clutched to his face. "But this is – you should not come in – you could catch it nah, doctor said."

"We won't keep you at the door, Stanley," said Eustace hastily. "We wish you soon well again and we will be back with a collection from our club while you are not working."

"Thank you," said Stanley, accepting the polite fiction that the collection would be for his keep rather than for his funeral.

Ellen was unable to say much except, "Oh, Stanley…" with a wealth of feeling.

"I know, lass," he said sadly.

"Come, Ellen, we mustn't tire Stanley. I will return very soon with some funds, I promise you."

"I can't say we won't be grateful for it," said Mrs Jagger.

Stanley had now shuffled off back inside, unable to remain on his feet for too long, and it was a very silent pair that set off to cycle back down the hill. When they reached the town, Eustace proposed they call into a tea room for some refreshment and Ellen agreed, for she was also feeling the need for some cheerful surroundings before they parted ways. Settled at a table in a quiet corner, they ordered coffee.

"Let us go directly to Noel," said Ellen eventually. "He can give some money immediately and we may collect at the Clarion Club later. I do not think we can wait."

"I agree," said Eustace. "Will you see him?"

"Yes. He is to dine with us tonight and I will ask him privately then. Noel is generous and I know will not stint."

"Bring it to me at the school then, Ellen, and I will take it. It is only to leave it at the door after all."

Ellen nodded, looking forlorn.

"Carrie will be very sorry about this. She made sure to have John, Peter and Stanley taken such good care of after the fire at the mill," she said.

Eustace looked at her for a moment.

"Ellen – at Wainhouse Tower – I heard you tell John, when he said you were not to blame, that you were. What did you mean, Ellen?"

"Nothing – I – you misheard me perhaps."

Eustace sipped his coffee for a moment before saying quietly, "If you are shielding Peter in some way, for you were answering for the two of you, I know, then I do not think you should feel obliged to do it. He is working there now, at Stanger's, or will be soon, he said – I would not like to think it was under any false pretences."

Ellen remembered again how Peter had told her about the fire at the flour mill. She felt she could only stall now, as Eustace might well feel he had to warn the owners of Stanger's Mill about Peter.

"I assisted him myself in getting employment with my brother, Eustace, so you need feel no anxiety about it."

"Very well. I thought you seemed troubled, but

perhaps it was only by Peter's abrupt departure. He is an impetuous kind of fellow and a bit flighty like that. I did think it a bit much that he struck Albert that day out on Ovenden Moor," he added primly, making Ellen smile.

"Yes, I suppose it was," she agreed. "And as for being troubled – no – it was just that Peter and I had been delivering the paper together that day and we both thought we should have seen the fire sooner than he eventually did."

"I see," said Eustace, his face clearing. "Yes, it *was* Peter who alerted the brigade, wasn't it? That was the route you took with the papers?"

"Yes, down to Sowerby Bridge, then along to Ripponden and Rishworth. I didn't go the whole way and came home leaving him to it," said Ellen.

"And then he noticed the smoke?"

"Yes – that's right. When he was coming back. He rushed to raise the alarm and get the Neptune out but it was already well ablaze by then. We both thought afterwards that if we had seen it on our way earlier, well, it might have been prevented from being so serious."

"But since you did not, you cannot blame yourself, Ellen. Nor should Peter feel guilty, if he tells the truth? I am glad that is all you meant. Put it out of mind now and let us concentrate on what we can do for poor Stanley and his family. They will not have money for – well, you understand me."

"I do," Ellen agreed glumly. "I will speak to Noel as soon as I can later on today."

She hoped she had covered their tracks well enough with her half truths and that Peter would not be at risk of discovery and punishment. Such a serious crime would mean a hanging for him, especially if it came out about the Bradbury mill. Once again, she realised how reckless Peter Lumb was and how he courted danger without a care for any personal consequences. He was not a safe man to consort with, even as a companion. Ellen knew she should put aside her thoughts about him, forget about the lightning kiss and the heather kiss too, as she thought of them. She must try to move away from any sense that she and Peter were bound together, even though she might feel that they were by what they had done together at Stanger's Mill.

"Ellen – I want you to know that you have a friend in me," said Eustace, still not entirely convinced, it seemed. "You are among the youngest of our group and I think, as your brother does not join us, I might offer to act as your sounding board if there ever *are* things which you are not comfortable about."

Ellen, although a little worried by his perception, thanked him for his kindness and they parted company for her to return home again. There, she was teased over her 'good works' with the town's poor children by Sylvia, a young woman who, naturally, would not be seen dead amongst such company. Sylvia and her mother soon went up to dress for Noel Ogden's evening visit. Ellen, ready in a hurry, kept watch from the window seat in the front room to make sure of catching Noel as he arrived, so as to have a private word about the Jagger family's pressing need for money.

A light varnish of rain had fallen outside, making the sandstone flags of the pavements shine like new conkers in the last of the evening light. She thought how sad it was that Stanley might not see even so ordinary a thing again soon, at which tears stung her eyes. Noel arrived and she hastened out to greet him as he stepped down from his carriage, which would return for him after dinner. He was dressed splendidly in a full evening suit, somehow managing not to have had his coat tails crushed by sitting on them. He was always immaculately shaved and did not affect the fashionable side-whiskers, moustaches or beards of many. A scent of spicy cologne drifted from his rosy skin as he greeted Ellen. She caught his arm to detain him from going straight in.

"Noel, Eustace and I went to see Stanley. He is dying and his family have no money for medicines or his funeral, which will come soon. Will you help? We will make a club collection as soon as we can to repay you?"

"No need, none at all!" Noel interrupted her hastily. "Of course I will. Poor chap, poor dear fellow. I had no idea of it."

Of course he had not, being busy with entertaining when Peter had broken the news and then stormed off from the party. Noel always preferred, anyway, to have no idea of real unpleasantness in life, Ellen saw, skirting round the edges of it wherever possible, and yet there was no doubting his generosity, self-centred as he appeared to be. Ellen knew that Noel always carried money, partly to back up his reputation for buying extravagant items on impulse, or, as rumour also had it, to gamble when the fancy might take him as well. Taking off his white kid evening gloves, he drew his wallet out of an inside jacket pocket to give her a number of large banknotes.

"Thank you, Noel. I will take them straight to Eustace tomorrow," said Ellen. "It is very good of you."

"It is what the Clarionettes do, Ellen, that is all it is. Those who have funds now help those who don't have it now. We always say that, don't we, at the Clarion Club? Not a word to anyone else, mind. Stanley and his family have their pride to think of."

The statement, as well as the action, showed the better qualities residing in Noel's nature and reminded Ellen of what she had admired in him, as well as his other attributes.

"Yes." She smiled at him. "Let us go in, it is still

damp out here in the air."

The carriage dismissed again until later, she went into the house with him, where he stepped up to his part of being an entertaining visitor with all his usual gusto. Soon, he and Sylvia were rippling through duets again before the family all dined together. Leonard joined them for that event and so they were quite a lively party. Carrie, he said, had stayed at home to keep her ailing father company, which was approved of, especially by Mrs Rastrick, who was pleased to be relieved of her daughter-in-law's presence at any time.

***

Eustace took the money up to Mrs Jagger under cover of the school dinner hour. She received it with some consternation at the large amount but was soon persuaded that it would be a necessity for the family, after the sad event as well as due to it. They spoke in hushed tones on the doorstep to spare Stanley from hearing them. Ellen remained in the school room marking exercises until Eustace returned, both to hear how Stanley fared and, if Eustace were asked for, to say he would be back at any moment. Fortunately, he was not missed. The news of Stanley was that he could no longer rise and it was likely to be only days rather than weeks now until the end came. Peter was still keeping night vigil at Stanley's bedside according to Mrs Jagger. After her session at the school, Ellen rode down to see John and Cyril in the stonemasons' yard and told them how things were now. They were very sorry to hear it and said they would make his headstone for nothing, of course.

The next time the Clarionettes met, it was for the very sad occasion of Stanley's funeral. Noel had bought a grave plot for Stanley in the cemetery above Wainhouse Tower, again an act of private generosity which only Ellen and Mrs Jagger knew of. After the short service in the gloom of the church, they all emerged again into an unlikely sunshine where crows cawed in October-bare trees. Their feet shuffled in dry leaves, which were drifting about them like mourners too as they processed to see Stanley's coffin lowered. Stanley's headstone was of polished black granite, picked out in gold. On it was an image of St Florian, the patron saint of firemen, carefully designed by John and Cyril, showing a Roman soldier pouring a pitcher of water over flames. It seemed a long time and yet no time at all since they had all been together in the Sunny Vale Pleasure Gardens, hopeful on their youthful excursion.

Peter was full of angry grief at the loss of his best friend and, as always in him, this made him want to lash out at the unfair forces working against them in life. When Ellen came to his side, as he seemed ready to be making off in a private dash from the churchyard almost before the ceremonies were concluded, he looked bitterly back at the company behind them from where he was at the gates.

"I'm done wi' it all, Ellen!" he exclaimed. "The Clarion Club's just become a rich man's playground and I'll have no part in it!"

He even wept fiercely, she thought, despite his evident desolation. But then, of course, he did not know that he wronged Noel here.

"No, it hasn't, Peter!" she began to say but he interrupted at once.

"It has! Our fireman comrades made him a fine memorial, I know that. But he shouldn't be lying there. Wouldn't be, if he weren't worked to death in a carpet factory!"

"It's our fault too, Peter," she said. "That smoke."

"Nay! I'll not be having *that*!" he fairly bellowed at her and shook her hand off his arm roughly, stomping off alone down the path, where she could see his turbulent figure marching away before he vanished round the curve of the wall.

Nobody else had heard them and she rejoined the crowd, which was still listening to the vicar's words, saying only to Mrs Jagger, who asked where Peter was, that it had all got a bit too much for him and he had gone now, at which the other woman nodded.

"Aye, he tired himself out for our Stanley. He's took it hard. Leave him to it, lass. That's best." And Ellen agreed that it was.

Among the mourners, Jane Ellison looked as if she wore weepers for herself, a pale face among the black of her garments turned only ever in one direction. When the group by the graveside began to break up, she moved to speak to Albert, overwrought by the occasion into a sense of time slipping out of their hands along with life passing by, while he delayed and dallied with others.

He frowned and said that this was not the day to think of themselves, at which she said in low, hot tones, "But, Albert, do you ever think of me at *all*?" making him frown a little more, the pleasant smile easily on his lips at most times vanished into gravity and disapproval.

"Today, we are all thinking of poor Stanley," he rebuked her, using the occasion as a rebuff of her demand on him.

"You deny me again!" she half-cried out.

Jane strode away, lost in her own grief, for her love, for herself, for Stanley's death and at the increasing futility of the situation she found herself in with Albert. All the while he, tiring of the strenuous feelings she flung at him, retreated like a tide going out. And that was how it felt, that stormy waters had cast her upon on some bleak shore and left her stranded there alone. This time, her distress went almost unobserved. Eustace was busy consoling Mrs Jagger, as were Peter Lumb's mother and the vicar. Ellen caught a moment of the exchange, the tone only, but, as she turned, Jane was going. Noel joined her, offering to take her home.

"Come, Ellen, let me take you back. I have my carriage and it is time I called upon Sylvia again. I have been busy with these sad affairs lately and must not neglect her. Our theatricals come soon and that will cheer us all up, I am certain of it!"

"You have not been inattentive to the fair Sylvia, I hope, Noel?" observed Albert lightly, as Hannah and Sarah came up arm in arm beside him.

"Noel has been very kind indeed to Mrs Jagger. So have John and Cyril," said Ellen as Noel went to say his farewells to others. Ellen felt that Albert needed to be sensible of some obligations himself. "Where has Jane Ellison gone rushing off to alone? I saw her speak to you."

"Jane is an emotional creature," he said easily. "She gives into it – I expect the occasion was too much for her."

"Aye. That'll be it," said Sarah with a snap of her dark eyes. "Nowt to do with Albert, Ellen."

"How could it be?" added Hannah calmly. "We're at a funeral. Of course she's upset. We all are."

Ellen looked between them and then directly at Albert, who made a small bow and took his escort away with him without saying any more. Subdued, the rest of the mourners all bade one another farewell and she shook hands with John and Cyril. Libby had been unable to escape her domestic duties and Albert had told them earlier that he had promised to pay her respects himself. John, Ellen could see, had not cared for the reminder of which family Libby worked for, even though Albert was rarely resident in the same house. She could also see that

Albert enjoyed needling John by saying it, in spite of his ostensibly serious demeanour. For all Albert's good looks and easy warmth, Ellen was beginning to realise that he was trouble too, in a different way from Peter of course, but trouble nonetheless.

***

That was the last of the good autumn days for a while and once more Ellen was housebound by heavy rains for several days. Here, all the talk was of one thing only, the wedding being as much of a theatrical production in the making in the minds of her mother and Sylvia as *Midsummer Night's Dream* tableaux were to be in Noel's big house on the hill. There were endless lists of things to be made and Ellen was required to join in with writing them. Her sighs of boredom were chastised by her mother with, "Really, Ellen. I do wish you would be more responsible with your time." Which Ellen thought rather rich coming from her mother, who did nothing with hers at present except fret about the forthcoming nuptials.

The wedding appeared to be an entity in its own right, quite apart from the couple it involved, something that had to be propitiated at all times with the right votive offerings to prevent anything from going wrong on the big day – the wrong person being omitted from the guest list, say, or even worse, somebody they did not want to come being included in error. Then there were the printed invitations and place cards which had to be absolutely correct, and the clothes, the endless clothes, for Sylvia's trousseau.

Ellen's excursion to the bookshop with Kenneth came round eventually. A fresher wind was blowing and there had been frost swirls on the windows in the mornings. Coming into the parlour on arrival, Kenneth was punctiliously polite to Sylvia and she was rather lofty in return, as if he had no right to any such pained disapproval. In Kenneth's mind at least, and certainly in some others, there had formerly existed a kind of understanding between himself and Sylvia. He would undoubtedly have proposed after courting her politely for some time longer. It created something of a prickly atmosphere and so Ellen was glad to go out with him as soon as it was decently possible to escape. If her father had been there (a man who took no notice whatsoever of so insubstantial a thing as an atmosphere) it would all have passed off, but he was not and so things congealed rather quickly. Ellen's mother contented herself with grumbling that she would have thought Ellen had better things to be doing than going looking for more books to read, but was mollified by Kenneth's offering that if she had any commissions in town, he would be glad to take Ellen anywhere required to get them for her. Luckily, she was unable to think of anything in particular, but the gesture had been made and honour was satisfied.

"Oh, I am so glad to see you, Kenneth!" Ellen exclaimed as she got in beside him in his two seater gig. "If I had to look at any more ribbons and lace I would be fit to strangle myself with them!"

Kenneth laughed, a warm and hearty sound, for he had a very natural manner when he was not on his dignity.

"I am not surprised – although I *do* remain surprised that – well…"

"I know," said Ellen sympathetically.

"Oh, you must not think that I bear any…or retain any feelings of…"

"I am glad of it!" she returned roundly, conveying richly that Sylvia would not deserve it if he did, at which he smiled.

"Then, let us enjoy getting at our new books!" he suggested, a pleasure which they were both looking forward to.

The bookshop was really a house, its rooms filled with floor-to-ceiling shelves crammed with cloth and leatherbound volumes. A smell of damp in this weather was inevitable, in spite of the small fires burning in grates in the rooms to keep them aired. The onion skin paper of more cheaply printed books, two tiny columns of text on each page, stuck together a little as Ellen looked through them. Kenneth had already ordered *Vanity Fair* as a surprise for Ellen and she was presented with the latest Caxton edition in a green binding.

"Thank you, Kenneth!" she cried. "That is so kind of you. Very kind indeed!"

"I wanted you to come away with something which I knew you had the wit to enjoy." He smiled. "I look forward to discussing it with you and laughing over it, when you have any time to yourself to read it, of course."

"Oh do not speak of that!" she cried, at his reference to the all-consuming wedding plans. "I will certainly make sure that I do!"

"I believe it is your eighteenth birthday soon, Ellen?"

"It is," she agreed. "In just a couple of weeks' time."

"An occasion of your own. Then I hope you will accept that as my gift to you for it."

"Very gladly!" she exclaimed. "And I am so grateful to you for thinking of me."

"Believe me, Ellen, I often do," he said kindly. "Let me ask the bookseller to wrap it especially for you and then you can keep it by until the day."

She handed it back to him with a smile. Kenneth went to have a pleasant exchange with the shopkeeper over the ceremony of thick brown paper and string being carefully squared off into a perfect parcel for her to carry.

"Do you have your own book in yet, Kenneth?" she asked. "The H.G. Wells?"

"Oh, he does, Miss Rastrick! I am fetching it for him

directly," the bookseller assured her.

Ellen idled to the front of the shop while they were busy and looked out of the window into the street. Opposite was a chemist's. Illuminated glass show globes of coloured water were on display to attract customers, gas-lit to make the rich colours of red, green and blue glow enticingly. Ellen was thinking how pretty the huge carboys looked, with something exotic and magical about them, when she saw Jane Ellison coming out of the shop door. Although she was no longer dressed in black for a funeral, her clothes were drab. She had a drawn look and a miserable air about her. She was pulling her reticule strings closed and had clearly just put something from the pharmacy inside it. Jane did not see Ellen looking out at her and walked away, abstracted from her surroundings altogether, lost in whatever her thoughts were. Ellen frowned at the sight and then recalled her earlier idea to reintroduce Kenneth to Jane. She was sure Albert Dewhirst was still behind this change in Jane's demeanour in some way, and it did not do to wallow where love was unrequited. She had learned that herself, she felt, even though she had realised in the end that she did not love Noel in the way she had fancied she did.

"Look, Kenneth!" Ellen called, turning round to him. "There is Jane Ellison just going home from the chemist's opposite. If you did not mind, once we are finished in town here, might we call on her? I do owe her a visit of my own and, well, it may be just my fancy, but she looks in low spirits. Perhaps our company might cheer her."

"And keep you out of that of your mother and sister's a little longer, eh?" perceived Kenneth, sounding amused. "I would not like to impose on the lady, though, if she has a mind to be alone."

"I think Jane spends too *much* time alone, Kenneth,"

said Ellen. "And that is the trouble."

"Very well," he agreed. "I have one or two things to pick up for my own mother and then we may proceed. I will be happy to pay Miss Ellison a visit. Perhaps the difficult cleric will not be there today!"

"Oh, indeed, I hope not. He is a glowering kind of man who makes a person uncomfortable. Not kind in a curate!"

"I agree, but perhaps we should not laugh too soon at his expense. He may have good qualities we don't know of," said Kenneth with mocking piety, making her smile.

Kenneth and Ellen called at the Post Office to send a parcel, a shawl his mother had knitted as a gift to her sister, his Aunt Beryl, who lived in Huddersfield.

"Mother is always convinced that Huddersfield, being higher up than Halifax, is a colder climate, and, it coming on to winter, likes to make Aunt Beryl something to keep her warm every year in good time. She speaks of it to people as if it is the Steppes of Russia, Ellen. 'My sister Beryl lives above the snow line, you know'," he said, imitating his mother's way of speaking with uncanny accuracy, making Ellen laugh. "Still – it is a kindness from her," he added, smiling.

"It is indeed very kind of Mrs Butterworth," Ellen agreed, smiling back and thinking that, although she always thought of her as an interfering gossip, some of Kenneth's own kindness must come from his mother too.

After this, there was some floral-scented soap which must be purchased from an emporium regarded as being sufficiently high-toned by Mrs Butterworth for her tastes, and then their shopping was done. They turned the gig towards the upper end of town and made their way to the Queen's Road rectory to pay their call upon Jane Ellison. A housekeeping day servant who looked immediately put out by their arrival admitted them.

"Vicar's busy in't study. Miss is upstairs, just lately come in. Taking her outdoor things off, I expect," she said grudgingly, a dusting cloth still poised in her hand.

"Don't let us disturb you, ma'am," said Kenneth, rising to the occasion. "I will wait in the downstairs sitting room while Miss Rastrick goes to Miss Ellison's room to let her know we are here."

"All right," she agreed ungraciously, nodding him through to the chilly front parlour.

"Oh, and pray don't disturb the vicar on my account meanwhile, either," added Kenneth.

"I won't," she bridled, as if the very suggestion of it overstepped the mark.

With a smile of wry amusement at one another, Kenneth went into the parlour to wait and Ellen went upstairs, the servant pointing which room to knock on the door of before she vanished into the back of the house again. Ellen knocked on the door.

"Jane?" she called quietly. "It's Ellen Rastrick. I saw you in town and am come to call. The servant said you were just gone up to your room. I hope you do not mind?"

There was no answer from within, not a sound at all.

"Jane?" Ellen called again, "Kenneth Butterworth is here with me too. Can you hear me?"

Puzzled by still hearing nothing, she thought the servant had perhaps been mistaken and hesitantly tried the door, which opened. At first Ellen wondered if the room was empty, then she saw a prone figure, fully dressed, lying across the bed.

"Jane? Are you ill?"

Hurrying forward, Ellen saw that Jane lay as if utterly stupefied, worse, was deathly pale, with a bluish tinge about her lips. On the dresser, an empty laudanum phial had been drained of its contents. Ellen touched the clammy cold face, felt the faintest flutter of a pulse in the neck and raced downstairs to Kenneth first.

"Kenneth, Kenneth! She has taken laudanum. An overdose of it, I think. She is quite unconscious. Near death even!" Ellen wrung her hands helplessly.

"What?"

Kenneth raced back up the stairs with her and saw that it was indeed true. While he shook Jane and slapped her face gently to no avail, Ellen saw a written page on the dresser in Jane's hand. The page looking unfinished, blotched and left open without intent. Perhaps she had been overcome while writing it? Without hesitating Ellen placed it, unseen by Kenneth, in her own dress pocket to protect Jane's privacy.

"There's no time to be lost, Ellen! I must tell her father to send immediately for the doctor. Stay with her."

Ellen nodded as he rushed off down the stairs to bang on the study door. Jane's father came out and joined Ellen as Kenneth himself raced with his gig to fetch the doctor and bring him back at once.

"Oh, Jane, my dearest child!" exclaimed the poor vicar. "She has not been sleeping, Miss Rastrick and – this potion must have been made far too strong. That chemist must be brought to book!"

"But sir, why would she take a draught of it now, in the day?"

"She sometimes sleeps a while in the day if she can. Jane says she needs the peace for her nerves. I do not know – she has been most unsettled in mind of late. I think that perhaps she feels the loss of her mother more deeply than ever at her age now. She has grown into a young woman without her mamma to be her guide and support in such times. And then…" He paused and went on, in a rush of such distress that he could not prevent himself from blurting it out. "She told me she had lost her faith, Miss Rastrick! A terrible thing for a vicar's daughter, and I, of all people, to be unable to help her in it!"

The distraught father clearly had no real idea of what might be troubling his daughter and Ellen did her best to comfort him.

"I am sure, Mr Ellison, that whatever troubles Jane, it is certainly not something which *you* have failed her in."

They rubbed Jane's hands and called to her, and then the doctor arrived, called for salt and hot water, brought a glass funnel and rubber tube out of his bag and prepared to administer an urgent emetic.

"You must leave the room, Miss Rastrick. You too, sir," he said to the vicar. "This will be a most unpleasant business but it may save her. The only hope is to remove the opiate and pray it has not repressed the nervous system fatally already. Too strong a dose in error, I have no doubt, and not the first time I have seen it."

"My thoughts too," agreed the vicar eagerly, anything else being too unspeakable to consider.

Kenneth and Ellen waited downstairs with the vicar and Kenneth rang the bell for the servant. He acquainted her, very briefly, with the fact that her young mistress had fallen gravely ill and the vicar needed a brandy. Tea would do fine for himself and Miss Rastrick. Shocked, the formerly begrudging woman made no protest and did as she was asked, flustered and upset by this unexpected turn of events.

Kenneth and Ellen did their best to console Mr Ellison, who could only keep repeating, as his cup of tea cooled and his glass of brandy went ignored, "I blame myself. Loss of her mother and then loss of her faith! The poor child's nerves have been far more disordered than I realised."

"No, no, Mr Ellison – this is a simple medical error

and nothing to do with Jane herself. I am quite certain the apothecary is at fault. Why, my mother takes a nerve tonic and sleeping draught daily and is no less lively for it – faith or no faith," Kenneth answered with kind patience, every time he said it.

At length, the doctor came down to them.

"She breathes and her pulse is weak but constant. I am afraid she will need to be sat with for the next twenty-four hours to make sure there is no falling off in her condition. I fear that she is not out of danger quite yet."

The housekeeper servant, rung for again, silently went to clear up the result of Jane's treatment with real distress for the young woman. The paper of Jane's letter crackled in Ellen's pocket like a guilty secret as she and Kenneth stood up to take their leave of Jane's father, who was anxious to go up to her side as soon as he could.

"I wonder if you would be so good as to call upon Mr Sykes at the next parish? The Reverend Craddock kindly asks his curate to stand in when I need his assistance, which I fear I am likely to do, having no curate of my own. I am sure they will be most concerned to hear that Jane is unwell."

"Of course we will, sir, and will come back tomorrow to ask after Miss Ellison and see if there is any other service I can do you," Kenneth assured him. "I wonder if—" He hesitated delicately. "I might offer to employ a nurse to sit with her by nights?"

"Well, my dear sir, if you felt…I would be most grateful," Mr Ellison agreed, this not being something he could afford to pay for himself.

"I will organise it at once, sir," said Kenneth, shaking hands.

He and Ellen left the stricken household to watch and wait.

"I wish I had not persuaded you to come!" exclaimed

Ellen. "This is dreadful and we had been enjoying such a pleasant time together."

"I understand you but I feel it is as well that we did. If you had not gone up to her room, Ellen, well, she might not have been saved." Kenneth cracked the reins and flicked the horse's ears lightly with a whip to make it set off again. "I wonder, given what the vicar told us, whether she may have taken more than was recommended with intent. A deliberate mistake, if you like. Not to die but to be seen to suffer. An indulgence of melancholy. If so, it was a cruelty to her father." It was quite a penetrating insight into Jane's behaviour, Ellen thought. She was surprised by his acuity but found his censorious attitude rather heartless, in spite of his kind actions. His main thought seemed to be about Jane's duty to her parent, with a want of sympathy for Jane herself. "To my mind," Kenneth went on, "her choice of reading suggests a brooding nature perhaps not best left to its own devices. I prefer things a little more lively, personally." Ellen presumed he was thinking of Sylvia again, but then he said, "I am more than certain that you will thoroughly enjoy your birthday book, Ellen, which I can assure you will not give *you* the glooms!"

"I am sure I shall," agreed Ellen, not quite sure how to respond to his observations, given what she suspected had moved Jane to this action. "Only, now we must see Mr Sykes and then – shall I come with you to engage a nurse?"

"No, I will see to it through our family doctor but, yes, we will call upon Mr Sykes and see if his vicar will share him for a while."

Mr Sykes was at home and expressed himself shocked and surprised by the unexpected news about Miss Ellison.

"Her poor father!" he exclaimed. "I must see if I can distract him. We have enjoyed many a lively debate sparring over controversial topics and if I can engage him in one or two again it will take his mind off things."

This put Mr Sykes's own view of how he conducted himself socially in rather different and better motivated light than Ellen had perceived before, as it perhaps did Kenneth, who could not resist saying, "Darwin's new theories, Mr Sykes. Now where do you stand on those?"

Felix Sykes surprised them by laughing somewhere amid his full, dark whiskers.

"I cannot shock him too dreadfully at such a difficult time," he replied. "No, something a little less sensational might be better, although I will be happy to discuss them with *you*, Mr Butterworth. I am not so unenlightened as you may think. I am sure that Miss Ellen Rastrick, here, is no stranger to debates either." He smiled, referring to the Clarion Club, much to her consternation.

"Ellen has very decided opinions, certainly," agreed Kenneth. "Even though I do not always think that she realises it."

"Miss Ellison and I debate also," said Felix, with a glance at Ellen that said he would keep her confidence, as he did Jane's, with reference to the Clarion Club. "I will endeavour to make her mind lively too once she wakes again."

"That may not be at once," said Kenneth, looking serious again. "My next stop is to see to a night nurse for her. The doctor says she must be sat with and watched."

Felix Sykes looked solemn too, said he was sorry to hear it and confirmed that he would go at once to Mr Ellison.

"The vicar here will be happy to allow me to assist. They are great friends, you know, and I hope that I have become a kind of one to them both too."

They left with a better opinion of Felix than they had arrived with. Then Ellen was returned to Saville Park with her book parcel and Jane's letter to take up to her room. She had not seen Felix at the most recent of the club meetings and he certainly did not cycle with them, so she hoped she would not have to speak to him more directly about it and reveal that her family did not know where she was really going, nor with whom. She drew Jane's note out of her pocket, scrawled, unfinished and left on her dressing-table as if she had been overcome before she finished writing it. After a moment's hesitation, Ellen glanced through it to see if it should be kept away from others' eyes or was something just unimportant. What she read showed her that Jane *had* intended to end her existence and that she blamed someone for it. *I can no longer endure the torture of knowing you are with others and I know that will never change*, it began.

Once she had seen that opening line, Ellen closed the paper again. This was a private anguish and she knew who it must relate to. Although it was not addressed, there was only one other person who should read it and she meant to take it to him. Kenneth had left her at the house and gone on his mission to engage a nurse for Jane Ellison. Nobody else was at home and, without thinking any further about it, Ellen set off again herself on her brother's bicycle. The Dewhirst Dye Works was reachable and she would arrive before close of the business day.

Within its gates, she made her way to the office area at the side of the factory. The man she approached in the yard had a slight smile lurking about his lips when she asked for Albert. She supposed young ladies bowling about on their own were seen as rather forward, especially when calling unannounced on the eligible young master of the family firm. He showed her up without comment, however, knocking on a door of a room and opening it to say gruffly, “Miss Ellen Rastrick for Mr Albert.”

Albert was with his father. Both were engaged in looking at some paperwork over a desk and Albert looked up from it in some surprise at seeing Ellen standing there.

“Miss Rastrick – all is well at home, I trust?” asked Albert, getting to his feet.

“Thank you, yes. You will recall my brother speaking to you recently about Stanger’s Mill?”

“Oh – yes, of course,” said Albert, picking up that a private word was being engineered. “Do come outside with me, won’t you? I know I said I would arrange a date to discuss it all further.”

“I mentioned that I would be passing by today after a visit and so…”

“Quite right and very good of you to act as our go-between. Excuse me for a moment, sir,” he said to his father, who was quite happy for him to speak about Stanger’s Mill to Ellen, as this upcoming concern was quite the talking point amongst the manufacturing community. Albert led her along a small corridor outside and into another area which overlooked the square courtyard of the factory building.

“What is it really, Ellen?” he asked with a curious smile. “Something to do with the Clarion Club we can’t mention in front of my father?”

“In a way, yes.” She drew the note out of her reticule and handed it to him. “Jane Ellison has taken a draught and is in a dangerous condition. I found her senseless in her room today. This was on her dressing-table. I saw one line of it and – well, I had no doubt for whom the message had been intended. You, Albert.”

Albert scanned the note as she spoke, a look of shock quickly followed by anger passing over his face.

“Me? This names nobody.”

"Does it need to?"
He had the grace to colour.
"Ellen..."
"We have all been witness to her distress. What really lies behind it is private between you. But you should know what she has done."
"This is monstrous!" he exclaimed, now in a great agitation. "Not a word about this note to anyone, Ellen. Jane's reputation! My own!"
"It is thought to be an accident, that the measure was made too strong as a nerve tonic. Nobody has seen Jane's note apart from me," Ellen told him.
Albert glanced up with hope in his eyes at that.
"An accident? Perhaps it was."
"Perhaps – and perhaps not."
A short, fraught silence followed between them. He shook his head
"I thought Jane sought *freedom* through the Clarion Club."
Ellen was not sure what he meant by that, except that his tone washed his hands of any responsibility for whatever that might have been if it involved him.
"Will you go to see Jane?" she asked, her own inflection suggesting that she, at least, thought he ought to.
"I will send word of enquiry, certainly, and visit if I may."
"I think you should if you can," she said, relieved that he had not refused outright, for his manner confused her. "I will go now."
"Ellen – I am very sorry that this has happened. It should not have done."
"No," she agreed. "It should not."
Composing himself, Albert returned to the office and Ellen made her way back downstairs. It was coming to

the close of the working day and a hooter sounded, followed by a milling crowd of men, women, girls and boys beginning to exit in a clatter of clogs on the cobbles.

"Ellen – what are you doing here?" a woman's voice asked her and she saw Hannah and Sarah, with their shawls pulled over their heads, among the crowd.

"I am just leaving," she replied and then hesitated. "I came to tell Albert that Jane Ellison has taken an overdose of laudanum. She lives but is not safe yet."

The two young women exchanged a long, deep look.

"I'm sure we're sorry for it. It were asking for trouble."

"I think she loves Albert," Ellen blurted out.

"Aye, that were plain for all the world to see."

They said no more, enigmatic as ever, and progressed along their way out arm in arm together without a further word to Ellen, who still did not know exactly what lay between them and Albert Dewhirst either. The two women shared a cottage, she believed, and there was talk of them posing for Albert's studio pictures, a knowledge that he was part of some set-up with them. But Ellen's class divide was still strong in her head in many ways. Involved as she knew they were together, the two women seemed a closer entity than the trio they made when they were with Albert. Besides, his hinted proposal to Sylvia did not suggest he felt tied to them in any future life. Socially, it would surely be impossible for him. Jane, too, was not of his moneyed station, although quite respectable in being a vicar's daughter.

Albert had brought Jane with him to visit Ellen only recently and spoken of calling at the vicarage himself. He had seemed quite set on demonstrating that he and Jane were on fond good terms in his usual flirtatious way then, it had seemed to Ellen. Was it really Hannah and Sarah who bedevilled Jane's jealousy? She did not know, but she felt that *they* would. On impulse, she followed them on her bicycle, with a curiosity to see where they lived, and how.

They walked down a cobbled hill further to the bottom of the town and when they arrived at the small enclosed yards they lived among, Ellen called out, "I say! Hannah – Sarah! Might I come in and talk to you. I – I would like to speak to someone who knows Jane as I do, from the Clarion Club. I found her you know, today, and…"

The shock that she had experienced was plain on her young face and the two more mature girls, who had no ill-feeling towards Ellen and understood her naivety, let her in, making no comment about her clearly having followed them.

"Tha might see more than tha's used to," Sarah remarked drily as they entered the small hall lined with the photograph portraits, but it was poky and dark inside and without any lamps on yet, so Ellen saw nothing until they entered the kitchen.

There, they lit the gas jets, very modern equipment for a small house like this and people like them to be enjoying, evidence of Albert's money being spent there. The one or two pictures featuring on the kitchen walls were not so overtly erotic as some of those in the hallway, although Ellen noticed them and asked guilelessly, "Are those some of the portraits Albert takes? I like you dressed up as an Eastern princess, Sarah."

"I weren't so keen. I'm washing her feet wi't jug of water," said Hannah ironically.

Sarah was cast in an imperious pose, Hannah as her lowly servant. The bare foot was the only nod to exposed flesh, but even so there was something about it that suggested private secrets, a slender ankle and the bottom of a supple calf shown. It made Ellen say, without thinking, "What do you think made Jane do it? I think you would have far more idea of it than I."

Hannah followed her eyes to the picture and gave her a softened look.

"Think thissen lucky, lass, that you haven't yet. You're far from ready. We understand his kind of love. It starts young in our worlds. She didn't. Jane Ellison. She couldn't take the pleasure of it without turning it back in on herself. Being a vicar's daughter mebbe."

"His kind of love? And what kind is that?"

"The physical kind, Ellen. Of the body, not that of the heart. He's not made for that. Not yet any road."

"We expect nowt to come of owt," Sarah said, "and that's why it works for Albert. For now. Till he tekks up his real place in't world."

"Aye – we'll see a bit less of free at heart then, won't we?" said Hannah with a laugh.

They sounded indulgent, the wise old heads in charge of their own futures. Something began to dawn fully on Ellen. Mistresses she associated with the old kings of France, or Charles the Second and his courtesans. They were elegant, palace-dwelling creatures with pampered roles, living in sumptuous apartments. A king's mistress was painted in rich robes to show off creamy shoulders, fine arms and an adventurous decolletage. But that photographic plate of Sarah's foot and lower leg, the pose, that *had* had something of the same about it, Ellen thought, recalling it now.

Were Hannah and Sarah, these sturdy-minded, ordinary mill women, really *Albert's* mistresses? And – had *Jane* been another? No. That could not be! She felt her own heart beat faster at the thought, the recollection of the lightning kiss and the heather kiss, the pull at her centre when she experienced them, the knowledge that things had stopped far short of something else, something which married people knew of. That thought. What was it like? She felt her blush rise, that envy of things she felt other women already knew and she did not.

"You – surely you are not – not – and Jane cannot be – Albert's...?"

She trailed off, unable to find the right word for what she wanted to ask, 'concubine' sounding ludicrously overblown and laughably out of context.

The two women regarded her with that self-contained, confident silence of theirs, smiling slightly but not answering.

"What – what is it like?" Ellen blurted out, making them laugh at her innocence.

"Ever been kissed?" teased Sarah.

"Yes!" said Ellen, lifting her chin and feeling she had to answer some challenge. "Peter Lumb has kissed me. Twice!"

She flushed right up from her throat at the thought of it.

"Peter Lumb!" exclaimed Sarah. "Who'd ha' thought it?"

"Well, from't colour of thee, that's give you a taste of it," said Hannah. "Now – what about Jane Ellison. Tell us what happened. Properly."

Ellen did so and they listened with grave attention, shaking their heads.

"Kenneth Butterworth was with me. My neighbour. You don't know him. He has gone to engage a nurse to sit with her."

"I nursed my mother," said Hannah, and again she and Sarah exchanged a look. "I'll sit with her. Talk some sense as well when she comes around. And I'll keep Albert away. It won't do her any good to see him."

"But – I asked him to go to her!" exclaimed Ellen.

"He won't," said Sarah. "Whatever he said to you, Ellen. He'll feel wronged by it, and angry. It will upset him about her, right enough, but I can tell you he won't be made to feel in the wrong because of what she did. It were a punishment for him, not herself, she meant by it, Ellen. Don't you see that? Albert will have done."

Ellen remembered Albert's expression at the news and knew that Sarah was right.

"I think I do. I like Albert, he's lively and different. But, why would she love him so?"

"She'll have told herself she had to, to do what she did. Some folk are made that way, or made to think they should be," said Hannah.

"It's so sad! Do you remember, on Albert Promenade, how happy we all were starting out together?" exclaimed Ellen.

"Aye, we do," agreed Hannah. "For some it's stayed a good thing and a new thing. You're one of them, Ellen. Be proud of it. Not many 'ud come to us as friends. But you have."

"Yes!" she agreed. "I have."

"Then let us do the same for Jane. She's one of us in't Clarion Club and we'll tekk care of her in that spirit. She deserves that, for all her daft-headedness now. You'll agree, Sarah?"

Sarah did not go quite as far as that.

"You go if you want." She reached up for the tea caddy, filled the kettle and put it on the stove. "I'll keep 'ouse. He'll not like it, but I'll tell him you went to stop any more trouble."

"Albert, you mean?" asked Ellen.

"You'd best be off, Ellen. He'll be in for his tea in a bit. Then home to Mother for t' dinner. Depends on the night. This is one of them nights."

A glimpse into these mysterious domestic arrangements between Hannah, Sarah and Albert, so intimately close in this small house, gave Ellen a little frisson of excited wonder at it. Albert living like a gentleman at home and like a – well, what exactly – here, with these two women? Ellen got up hastily, realising that Albert would surely not want to find her here with them.

"Peter Lumb, eh?" asked Sarah with a sardonic chuckle. "Peter, who clouted Albert on the nose for messing wi' Jane's feelings!"

"Peter isn't like that!" Ellen burst out hotly, not able to quite explain herself but meaning that Peter had morals about people and their feelings.

"No, he's not. He's a firecracker, but he's straight up, is Peter," agreed Hannah.

"He's just my friend really," added Ellen, for this was how she had felt it. "Well, he was, before Stanley died."

"He'll come round from that," said Sarah more kindly. "But don't give him no ideas, mind!" she teased.

"Certainly not!" declared Ellen.

"I'll go up to t' vicarage in the morning," said Hannah. "Tell them she did me a kind charity turn once and I'm repaying the favour. Vicar'll take that as a reason for my offer, only being a mill lass. Nobody will have to pay for a nurse after I get there."

"Thank you, Hannah!" said Ellen. "I feel very relieved you will be with her," and she did because she genuinely felt there was a bond of fellowship between them all, and certainly more with Hannah than Sarah. *She* was a more disturbing and satirical character altogether, whom Ellen could not quite fathom. She had a chippy edge rather like Peter's. "But what about your job at the mill, Hannah?"

Hannah gave a low laugh.

"Albert'll see me right there. A favour deserves a favour. I'm keeping him out of bother, aren't I? And her, if I can."

On that note, Ellen bade them good evening and cycled off into a gathering dusk to get home in time for dinner. Fortunately, nobody was at home except her father and herself. Sylvia and her mother were dining up at Noel's house tonight, it turned out, so she had nothing to explain to anybody about her day, apart from her father asking, over the soup, "How did your trip with Butterworth to the bookshop go?"

"It was very enjoyable, Father. And Kenneth has bought me a book for my birthday, but I am not to read it before."

"Oh, yes? And do you think you will be able to hold yourself back from it until then?"

"I will try," she answered, with a grin at his mocking tone.

Her father, she knew, had no interest in books, regarding them with the same slight foreboding as the family Bible, the contents of which he had been bored with in his youth on many an occasion of Sunday readings at home, occasions at which he would often shudder when recounting them. Parliamentary affairs and business matters, things of the day, now that was something else – as he would also often say himself. He did value an excellent newspaper; one of which he buried himself in after their meal.

"Facts, not fiction, you see, Ellen," he said, rattling the pages. "Realities – that's what make the world turn. Read the reports and opinions of others and come to ones of your own."

"Yes, Father," she agreed absently, thinking of Albert, Sarah, Hannah and Jane.

Her mind was full of the other world she had glimpsed and the shocking pictures she had caught a glimpse of in the hall on her way out, those bare limbs and tangled poses. Images suggestive of the bodily love which they had told her lay between themselves and Albert. She wished Libby were still here to ask about it. Libby was bound to understand more of it all than Ellen did, she was certain. Libby and John were courting – were there more than kisses, or not until the marriage bed, whatever really happened there? Was Jane now a fallen woman? She pictured Jane cast out into a snow-filled night, but the vicar's concerned and gentle countenance did not match a stern patriarch exacting moral banishment, closing the door behind his erring daughter. No, she could not imagine that. Besides, Hannah was going to look after Jane. Ellen felt a great comfort in that. It had been hard for her not to share it with them, but she had not betrayed Albert's wish that nobody else should know of Jane's note. She had not blurted out its existence or its contents. She felt that this was a kind of trust. He would have to let Hannah do as she planned to and be grateful for it. Perhaps Hannah was right that it would not do Jane any good to see Albert, or not, at least, until she were fully recovered, which Ellen hoped very much that she would be soon.

Chapter Ten

Peter was glad to start at Stanger's Mill. He wanted to get away from where he and Stanley Jagger had always lived and Stanley had just died. The walks they had gone on since boyhood, rambling over Ovenden Moor's heather-covered hillocks, old spoil heaps from open cast mining beneath them, were lonely now. He had thought he might feel Stanley's friendly presence silently by his side, just as they had often gone along together, but all he felt was the loss of him. Peter had sat and wept up there alone often for his old friend and then gone back to do what he could for Mrs Jagger. But now Eustace had brought a collection from the Clarion Club for her family and his responsibility was relieved a little. Peter thought Eustace was not his type of man at all – too prissy somehow but still – so he felt he could make his move away without feeling so badly about it. His own mother was pleased because he could send more home and make space in the back-to-back for the growing brothers.

Any road, he thought to himself, there were two of the young'uns doing a bit too now, old enough to start working. It was Peter's wish to pay towards apprenticeships and keep them out of the mills, if he could. Billy had already started as a cordwainer with the Co-operative Society's Boots and Shoes and Ted was soon to be an apprentice engineer because he was talented with mechanical things. Better to be building machines than get killed working with them, was Peter's view. Their father had been dragged into one by the arm, his sleeve caught, the injuries horrific and lethal almost at once. Peter meant to put his new opportunity to good use and set his brothers on safer paths in life, if he could.

This, for Peter, was a combination of fresh start and atonement. He did not feel guiltless about the fire at

Stanger's Mill. With this new position he could make amends, not to the Stangers themselves, of course, but to the workforce whose jobs had been blighted as a result. Because he had lost his own job too after the flour mill fire, another rebellious act that had got out of hand, he did not feel the same about that. Besides, that fire had indeed been an accident waiting to happen. He had meant a small blaze to point up the ever present danger of fire in the drying room and force the employer to do better by them. The men had been underpaid for years, the bakers' own jobs in the adjoining building done in gruelling conditions. They lived short lives sweated out in a heat and toil during long hours that gave them distortedly strong arms but sapped their hearts and lungs. To live to forty was a rarity. He had acted alone but with plenty of influence from others, who complained as he did that something ought to be done to change things.

In terms of reparation at Stanger's, though, there was also the injury to his fellow firemen to take into account. John's maimed hands and Stanley's early death lay heavy on his conscience. It was after the smoke damage that Stanley's condition had worsened so fast, even if the outcome *had* been inevitable. While Peter's innate anger led him to feel justified in his acts against the powerful, he was mature enough to realise that he indulged his own violent impulses through them too and that it was not as pure a 'fight' as he had liked to think. Especially when the consequences were far more catastrophic for the people around him than they had been for the owners of the two places he had burned. For all this awareness, Peter still believed that, in principle, he was right.

All these thoughts passed chaotically through his mind as he sat now on an open cart end, being driven with his few belongings up to Stanger's Mill and the cottage which was to be his. It struck him that anyone looking would just see a young man sitting on a cart, his legs dangling over the edge and idling through pleasant scenery, the turmoil of his inner self and thoughts quite invisible as he passed under the avenue of trees which protected him from the drizzle which had begun to fall. The carter dropped him off past that turn of the road which hid the little line of cottages on the bend and around it. Peter took down his sack of clothes and a few parcels of other things. The door was open for him, the key left inside on the windowsill, as he had been advised it would be. Going in he looked around and noticed that, in spite of his refusals, a new kitchen table, with two chairs and a better armchair, had been supplied. He headed with his sack of clothes up the narrow, unrailed stair and found a bed and chest of drawers for his things. Peter had thought to acquire a plain, straw-filled pattress, intending to sleep on that on the floor, for of course, he owned no bed in reality. He shared the pattress on the floor at home with Billy, end to end with the one the two youngest slept on, old coats for extra warmth when needed. Here, there was a woollen bed blanket and a patch quilt, he saw, looking about the place with reluctant appreciation.

It was a discreetly generous welcome and he felt he knew who he had to thank for it. Ellen had been present when he had seen the cottage and no doubt she and Len had agreed on some simple furnishings in spite of what Peter had said at the time. She saw past his defensive façade better than anybody, he felt – to an extent, anyway – in spite of her sheltered youth. Ellen had a kind heart, with true principles and a natural sense of fairness which had led her to the Clarion Club, he believed, and he liked her for that. He knew, with her brother now being married to Carrie Stanger, that he had placed a great burden on Ellen by involving her in setting the fire.

At the time, he had wanted her to do it to understand that you had to try to live by what you said, to take action for the cause, not just wait for slow reforms through talk and changes made by politicians miles away. They were people from the other classes in any case, so what did they know? He had wanted her to see through his eyes and he had thought that she did. He hadn't given that other aspect any thought at all, caught up as he was in his own feelings. Now, he felt a prick of conscience that he had rather forced than persuaded her. It was taking advantage because she was young and untried, so had hesitated to resist. But still, he told himself, Ellen had shown that she was not afraid. They had acted as comrades. The flame had burned pure from that point of view!

Even so, he had never asked her how she felt about it and he had put her under further duress to keep the faith with him when he had been in hospital, hadn't he? Any guilty pain about what happened was his alone, though, and Ellen understood that to be the case, didn't she? Stanley and John were *his* fellow firemen and friends, Stanley his dearest and oldest. He brooded for a moment or two, frowning, then his expression cleared. Ellen had only set a match symbolically, really. She must know that and she had been alone with him since then and never said otherwise, had she? They had even kissed like sweethearts in heightened moments. Peter had never had much time for spooning in his life so far, being fired up by so many other things, but, for all that, it was fun to do and harmless kisses were freer between youths and girls in his world than in Ellen's. He'd enjoyed his share of them but he had a more serious feeling towards Ellen. The fire they set had lit another spark between them and they both felt its pull from time to time, he believed. Ellen was fine, she was a brave one, 'a good lass' being the only way he could put it to himself, a rare accolade from Peter, especially for a mill owner's daughter, a class to be despised in general.

He recalled, with some regret, how he had gone off from her in that angry distress from the graveyard, seeming to blame her along with others for being rich and insincere. Part of him – the selfish, difficult part – believed she ought to understand anyway, but part of him knew it was unfair to presume she had not felt it keenly when he shook her off. He decided he would write a letter to her once he had put his new worker's cottage straight. He would also, when he could speak to her alone, reassure her that she bore no blame for setting the fire at Stanger's Mill. He didn't want it lying on his conscience that it might be lying in some way on hers. He had enough to deal with as it was, feeling to blame for John and Stanley, didn't he? He didn't need to feel any worse about it because of Ellen! Already, his resentment rose a little at that thought and then subsided again, in a recognition of how underserved by Ellen any umbrage on his part about that was.

"Peter Lumb," he said sternly to himself, putting his father's pipe on the mantel with care (a keepsake which, as eldest son, was his), "you're a miserable sod when you want to be. Get your manners straight and thank Len Rastrick for this when you see him today. And what's more, you can like or lump it and write a proper letter of appreciation to Ellen too. So that's settled."

***

Peter had not been wrong in his assumptions about the cottage furnishings. While Len, Carrie and Ellen had been having tea together later on in the day when they had first shown it to him Ellen had said, "You know, Len, there is very little in the cottage there for feeling homely."

“I am sure there were more pieces in the place before. Shall we just put some basics in anyway, then?” he asked, spreading jam on a thickly buttered scone.

“Of course,” said Carrie. “It’s usual when we have a new tenant. People have so little furniture that we turn a blind eye to anything going off with them when they go.”

Ellen smiled at her, saying, “That is kind. And I am quite sure Peter has nothing to bring. Even if he did, he’d leave it for his mother and the family. She’s a widow, you know. So many of the men are already having to be the father of the family with their own already gone. It seems hard, doesn’t it?”

“What young men?” asked Len.

“Why, the young men who work in all our factories and mills, Len! Don’t you look around?” Ellen had said.

“Hah! You’re turning into a radical thinker, Nell. Where are all these ideas coming from? Is it going out with that cycling club you’re so keen on? What is it called again?”

“Never mind,” Ellen responded hastily.

She and Carrie exchanged the slightest of conspiratorial glances, missed by Len, who was reaching for another scone.

“Anyway, Peter Lumb strikes me as a man with plenty of ideas,” he continued, as he was only half trying to get a rise out of Ellen. “We’ll see how he goes on. New furniture for the cottage it is.”

In fact, Ellen was far from being as confident as Peter thought about his underlying opinion of her and, besides, she had not quite been able to shake off the social differences between them herself yet. What she believed she ought to feel and what she sometimes did feel were not one and the same. For instance, Libby was her friend at the Clarion Club but at home she was her maid. Or had been. The conflict was still not resolved in Ellen’s mind, any more than it was in Peter's. It was new to all of them, as Libby had said, but the Clarion Club had opened doors which had been firmly closed before and let them look one another directly in the eye.

Ellen wondered if Peter meant it when he said he had done with them all at the Clarion Club, or whether he had said that in the heat of the moment, the way he did? Time would tell, she supposed. She hoped he had not meant it so finally, but even if he had, she felt a kernel of inner happiness in knowing she would not lose contact with him as a result because now she might see him at Heatherfield instead. She knew she would have gone home from this visit before Peter's arrival, but there would be many others to come.

Carrie and Ellen had not told Len, of course, about going to the Peterloo Massacre rally, nor that Peter Lumb had been Ellen's companion there. Ellen was careful to follow Carrie's lead in anything she did tell Len about the stay with her old friend, Fiona, in Manchester. Carrie camouflaged it subtly while telling no direct untruths.

"Oh, still supporting all her lame dogs, Len," Carrie had said when he asked how Fiona was.

"Still thinks women should be doctors?" he asked, lightly enough.

"She does and you know I don't see why not, if you have the right kind of mind."

"I know that you don't," Len hastily agreed. "No more do I, if it comes to that."

But Len didn't think seriously about it, nor about what particular lame dogs were being referenced. Ellen knew, though, because Fiona and Carrie said that the women campaigners were seen as no threat by the *top* dogs, the men. They were just seen as lame dogs, hobbled by their own apron strings. To Len, it had another meaning, that the women she mixed with over there were good-heartedly engaged in various charitable lost causes and had their ladies' cycling club for recreation together. That was his wife's woman's world and he was happy to leave her to it. Ellen perceived here that their marriage was founded on an understanding that had become affectionate respect for each other's forbearance.

Len supplied Carrie's father with an efficient son-in-law to run the business, increasingly less with him than for him already. Carrie supplied Len with his place in the world and a role for himself in it which was not subordinate to his own father. Meanwhile, Ellen enjoyed sharing the secret confidence of the Clarion Club and each of their other lives with Carrie, who knew that there was more to Ellen than her family thought, just as there was more to Carrie herself than anyone here, including her own husband, knew.

***

Newly arrived in his cottage and settling in for the evening, Peter lit the wood kindling left ready in the fire and carefully added small pieces of coal. It was the kind of place, set against a hillside, which was always likely to be dark and cold inside if you didn't keep the damp off. Not that he could complain about that aspect. What he had seen of the mill owners' house, Heatherfield, suggested the same. He preferred to have the four winds blowing about his head himself, as he did on tramps out across the countryside, where you seemed to be striding the hilltops along with the clouds. Still, Ellen had shown him the moors above here and he could head out that way some days. They were bleak and barren looking in the distance on the Saddleworth side. He wouldn't care to get lost up there, he felt, especially as winter came on, and they were headed into autumn now. There were a couple of bundles of candles on the shelf for him and a single candlestick-holder to light his way to bed, like Wee

Willie Winkie, he thought, with a smile to himself. He lit one now and set it on the kitchen table to brighten things up, ready to eat the pasty he had brought with him. He boiled the kettle over the fire to make tea from the paper screw of leaves his mother had given him to bring. She had also passed on the brown betty teapot with the cracked lid that had once been her own mother's and they'd used for years. Peter had bought her a new one long since but that had still remained a treasure, set aside on a shelf until she gave it to him now that he was 'setting up for himself', as she put it.

After that, he set off for Heatherfield to meet his new employer formally in his role as foreman manager. How would the other men take it when he met them, he wondered? Would there be someone who thought that job belonged to them and others who thought it did too, which would have him resented from the start? He was young to hold the position but he had persuaded Len it was his forward-thinking planning he was needed for, to modernise the place. Len had also said that it was a new position and he would not be directly in charge of the factory workers' shifts themselves but in a parallel role to the man who managed that. Not that anyone was back in the workplace yet, of course.

"I see myself as a sort of architect, and not just of bricks, but of ideas here, like I told you before, Rastrick," Peter announced, planted on the rug in Len's office (once Mr Stanger's domain). Len's eyes widened slightly at the lack of 'Mr' prefacing the address but he did not flinch. "Working side by side wi' thee as much as under thee. That's if we're to achieve any vision here."

"Understood, Lumb," said Len, answering manfully in kind, so that Peter's slightly challenging stance relaxed. Seeing that, Len added, "There is no point in us lacking co-operation at any level." Putting out his hand. Peter, smiling now, stepped forward to shake it, whereupon Len added, "I will always hear your proposals", to remind Peter who would have the final word on things and that he was, after all, the boss, but it was gently said. "Well, then. Let us step down to take a look at the mill itself and how the building is going on. I want you to show me again where you are thinking of making changes for safety. The chimney base is all but completed. I wanted them to concentrate on that until you came, now that we are agreed on your appointment here."

"Aye, that's grand," said Peter, looking pleased.

"We will return for some tea and you may tell my wife too about the plans."

"I'll be glad to. One favour, Rastrick – may I beg some stationery to write letters with? I've not had an opportunity yet to get any."

"Certainly. Help yourself to paper and to pen and ink. There is plenty of all in the office here."

"I'll buy my own of course, when…"

"Of course," Len finished for him, the words 'when I'm paid' left politely unsaid.

It felt strange to Peter, finding himself back at the scene of the fire, some of the blackened brickwork knocked down and cast aside for new footings for different buildings, the main factory destroyed at one end altogether and a new chimney beginning to rise from its old ashes.

"Tha should make that fancy topped," said Peter, thinking of Wainhouse Tower with its balconied, tiered lantern top, and also of the grand crown top of the Dean Clough Mills' chimney towering over the other end of the valley. "Worth spending on so folk see it and look at it. Then they'll be saying from't road down, 'See that? That's Stanger's Mill right there.' And it'll be a landmark."

Len considered.

"I think you're right. You can see the mill from Ripponden Road and from the hills. It's set back a bit from the fields in a prime spot. What are you thinking of?"

"Something in tiers, looking like it's got arch windows, going up to false balconies. Like summat in Venice, or mebbe India. Build it taller than it has to be. Top t' chimney out in different coloured brick layers. Keep it bright. Make your mark. Advertising Stanger's to all t'world as top notch. I've seen chimneys like that in Lancashire."

Peter had been very struck by the warehouses and factories of the Manchester cotton merchants he had seen. Whitworth Street was a series of ornate palaces, hard to credit as being warehouses, working buildings made to show their owners' stature, that they were gentlemen of culture building something beautiful to show off their position, or make it look greater than it was.

He did not add that, if Rastrick agreed, for Peter it would be the finest monument he could offer to Stanley and also a private recognition of John, whose bravery on that night of the fire, at such a price to himself, had saved Peter's own life. He felt a terrible guilt over John's maimed hands, only now lessening as John Henderson managed to get his skills back gradually. Peter was deeply ashamed but it took him into avoiding John, when he knew he should have tried to support him. Perhaps this would be some kind of recompense and he'd bring John to see it one day and say, "I had it done to thank thee."

Even as he thought this, he spoke eagerly to say, on impulse, "John Henderson could draw the design for you – the fireman who brought me down when I fell unconscious. He's been badly affected and it would be a great thing to thank him with that job!" His eyes lit up at the prospect of the idea. "He is an excellent stonemason and artist."

"A splendid start to our work together, Lumb!" declared Len, impressed. "I knew you had vision, and you certainly have. Will you write to him too for us please, to suggest it?"

"I will and gladly!" said Peter, delighted to have some possible way to make some of the amends he felt were due from him to John.

"We will talk to Carrie and I am sure Mr Stanger will be persuaded of the advantages of it. Next, take some string and mark out where you think these building extensions ought to be for enough space and perhaps your friend can design that too with the windows you envisage. You could work together on it."

"Aye!" agreed Peter eagerly, feeling a lump melt off the rock of bitterness he carried in his chest and melt into warmer emotions.

There wasn't room for too much sentiment in his life, Peter believed, if he were to stay focussed on what was right, what should be battled for, but being a man of strong feelings, they were always likely to break through and be as powerfully felt as his anger was. Borrowing a ball of twine and some pegs from the builders already on site, he marked out where he thought the new building should be added on to the surviving parts of the mill which were still sound. Most of the machinery had been salvaged but he and Len between them hoped to buy more modern ones, with higher safety levels built in. Losing himself in the moment later, when he was back at Heatherfield and talking through it all in Carrie's presence too, Peter revealed how the dreadful death of his own father was the inspirational source of his zeal for better working conditions and his hopes that his own younger brother would design safer machines and engines in the future. He stopped short suddenly, while he was in full flow.

"I'm making a fool of missen in front of you talking about all that," he said gruffly, burying himself in his tea-cup.

"Far from it!" said Len, who had found himself unexpectedly moved and was reminded of what Ellen had said to him about being blind to the circumstances of those who worked for them. Peter looked up and, still emotional, presented a far more engaging expression than he usually did. "We will do very well together, Lumb. Very well indeed," Len, touched by it all, assured him.

"Thank you, Rastrick. Mrs Rastrick," said Peter, with a proud and grateful nod to each. He left them with a bundle of notepaper and envelopes, also equipped with pen and ink, having assured them that he would be quite comfortable in the cottage now and would return in the morning to resume discussions. "I'll draw up some plans myself too now," he said, gesturing to the paper.

"Your powers of description are such that I almost feel we have seen them already," said Carrie warmly. "Good evening to you, Mr Lumb."

With cordial handshakes all around, Peter left them and walked quite happily back to the cottage, where he put some more coal on the fire, lit a candle and settled down to write his letters, one to Ellen and one to John Henderson.

Dear Ellen, he wrote, *I hope I find you well. I came to the cottage today, where I am very comfortable. Thank you. I know I was out of sorts when we last met. I am sorry for it and hope you will forgive me.*

Your friend,

Peter Lumb.

In his usual way, he left much to be inferred from little said about what he expected she would understand anyway, especially since he found it difficult to express in writing any more than the basics of what he felt. A kind of shyness came over him as he put pen to paper, even though far more generous words were in his head and greater warmth in his heart towards Ellen than seemed apparent from what he wrote there.

"Well," he said to himself, "when she comes here, or we meet next, I'll just tell her, like, to her face, how much what she's done getting me this position means to me. You daft beggar. You've told her brother and sister-in-law more abaht that already than Ellen, and she's stood right by your side since that damned fire here. And been the best of comrades." He thought about the winter to come and walking up on the Moor again with her to see the snow drifts up there that would make a spectacle then. "I've kissed you in't summer lightning, I've kissed you in't autumn heather, and I'll kiss you in't snow, Ellen Rastrick. And we'll see how you like it." He smiled to himself, anticipating another tender moment in their unusual friendship, liberated by the Clarion Club to enjoy it.

He saw Ellen as a freshly freed spirit, not in the way Albert Dewhirst presented it but more as a young girl striding forward into a better future, with that hopeful friendly face of hers lifted up to the sun of it. He was glad to know her and he hoped now that she was glad to know him too. He would be pleased to send that letter and put things to rights again. She never did take him to task for storming off and that wasn't the first time he'd done it, he knew, but she hadn't deserved to be included in his harsh words about Dewhirst and Ogden. That put him in mind again of the others and he sat down to write a second short letter to John Henderson, inviting him to come and meet him and Len Rastrick. He explained that Len wanted to explore commissioning John to design and build a new chimney top for him – one which would stun the Calder Valley and make Stanger's a byword for *a right rare piece of masonry. Let's knock the socks off Noel Ogden and his Wainhouse Tower*, he concluded with a flourish, thinking that this, at least, would be well worth it.

"Hah!" he laughed to himself, sitting back with a pleasant mental picture of the Clarion Club standing around his and John's achievement admiringly. "Made with our own hands, see, not just bought up because you can," he told an imaginary Noel, the completed chimney conjured up in his head already as a magnificent edifice.

He rocked back on his chair, hands behind his head, looking contentedly out of the window at the darkening road and lost in these pleasantly self-aggrandising daydreams, when a rap on the door brought his chair feet down sharply. He opened up to see the woman who had been shaking out a mat the day he, Len and Ellen had looked around.

"Nah then," she said, thrusting a covered dish into his hands, something wrapped in a cloth on top of it. "You'll be wanting this. I don't see any tea on that table."

She spoke in the slightly challenging way common to the neighbourhood,

"Thank you, missus," said Peter taking it gratefully. "You're right there, there in't none. I only got here today."

"Ah know," she said. "Well, I'll let you get on." And with that she went back to her own cottage.

Peter shut the door and took the food to the table. A stack of griddle oatcakes was in the cloth, which he could eat for supper and in the morning, and there was a stew with a suet cobbler on the side for his meal now, making an appetising sight when he took the cover off. He ate it gratefully, thinking that it was all right round here, really, wasn't it? He would post his letters in the morning. Having eaten, he took down his father's pipe, packed it with some of the tobacco he had brought with him and enjoyed the ceremony of lighting it. He smoked it sitting in the armchair by his warm fire, with plenty of coal in the scuttle by it, unlike at home, and feeling quite the king of the castle for once in his life. He enjoyed the restfulness of being on his own, surrounded as he usually was by the others of his family in a small house, where there was always noise and somebody wanting to talk. Peter wondered if his own mind would quieten here, for his thoughts were forever racing and keeping him awake at night.

He'd have time to read here a bit in the evenings. If he had any books. Ellen had books and she liked reading. Maybe he could add something about that to his letter and ask if she would mind lending him the odd one to read when she came, if it were not too much trouble. A further thought came to him. Why shouldn't the proposed Clarion Club's free library allow members to share radical books as well? Ones the municipal library would frown on. That would be a wonderful thing for a lot of them. For all his churlish words before about most people not being able to read, access to books for those who could and encouraging others to learn to read, as Eustace wished to do, would be one of the ways forward for everybody. He'd suggest it at the next meeting.

Oh! He had said he wouldn't go to any more meetings though, hadn't he? But only to Ellen. And she knew he didn't mean half of what he said when he was worked up, didn't she? Of course she did. That was the thing about Ellen. You didn't have to tell her. At least, he didn't think he did. He shook his head, knocking his pipe out and telling himself to stop babbling on to himself.

"That poor lass's ears will be burning toneet, Peter,

lad," he said to himself. "Give her a rest and think about summat else."

He finished tidying the place up with his few belongings put away in the chest of drawers, his one outdoor jacket hung on the back of the door, and sat a while longer before going up to bed, drawing out some of the plans he had told Len of and looking forward to showing them to John Henderson too. Peter had missed John and he'd be glad to have a good reason to see him again. It struck him it would be something good to tell Ellen of one day soon, too, properly in keeping with the Clarionettes' aims to benefit one another and others if they could – even if it *was* partly to salve his own conscience by having John rebuild the very chimney that had injured him when he rescued Peter.

***

Albert was at the family home to dine on the night he got the news from Ellen about Jane. A smile was not so ready on his lips as usual and his dark eyes darted about with a slightly hunted look. Now and again, he caught Libby's glance, as she came forward to serve at table alongside the butler. This household boasted a butler, a cook, a boot boy, a kitchen maid and Libby doubling as parlour maid and ladies' maid to Albert's mother and sisters. Libby knew him well enough to see that he was rattled and wondered why. Long windows were dark, the curtains left open to reflect the candlelight, since it was Mrs Dewhirst's boast that they were not overlooked by any neighbour in their extensive, hedge-surrounded garden with rolled lawns.

"Albert, my boy. Share with us what news it was that Miss Rastrick brought to you today," Mr Dewhirst suggested in all innocence. "I am sure your mother and sisters will be interested. If it is a good notion we must be sure to tell your brother too when he next sees you. Why you can't both dine here together I fail to see the reason of…" he concluded with a baffled expression, cutting vigorously into a slice of meat on his plate.

Albert jumped at the mention of 'Miss Rastrick' and with a very odd expression, Libby noticed. Had *Sylvia* come to call? Libby knew all about Albert's sotto voce and provocative proposition because Ellen had told her. Perhaps Sylvia was exploring her options after all?

"We don't see eye to eye, Father, as you know. My brother does not approve of my artistic side," said Albert.

Libby smiled to herself, thinking it was probably not all that the rather more fastidiously proper first born did not approve of.

"Is photography really art, I wonder?" mused his father.

"Not to you, Father, no. Or my brother. But it is to me," said Albert firmly. "I work for you both in the firm but I must have my own occupations too."

Albert's mother gave him an indulgent smile for he was, naturally, a favourite there, and his father said, "Well – you have your studio and you have made some very good family portraits for us, certainly. So, you were about to tell us?"

"Why, there is nothing greatly to say. Ellen merely wished to arrange a day for me to meet with her brother Len to discuss the progress at Stanger's Mill. I thought if I paid a visit and found out more about their ideas for it, we might look at modernising ways ourselves. I will be going on Wednesday morning, if that is convenient to you, sir?"

"Certainly! I will be most interested to know more. I know you call to visit the Rastricks on occasion and are acquainted with Leonard and his father. Good of young Miss Ellen to act as messenger. Wasn't she on a *bicycle*?" he asked, rather as if she had appeared on something as bizarre as a dromedary.

"Yes, Father. Women do ride them too, you know."

"Most extraordinary. I wouldn't care for Phyllis and Anthea to do it."

"Why not? They can have a tandem," said Albert, with a wink at his younger sisters.

"Oh, yes!" declared Anthea, the youngest, earning a rebuke from her mother for it.

"Don't be pert, Anthea," she said, smiling nonetheless.

Albert had now committed himself to a visit to Stanger's Mill. He would have to send a message to that effect now to Leonard Rastrick, but he found himself glad of the idea of getting well away from anywhere Jane Ellison might be talked of. Well, he would be, if Ellen were not visiting Heatherfield too, which he hoped she would not be. At the thought of Jane, his appetite and spirits deserted him again and he fell silent. He caught Libby's eye and realised she was studying him from aside, wondering what was on his mind.

"Dobson," he addressed her, rather peremptorily. "I believe I have finished. Will you show me out and fetch my hat and coat, please? I won't stay for coffee, Mother, and will be out until later. I may stay at my club tonight."

"Very well, dear," said his mother, used to his comings and goings as a young man about town, a veil of decency habitually being drawn over what those many nights away might entail.

What Albert's club was a euphemism for was never questioned, although the rest of the household, that is, the servants, were known to gossip about it. Not that any of them knew Hannah and Sarah except Libby and she kept her counsel about them, to Albert too because it was not a very open secret even among the Clarionettes, whatever they might imagine. She came out into the hallway and handed him his outdoor things, saying, with pointed crispness, "Your coat – *sir*. Your hat – *sir*."

"All right, Libby," he responded edgily. "You know I have to talk to you like that here."

"Not *quite* like that," she said. "What's really going on? You're well out of sorts. And *Ellen* came to the factory? Why?"

He glanced about, anywhere but at her at first, and then, looking right into her eyes with a plea for something – understanding, or perhaps sympathy for his own situation here – confided in her.

"It's Jane Ellison, Libby. She has taken too much laudanum. Not – well, Ellen does not think by accident. She found her."

Libby drew in a sharp breath.

"Not – *dead*, Albert?

"No, near to it."

"And Ellen came to tell *you*. I see."

There was a wealth of meaning in her few words.

"Don't condemn me, Libby," he said indignantly. "And do something to get rid of this, would you? *I* don't want her letter!" From his pocket, he took the note Jane had written, either to him or about him. He now thrust it into Libby's hand, saying, "It isn't my fault."

"No?" she said thoughtfully, looking back at him so coolly that he banged angrily out of the house after all, uncomforted and leaving her to close the door after him.

Libby could see the possession of the note burned him, that he would not dispose of it himself but wanted it to vanish by another's agency and absolve him from having it. In a way, she pitied him, but vanity had led him to make Jane his lover and give in to her desire. They had all warned him that with somebody like Jane it could not be right. Jane would not understand that he did mean what he said, that he was the bohemian artist he posed as – or at least, he was for the present.

She went up to the attic bedroom where there would be no other servant present and read the letter. It was incoherent, full of irrational pain, a distraught love of a kind which could never bring happiness to either party. Even so, it was couched in veiled, high-flown words which, if you did not know the person it was written to, did not accuse Albert directly. He had trusted Libby with getting rid of it without thinking, but really, at no great risk to himself should other eyes see it, she thought. The letter stopped where it was blotched and smeared, the writer's hand and mind overtaken by the draught she had swallowed. Irresponsible and self-indulgent, the pair of them, in Libby's view, not to mention being blind to the realities of their circumstances. As if Albert would ever run away with, or marry, a penniless clergyman's daughter! Well, Jane had created her own hothouse and it was full of blooms that would wither in the cold, harsh light of day.

Ellen must have brought this to Albert, so that meant she had read it, or at least scanned it to know for whom it was meant. Libby pondered. What if there were another reason for Jane taking that laudanum? Could she be with child? If so, that note ought to be kept against an uncertain future for Jane. Where there was a child, there was a father. She ought to have her letter returned, since she lived.

The following morning, donning her shawl and outdoor shoes, Libby used the excuse of posting the household letters and having some commissions for her mistress to leave the house, and she headed for the Rastricks. Ellen should put this back in Jane's possession, hidden in a drawer perhaps, but somewhere she had it if need be. Ellen was at home, and pleased to see her when the new maid said there was a person at the back door calling for her.

"Libby! Why are you out here?"

"Because I only came to see you, Miss Ellen," she said, using formal address as she was in the hearing of the other servants, "and to see how you do on my way about some business."

"Let me walk with you!" cried Ellen at once and they stepped out together, smiled at by the cook, who knew them for old friends and girl confidantes as well as servant and mistress.

"Ellen – Albert's told me about Jane," Libby said at once. "He's read the note you brought to him and he can't stand it. He gave it me to get rid of. I think you should give it back to the lass on t' quiet. She might need it or want to get rid herself. It's best she dun't know he saw it. I can tell you it's done her no good in Albert's eyes."

"No," agreed Ellen, looking fretted. "Did I do wrong to tell him and give it to him?"

"Not in my view," said Libby, squeezing her arm and linking hers through Ellen's as they walked. "But he won't go to her. That I am sure of. I hope she won't find herself ruined."

"Ruined!" cried Ellen, catching the import of this at once. "I did not think that – well…"

"Let's hope not. In them things, it's the woman's word against the man's."

"Poor Jane! Hannah has offered to nurse her. She and Sarah said Albert would not go to her, either."

"Then they, at least, know him well. Are you to call?"

"Yes, later this morning, with Kenneth Butterworth. He was with me when we discovered her. We had seen her when we were in town, you see – well, I had. And I felt she looked in a poor way then. We found her only just in time for the doctor to come and try to save her."

"Mr Butterworth? I am glad you are friends, Ellen."

"That is all we are," said Ellen firmly.

"Are you determined only to be friends with all young men?" Libby asked, with a knowing smile.

"For the present, certainly!" declared Ellen. "Wasn't it you who told me I am too young to be thinking of any courting?"

"Aye, but I think for you, better him than Peter Lumb," commented Libby, upon which Ellen coloured slightly.

"Oh, Peter!" she said, in a dismissive way she did not really feel. "He is working with my brother, you know, on the mill restoration."

"Is he now? Thanks to you, no doubt," laughed Libby. "Here." She passed Ellen the note. "Take it to her and hide it for her. Now, I must get back."

Once more, the unfinished letter was in Ellen's possession. What had Albert really felt when he read it, she wondered? He was far from heartless and she rather pitied him for being the object of such an abject devotion. She hoped that she would never feel like that about anybody herself. Sighing, she went back to the house and readied herself for Kenneth to call for her. When he did, it was clear they were both steeling themselves for the necessary visit. They found the invalid feeble but awake and able to receive Ellen, at least. She was in the parlour with a wrap around her shoulders before a fire. Whilst Kenneth discreetly left them together and went to speak to the vicar in his study, Ellen gave Jane back the letter.

"Jane – I found this and hid it for you. I did not think you would wish other eyes to…"

Jane took it and glanced at it with a strange indifference. She gave a short, bitter laugh and thrust it upon the fire herself, where the heat of her written words was quickly consumed and reduced to ash.

"That is all done with. Thank you, Ellen," she said.

"Where is Hannah Robertshaw?" asked Ellen.

"Gone. I sent her away again as soon as I was able. Why would I want *her* here? She told me – she told me…" Jane's face changed as her words trailed off.

Ellen bit her lip, in no doubt of what Hannah *would* have told her. That Albert did not wish to see her and Hannah was guarding the gate at Jane's own house to prevent it.

"You needed a nurse and…"

"I have no need of one now. Felix Sykes will be here shortly. He reads to me often. He is kinder than I thought."

"Oh. That is good," said Ellen, feeling rather helpless.

Jane looked at her with a fretful kind of exasperation and rang the bell.

"I suppose you want some refreshment? Didn't Mr Butterworth arrive with you?"

"He did."

"Then they may as well join us – he, my father, Mr Sykes. Come one, come all."

She had a restless glitter in her eye and plucked at the fringe of her wrap repeatedly. There was something about her demeanour, changed and damaged, which Ellen did not like. This was not the young woman she had met at the Clarion Club, shy but self-possessed, wanting more from life as they all did but not, surely, this? She could not ask her about what Libby feared might have come to pass and the moment alone was soon over, for which Ellen found herself grateful. There was no gratitude in Jane herself, only a strange kind of resentment. At finding herself still alive? Did she blame Ellen for saving her? She seemed a little mad, as if she were sinking herself into some other state of mind now. Or it could be that the dose of laudanum still afflicted her in some way? Perhaps other nerve tonics were being given to her too?

Ellen was touched to see how gently Mr Sykes

addressed Jane when he came in, asking if she were quite comfortable and putting more coal on the fire beside her. Ellen felt she was seeing quite another side to him and when she and Kenneth took their leave after the smallest of polite intervals and a cup of tea, she saw how Felix Sykes at once took up a volume and tried to engage Jane's wandering interest in some poetry. It was a while before Ellen and Kenneth spoke, both affected by Jane's altered manner.

"I expect Miss Ellison may have a long convalescence from such a serious event," Kenneth remarked finally. "But I think we may be quite happy that the vicar is being very well supported in caring for her.

"Yes," Ellen agreed. "Perhaps we should not call again for a while to ask after her."

"I quite agree," said Kenneth firmly. "I think Miss Ellison already has all the company she can presently manage to enjoy at hand already."

They found Sylvia at home with Noel when they returned to the house and, after they had made as little as might be out of Jane's illness, conversation turned to Ellen's forthcoming birthday and the play tableaux being rehearsed at Noel's house, ready for performance, he believed. Ellen found that her eighteenth birthday was to be the occasion of setting a date.

"I am happy for that, Noel, as long as I may be in the audience and not expected to take part myself."

"Of course, Ellen – it will all be for your pleasure."

"Not mine alone, I am sure," she observed drily, making Kenneth glance at her with an answering amusement in his own eyes.

***

Ellen received Peter's letter the following morning and immediately found her spirits lifting – he was happy there at Heatherfield and Stanger's and he regretted his former rudeness to her, both good things. It was a relief to find something positive going on out in the world after the gloom of Jane Ellison's self-destruction. Made light-hearted by Peter's note, she cycled down to tell John Henderson and Cyril Raynor all about it. She had not been to help out in the workshop for a while. Although she was not really needed to do so any more, she enjoyed learning more of the skills they shared with her when she was there.

"You're not the only one to have had a letter from Peter Lumb," John told her. "He has a proposal for me and a good one too."

Ellen was delighted to hear about the idea of John designing the new mill chimney top.

"Why, that's a wonderful idea, John! Will you do it?" she asked eagerly.

"Aye, I think so. I don't see why not," John said, understating his evident pleasure because that was the way round here, rather than being overtly enthusiastic about anything.

"He owes it to you," she said unguardedly.

"What for?" asked John curiously.

"You wouldn't have been hurt at all if you hadn't saved him from that very same chimney," she declared.

"He owes me nowt for that. It's what we all do for one another as firemen," John said.

Ellen shuffled a few things around on the work bench to cover her momentary confusion.

"Well," she said, looking up again. "That's all right then."

"Aye," said John, looking satisfied. "It is."

"I can manage here, I suppose," said Cyril, smiling too. "You won't be there all the time anyway, will you?"

"Nay, I'll not," agreed John. "I'm invited for a first meeting with Peter and your brother in't week, like,

Ellen. Wednesday, if you might be calling yourself?"

"I will make sure I do!" she said. "Oh, and don't forget, Noel has his play on very soon. For my birthday. Will you both come?"

"Both come? We're both in it, aren't we?" said Cyril. "He has me as Puck. John here was to be one of the nobles of Oberon's court but he's made his excuses. What a palaver dressing up for it is. Still, at least I have my lines learned. Rather beautiful ones too. Of course, Noel has hogged the best. 'I know a bank where the wild thyme blows'," he began mellifluously, quoting the speech.

"How well you speak it!" Ellen said, impressed.

"Thanks to Eustace. He's not rested till he had us all loving the language, if we didn't to start with," said Cyril. "The orphanage youngsters an' all."

"He's a good teacher, isn't he?" said Ellen.

"That he is. And a good fellow too. The kind that gets overlooked. Speaking of them as doesn't – what's been going on with Albert Dewhirst and Jane Ellison?" John asked. "Libby let me know something of it but wouldn't go into any detail."

Ellen looked down.

"Oh. She has been ill. That is all. A mistaken dosage of laudanum from the apothecary. She is getting well now."

John and Cyril looked at one another and shook their heads.

"I thought as much," said John. "He's not worth that, is he, for all his carry on?"

"No," agreed Ellen. "But he did not intend her any harm, you know. Albert is not a cruel young man."

"I'd agree there," said Cyril thoughtfully. "The trouble is that he's another who won't blame himself for any hurt felt because he made somebody love him."

“They’ve got too much money, him and Noel, and too much time on their hands,” said John. “I’d hoped they’d learn summat through the club. Mebbe they have and mebbe they haven’t. I’m glad t’lass is on the mend and let’s hope no more comes of it.”

***

On Wednesday, Ellen asked if she could be driven to call at Heatherfield. At first, her mother appeared tempted to join her, always keen to seize an opportunity to see her beloved Leonard, until Ellen said, “I am really to visit Carrie, Mother, but I am sure she will be happy to see you too.”

Then Mrs Rastrick found that Sylvia would probably have need of her after all, with so much in preparation for the *Midsummer Night’s Dream* tableaux.

“And it is for your birthday, Ellen, so I am sure you will not object?” her mother concluded as she withdrew her initial intention to go with her daughter.

“Not at all, Mother,” said Ellen with a smile, and set off alone with a small sigh of relief.

She arrived to take coffee with Carrie in the drawing room, learning that Peter, John and Len were already in the study discussing the proposals for the mill chimney. Not long after that, much to their mutual astonishment, Albert Dewhirst was shown in.

“Ellen!” he exclaimed in surprise. “I did not expect to find you here. I have come to see your brother.”

“I did not expect to see you, either,” she responded.

Carrie looked from one to the other of their flustered faces and drew a wrong conclusion.

“Excuse me,” she said in her blunt way. “I will let Leonard know that you have arrived.”

Albert and Ellen found themselves alone and viewing each other with some dismay. Albert got up and walked about the room before saying, “Ellen – I know that Jane is well now. I would not have you think I had not asked after her."

"But you won't go to see her, Albert?"

"No," he said. "Her spirit must heal. Then perhaps we may be friends again. I hope that you understand a little, Ellen."

His eyes brimmed slightly and she saw that he was indeed distressed, on Jane's account as well as his own.

"A little, perhaps," she conceded. "I hope that – I trust that Jane's reputation will remain safe."

The veiled reference did not escape Albert, who looked startled to be asked but answered, "Most certainly, Ellen!" in a very definite tone. "There will be no doubt of that at any time in the future," he added. "Although I am surprised to hear *you* ask me!"

"I dare say you are," said Ellen, "but I will be eighteen next week and I have learned something of life now in the Clarion Club."

Whatever she meant by that remained unexplained, as Carrie returned with Len in tow, finding the two young people at a very safe distance from one another, one staring out of the window and the other at the floor, quite silent after their short exchange.

"Ah, Leonard, my dear chap!" exclaimed Albert with clear relief, going quickly forward to shake his hand. "I am come to hear all about your new ventures here. It is quite the talk of the valley, you know!"

"Come into the study, Albert – Peter Lumb is here, my new foreman manager, and this is John Henderson, who is to build me a chimney the like of which you will never have seen before!" Leonard announced. "You are welcome to join us!"

"I should be delighted!" said Albert. "I know them both, you know."

"You do?" exclaimed Leonard. "You surprise me."

"Often, I surprise myself," returned Albert wryly, with a glance at Ellen, but he made no mention of the cycling club just then and followed Leonard back out of the room, leaving Ellen alone with her sister-in-law.

"Is anything amiss?" asked Carrie, as directly as ever.

"Not with me, Carrie. I will wait until Albert has gone before seeing what plans the others have, but I should like to do that."

"Certainly. Meanwhile, will you look through this speech that Fiona intends to make at the Women's Guild she has set up recently and tell me what you think. It reads well but might be rather long to hear!"

She passed Ellen a letter about universal suffrage to peruse. Ellen agreed that it was perhaps rather long for an audience to sit through and she and Carrie suggested some edits, which Carrie assured Ellen would cause no offence.

"I say too little and Fiona says too much," she smiled. "We were always the same. But she will listen to me about it."

This done, Carrie returned to the topic of their unexpected visitor.

"You know Albert Dewhirst already, of course? I do only slightly. I believe he is considered a good-looking young man."

"I expect so," agreed Ellen coolly. "He has called at our house and seems to get on well with my brother. He is a Clarionette too, you know. He comes out cycling and was at the meeting where you spoke."

"Was he?" Carrie laughed aloud. "You surprise me and I had forgotten it."

"Yes," and Ellen laughed too. "But we must not mention it to Len."

"No," agreed Carrie, a mischievous look in her eye. "I agree. Were you having words to do with the Clarion

Club, then, Ellen? I felt there was something in the air."

"Yes," said Ellen, choosing not to elaborate.

"Politics can be easy to disagree over." Carrie nodded, taking it as read now that this was the cause of the friction she had noticed.

Ellen said nothing to disabuse her of it because Jane's business was not hers to share and nor was Albert's, if it came to that. A few months ago she would have confided it but she had matured in discretion as well as in herself.

"Carrie – in the club we have benefits for people who are not in work or cannot work at present. I wonder – for the mill people who cannot return yet since Stanger's is not up and running, could we not do the same? Or do something for them to know they are still thought of?"

"An excellent notion, Ellen. Let us join the men now and see how they get on. You can suggest it to Len."

Their entry to the study was Albert's signal to bid everyone a polite farewell, having expressed much interest in the work to be done.

"I expect to see you at Noel's theatricals, Miss Rastrick, next week?"

"Of course," agreed Ellen.

"Until then," said Albert politely, bowing slightly and making his way out.

Peter and John greeted Ellen now. Peter, in particular, was looking highly delighted with the way things were going, an unusually lively colour in his face from the pleasure of it all, that and the sense of having done something good and positive for somebody else.

"Nah then, Ellen – John here's to work wi' me and your brother on designing a grand new mill chimney – what do you think of that?"

"I think it is a wonderful idea!" said Ellen. "John, I'm so glad!"

Everybody smiled at one another and it was clear the

three of them were on the best of terms. Len looked between them curiously but smiled too and together they looked at the first sketches of ideas which John had brought and Peter had tried to realise in his plans. After admiring them, Carrie said, “Ellen has had an idea too. Tell them.”

Ellen repeated her thought of some kind of benefit activity and Peter exclaimed, “I know! The moors up by are perfect for a bout of Knurr and Spell! Let’s do that before the winter comes on altogether, for the men? It’s coming up Halloween. We can have apple-bobbing for the children and the women can sell food and things they’ve made. We can get folk from Rastrick’s Mill to come? Mebbe Dewhirst’s if Albert were on board wi’ it.”

“Yes – ones in work to support those who are not by joining in. It hides that any charity from the owners is involved,” agreed Carrie, intervening before Len demurred at expense. “Father has always been a benevolent employer, Len.”

“As will I be!” he hastened to say. “We must tell him, it will brighten his day to hear of it.”

“Yes, indeed,” agreed Carrie.

It was time for Ellen to leave now, the driver having waited for her for upwards of an hour. Both John and Peter came out with her, leaving Carrie and Len to bring the failing Mr Stanger out of his room to the parlour fire and hear of their plans for a sports and benefit occasion.

“Let me give you a lift back into Halifax, John?” offered Ellen. “If your meeting today is over?”

She saw that he had gathered up rolls of drawings to take back with him to work on.

“I’d be grateful for that, Ellen. What about my bicycle?”

“It can go in the back of the carriage easily I think!”

“Ellen!” Peter called out to her as they made ready,

heaving John's bicycle for him into the back of the light carriage. "It's been a good day's work all round!"

"It has," she agreed.

"You'll be back to plan for our benefit wi' us all? It were your idea."

"Oh, yes," she agreed happily. "I will be very glad to!"

"And – happy birthday for next week. I'll write to you."

"Please do!" she encouraged him as they shook hands, relieved to be back on good terms together again.

"Oh aye?" said John Henderson, as they set off in the carriage leaving Peter waving behind them on the road. "It's like that, is it?"

Ellen just smiled and decided to say nothing. Not having made her rise to it, John just laughed quietly to himself and let her turn the talk on to the chimney and mill plans again, and what might be done for the sports and activities day. She asked where he would stay when he was to work at Stanger's and he told her he'd have digs with one of the millworker families nearby to it. When he got down, he said he too would see her at Noel's theatricals next and, one way or another, Ellen found herself looking forward to her birthday occasion.

Peter would not be able to come now with his new work commitments, and perhaps still would not want to associate with either Noel or Albert. What would he say if he knew about Jane? Ellen wondered, imagining that his ire would be fired up immediately against Albert again and remembering that thump on the nose he had given him already for far less. No, Peter could not go but she would ask Kenneth to join her in the audience, as a thank you for her book. He had come to the statue unveiling and she did not think he would refuse. When she returned home, she wrote him a note of invitation, saying she would take it very kindly if he would drive her up there for it, since Sylvia and her mother would already have taken the household carriage. Mr Rastrick senior, she had no doubt, would duck the theatricals altogether as being far too frivolous an outing for him to trouble with. In this she was right, she discovered a few days later, having secured Kenneth's agreement by return of post that he would be delighted to join her.

"I'll see enough of Mr Ogden in his finery at your wedding, Sylvia. I have no wish to witness either of you making a show of yourselves prior to it. No, I'm sorry, Ellen – you must enjoy your birthday party without me."

"It isn't my birthday party, Father," said Ellen calmly, passing him the gravy boat at dinner. "Not really. It's for Sylvia and Noel."

"How ungrateful," said Sylvia with a little moue, laughing anyway because it was so blatantly true.

"I'm sure I will enjoy it anyway," responded Ellen. "Kenneth is taking me in the evening, so Father need not be troubled at all about it."

"Excellent," said her father. "Very kind of him to waste his time on it, being the sensible fellow that he is. And thoughtful towards Ellen on her birthday. I am glad somebody is."

He harrumphed into his plate with a meaningful look at his wife, who had the grace to look a little discomfited, although exclaiming at once, "Really, Harold! When I have so much on my shoulders with the wedding, and I have helped a great deal with the theatricals."

"Doubtless," said Mr Rastrick drily, with a little smile at Ellen. "You will be able to read that book he bought you soon enough."

"I will and I am looking forward to it," she answered.

Chapter Eleven

Ellen had enjoyed her eighteenth birthday so far. The post had brought a short letter from Peter, wishing her many happy returns of the day and hoping they might meet again soon. She had unwrapped her gift book and enjoyed beginning its lively sprint through the life of Becky Sharp. Carrie and Len came for lunch and cook had made a light sponge birthday cake for them all to have. Len made her a gift of his expensive, new-fangled bicycle for good, and Carrie gave her a leatherbound book with clasps to begin writing her thoughts or ideas in, wanting to encourage her in that. Her mother and father presented her with a new winter cloak and the pair of handmade boots she had recently been to be measured for. Sylvia had bought her a soft woollen stole to wear. The new maid dressed her hair for the evening's theatricals. Sylvia and Mrs Rastrick had already gone up in advance to Noel's gothic mansion. Ogden Towers was situated on one of the hillsides outside the town's industrial smog, with very fine views from its vantage point.

When Kenneth came to collect Ellen, he wished her a very happy birthday and looked with admiration at her appearance, rarely seeing her dressed up in the ordinary course of events. Coming down the stairs and putting her gloves on to greet him, she enjoyed the look of slight surprise on his face and also the approval.

"I have begun *Vanity Fair*," she told him. "And I love it already!"

"I knew you would," he said, looking pleased. "Well – let us go and be entertained. I can hardly wait, can you?"

This last was said with slight scepticism for the benefit of Mr Rastrick, who had come out of his study to say good evening and rejoined, "Rather you than me, my boy, but I wish you both well of the event!" as he waved them out on their way.

***

Ogden Towers was effulgent with lights, to create at least the impression of a summer evening. In the entrance hall, Alexander the Great already sported a hat at a jaunty angle, placed there by some satirical guest. Ellen thought she recognised it as Albert Dewhirst's. Children from the orphanage school were still running about excitedly in their various tunic costumes, not settled yet on the platform or at the back of the room to wait their call to pose. She knew some of their faces, transformed with excitement now and without that look of amusement at her, the 'lady', which she had seen in their eyes when she read them their letters. There was something of the same in Hannah and Sarah's look, she thought now, and in their knowing aloofness from Clarionettes like herself. Lines of chairs were arranged for the audience and she and Kenneth went to take their places, ushered to the front by Mrs Rastrick to sit by her. Mrs Rastrick was in a state of high tension, being caught up in the occasion, but said when they arrived with flustered satisfaction, "Noel has told me I have done all I possibly can and must sit and enjoy it all with you now."

"I am sure you have, Mother," Ellen assured her, unable to resist adding, "You must save some of your energy for the wedding itself, you know."

"Oh!" exclaimed Mrs Rastrick, fanning herself. "You have no idea, Ellen, truly you do not!"

Ellen refrained from saying that she most certainly did know, since she was entertained with it on a daily basis. She looked about the seated audience, recognising plenty of local faces, but could not see many of the Clarion Club members, although she spotted John Henderson and Libby together. Of course, some were in the play itself but not many of those were of her close friends group,

The series of tableaux, performed with some of the most famous speeches from the play, took place on the stage. It all began, of course (not as the play did), with Sylvia and Noel in full costume as Titania and Oberon, seated on throne chairs to greet the guests. Before them was Albert Dewhirst's box camera, with him as master of photographic ceremonies, each tableau to be pictured as they took place. Albert himself fussed about the placing of everybody on the set, so that arranging them all seemed to take twice as long as the actual piece itself. Ellen saw Eustace looking anxious about his charges doing their best and encouraging them along if there was any hesitation from the various 'fairies'. One of the older boys, particularly affected mentally and physically by his starved early years and who had to stay down in classes with much younger pupils, was enjoying playing Bottom, looking constantly to Eustace at the side for the approving smile that he was doing very well in the few edited speeches he had with Mustardseed, Peascod and Peasblossom, all spoken in the broadest of local accents. The tableaux, strangely, were not performed in any particular order, adding to the confused sense of a fragmented dream, but it was not, of course, so much about the play as the players themselves.

Noel and Sylvia looked quite extraordinary in elaborate costumes and headdresses but when Cyril made his appearance as Puck, everyone drew a breath, for his was a real and witty piece of acting, his neat features and figure (hair sprited up so that it stood out in a fair halo) being very well suited to the nimble way he played the role. Of course, as a fireman, he was gymnastically fit and he made great play of climbing up and down a pole with ropes, from the pinnacle of which he made his speeches, standing or crouched on a plinth. The applause for Puck was particularly loud.

Part way through the chaotic evening, when there was a pause for interval and refreshments, the guests got a chance to mingle. It was now that some others arrived. First, Ellen looked up to find the looming figure of Felix Sykes before her, with Jane Ellison, head slightly bowed, at his side.

"Mr Sykes! Jane!" she exclaimed.

"Miss Ellison wanted to wish you many happy returns of the day, Miss Rastrick. It is her first occasion out and I believed the play might entertain, those of us being fellows of Mr Ogden elsewhere all being invited, of course."

Oh, yes, the Clarion Club, thought Ellen! Jane herself had not spoken but Ellen said thank you to her anyway, while the restless eyes of the other girl sought about the room until they found Albert and settled there.

"How are you now, Jane?" Ellen enquired, trying to bring her attention away from him.

"Quite well, thank you," she answered, in an empty voice.

"Do you wish to stay, Jane?" asked Mr Sykes.

"No. I am already tired," she replied. "May we go?"

"Yes, I have kept the hansom cab outside in case it was too much for you," he answered kindly. "Well, we have wished Miss Rastrick a happy birthday and I have congratulated Mr Ogden on the event. We did see the last tableau take place. Unfortunately, we were rather late in setting out as Miss Ellison was not quite sure about coming. I think it brave of her to have done so," he concluded gallantly, seeming unaware of any particular person being the possible reason for her reluctance and referring only to her health.

Ellen doubted that Albert had noticed Jane's arrival, involved as he was with all his attention on the players. She had looked about for Hannah and Sarah but tonight it seemed that Albert was without their attentive escort.

"Was that Jane Ellison I saw speaking to you for a moment just now?" asked Kenneth, arriving back at her side as they stood in line for the punch bowl.

"It was but she has left again now, I think."

"How was she?"

"Distracted, quiet, not herself," answered Ellen.

"A pity. Ah, excuse me, I must just speak to somebody else here," he returned, and went to greet another of the neighbourhood business people nearby.

Just then, Noel came up to her and said, "Ellen – happy birthday to you! After you have had some refreshments, will you allow Albert to take your portrait in celebration?"

"I will, thank you," she agreed, and she went to sit for it while the interval continued.

Albert was civility itself to her as he put her into a pose on a chair and took her portrait with his box camera, while she kept as still as possible for the necessary minutes. It was after this she decided to tell him that Jane had been briefly present. He bit his lip a little at that news.

"I did not see her, I assure you, Ellen," he said.

"I know. She saw you, though, Albert. Felix Sykes is looking after her."

He raised an eyebrow at that but said nothing against the man, remarking only that he was glad somebody did. It was as well Ellen had prepared him, for in a sudden rush through the milling guests, Jane Ellison unexpectedly returned alone but, finding herself before Albert at last, seemed unable to speak to him, pale and trembling but gazing at him intently.

"Jane," he said low, clearly shocked by her changed demeanour.

"Albert—" she said, great appeal in the one word of

address.

After a moment's pause, he said, "Jane, I will come to see you soon now you are well again."

"You promise it?"

"I do," he repeated, and with one transformed smile, she rushed away again, making whatever excuses she had invented for Felix Sykes as he waited by the door for her.

Since Ellen had been with Albert having her portrait taken, no doubt Jane had said she wanted to speak to Ellen again, possibly to thank her, for Felix waved across in farewell to Ellen and led Jane out again.

"Albert – did you mean that?" Ellen, the only witness to the exchange, asked of him. "Or did you just say it to buy time and prevent a scene?"

"Her poor face," he said, almost to himself, visibly moved by the actual sight of the distressed girl, as he had not seemed to be by knowing of her plight, although her letter had certainly upset him in various ways. "Yes, Ellen, I made a promise I will keep. I will call on her at the vicarage now that she is recovered."

Ellen was left knowing no more of Albert's feelings about Jane than he seemed to know himself, caught unawares as he had been, but the last of the evening's tableaux were about to begin and she had to resume her seat with Kenneth Butterworth again. She was among the crowd of guests congratulating their hosts and performers at the end when she was excitedly hailed by someone calling her name and laughingly pushing their way through to her.

"Ellen! Nell! Many happy returns of the day to you!" And she turned to see Peter, chilly night air caught in his hair and around him, vivid cheeked from a lengthy cycle ride. "I've missed it but I was determined to see you on your birthday and cycled all the way after work. Come!"

Pleased to have surprised her and still laughing, he

pulled her aside and out of view momentarily, catching both her hands and kissing her briefly on the lips, his face cold against her hot one.

"Happy birthday, Nell!" he said to her again and she laughed back.

"Peter, how you have surprised me! I got your letter today. Thank you."

"And now you have me too," he said. "I'm sorry I had nothing else to bring you."

"Oh, I am so glad you came! What a pity you missed the show though."

"I hope Noel looked proper daft."

"He did, rather," laughed Ellen. "But you must never tell him I said so."

"Would I? We never share our secrets, Nell, you and I, do we?"

"Never," she answered, knowing precisely what he referred to.

Their moment alone was already interrupted.

"And what might those be, I wonder?" asked a light, questioning voice.

"Nothing to trouble *you*, Cyril," answered Peter. "By 'eck! *Look* at you!" He scanned his fireman friend with amazed incredulity. "Had a scare? Summat's made your hair stand up."

"Cyril was wonderful as Puck," praised Ellen. "You would have loved it, Peter! Peter came all the way here on his bike to wish me a happy birthday, Cyril."

"Aye, and having done it, I'll be happy to cycle all t'way back again," declared Peter.

"Have a drink first, Peter," urged Cyril. "Come on. John and Libby are here. You must come and say hello."

"Aye, I suppose so," answered Peter, in the droll way Ellen now recognised as his dry humour, with a glance back at her as Cyril made to pull him aside in turn.

Ellen smiled and returned to the guests where she saw Kenneth looking for her.

"There you are! Where did you get to, Ellen?"

"I saw Cyril and wanted to tell him how brilliantly he played Puck," said Ellen, deciding not to mention Peter and hoping now that Peter himself would not see her with Kenneth. "Let us make haste to Mother, Sylvia and Noel," she added, eager to be seen with a family group rather than Kenneth alone.

They made their way through to Mrs Rastrick, and the key players, who were all clustered together by the stage looking like royalty receiving tributes, as the various guests congratulated them. Ellen did not think either man would be jealous of seeing her with the other. It was more that Kenneth would disapprove (as he had when Peter had been at the concert with her) and Peter would simply be resentful to see her in Kenneth's company after that earlier encounter. In her own mind, though, it was Peter whom she did not wish to upset because he had been so happy to surprise her by coming and she had been very happy indeed with her light-hearted birthday kiss. Noel's carriage was soon ready to take Sylvia and Mrs Rastrick home, with Kenneth and Ellen following on.

The several orphans had been spirited away with Eustace in a hansom cab. Cyril lingered with Noel, who was making much of him after the event. Ellen looked about for John, Libby and Peter but could not see them anywhere among the departing crowd. Either they had gone already or were still talking somewhere in the house. Albert was packing up his photographic equipment and plates carefully with his own driver and she decided to say no more to him. It was time to go. There was plenty to remember about her birthday night as it was. Kenneth, though, had conversation he wished to make on the way home.

"I saw those firemen we chanced on that day doing their drill and met again at the concert hall, Ellen. They were at the theatricals and in them too! I had not realised that Puck was one of their group at first. I noticed Mr Henderson and I went to have a few words. Did you know that your old maid is engaged to him now? I was giving them my best wishes when I recognised Puck. He was nearby speaking with that other fellow, who was also with you that night. What is his name again?"

"Mr Raynor played Puck, but I think you mean Peter Lumb. He and John Henderson are working with my brother at the new mill chimney for Stanger's, you know."

"I didn't! Another strange coincidence between those I had not imagined linked in any way."

"It is not so strange. John Henderson is a local stonemason and my brother was in need of one. Peter Lumb is his new manager foreman. I expect he recommended him. My brother said he liked Peter's forward-thinking ideas when the position came up at the mill."

"Oh. *His* forward-thinking ideas. And you know all about them, Ellen, presumably, do you? How goes your cycling group? Didn't you say it was called the Clarion Club? I read about it recently – a more radical-seeming affair than you described it to me as being perhaps?"

"I don't know what you mean," hedged Ellen. "But it goes quietly enough at the moment now that winter is coming on. It hasn't been the weather for cycling. But I will keep up with it by myself when it is fine. Len has given me his bicycle today. Mother did try not to be scandalised."

"Then – neither will I be," answered Kenneth lightly. "Perhaps I may hope to find you at home one day? That is if I make sure to call when it is *raining*, of course?"

"Perhaps," said Ellen, with a smile at the humour in his voice.

"I wonder how Mr Dewhirst's photographic plates of the tableaux will turn out?" Kenneth remarked next. "I am surprised he did not take one of that fireman fellow, Lumb. He has a good, strong profile for such a portrait. Don't you agree, Ellen?"

"Do you think so?" she answered noncommittally. "I hope my own portrait will be successful. It is so hard to sit still for long enough. Albert was very patient with my fidgeting."

Would Albert really go to see this strange new Jane Ellison? Ellen wondered, reminded of it by Kenneth talking of Albert. She also wondered at Kenneth's persistent mentioning of Peter Lumb. Had she been wrong that they had not been seen together? Nobody had seen their kiss, she was sure of that. Well, what of it if he had seen her speaking with Peter? These were only hints and nudges from Kenneth and all she had to do was stonewall because he surely would not presume to ask anything too direct. All he said next, however, of the photograph Albert had taken of her, was, "I am sure it will be a great success and I am looking forward to seeing it."

"That is more than I do, although I am simply dying to see the ones of the stage set pieces. They were all rather wonderful, weren't they?"

"They were. Your sister looked at her most beautiful – quite otherworldly."

"Oh, you must not think her at all spiritual, Kenneth. She never even reads poetry, let alone writes any!"

"No – she merely achieves the look of it. Rather, I imagine, like Mr Ogden. Although perhaps I do him an injustice?"

"I don't think you do," Ellen answered and they

shared a mischievous laugh together as they arrived at the gates of her house and he got out to help her down.

Just as he did so, her hand in his to step out of the carriage, he said, "You know, it is all very well to be modern, Ellen, but it is better to remember where we belong, too."

"Is it?" said Ellen. "Thank you, Kenneth."

She spoke mildly but was far from submissive in manner. Kenneth dropped her hand and drew back slightly.

"Well, then. Happy birthday, again, Ellen."

"Thank you, and for going with me to Ogden Towers," she answered with great politeness.

Removing her hand, she went into the house after her mother and sister, leaving Kenneth to drive on to his mother's, rather rudely not invited in. Her mother was in full flow already to Mr Rastrick, whom they found peacefully reading his evening paper in the parlour in the quiet glow of a comfortable lamp.

"Such an evening you have missed, my dear!" she exclaimed, all in a flutter of hands and draperies.

"I shall not miss it," he remarked, shaking pages straight. "For you will share every last moment of it with me, I have no doubt."

"I am simply exhausted! Oh, Ellen, where is Kenneth? Did he have to go directly home?" (Not waiting for any reply.) "I expect he did. His mother will be wanting to hear all about it! Sylvia and Noel were quite wonderful, Harold!"

Post performance lassitude was overwhelming Sylvia, however, and she begged the family to excuse her, for she simply must retire.

"Happy birthday, Sister. I hope you enjoyed our present to you this evening," she said to Ellen, pausing at the door.

"Oh, quite as much as it was intended for *me* to enjoy it," rejoined Ellen. "Thank you, indeed."

Any note of sarcasm was not felt, or at least not acknowledged, as Sylvia simply smiled nobly and went upstairs while their mother exclaimed on.

"I should certainly think she did enjoy it! What an occasion for her it was, Harold!"

"For which of them, my dear? Sylvia, or Ellen?"

"Why – why both of course!" she cried, her words tumbling out in a tidal wave of voluble description.

When Mrs Rastrick was in this mood, she was quite as capable of overtalking herself as she was anybody else. After a while Ellen left them together, having played her admiring part again for as long as seemed polite. She went to her room to enjoy another chapter of *Vanity Fair*, deciding not to feel at all guilty about Kenneth, since he had been far too given to offering her unwanted advice, not to mention offering strange opinions about those she knew and he didn't on the way home! She had felt rebuke somewhere in his manner about them, in particular Peter, of course, and she did not at all care for it, she thought. Kenneth was stuck in his notions of station and she had been freed of them, or was learning to be, through the Clarion Club. A recollection of words Kenneth had once used when Sylvia's new engagement was known of passed uncomfortably through Ellen's mind as well, however.

"I am afraid, once my good opinion is lost, it is difficult for me to find it again," he had said, lightly enough at the time. "I may want to do so but it simply refuses to do as it is told."

She would not care to lose Kenneth's good opinion of herself so quietly and completely, she knew that. He had spoken of it amusingly, as a character fault which he regretted having, like a disobedient dog, but Ellen had still felt something implacable behind the words. His change of feeling had never been expressed by the slightest coolness or incivility but the new barrier between him and capricious Sylvia, invisible as it might be, was quite impermeable. Ellen thought of his quiet, playful humour when she was in his company, the friendliness between them and the way they loved to discuss books. Part of her could not believe that Kenneth would really be so intransigent towards *her*, whatever happened, while another part knew that the conversations about books might continue but the heart would have gone out of them, if she *did* lose his good opinion of her. Kenneth had not liked her talking to Peter at all, that much was clear.

This was interrupting her reading and she banged *Vanity Fair* shut again, feeling that while she might not be unwittingly eating hot chilli peppers at table like Becky Sharp in the book, she had plenty of overheated thoughts making her mind work overtime instead. What did she mean by thinking to herself, 'whatever happened'? That she crossed the class divide Kenneth felt so important by consorting with the like of Peter, John, Cyril and the Clarion Club and that this might go further? Or that he might find out she had set the fire at Stanger's Mill with Peter? The thought of this made her go cold all over. He would certainly never forgive her for that. Nobody would – except, of course, for Peter himself.

This brought her round to being angry about that again, even as she felt closer to Peter all the time, and now felt again the attraction of the birthday kiss and his other lightly given kisses, ones which told her that Peter saw her as a growing woman and not a callow girl as others did. But did he presume her a sweetheart as well as a comradely friend? And what might that mean? This took her mind back to Jane with Albert, to Albert with

Hannah and Sarah, to those pictures on the walls where bare skin as pale as pearls was silver and black in the flicker of gaslights in a cottage hallway. Thoughts of it all made her restless on her birthday night when she went to bed.

***

Plans for the moorland benefit gala were soon in place under Carrie's efficient stewardship of getting the working women on board. She had never been standoffish and, due to her down-to-earth ways, was more accepted than many in her position would have been by them. Bread and cakes were made to be sold (the makings of which were donated by her in the name of her father) and games were to be enjoyed. It all helped Peter to become better known to the laid-off men he went round door to door to speak to, talking about what he hoped for them once the mill was back up running, and it would be before the year was out, he assured one and all. Beating the winter became the spur for the chimney design and build, while the rest of the mill buildings developed quickly back from the ground, the plans agreed. A breadline wage was paid out to the whole workforce. Those who could learn them or had building skills were brought back to work on the construction before they could spin worsted again.

"It's only putting one stone on top of another," Peter encouraged. "If tha can work a loom, tha can do that! I don't want to bring in Lancashire brickies if I can 'elp it for t' chimney, do I?"

He whipped up a fresh loyalty, backed by Leonard Rastrick's young face and new approach to both mill and improving conditions for the workforce, alongside Peter as his new foreman manager. The old foreman of the mill workers was always carefully deferred to by Peter, his views respectfully listened to in meetings between them, so for now there was no resentment there or clash of wills, since all was theoretical prior to the mill starting up again. The inexperienced builders all worked under hired men under John's direction, so that they really acted as the unskilled labourers needed to support the construction professionals. With all this going on, feelings were friendly between owners and working people on the day of the gala.

It was a lucky day for weather. For once, it was quiet over the wind-troubled moorland. By mid-morning, there was even a little heat in the sunshine to warm the crowd gathered around the makeshift stalls. Leonard invited all and sundry to the occasion. He had laughingly asked Kenneth Butterworth to join them when they had coincided one day at the Rastricks' house, painting so lively a picture of the coming festivities that Kenneth agreed.

"How could I resist, Leonard? Is your sister coming?"

"Ellen is, yes."

"I meant, Ellen, of course," said Kenneth, as if there were no question of his referring to Sylvia at all.

Sylvia was present at the time and paused in pouring coffee from the elegant spout of a silver pot to say coolly, "I am glad you did", inferring that nobody in their right mind could expect *her* to attend such a socially crude occasion.

Now Kenneth, in tweed plus fours and Norfolk jacket, stood next to Ellen clapping the competitors in Knurr and Spell. It was a vigorous game, in which individuals took turns at striking a small ball with a four-foot-long pole with a hardened wooden pommel on the end. The winner was the one who sent it furthest. There was no limit to the number of competitors and they were many, for all the young men enjoyed trying to excel at this local game. There were prize rewards for each round, the aim being to spread money about as widely as possible.

The walnut-sized wooden knurr first rested in the spell (trap) on the ground. The player struck the spell's lever to fling the knurr up, then hit it hard as possible with a wild swing of the pole. It was wise to steer clear of *that*, the energy going into the strike creating a lethal speed. Others were busy checking at the wooden pegs driven into the ground every twenty yards for a distance of about two hundred yards, to see which knurr had landed furthest away. It was a chaotic kind of race with great excitement about it, taken very seriously though, with a slate chalking up the distances against each player's initials. A cheer had gone up for John, who struck well but not as far as the previous man, with whom he joked that if it had not been for his bad hand he'd have thrown up the knurr better and hit it harder as a result.

"Nay, tha's just a sore loser!" responded the other, clapping him on the back.

Peter came to take his turn next, delivering a swingeing hit which took the knurr way out into the field, to great acclaim from the crowd. A roar of appreciation went up for the strike.

"Your firemen seem rather good at this workman's game," observed Kenneth, somewhat patronisingly, Ellen felt. "More Lumb's natural recreation than Beethoven, I imagine."

"Oh, I cannot resist! I must take a turn!" shouted Len, flinging off his jacket and striding forward in his shirt sleeves. "Who will lend me their pole for a go?"

"May I join in too?" Kenneth surprised Ellen by asking.

He walked forward alongside her brother, who exclaimed, "Of course you must, Kenneth! Here, who goes next?"

Politeness among those sensible to whom they owed

all this and what was to come out of it, meant that both Len and Kenneth were urged to go next. Peter came to stand beside Ellen, watching in turn and said, "Reet, then. Let's see how *he'll* do!"

"Len, you mean? He'll be hopeless. He couldn't ever play cricket. Kenneth can though. He might be all right."

"It were 'im I meant," said Peter, who hadn't forgotten the concert evening either.

He was still aglow with his own success and looked well on it to Ellen. He had his shirtsleeves rolled up, too warm to put the jacket back on which he carried slung over his shoulder.

"You were so good at it!" cried Ellen. "Really, you were, Peter!"

"I did me best," he answered modestly. "You've seen *'im* play cricket, then, have you?" he asked, scanning over at Kenneth.

"Yes, often in summer, at the church fête sometimes, or garden party teams on the Moor Field below the Crossley orphanage school. He's quite a hitter," teased Ellen, rather enjoying what she realised, this time, was definitely a rival jealousy between them of sorts, and one quite possibly, just possibly, about her, of all things! "Kenneth is a neighbour, so of course I have known him for years. I don't know anything about how he kisses a person, though," she added with pretend nonchalance.

Peter's mouth twitched with amusement at that but he continued to stare intently at the game, saying, "Oh, aye?" He glanced down at her, adding drily, "Don't distract me. I can't be missing this! Oooooh! Bad luck, Rastrick!"

Len struck wildly but did not manage to send the knurr in any straight line, so that it curved out into the dead bracken and had to be searched for. Next, Kenneth stepped up, taking a cool measure of distances and planting his stance for a sportsman's balance.

"I've never tried this!" he called out to everyone. "Here goes, then!"

He cracked the lever smartly, released the knurr like a grouse whirring up to be shot and struck it a deadly accurate blow which sent it far down the lines of pegs. Peter narrowed his eyes into the sun.

"Hm. Not bad," he grunted as if having teeth pulled.

"I'll bet it wasn't as far as yours," said Ellen loyally.

"It better not be," Peter answered. "I'm off to check. No cheating by the toffs in *this* game." He strode off to see whether Kenneth's hit had matched his own.

Kenneth himself, with Len alongside, were already headed to look too. The measures were soberly taken by those umpiring the match and the players continued. For the rest of the competition, though, it was Peter and Kenneth's shots which had gone the greatest distance and lain pretty much side by side at the far length of the two hundred yards.

"You do realise it means a duel to the death if it's a tie, don't you, Kenneth?" Len said to his friend. "It's an old tradition of the game."

"Aye, that's right," said Peter, for the three of them had drifted back to where Carrie now stood watching with Ellen in their part of the audience. "We crack each other round 'ead wi' t' poles till one of us is done for."

"You rather sound as if you mean it, Lumb," said Kenneth.

"Do ah?" returned Peter blandly, after a beat. He turned to Ellen and said, "Ellen, I've been meaning to ask you – in my cottage, I'm a bit short on books, tha knows. Could you spare me any?"

Ellen gave him a startled look. She had not told him before about talking to Kenneth Butterworth about books, she thought, but this request of Peter's was unfortunate, since that was the source of her intimacy with Kenneth. She knew at once that *he* would not like the question.

"Of course, although I am sure Carrie has books too," she answered lamely.

"But I haven't asked Mrs Rastrick. I've asked *thee*," said Peter, that look of truculence passing over his face which closed him down. "Some of them we've talked about together."

"I will be happy to bring some volumes and drop them at Heatherfield for you, Mr Lumb," said Ellen.

"I see. Thank you," he said rather heavily. "How extremely good of you."

Such formal address and mention of leaving books for him instead of giving them to him directly struck him to the quick, Ellen could see. His pride was very stung, not to mention his feelings. Only, she had been so aware of Kenneth, who was standing by, overhearing. She was furious with herself for falling back on her own social standing to push Peter off, but then it had not been fair of *him* to force the issue of their private intimacy in public like that either, had it? Or, hadn't it been? She was suddenly furious with both Peter and Kenneth as well as herself.

"Oh, Carrie! We must go and help with the stalls over there. I promised before but I've been so caught up in the game," she said, turning to her sister-in-law.

"You are quite right, Ellen," Carrie agreed, picking up on her discomfort, but before they could get away, Kenneth remarked…

"Perhaps we may bludgeon each other with novels instead, Mr Lumb? I am quite a reader myself. Ellen and I share many a lively discussion on the subject. In fact, I gave her a particular book for her birthday last week, *Vanity Fair*. Have you read it?"

"Nay," returned Peter shortly.

"Then she may lend that volume to you as well when she has done with it. I am sure *I* don't mind," concluded Kenneth. "If you will excuse me, Carrie, Len, I find it turning rather cold and will take my leave. It has been most pleasant to take part. I hope you enjoy the rest of your day, Ellen, and wish you every success with it."

He spoke with the same friendly, cordial voice and expression as he always used with her, but Ellen already feared that departure of his good opinion, ridden over roughshod by Peter and disappeared into some hinterland.

"But, Kenneth!" Len called after him. "You don't know if you have won yet?"

"I do know, and I didn't," he returned, walking on to get on his horse. "Congratulations, Lumb!"

"Actually, it weren't Peter Lumb what won," observed one of the umpires, who had just finished checking over all the initials and distances marked with his fellows. "It were Tom Berry!"

One of John's builder's, a stocky fellow with a burly arm, stepped forward looking delighted with the news. Peter laughed and said, "All that for nowt! Butterworth!" he called over to Kenneth. "We can spare each other a fight to t' death! We're beat fair and square by Tom Berry 'ere! Come and shake 'ands wi't victor, won't you?"

This left Kenneth with no alternative but to return to do so, or look a bad sport and rude with it, which his gentleman's manners did not allow him to indulge in being. Ellen and Carrie were still alongside as the result was called out and Ellen was impressed by the way Peter took command of an awkward moment to dispel it. For Peter, though, there were more relations at stake here for him than scoring points off Kenneth Butterworth as any kind of rival for Ellen's friendship or affection, which he hardly admitted even to himself had been his concern. He did not want his employer to think he had caused dissent with an old family neighbour at a public event designed to build future harmony between employer and worker. He could not afford to be seen as a trouble maker here, tamping down his instinct to flare up in response to the considered disapproval which he intuited was being directed towards him by Kenneth Butterworth.

Peter shook Tom's hand warmly, as did Kenneth. Then Peter shook Kenneth's hand, saying, "Come on, man. We can look each other in't eye, nah – we both played a blinder theer, Butterworth, even if t' best man won in't end!"

Kenneth shook his hand back, with a glad response. They did indeed look each other in the eye and Tom Berry clapped them both heartily on the back, saying, "Come and sup a bit of ale wi' me over there! Thee both were as good as I were." So that the three men went along together, with Len alongside, to take a bumper of ale from the casks brought up to refresh thirsty players.

Ellen watched covertly from where she and Carrie now helped out serving cuts of fruit loaf and barm cakes filled with slices of ham, in return for whatever a giver felt able to offer to the cause of supporting the laid-off workers. The more affluent were generous and there were plenty of those present due to Len and Carrie's invitations. Kenneth did not leave after all and circulated with Len around their own people, for after the game the crowd separated out into those who knew one another best, which of course divided owner class from worker class again. Still, the way money had been collected was going well. Ellen caught up with Peter again after a short while when he came over for some food. He made sure to find himself precisely where she would serve him, which she was pleased to notice.

"Well done, Peter," she said. "If Kenneth had been

you, you would have stormed off anyway!"

Peter had to laugh at that accurate hit.

"Aye, well. He isn't me. Is he?"

"No," agreed Ellen.

They exchanged a private look which seemed to give Peter all the assurance he needed, although he said, "About them books…"

"I will bring them to you in person, of course, at the cottage if you like?" she suggested with slight defiance.

"Nay, meet me at the house. You were right enough," he conceded. "Neighbours would see thee and talk and thy brother might tekk on an' all."

"He might," agreed Ellen, relaxing now that any wrong-footedness on her part (not that Peter had misunderstood at the time at all, of course) seemed to be cleared up. "Very well. I will do that and call up soon to Heatherfield with them. It is going so well, Peter! It is just like the Clarion Club, isn't it? The better-off people donating more but everyone giving a bit of something, even if it's only themselves."

"Aye, lass, it is," he agreed, smiling at her naïve enthusiasm.

Other people were waiting to be served now and he had to move on. After a while, her turn done, she went to look for Kenneth, who was still circulating with her brother. Peter was somewhere with John and others, not presently in her view.

"Kenneth," she said, trying to get his attention, which always seemed to be at one remove away and given elsewhere, reminding her of Albert avoiding Jane in the same way.

He turned to her finally and she blurted out, sotto voce, "Of course I will not lend the book you gave me as a present, not to Peter, or to anyone. Why did you say that?"

"It is only a book," he returned. "And you may as well share *that* as well as your liking for discussing them with others."

"I don't think you are fair, Kenneth," she retorted. "I cherish that gift."

"I am glad to hear it," he answered after a considering pause.

Ellen was to stay overnight with her brother and sister-in-law, dine with them and return home the following day. Len now invited Kenneth to stay for dinner with them as well but he politely declined, apologising that he had already agreed to accompany his mother elsewhere in the evening. Although this was more than likely to be the case, Ellen still wondered if he were being cool with her because of Peter, whom of course he did not see as any kind of social equal to either of them, as she knew. She walked with him to his horse and went so far as to say, catching at his bridle as he gathered up the reins of his sorrel mare, "I hope you leave me as good a friend as you arrived, Kenneth?"

He looked down at her slightly anxious face and answered politely, "Of course, Ellen. Why ever would you imagine otherwise?" And he smiled, so that she was glad to believe him.

Kenneth's good opinion of her was not lost yet, then. Ellen found herself relieved about that. She realised, suddenly, how much she relied on his visits now to bring her some congenial company at home. Kenneth needed to stop being so stuffy about mixing outside of his regular circles, that was all, and living with such a mother, was it any surprise that he found it hard to shake those attitudes off for very long? He could not help it, any more than Peter could help himself about the way he was with people, she thought magnanimously. Besides, she rather liked feeling that Kenneth and Peter had jostled together over *her*, an entirely new sensation for Ellen! Kenneth turned in his saddle to wave at her, just as Carrie and Len joined her to see him go too, all waving back, and she felt that they *had* parted as friends after all.

Peter and John Henderson remained afterwards with some of the people putting things away after the gala, helping to load carts with trestles and other goods. Ellen went over offering to help pass things, admiring the way John and Peter, so used to working together as firemen, hefted things up between them with athletic ease and speedy efficiency, changing positions turn and turn about, jumping on and off the vehicles, one above on the cart and one below. She was not alone in this admiration, and the men altogether were enjoying making a spectacle of their physical strength to the women who were assisting with the packing up. Quite a few of *them* were just as fit too, from working in the mills and walking miles to anywhere anybody needed to go. Those in the Clarion Club, on their bicycles, were aristocrats of the road to the other working people of the district, going about on shanks pony as they had to, Ellen realised.

Peter, dusting his hands off, jumped down to smile at her, saying, "All done! John's away now to meet Libby for a sweetheart walk in't evening. She's allowed a call once a week now they're engaged."

"Once a week…" Ellen repeated, struck afresh by the unfairness of others' lives, even though she knew the domestic servant regulations as well as anyone, having always had them in the household at home.

"Aye, but they'll be wed soon enough. Before Christmas. Like thy sister will. Only not at t' same kind of do!" And he laughed at the idea.

"I had rather go to John and Libby's wedding any day than Sylvia's!" declared Ellen. "I quite dread it. Mother is driving everybody mad with it all. It is a very good job that my father is so even-tempered – but then, he never really listens to her going on anyway."

Peter laughed at that and, seeing him still sunny, she said, "You know, Kenneth Butterworth isn't as much of a stuffed shirt as you might think about things. He's done a very kind thing for Jane Ellison."

"He's not a ninny like Noel Ogden, I'll give him that – and at least he can hit wi' a bat and shake a man's hand after. Any road, what do you mean, he did summat for Jane Ellison? It were *you* he bought a book for, weren't it?"

"Yes, as an old family friend and neighbour, for my birthday, Peter. I don't have many people I can discuss books with. That's about the only thing you and he have in common!"

"Good!" said Peter decidedly. "I know you're well-acquainted with folk who are already in your life. I'm not daft, Ellen. And you have to stay on good terms with them at home. I know that too. It's just…"

"Just what?" she asked as he was poised to say something with meaning to it, she knew, and she wanted to hear it, quite as much as she had been most anxious not to lose Kenneth's good opinion before he left, if not more so.

"You know wi'out me sayin' it," said Peter. "And I'm not going to talk soft in company, am ah?"

Ellen smiled, for this did mean something.

"All right. Well, then, I'll tell you about Jane but you must never breathe a word of knowing. It's her secret."

"Then why tell it?"

"Because, it was awful! She took an overdose of laudanum. I found her in in her room and Kenneth went for the doctor only just in time! We had been in town. Kenneth took me in his gig for things our mothers wanted" – (a slight untruth but never mind) – "and I saw

Jane coming out of the chemist. She looked so downcast I asked him to take me to see her, and he did. If he hadn't raced to the doctor her life would have been lost!"

Peter took this rush of words in and asked, "Did she mean to die?"

"People believe it was an accident."

"People? But not you, then, Ellen. How about him? Butterworth?"

"He doesn't say. I found something that meant, well that I think…I gave it back to her when she was well again. She burned it."

"A letter?"

"A scrawl, a note of some sort, not finished. It was not addressed to anyone," she hastened to say.

"Mebbe not but we can guess what man drove her to that, can't we?"

"We can't know, though. Nor if it were deliberate or an accident. I just told you so that you knew Kenneth will help people too."

"Why do you want me to think well of him?" asked Peter. "I won't, tha knows." But he said it with a glint of humour in his expression that told her he was teasing her.

"I don't care what you think of him," returned Ellen. "I just wanted you to have a fairer view, that's all."

"Oh, aye. All reet, then. If I need a doctor, I'll know who to send on for one."

Ellen could not help but laugh and, for a moment, the backs of their hands brushed covertly, hidden in the company around them, her brother and sister-in-law nearby and people making ready to leave. The warmth of skin on skin was matched by the flush on each of their faces and then, of course, the moment was broken.

"Goodbye, Lumb! We are going on back to the house now. Will you be all right getting back on one of these carts?" Len called across.

"Aye, right enough." Peter scanned up at the sky, which in the way of this part of the world, had darkened over now and threatened rain soon enough. "We'd best all crack on if we don't want a drenching. It's been a grand day for it, though."

"Carrie, Ellen and I will tot up our takings and draw up the list of who should have what out of it – Carrie's had her ear to the ground there and I know you have, Peter. We'll look at that together tomorrow, shall we? Go and have a good night's rest now. You've earned it!"

"Aye. I might take myself off out for supper first to the tavern. Royal Oak does a fair dish of stew."

Ellen here murmured in Carrie's ear, and she, nodding, said, "No, I won't hear of that. You'll come and eat with us at the house tonight, Peter. Then you and Len can do the counting-house work. I think Ellen and I will start off the lists."

"Fair enough, if I'm wanted there for working after," said Peter, as if the concession were entirely his.

"Yes, do dine with us, Lumb," agreed a slightly startled Len, recovering himself enough to invite Peter too, working on the gala's takings afterwards giving less of a social feel to his being asked to join them at table.

"All right, then – I'll freshen up at 'ome and call up at the 'ouse later on."

"We dine early, Peter, for Father's sake," said Carrie. "Will six o'clock suit you?"

"Thank you, Mrs Rastrick, it will," said Peter.

He was always polite to Carrie, a woman who commanded his respect because of the Peterloo meeting in Manchester and, of course, for championing his approach to Len Rastrick for the job he now had. Her unvarnished manner quite matched his own, so that Peter saw nothing off-putting in that and they got on very well whenever they had occasion to meet.

Ellen said quietly, just to Peter, "I am glad to see you happy again, Peter."

He answered, catching her meaning at once, "I've not forgot him – Stanley. Ah'd never, but at least this – this is *doing* summat abaht things."

Things like the conditions that had done for Stanley and the fire that had hastened the damage to his ailing lungs, Ellen knew he meant.

"I know. And I think you're right. I am sorry I reminded you."

"No. You didn't remind me of the friend I remember every day, even if I don't wear me heart on me sleeve abaht it. It'd pain me more never to hear him mentioned."

"In happier times," Ellen suggested.

"Yes," he answered, smiling slightly at thoughts of those. "In happier times. We'll talk of them. I'd best be off to smarten missen up, then."

"I'm glad I will see you at dinner, Peter."

"As am I," he agreed, putting on his cap and departing to jump on one of the carts as Ellen went to join her brother and Carrie in saying their last goodbyes to lingering guests. "I can't afford to be eating out at no inns!" he grinned, to tease her as to what pleased him about the invitation.

***

The evening meal was simple, since all the day's efforts had gone into the benefit from the Stangers' own kitchen too, but cold cuts and boiled potatoes with greens and gravy were welcome enough. Peter appeared in his Sunday shirt and looked cool and refreshed, hair brushed down into smoothly laid short feathers instead of the ruffled crown he had sported on the Moor after all the energetic activity. His manner seemed a bit defensive at first, perhaps wondering how he would be received after all when it came to it. He need not have been concerned, however, because he was greeted and seated as courteously as any gentleman guest might have been at Heatherfield, where nobody except Len (and he little enough) stood on ceremony. Old Mr Stanger had come out of his room to eat too, wanting to take part in the evening after the gala, which they were all able to tell him about over the meal, so that it was a lively enough affair. He made approving grunts at intervals and concluded, with a still sharp glance from under his bushy brows, "It weren't a bad do, then. Who's idea was it again?"

"Actually, my sister's to begin with," said Len, rather proudly. "Young Nell, here."

"Can we afford it, though, that's the question? Paying people when we have no work on. I never heard of such a thing."

"We can't leave our people to starve, Father," said Carrie.

"And if they seek work elsewhere in the meantime, sir, then we have lost our skilled workforce. Look after them now and they will come back to us when we *do* have work back on," pointed out Peter.

"*Our* workforce," said Mr Stanger. "Is that loyalty or ambition speaking?"

"Both, I hope," said Len, before Peter could answer and put his foot in it. "I want a foreman with vision for the future of Stanger's Mill. Lumb has it."

"Hmph. And they'll be calling *thee* Mr Stanger soon an' all. No mention of Rastrick to be made in the name of it?" asked the old man, gruffly mocking of it but sounding appreciative nevertheless.

"None at all, sir. This is Stanger's Mill. Your mill. I am honoured to work for its renewal. Besides, Carrie is still Miss Stanger to the people round here, for all she is married to me," said Len, laughing at it as he wiped his mouth on his napkin. "They're slow to take to things round these parts."

(He glanced at his wife as he said this, but she just shook her head indulgently.)

"And that's why it's good to care for them while their lives are still tied up in your business," said Peter. "Why, Mr Stanger, if you could have seen the people up there together today, you'd have no doubt of it!"

"I believe you, my boy. I believe you," said Mr Stanger, nodding slowly. "Well, I've handed over the reins to the next generation, so I have to trust in all your judgements."

Having earned his approval, they relaxed over dessert and then Len and Peter went off to count money, whilst Carrie and Ellen talked quietly over the lists of family and individual names. Mr Stanger remained dozing by the fire in his cushion-filled basket chair. He soon dropped off to sleep after eating any meal these days but wanted to stay in company a little longer before being taken off back to his room. When he was deeply off, Carrie rang the bell and the manservant now employed to care for his needs came to steer him carefully out and put him to bed. She and Ellen carried on over their work and then Ellen said, "Do they really still call you Miss Stanger, Carrie? They did in Manchester, I remember."

"They do, often," Carrie answered. "Well, it makes no matter. Len will be happy with his new mill and he may call it what he pleases one day. This is to be kind to my father, keeping the name of Stanger alone at present."

"But it will be your new mill too, Carrie?"

"No, after my father is no longer with us, I will leave him to it."

"Leave him to it! But – where will you be, and what will you be doing?"

"Why, living in Manchester with Fiona, of course, and

continuing our work. I shall certainly revert to Miss Stanger in name then, if not in fact. That will depend upon what Leonard wishes. There will be some pretty young miss one day, and meanwhile, he knows he may please himself."

Ellen recalled Len's sideways glance at his wife at the dinner table and the way she had shaken her head at him, smiling a little.

"Carrie – when Len said people were slow to take you being married to him – did he – did he mean you were too?"

"I doubt he meant anything by it," said Carrie in her flat way. "But you know I keep my independence, Ellen, already. Equally, so does Len. For the present, he is all caught up here. It is still new to him, you know, having so much scope for responsibility. I am glad it is good for him. And, I think, for Peter too. They are young enough to make a good team to start afresh. Oh, do not look so astonished, Ellen! Surely you did not think your brother had married me for love?"

"Perhaps not," admitted Ellen. "But, Carrie, I believe he has come to love you. I really do. I know my brother and he's the decent kind really – he has never broken any hearts that I know of, for all he goes out to his club to drink and play cards. Or did. And he always speaks of you with the greatest of warm feeling."

Carrie put down her pen, with which she had still been carefully marking up lists and said, thoughtfully, "I see. I had heard – before we married, that he was particular friends in that way with Noel Ogden?"

"Drinking and playing cards? Only when they were living their carefree young bachelor days. They do go to the same club in town. But Noel is engaged to my sister Sylvia now, don't forget."

"Yes, but I doubt that cramps his style, especially,"

remarked Carrie wryly. "Your brother and I have an understanding of how things are between us, Ellen, and I thought we were clear on it. If love is mutual respect, then I am happy he feels it for me."

"How strangely you put it, Carrie! I should wish to love someone passionately and be loved back the same way."

But not, she thought, in a destructive way, the way Jane Ellison loved Albert.

"Of course you would, Ellen. You are eighteen to my forty-one. There is a world of difference in our expectations," Carrie said with a laugh. "I wish to carry on my work for women's futures with Fiona and the others. I could see at once that it was not for you, Ellen. No, you carry on as you are with your Clarion Club. It is far more your forte than the world of campaigning."

"Do you think less of me for it?" asked Ellen.

"Not at all, Ellen! Absolutely not. And I have no plans to abandon Len to Stanger's Mill quite yet, although I am sure he will be happy about it when that day comes."

Ellen did not think that Len would be, not if it were intended to be any time soon, and not if it meant that Carrie would decamp wholly to Manchester and her old best friend. A friend was not a lively young husband, after all, was she? Ellen was glad she had told Carrie that Len loved her, and perhaps now Carrie would not think herself a dowdy spinster who ought to free him of her and go off to do good with other unmarried ladies, having got him to marry her to please her father and give Len a status he wanted. For this was what Ellen thought lay behind it all. That Carrie believed once her father had died she and Len would be free of any unwanted obligations to one another. Thankfully, if that were the case, thought Ellen, although Mr Stanger failed gradually, his constitution was a strong one and the doctor saw no immediate danger in his condition. Ellen and Carrie said no more of it for the present and finished their lists in time for Peter and Len to come triumphantly back in saying it had been a very good outcome for the benefit, with plenty of money raised to go round.

"It's getting late now. I'd best be off back to my cottage," said Peter. "We can put all this together tomorrow if you've a mind to?"

"Oh, yes!" said Ellen. "Before I go home, Len? I want to finish this with all of you."

"Then so you shall," he agreed. "Call back at our usual time in the morning, Peter. We will have breakfasted and be quite ready, won't we, Carrie?"

He looked to her for approval of the plan which she nodded at, saying, "Of course." And Peter said goodnight to them.

Ellen would have liked to go to the door but the servant had come to show him out and they had to content themselves with a bright glance at one another under cover of a handshake. This, being visible and just a short formality, carried nothing of the frisson of earlier when the backs of their hands had brushed together, softly and deliberately lingered over. When he had gone, Len said, "I am glad to see you and Ken Butterworth are such good friends, Ellen. Father likes him."

"He does, yes," agreed Ellen briefly, who did not especially wish to be thinking of Kenneth just then.

"Two bookworms together, they are, Carrie – eating their way through dusty old volumes. It is good to have a shared appetite."

And again, if he intended anything by it, his tone was too light and his manner too open for there to be more than a shade of meaning. His wife glanced up at him, a steady look, and he turned aside, declaring that he would have a nightcap before turning in, if nobody objected.

Nobody did, so Carrie and Ellen left him to his brandy and cigar by the dying fire, saying goodnight to him and to each other, going to their own rooms. As she was dropping off, Ellen heard knocking on a door across the landing. It woke her up to voices. After a short, murmured conversation, Carrie's voice said audibly, "Goodnight, Len", with gentle firmness.

Ellen thought Len must have had more than one brandy and been sent to sleep it off in his own bedroom then. Well, what harm, he had had a successful day to celebrate, Ellen thought, settling back down to sleep with a yawn and a smile to herself. Her brother and Carrie were such an unlikely pairing to start with and, yet, they seemed happy enough, or were getting to be as they came to appreciate one another. It would not do for me, thought Ellen, as her mind wandered between Kenneth and Peter. Would it be one of them she loved and who loved her? Or would that be like Noel and John, a transient fancy, and it would be somebody else she loved whom she did not even know yet? In her dreams, Peter and Kenneth drifted through tangled scenarios with her, neither being quite themselves, although she knew she recognised them.

For a few moments on waking it remained a disturbing confusion, but then it cleared and was forgotten as she got up and remembered, with great pleasure, that Peter was coming to the house after breakfast and they would spend the morning working together. It was a very optimistic group that shared out money against names and worked out the fairest allocation according to need as far as that was possible. The next question was how the money would reach people.

"Why, that is simple," said Ellen. "Let Carrie, Peter and I do it on our bicycles together, door to door. That way it is all discreet, with nobody having to come out in public, cap in hand, to Heatherfield."

Len considered this, looking dubious, and then Peter said, "I wonder, though, if it were just done here, as if folk were collecting their wages, that it might seem even less like a charity effort. We've made it so there's none gets nowt, even if others get more. And if some people do grumble at it, that was how it were all agreed and everybody knows it. Besides, it were a joint effort, so it in't charity."

"What do you think, Carrie?" asked Len, turning to his wife. "I'm inclined to agree with Peter. Besides, scrambling up and down these hillsides to get to everybody between you would surely make even more of a spectacle of it. Calling direct to people's doors!"

"It's what we've done in the Clarion Club," objected Ellen incautiously. "Eustace Horsfall and I went twice to Mrs Jagger. And Peter, Noel isn't always a 'ninny' as you call him. You don't know that he paid for Stanley's grave plot, do you, and that he stood the whole cost of the funeral and casket with never a word to anyone?"

"Ellen…" said Carrie, but it was too late.

A few cats were out of the bag in Ellen's eagerness to let Peter know that Noel, like Kenneth, was better than he thought.

"*I* were looking after things at Stanley's!" Peter burst out, his face darkening.

"Of course but…"

"What do you mean, Ellen? This Clarion Club is a charity as well as a cycling club? And who is Eustace Horsfall?" asked Len at the same time, missing Peter's level of anger.

"He is a teacher at the Crossley and Porter Orphan Home and School, Len. I go to read with the children there."

"Oh, I see," said Len, subsiding, as this just seemed, to him, acceptable women's work for his younger sister to be involved in.

Ellen was looking at Peter's expression and realising how badly she had blundered by sharing this with him, making his angry pride burst the banks immediately and overwhelm their happy calm together this morning. He looked aside, his face working.

Carrie noted it and said evenly, "In any case, Ellen, you do not have your bicycle here and are due to return home. I will drive you myself shortly in our small carriage and we can lunch with Sylvia and your mother. I must call sometimes," she said with a wry smile, "and if you remember, that was your own suggestion for the day? We will be expected on time."

"Of course," agreed Ellen hastily.

"Let us leave Len and Peter to make the rest of the arrangements about the benefit money. I am agreed with Peter that it would be better if people received it as if it were a wage."

"Agreed, too, then," said Len. "Lumb?"

Peter, having collected himself a bit, nodded his acquiescence, not quite yet able to speak. Swallowing (for he had also been caught unawares by the instant emotion he had felt at a mention of Stanley's funeral which he had not been prepared for) he said, rather gruffly, "Aye, reet enough."

Len said if that was agreed, he would go and get the carriage harnessed up ready for Ellen and Carrie.

When he had gone out of the room, Peter looked at Ellen and said, "Ah should've known. I were too caught up in grief then, and John let me think it were another all round do for a collection. But that were too much, weren't it, for one go?" His expression cleared like the sun coming out, the brightness back in his eyes instead of hot temper. "It were thee asked 'im to do it, weren't it, Ellen? Don't go shaking your head. Noel Ogden wouldn't

’ave a thought of putting a hand in ’is pocket wi’out that. I’m sorry I took on just then.”

“I shouldn’t have said it,” Ellen regretted, looking chastened. “He didn’t want anyone to know. And now I’ve told you all.”

“Len wasn’t listening, really,” Carrie assured her. “His mind is too full of his plans to pay attention to much for long. Besides, he is keen to be busy today. I will leave you to say goodbye and go to get ready.”

“And I shouldn’t have told you about Jane Ellison, either,” Ellen went on to Peter after Carrie had gone out, fretting over her several indiscretions.

“Mebbe not. But you did. And who else would you tell things to if not me? You didn’t mean any of it for your family’s ears just then. Carrie won’t say owt and, like she said, Len weren’t listening. He’s on edge wi’ her today, seems like he feels in the wrong some’ow.”

Ellen remembered that night-time knocking on the door she had heard, the feeling that Len had been sent unwillingly away.

“I think he had too many brandies last night before turning in,” she said.

“Oh, reet. Sore ’ead and she ’ad some words to say, I’ll bet,” said Peter. “That explains it, then.” But, somehow, Ellen didn’t quite think it did.

She recalled her conversation with Carrie earlier that evening, although she could not have defined quite exactly what had lain behind Carrie’s thoughtful “I see”, when Ellen had told her she believed Len did indeed love his wife. Ellen had drawn her own conclusions then but perhaps they were not correct ones? She had no idea and time with Peter was short now. She did not want to waste it speaking of her brother and Carrie.

“I will come soon with your books, Peter,” she assured him, as they both took a step forward instinctively to stand close.

"Good," he said. "I'll look forward to that."

They smiled at one another but, just then, Len and Carrie came back in, so they had to stand back and shake hands instead of exchanging another kiss, a kiss that hovered between them, invisible to others.

"I'll bid you good morning, then, Miss Rastrick," said Peter, with a grin of chagrin echoed by her own.

"Until next time, Mr Lumb," she replied in kind. "I hope it goes well for you with the benefit money and rebuilding the chimney and mill with John Henderson."

"Do hurry up, Ellen!" Len, reminded of the lunch engagement, urged her. "You know what Mother is like with Carrie and if you make her late..."

"I know, Len. Don't worry, we will be in plenty of time! Are you ready, Carrie?"

"Quite ready," she answered and, Ellen having fetched her own things, the two women left to go out into the two-wheeler. Then, in the mannish way which Mrs Rastrick had decried on several occasions previously as being unladylike, Carrie drove them herself to the Saville Park mansion, Ellen seated beside her.

When this habit of Carrie's was criticised in the early days of their marriage, Len had said, when he had called in alone and been taken to task for his wife showing them up to the neighbours arriving in such a style, "Carrie has had to be businesswoman for her father this long while, Mother, and is quite accustomed to going about without a driver wherever she needs to be."

"She does not have to be one now she is married to *you*," Mrs Rastrick had pointed out, but this had made no difference whatsoever to Carrie's way of driving rather than being driven, especially as Len never told her about it.

"You must get used to more modern ways, Mother,"

Ellen had said then, coming instantly to her sister-in-law's defence, already fonder of Carrie than she had ever been of Sylvia.

"Like you on your *bicycle*, I suppose!" Mrs Rastrick had retorted. "At least if Sylvia goes out herself, it is riding side-saddle on a horse as a young lady should and where she may be seen riding well."

"Oh, *Sylvia*!" Ellen had snorted.

"Both daughters cannot be paragons of virtue, my dear," Mr Rastrick observed to his wife. "Or how could one of them ever be held up successfully as a good example to the other?"

"Harold – *you* may be waggish if you please, but somebody must consider decorum," Mrs Rastrick had answered, sweeping out to see if the maid had brushed the mud off the hall carpet as requested before today's visitors might arrive with their calling cards.

Mr Rastrick sighed slightly and smiled over his newspaper at Ellen, who smiled back.

"It's all right, Pa. One day Sylvia will put a foot wrong. And then where will Mother be?"

"Ah. Now there's a question," he had answered, with a quiet chuckle.

Ellen remembered this conversation with amusement as she and Carrie bowled along smartly together. She thought what an utterly different world her mother lived in. It was years behind the one Carrie hoped to build for women and the one Ellen herself hoped to belong to – moving into the modern future with the Clarion Club and its ideas, in its mixed company. Kenneth belonged far more to her mother's world, she suddenly realised, much as she liked him, than she and Peter did. She enjoyed Kenneth's company and his sometimes playfully waspish conversation, certainly. She had even warmed to finding him attractive in his plain, understated way, for he was always animated by some interest or other.

There was, though, undeniably, something very old fashioned about Kenneth Butterworth. He had a propriety which could be irksome, especially when rebuking Ellen for lacking something of the same. Above all, he liked things as they were and saw no need for change. That, she thought now, yes, that, was the principal difference between them. Ellen and Carrie travelled along the road to Halifax in companionable silence, each quite at ease to think their own thoughts.

"Carrie," said Ellen after some time, thinking of their talk last night. "Are you planning to visit Manchester again soon?"

"Yes, Ellen. Quite soon," Carrie answered. "The Women's Guild Fiona has begun will have much work to do, being new. I would like to be there to support it. Len has Peter with him now and will be quite happy getting the mill raised again before year end. A month or so without me will not be too trying for him, I dare say. Father is well cared for and I have no anxiety there, for he has company all the time."

"A whole month? A proper visit, then. I will miss you," declared Ellen. "And so will Len."

"Perhaps," agreed Carrie equably. "But I will soon return and everybody has plenty to do in the mean time. You will pay a longer visit of your own to your brother, of course, while I am away, to make sure all is well?"

"Of course!" Ellen was happy to agree, thinking that she certainly would, for in that way, she would be able to see Peter, and perhaps John Henderson too.

If she were visiting her brother to keep house for him during the time Carrie was away, her mother could hardly object, could she? And she would escape the wedding-planning for a welcome respite. Carrie smiled at her, knowing this and that the company at Heatherfield would be more than welcome to Ellen. Peter was beginning to impress Carrie now that he could remain steady, in spite of the undoubted chip on his shoulder. She saw him subdue his temper at times, as he had done this morning, which showed that he was sensible of it. Like Ellen, Carrie saw Peter's unpredictable nature as being born of his frustrated potential rather than being an inherent character flaw. There were many men and women in the same social predicament, which the two women hoped the future would alter for people.

"That's settled, then. I will raise it with your mother at luncheon so that she is prepared."

"Is Len prepared?" asked Ellen.

"Not yet. But he will be," answered Carrie in her pragmatic way, making Ellen smile to herself because it was clear that Carrie's mind was quite made up on it all, whatever her husband might wish to say about it.

Carrie's calm firmness carried the day over luncheon with Mrs Rastrick and Sylvia too. Mr Rastrick was at his works. After making perfunctory enquiries about the forthcoming wedding arrangements (in which she was clearly not the least bit interested) Carrie proposed that Ellen stayed as companion with Len while she was away on a long visit to friends whom she had been long absent from since her own wedding. They had been such companions since early girlhood that they were almost family too, she said, and she must not neglect them.

"I lost my mother quite young, Mrs Rastrick," she explained, "and Fiona's took me under her wing on many a school holiday when Father was so busy at the mill. We boarded together with some others – a small girl's school in West Vale. I must not neglect them now that Fiona's mother is rather ailing. They moved to Manchester some years ago to be near other relatives after Fiona's father died."

It was the first Ellen had heard of Fiona's mother playing any part in the Manchester visits but she managed not to look surprised. Mrs Rastrick, on hearing that another person's mother was to be paid due respect (rather skilfully played by the tactless-seeming Carrie), saw nothing to object to. Besides, anything that separated this odd woman from her beloved Leonard was to be welcomed, and if Ellen were acting as his companion, she could exert influence to bring them back home more often to visit and dine.

"Can you spare your maid of honour for such a long spell, Sylvia?" asked her mother.

"Certainly. There will be little for her to be needed for now until nearer the day. You have everything in hand so early, Mother, that not a single guest could possibly plead a prior engagement," remarked Sylvia. "So they will all be forced to come."

"Oh, you know I cannot rest until everything is arranged to the best possible advantage!" exclaimed Mrs Rastrick, taking this as praise despite a certain edge to Sylvia's tone (for even Sylvia was feeling rather overwhelmed by the complete fussiness being given already to every aspect of her forthcoming wedding by her mother).

"Noel and I will be going abroad immediately for a tour of Europe, so Mother will have a long rest then," Sylvia told Carrie. "He has a yearning to see it all and bring back his own treasures to Ogden Towers. Not content with having his own statues sculpted, he is determined on real Roman ones, it seems. I would have thought there were paintings enough at Ogden Towers, but Noel does not agree."

"We are going up there this afternoon, Ellen. You may join us, if you please," said Mrs Rastrick.

"Oh, yes, I should like to, Mother," said Ellen, who

was glad to think of seeing Noel.

Arrangements agreed that Carrie would write when Ellen might go to Heatherfield, probably within the next fortnight, she left to go home, her back straight as she drove away in her usual solitary splendour.

"That hat," said Mrs Rastrick, looking after her daughter-in-law and frowning now that she had put her outdoor things back on. Carrie sported what looked very like a top hat on her piled-up russet hair. "Why does she not put a veil, or a feather upon it, as other ladies do? She wears it like a man would!"

"Oh, Carrie is not one to bother with ornament, Mother. She just sees it as her outdoor driving hat."

(Actually, as Ellen knew, it was Len's hat and not his wife's at all because he had joked with exasperation that she was wearing it out and he would have to buy another. Carrie had just laughed at him and said that he should do because she liked this one.)

"*And* still driving about alone," said Mrs Rastrick, shaking her head. "I am determined to persuade Len to employ a man for the task. Carrie has lacked guidance, I believe, with her father being a widower, poor man. She has not the first idea of how eccentric she appears. But then, she has not had the advantage of having a mother like me, as you girls do," she concluded, trying (and failing) to sound charitable about it.

The day had clouded over after lunch and they arrived in their own closed carriage at Ogden Towers in a barrage of heavy rain. In such light, the house looked less baroque than gloomy, with its windowed turrets sinister and dark, places you would be afraid to see a face looking out of in case it did not belong to the living. The two-sided set of steps leading up into the cavernous stone doorway ran with water, which dripped off the fangs of the peculiar gargoyles staring out from above it. It made

Ellen shiver and feel glad that there was no danger *she* would have to live in it in the future. But when Noel appeared, after a short delay when they waited in the lobby to be announced, all was as lively as usual.

He was delighted to see them and ushered them in with great enthusiasm. Ellen was the last of the group, for he had taken Mrs Rastrick and Sylvia on each arm as if to lead them into a ball rather than his drawing room, where a great fire blazed in welcome. Hearing a light step behind her, she looked back and was very surprised to see Cyril hurrying silently down the main staircase from the upper bedchambers, very much as if he meant not to be seen. But Ellen exclaimed, "Cyril! I did not expect to see you here."

Cyril stopped short and looked a little confused. Noel, hearing Ellen call out to Cyril, came to his rescue, announcing smoothly, "Oh, our Puck, Cyril, is staying here a short while to complete the inscriptions around my new fountain in the garden alongside my nymph. He has been rained off this afternoon. I have a marble wall with ovals carved about with laurel wreaths, and he is inscribing on them the names of my ancestors and their dates of birth and death. I mean to commemorate them all, as far back as I can go, which I think is about two hundred years or so, when the Ogdens had a manor here after being rewarded with it for some part in the Civil War. Who better than a monumental mason to do that job?"

"I did not mean to interrupt your visit," said Cyril, going on to pass off his appearance from the upper chambers with, "I had to go up to my *servant's* room to change my clothes. I worked as long as the rain held off but got caught in it anyway."

(He said the word servant with an odd inflection of emphasis and surely the servant's quarters were not accessed via the main bedchambers upstairs, thought Ellen, puzzled, watching him fuss over tying his neckerchief.)

"Good man. Thank you," said Noel with debonair ease. "Since you are passing, take tea with us fellow thespians, won't you? I am sure nobody will object."

"Thank you, no," said Cyril, rather on his dignity again with Sylvia present as fiancée rather than theatrical participant, Ellen realised. "I have the next inscriptions to research and write out from the family Bible."

"Very well," said Noel graciously. "I will send tea for *you* to the room where you work on it."

"Thank you," said Cyril. "Mrs Rastrick, Miss Rastrick, Miss Ellen Rastrick."

He gave a short bow and met Ellen's eyes with a spry twinkle in his own that she smiled privately back at, her mother and sister both, of course, being quite unaware that she had ever spent time at the stonemasons' yard with John Henderson and Cyril Raynor. Sylvia simply smiled with the saintly distance she affected when paying little or no attention to people she did not think it important to notice. Then she, her mother and Ellen were swept off by Noel to admire some recent gilding of plasterwork on cornices and ceilings he had been having done. Cyril disappeared into the building elsewhere.

"This house is not like any other in Halifax, Noel!" Ellen exclaimed.

"I do hope not," he replied complacently, hands clasped behind a jacket with very bright brass buttons ornamenting its coattails. "I had far rather be *rococo* than run of the mill."

They all laughed at this sally and then sat down to take tea.

Chapter Twelve

Albert, when he finally did call to see Jane, although made welcome by an unsuspecting Mr Ellison and as charming as ever in his own manners, had the restive air of a man who felt himself to be under pressure. Pleasantries were exchanged and eventually he suggested a very short walk, if Jane felt equal to it now.

"I am sure it would do her good," said her father. "Fresh air and a little exercise. Although she is not back to riding that bicycle of hers yet."

"It is near winter, Father," said Jane. "And not often fit for that. But I will walk a little. It is a brighter day."

She had refused the same previously when Felix Sykes had suggested it yesterday, and her reference was to Albert's arrival rather than the weather. Her outdoor things carefully assembled, with a fur collar about her neck to keep off any chill, she took Albert's arm to step outside and they took a turn along the street, then headed downwards towards People's Park, which they strolled through. Only when they found themselves quite alone on one of the ornamental iron bridges overlooking the lawns, bandstand and snaking pools, did they speak properly.

"Jane – tell me truthfully, why did you take it?" Albert asked.

"Because this life stifles me and I would not continue it feeling so."

"Yet why, when I taught you to feel free?"

"You tried to but then I trapped myself. I realise it."

Albert looked at her and saw no recrimination in her face, which seemed to encourage him to continue.

"Jane – listen to me. I have something to offer you today."

She gave a short, odd laugh.

"Only to me, Albert?"

"Only to you, Jane. I am going on a tour of Europe, for my art – a mini Grand Tour, if you like. Come with me, in secret. Then you will have your freedom and be with me."

"They…those other women will not…?"

"Hannah and Sarah? No. They will remain here working and keeping the house. I will be away for six months and, Jane, you can be with me. You will never have to come back here if you do not wish it. You are an educated girl – you could give private lessons in English to maintain your independence. We will find somewhere excellent for you – a place you choose to be in from those we visit in Paris, Venice, Rome. Think of it! Six months at least of seeing all that beauty with me, absolutely at our liberty."

"Six months – and after that, you will leave me to return here," Jane stated.

"But I will also return to you – to wherever we live alone together when I am back over there. And I will be."

Jane felt her mind fill with heady images and that recklessness which beset her whenever she was physically with Albert quickly possessed her.

"When?" she asked.

"I leave in but a week – it has been hastily agreed because my father long resisted the idea. I have persuaded him to allow it."

He did not add that the weight of certain rumours which had reached Mr Dewhirst's ear had added to persuading him that his youngest son needed to be got away from them, nor did Albert reveal that this was his own way of trying to make sure any scandal attaching to Jane which could impugn him was removed along with her.

"A week!" she exclaimed.

"Yes, but you shall join me in less than a month or

two. You will become a companion to a lady of means who wishes to travel – we will say that you met her some time ago at some charitable functions and she has asked you now to go with her to convalesce."

"But, however would my father be persuaded of such a thing, Albert? And what lady?"

"She will write to him with every possible respectable reference – and you will tell him of her. That she has corresponded with you and, hearing of your recent indisposition, thought it a solution for both of you. You need a change of scene and stimulation of mind and spirit. *She* needs a companion of the right education and background to accompany her. As a clergyman's daughter you suit her perfectly."

"Who will write as this lady?" asked Jane, presuming her to be some invention.

"She will."

A look of bafflement crossed Jane's face.

"It sounds a cruel trick to play," she said, clearly assuming him to mean some subterfuge, that Albert would play that fictitious lady's part himself.

"No, not at all. Would you have your poor father worry himself to death when you disappear?"

"Of course not."

"Then you will meet Miss Tordoff of Bradford," said Albert, with a grin which made her smile back. "I assure you that she does exist. I will rescue you, Jane, from this wretchedness you feel, if you will allow it."

"I will," she answered, in a parody of accepting a marriage proposal, which she knew that this was not.

She did not care, she told herself, so long as she could be with Albert. How often had she sat in the dull, dark rooms of the vicarage as the clock ticked on, feeling that the days wearing out so pointlessly were unbearable? Jane believed she was born for love and, thinking it denied her, had swallowed the laudanum. In a perverse way it had brought Albert to say that he loved her too, in whatever manner he did so, and this, yes, this *would* be liberty from the life she chafed against so much in the Yorkshire mill town. With Jane persuaded, Albert talked on of his own ideas for a different future.

"I have great plans, Jane. Since joining the Clarion Club I have met like-minded people with artistic vision. We think of making a society of our own, as William Morris and his Arts and Crafts group did. John Henderson cherishes sculpting ambitions. Noel Ogden would like nothing better than to be a patron of the arts, and he has enough money to live as he wishes without caring a jot for public opinion. Cyril Raynor, for one, would be delighted to have a reason to live and work alongside Noel," he added, with a lively laugh.

"You think of it being at Ogden Towers, then?" asked Jane in some surprise.

"Indeed we do and there will be ample space for us all."

"But – Noel is to marry Sylvia Rastrick. Surely, *she* will not stand for all that!"

"Noel collects her for her beauty and because he is expected to marry *someone*. By the terms of his father's will, he is reaching the age of that necessity. And she marries him for a better social position. I think you may rest assured that she will stand for all that is required. Besides, Sylvia likes to be admired and that way will always have a court around her."

"I doubt she is the only one," remarked Jane, rather tartly for her. "Ellen Rastrick warned me one day that she heard you say to her sister, on the very day that Noel proposed to her, why settle for Noel when she could have you?"

"Me?" said Albert with another laugh, for things had

quickly moved on from that day and he had forgotten his momentary flirtation with Sylvia. "Ellen does not know when I jest, Jane."

"And this was all it was?"

"Certainly! I did not recall it at all until you mentioned it just now. Pray tell me that you have not added this to your list of my wrongdoings for you to brood over?"

"Of course not," Jane denied hastily. "And I have accused you of none."

"Not directly, no," he said, looking at her sideways under his long lashes and presenting her with his profile as he looked over the neat grass of the park gardens. "But to take that suicidal dose...you never would again, or I will take back all we have just agreed upon?"

"Never!" Jane agreed with a shudder.

This she meant entirely, for while the treatment which saved her had been appalling to endure, the dreadful sensation of sinking so horribly into nothingness which had preceded it had been truly ghastly. Never again would she view any print of the portrait of the death of the poet Chatterton in any romantic light, or see death itself as an escape. She had fought hard with every breath to stay alive when they had brought her round, even the twilight days of her recovery a precious boon to her, although her personal misery had continued. For a moment, the bewhiskered face of Felix Sykes, who had read so patiently to her for many hours during those days, appeared to her, but then she dismissed it. While Jane's former plight might have touched the curate, she was not drawn in any way to him, although she had appreciated his kindness. Besides, she was not *that* Jane in reality, was she? Felix Sykes belonged to harvest festivals and the church, her father's world. Jane desired a far different one.

"I promise it," she assured Albert, quickly changing

the subject. "This society at Ogden Towers…it comes after your tour of Europe?"

"We have set no time on it," said Albert airily. "There will be much to plan. John will be marrying soon and setting up house with Libby – not everyone will be at Ogden Towers itself except as the working community."

"And I?" she asked. "Will I join you in it?"

"Jane, you will be free to decide on your own wishes. After all, you may prefer to remain abroad and have us live entirely by ourselves when I return to you there."

"But, Albert, what of my father?"

"If you decide to stay on, or to return and keep house for him, then that too is your choice, Jane. All I offer you is a different choice. An escape to live freely, with me often at your side. You will have a couple of weeks to consider it after I leave. Then I will write to you. You will write back to advise whether Miss Tordoff shall come to life."

"Albert, this is sheer fantasy! My father will not let me go travelling with a lady he has never met!"

"Oh, he *will* meet a lady. There is a real Miss Tordoff, Jane, as I have said. I can trust her to play her part in our plans."

"Who is she?" demanded Jane.

"An old friend," said Albert. "I began my adventures early in life, Jane, and everyone has to learn from someone."

"One of your free spirits?" asked Jane caustically.

"The very first, from whom I learned to be one. Give me the word and I will give *her* the word. Miss Tordoff will pay for her journey and I for yours. She is a lady of means and often travels independently. I am sure she will be happy to oblige me."

Albert's first lover, Jane thought, if his word was to be trusted! Was it, and did she?

"I will take you home now, Jane. I kept my promise to come to you. I demand none of you in return. You see how generous I am?"

"And you truly wish me to do this?"

"I truly do."

Jane, of course, very much wanted to believe that he did. Albert's smile was so sunnily upon her (quite carried away with the notion himself by now) that she was convinced. He would give her time, he said again, before he wrote, so that she could consider it all without feeling under duress. Her father was pleased to see some roses in Jane's cheeks on her return after saying goodbye to Albert at the door. Albert said he was expected back at home now for visitors of their own.

"I believe your walk has been good for you, my dear!" the vicar exclaimed. "He is a lively young man, is he not, Mr Dewhirst?"

"He is but he came to say farewell for the present, Father. He is to go away for a tour and see all the arts abroad, leaving very soon."

"Indeed? How very grand a style to live in! We will miss his occasional calls here. Now, you see you have another visitor, Jane. Mr Sykes has called in to see how you do."

Mr Sykes was looking rather gratified to learn of Albert's imminent departure, perhaps resentful that Jane had taken a walk with that young man today when she had refused one with him only yesterday.

"I am pleased to find that you are feeling stronger today, Miss Ellison," he said, in a tone of Christian charity which showed that he felt the slight.

"I am, thank you, but the walk has tired me now and I will rest a little, if you will excuse me, Father?"

"Oh, certainly, child. Mr Sykes and I have parish matters to discuss. Come and sit down, sir!" Mr Ellison invited as Jane, receiving Mr Sykes's bow, went off upstairs to her room and left them to it.

It was not kind of her, she knew, but just now, Jane did not care a jot about seeming rude, all her thoughts elsewhere again. She had a great deal to think about following Albert's visit. Would she feel able to follow through his plans, and would he himself do as he had said? She told herself that she did not have to go through with it when fear of what such a drastic change would bring overwhelmed her. Next, she would find the thought of being stuck here without Albert at all was equally, if not more, terrifying.

Over the next days, growing physically strong again, she drifted between these sensations. She told herself that if and when Albert's letter of invitation arrived, she would instantly know her own mind. Then, when the charade was played out, if she had cold feet at the last, after meeting 'Miss Tordoff' with her father, she still did not have to go through with anything. There was a vision promised her where anything was possible and yet, it had no solid foundations, did it? How could she know that Albert would really either stay at her side or return to her later if she remained abroad herself (a heady prospect which was exciting and alarming in equal parts)?

There was, too, that usual underlying cold draught of reality chasing away her rainbows. The choice would be hers alone to make. The responsibility for it and for herself would also be hers. Although she had longed for that independence, she had never been brought up to expect it in any way. There was marriage, or keeping house for her father. Now, she was to earn a living and not be kept – very good, this was the modern liberty they all aspired to for ladies in the Clarion Club. If she went ahead with that, though, she would have no financial certainty if it failed, whilst Albert's remained secure.

The Ogden Towers artists' community, if it came to fruition, *would* be on home ground, but living there would deny her any respectability ever again, unless Albert married her. If he spent six months with her away, would he love her in that way too and marry her in secret abroad? Her romanticism longed to believe it, whilst everything that Albert had actually said told her it was a foolish dream. She remembered, too, the brief few days when Hannah Robertshaw had come to nurse her, in what seemed some spirit of sisterly compassion, although Jane had rejected her as soon as she was able to do so.

"You must not have false hopes that will only hurt you more, Jane," Hannah, sitting by her bedside, had said, when she seemed more wakeful one morning. "Albert pursues his own world, you know – and he is what he says he is."

Jane had barely been able to speak in return, her eyes drifting closed again, but she remembered the words now, said with great kindness but deeply resented by Jane, and, even now, it was a caution which she did not wish to heed. One day, Albert's letter came, just as he had promised her it would. He asked Jane again to join him. He wrote assuring her that all travel arrangements would be made with 'Miss Tordoff'. She would be with Jane until they arrived in France to meet Albert. Then Miss Tordoff would leave them to go on alone. Albert was already in Paris, 'waiting', a word which gave Jane great pleasure to read. Seeing all this in writing, her impulsive feelings for him made all fears fall away. She wrote back to say that she wished to go to him and everything was set in train.

An exchange of letters began with the lady, which Jane began to share with her father, almost convincing herself, too, that she really did know Miss Tordoff in the way described. Mr Ellison's doubts about her journeying abroad so unexpectedly were allayed by his fears for her mental state at home. In this way, she would have a chaperone to protect her rather more than she did at the vicarage, where there was nobody except himself to perform that office, and she had been in the habit of going about rather more freely than perhaps she ought to have done. Had this made her spirits vulnerable after the loss of her mother, he had often wondered?

Miss Tordoff wrote that she preferred to travel in autumn, winter or spring, so avoiding the most strenuous times of year for heat and consequent disease, she said, and Mr Ellison felt this was rather sensible too. By the time she came to introduce herself (a neat and composed woman somewhere in her thirties, whose demure air belied Albert's description of their former relationship) Jane's father was already certain that this would be a great opportunity for Jane to benefit her experience and education, limited as it presently was. Meeting Miss Tordoff confirmed it.

"I saw at once, Mr Ellison, that Jane was a young lady of sympathetic character, and from quite the right refined background as a parson's daughter to make the ideal companion for my tour of Europe's cities. It has long been an ambition of my own to see them and, you see, I have the means now to afford it from my annuity. Such travels will surely benefit Jane's constitution after such trials recently."

Mr Ellison, who would also like to have Jane away from the rumours of attempted suicide which dogged him round the parish, was soon quite gladly persuaded that it would.

"You will have enough company without me, Father?" Jane asked.

"I will miss you greatly, my dear, but I have my work, my parishioners, my faith and my neighbours to occupy me. I will do very well, knowing that you do." And he patted his daughter's hand in a way which made the guilt start up in her heart at once but she glanced at Miss Tordoff, who gave her the slightest of reassuring nods, so that she said nothing.

Besides, she meant to use her time alone with Miss Tordoff to find more out about Albert's world. If Jane were to become a part of it, she must surely learn to understand it better, she felt. Miss Tordoff's appearance did not suggest a bawdy past, but rather more that she was her own woman, as Albert seemed to wish Jane to be. Jane herself made sure she did nothing at all out of the way on the approach to leaving, keeping very clear of all the Clarionettes and in particular, Hannah and Sarah. Albert had told her their arrangement would be secret from them and she was happy for it to remain so.

Mr Sykes was no longer involved in helping with her father's parish duties now Jane was well. He was too busy with his own vicar's demands to call very often at present, which was rather a relief to Jane. For privacy's sake, she had asked her father not to make her plans widely known anyway and he shared her discretion. Whatever views Mr Sykes did have about it when he came to hear about her travels, he had no opportunity to share them with her before she left.

When the day came, Miss Tordoff's carriage and a servant collected Jane and her baggage from the vicarage and took her to Bradford, where after an overnight stay they would take the train down to London for the boat train together. She waved farewell to her father and settled back to anticipate her liberty, with a growing feeling of fluttering excitement she had scarcely allowed herself to feel until the very moment of departure.

***

Ellen was glad to be going to stay at her brother's house and to have no further obligation to visit Jane now that she had recovered. Ellen had tried to like her better but did not find Jane at all congenial. Kenneth called with his mother instead of alone before Ellen left for her visit and so the talk was general, with Mrs Butterworth full of lively interest in all that was being done for Sylvia's wedding. Finally, the conversation turned to Ellen's prospective visit to keep house for her brother and help look after his father-in-law, while his wife paid a long overdue visit to old friends.

"Well, Ellen will certainly be able to enjoy reading to the poor invalid, for so Mr Stanger is now," said Mrs Rastrick. "I am sure her time will be much occupied with it, and her brother's with the new mill building. Of course, I hope to receive them often to dine here while Carrie is away."

"Very pleasant for all," said Kenneth, sounding approving of arrangements, which would ensure Ellen was busy in the house keeping Leonard's father-in-law company.

"I have finished reading *Vanity Fair*, Kenneth," Ellen offered.

"Then I must call upon you and your brother one afternoon and we will talk of it." He smiled at her.

"I would enjoy that," she agreed.

Before she left, she was at the school again with Eustace. It being a half-holiday for pupils and staff, the two of them had one last 'Clarion Club' winter cycle together up to Beacon Hill, for it was a bright enough afternoon to enjoy the view from its 'blasted heath' top. Ellen had last been up there with John Henderson she remembered as, having laboured up the cobbled incline in part on foot as it was so steep, they reached the summit. The chimneys of the Halifax mills all along the bottom smoked up in grey columns, dimming the air. The view was of dark, sooty buildings down there, with greener hills criss-crossed with walled fields all about them beyond the mills' reach.

"Did you know, Ellen, that a hundred years ago, they left hanged men, like the Cragg Vale coiners, dangling in chains up here as a warning to the populace?" observed Eustace, who always knew a bit of history relating to whatever part of the area they visited.

Ellen shuddered, for seeing all the mills and thinking of John meant thinking of Peter and what she and he had done together to a different mill. She tried to shake the fear off of what might still befall Peter if it were ever discovered.

"Ugh!" she exclaimed. "And there's the gibbet too, where they chopped people's heads off. What a very bloody town we have been in the past, Eustace! Thank heavens for civilisation today."

"Yes. From Hull, Hell and Halifax, may the good Lord deliver us," intoned Eustace, repeating the mantra former criminals were said to have prayed with, that they might escape dire punishment in all those places. "I expect people still fear justice here now."

Ellen decided it was time to change the subject and that it was Eustace's turn to be made uncomfortable. She was never entirely sure that she had convinced him about that mill fire, or that the things he sometimes said weren't meant to probe and warn. He harboured a distrust of Peter which he did not altogether hide.

When she had told him that both John and Peter were working with her brother to restore Stanger's Mill to more than its former glory, he had frowned and exclaimed, "Peter Lumb!" in such a way that it was clear Peter was the last person he would have expected to find engaged in such a position, and that, in Eustace's opinion, he ought not to be.

Now, she said, "Speaking of people being delivered from harm, Eustace, have you heard that Jane Ellison has just gone off as companion to a Bradford lady on a tour of European cities for several months?"

"No, I had not heard that! I am glad she is away from here. I fear she made herself unhappy over Mr Dewhirst. But what harm do you mean she is delivered from?"

"She fell ill for a while is all, Eustace, but being quite recovered, this will be a new opportunity for change."

"Ill! I wish I had known, I would have called upon her father to give my best wishes for her recovery, or at least written to convey them. And to go abroad, that is a great change of circumstance indeed!"

"She is quite well now, I believe. I think you were fond of Miss Ellison, Eustace?"

Eustace smiled ruefully.

"I tried to interest her in my poor pupils too but it was not something she relished at all. Perhaps I thought her other than she was."

He left his conclusions at that as far as Jane was concerned and Ellen, feeling she had been rather cruel now in telling him Jane had been ill and since gone away, changed the subject again.

"Will you come to John and Libby's wedding party, Eustace? It is to be very soon now. They have asked all of us to join them who were riding together in the summer. Not everyone can, of course. Albert Dewhirst is away and Noel is always doing something with Sylvia these days."

"Yes, they have invited me and I will certainly go to their wedding. A very happy union, I think, as a result of our Clarion Club. At least one such will be."

"Do you remember the first time we all cycled out together, Eustace? When John and Cyril carved their names and the date on the rocks at Albert Promenade?"

"I do indeed and a very good day it was, ending in the Hipperholme Sunny Vale Gardens!"

"It was. It's cold up here now, Eustace! We have been standing too long. Let us go back down."

"Of course," agreed Eustace. "By the way, I have been to see Stanley's mother once or twice and I think they are managing well enough for money. A couple of the younger ones are set on to work now and a wage is coming in."

"You are good to do it, Eustace."

"No – he was our comrade and friend and I feel a duty towards him for it."

Once again, Ellen warmed to the inherent kindness and principled standards in Eustace's character.

"I will tell Peter of it when I see him at my brother's house," she said. "He will be relieved to know it, I am sure. He felt it terribly, you know, Stanley's death. His eyes still fill whenever he is mentioned."

"I do not doubt the depth of Peter's feelings, Ellen. It is how he acts which concerns me. And…"

"And?"

"And I should not like to think *you* were in any way misled by him, Ellen."

"I am *not* misled!" she said, so roundly that he dropped the subject with a sigh, unconvinced, and they made their way back down with no more said about it.

***

Ellen was excited to arrive back at Heatherfield and find herself, if only temporarily, the mistress of a household. She was looking forward to seeing Peter and John, especially Peter. At first, she did not. Len was meeting them on site at the mill and she was tied to the house, by domestic arrangements and keeping old Mr Stanger company while his manservant saw to the nursing side of things. Her walks, when she took them, were solitary. In addition, Len himself was less company by night than she would have liked. Restless, he often went off riding into town, to visit his club or taverns with business associates, he said. He was excitable in the mornings, somewhere between exhilaration and being irritated.

"I must woo investors in the new mill," he said when she questioned him about it. "Hah! And when my wife is away I am to entertain myself too," he added on an odd note which Ellen could not interpret.

"What do you, mean, Len?" a puzzled Ellen had asked but he had told her not to worry about it.

He said that the stress of getting the mill finished and not bankrupting them all in the process was making him full of nervous energy which kept him in need of constant occupation, but he did not mean to neglect Ellen, he apologised. Sometimes, after Ellen had retired for the night, she was aware of company below that he must have returned with, woken by men's laughter and once a skittish giggle which sounded much nearer by, surely a woman's? But, after sitting up and listening for a minute, she heard no more and went back to sleep. One day, she persuaded him to take her with him to see the mill, where John and Peter were busy working and using a makeshift office in the old part which had escaped the fire. She was impressed by the mighty, striped brick mill chimney rising to a decorated top to rival that of Wainhouse Tower. John was standing by her looking up at it, while Peter and Len were busy inside on other calculations to do with new machinery which would be needed.

"It's very fine indeed, John!" she exclaimed. "There are so many tiers to it up there!"

"The men are happy – the more ornate, the more pay per brick," he explained with a laugh.

"Len seems to be worrying about it all – he says this is

why he goes out so often in the evenings to town as he must keep busy. I think it is because Carrie is away too, though."

"Your brother is a young man, Ellen and must be one sometimes. It is an unusual marriage he finds himself in, a disparity in age and with much responsibility attached."

"I suppose you are right. I have thought, sometimes, that Len brings company back, after I am abed in the house," she added with a frown.

"Well, I suppose that he is young enough to burn the candle at both ends for a while," said John, not taking this particularly seriously, it seemed. "Perhaps you should say that you are finding yourself too much alone."

"I am too *little* alone, for I am forever with Mr Stanger!" she cried and then said, "No, that sounded mean indeed. He is very kind and polite, and thinks I do not realise he allows me to win draughts and cards very often when we play together in the evenings."

John laughed and offered to have a gentle word with her brother himself, if a likely opportunity came up to do so. Like Len, Ellen found that Peter too was much taken up, even rather obsessively devoted, to the work of raising the mill. On the second Sunday afternoon, though, he called up to the house from his cottage to take her out for a walk. Leonard had gone out somewhere and Mr Stanger was dozing in his invalid chair by the fire, a blanket over his knees. Delighted to escape, she rang for the manservant to sit with the old man, eager to join Peter. It was a vigorous winter's day, where they could walk off onto the old paths criss-crossing the moorland, desiccated by frosty winds which had dried up the usual mud. Old bracken made russet mounds and the hilltop grasses were bleached a pale blond.

"You can still see my great tower from up 'ere, Ellen!" cried Peter boastfully. "That's *my* monument. A working place! I'm bound for Leeds on Thursday with Len so we can look at the new machinery we want to buy in person. We're almost done now!"

"It's wonderful," admired Ellen. "I thought I might see you more than I have done, though, Peter, since I came to keep house for Len while Carrie is away on her visit."

"Me? I'm up to my eyes, lass! It's grand, though, isn't it?" he asked, his gaze still fixed on the tower. Then, emboldened by her words and the rush of achievement he was feeling, he bent to snatch another kiss from her, for her face was turned to his. "I said to missen I'd kiss you again in't snow up 'ere, Ellen, and so I will! This un's for now." Carried away by the moment, he suddenly exclaimed, "Marry me, Ellen!"

"Marry you…?" she cried, utterly taken aback by the unexpected kiss and declaration.

"Why not?"

"I…"

"Nay, leave it then!" he retorted hotly. "I never meant to blurt that aht. I've no time for all that now, any road!"

He began to start away, his face flushed.

"Wait!" she called after his rapidly striding figure. "Let me think!"

"Forget I said it!" he called back. "Follow me to the road back."

He continued to dash off, leaving her to follow, chastened. The kiss and the occasion were as spoiled as if he had torn up his proposal in front of her and burned it on the fire as promptly as he had made it. She concluded the walk back alone, for he had long vanished ahead, and when she hesitantly knocked on his cottage door, it was locked, the window showing it was dark and empty inside. Wherever he had taken himself off to, it was not there. She looked back behind at the moorland hills, the tops bleakly frost-lit under a strange sunbeam fanning down momentarily from a sullen cloud shelf banking up over them now. Then it was gone, the gap closed. The sight seemed to capture what had just happened between herself and Peter.

Awkwardness kept them apart until Peter went with Len to Leeds. In the meantime, Ellen told nobody about it. She and Leonard paid a call back to their parents' house for dinner on the Tuesday night and stayed until Wednesday morning anyway. She could not even go down to see John at the mill, for during the few days Len and Peter would be in Leeds, John returned to the stonemasons' yard to work with Cyril because there had been funerals too numerous for Cyril to make headstones for alone. It was at this time that Kenneth Butterworth happened to call. Finding her alone, he returned on other afternoons, staying for tea and into the evening to help her with entertaining Mr Stanger. She found herself, being very disturbed by Peter's abrupt proposal and even more abrupt departure, happy to be in Kenneth's familiar company, discussing books and passing an hour in pleasant conversation underpinned by his quiet humour. They even read some of *Vanity Fair* to the old man in turns, taking parts each and keeping him highly amused. She appreciated Kenneth's kindness more than she could say. Finally, he presented her with quite a different kind of proposal from Peter's.

"Now that you have had one visit away from home, Ellen, I wonder if you might consider another? I plan to rent a house for the early summer up in the Lake District and will take my mother there. The air will do her good, for she struggles much in winter with the fogs and smoke of Halifax. For myself, and this might entice you too, that is the place of the Lake poets – Wordsworth and Coleridge! We might see the places that inspired them and study their poetry together. Where better to quote it than where it was written? You see how I bribe you, when of course, I am also asking you to be a companion for Mother too? She will need a lively young lady about her in a strange place. And since we are all such old friends, I hope your parents will not object, with Mother present as chaperone? I thought, too, that after Sylvia's marriage, without either your brother or your sister there, it might feel dull for you at home alone at first."

"Why, thank you for inviting me, Kenneth," said Ellen, who was surprised but thought it would be a pleasant diversion for her as things were, even if she had to be in Mrs Butterworth's society rather more than was comfortable. "You are quite right that home is, well, rather different for me now. It is very kind of you and your mother to think of asking me to join you and I have never visited the Lake District. I would like to come. That is, of course, if I am let. I think I may be. Mother will still be wanting to spend all her time with Sylvia and Father is always so busy at work that he only wishes to read his paper and be quiet in the evenings."

"Well, then, it is all but settled," said Kenneth, sounding pleased. "I will make my enquiries and discuss with you where I intend to take a house and you may tell me if you find it suitable or not. I am sure there will be plenty available to us."

"Thank you," said Ellen gratefully.

"Speaking of going away, I meant to mention to you that Jane Ellison has gone abroad as companion to a lady. I called upon the vicar to pay my respects the other day and ask how Miss Ellison did. You remember we talked of it recently here and I said I would go on both our behalves? Well, he told me about it all quite cheerfully. Surprising, isn't it?"

"Oh, yes, thank you for doing that, Kenneth. Gone away? Yes, that is surprising but perhaps it is for the best," answered Ellen.

Little knowing that Albert was abroad as well, she thought that being apart from him would certainly be good for Jane's recovery.

"Let us hope so. Mr Sykes was present, having called in upon the vicar too. Do you know, I had thought him rather sweet on Miss Ellison at one time but perhaps not if she has gone away. Besides, the overdose and her melancholia suggest hysteria. *That* would be enough to give any man pause."

"How heartless of you, Kenneth!" exclaimed Ellen, laughing at herself for her old matchmaking idea of introducing Kenneth to Jane, which had certainly not born any fruit. Without thinking, she added incautiously, "Anyway, it was not Mr Sykes that Jane was sweet on herself."

"Oh?" asked Kenneth with interest.

"No, it was Albert and he is a dreadful flirt anyway. In the Clarion Club, you know..." she began, then stopped short at her blunder.

She remembered in time to whom she was speaking and that regaling Kenneth with Peter punching Albert on the nose, Eustace warning Libby off Albert and Albert's real relationship with Hannah and Sarah, would be far from wise. Not to mention betraying the very secret she had kept for Jane so far!

"What, Ellen?" he asked. "Albert...?"

"Nothing," she said awkwardly, not enlightening him further, and Albert was a common enough name. "It was only talk. That's all."

"Gossip in the cycling club's ranks, eh?" he joked. "Well, whoever she was sweet on, if she was, she's been whisked away from such trouble now, hasn't she? Just as well, if you ask me. You do realise that the mountainous terrain of the Lake District will not permit us to ride bicycles, Ellen? I should not like you to be disappointed in that."

"I will not be, you may be certain of it!" she laughed back. Their meeting ended very cheerfully, with him promising to call again very soon and chivvy Len into being a better brother to the sister who had kindly come to keep house for him. "Oh, I am quite happy now," she assured Kenneth. "I am enjoying being away from home and ordering my own days as I wish, for nobody prevents it!"

"Then you are getting far too much of your own way, Ellen, and it is high time you went home again," he answered drolly, putting on his hat and stepping firmly out of the door for her to wave him away in his carriage and return, laughing, to the house.

It was quite true that, by now, she had settled into enjoying being able to order her days at Heatherfield, with plenty of time, in fact, to enjoy her reading, or walk out alone with her own thoughts and take in the surroundings. Mr Stanger slept a lot during the day and her time with him was more intermittent than she had told John it was. She liked planning meals with the cook, who came in, and even sorting out laundry lists. It was a responsibility of her own and not marred by her mother's chivvying of her as falling short in some way, or Sylvia's patronising and superior manner floating about to spoil her mood.

Sometimes, she tried writing a poem in the diary book which Carrie had given her for her birthday, trying to capture something that had struck her in the landscape, or the people living in it. It made her feel alive, tranquil and complete all at once to do it. Perhaps if she did go with Kenneth to the Lake District, she might brave sharing them with him in that significant countryside. It was only afterwards that she wondered how she would bear so much of Mrs Butterworth in close proximity, but surely everything else would be ample compensation for that inconvenience, if the Lake District visit ever really came about? Kenneth's collected manner pointed up Peter's rash impetuosity once more.

Peter's proposal of marriage to her had seemed to come as out of the blue to him as it had done to her, and then to be so put about that she did not instantly accept, giving her no opportunity to respond either then or later! Worse, to abandon her so abruptly in his temper at such a moment! If he could treat her so then, how reliable might his mercurial nature be as a husband? Might he just abandon a wife after cross words? She pictured herself in some poorly clad place instead of the comfortable homes she was used to being in, swung from joy to panic without warning. If that were to be what marriage to a man like Peter was, then she wanted none of it, she told herself, in an angry misery towards him.

She knew that Kenneth Butterworth would never have left her alone on the moorland to find her own way back and yet, wasn't that one of the things that had made her welcome the Clarion Club's freedoms, that men and women were treated, and treated one another, as adults in their own right? It wasn't as if she had been in any danger up there and Peter had led her back to the road in front, but in so rough a manner as to show little care for her at all, the girl he had just asked to wed him! If John did that to Libby, she would slap his face and jilt him, Ellen thought, which made her smile and again woke her to the realities between people. Well, if Peter wished to stay away from her now, she was equally happy to stay away from him! And when she returned home a short while later, she had still not seen him again.

Leonard took her back the day before Carrie was due home because he wanted to greet his wife alone, and

Ellen thought it quite right that he should. She also wondered if he hoped to avoid her speaking to Carrie about how he had gone out by nights when she was away, carousing, in Ellen's opinion, more than he ought to have done when he said he had been told to entertain himself by his wife.

"We will call upon you soon, I promise!" he had said, embracing her upon leaving their parents' house, which they had often been to and fro from in the intervening days, pleasing their mother at least.

Ellen returned to her usual life in Saville Park. She wondered when Kenneth would bring her any news about the proposed holiday and now it suddenly occurred to her that this might be his way of discovering what life together would be like. For where Kenneth married, his mother would live too, of course. He had recently seen a good example of her ability to care for and live alongside an elderly, ailing parent, which could make life difficult. But no, she was surely imagining that motive, she hoped. There was no word from Peter and she presumed him sulking in some fashion. In fact, though, he was as deeply perturbed as she had been.

When he and Len returned from purchasing machines to be delivered and John, back too, wondered why Ellen had not been again to the mill to see their progress, Peter admitted, "I might have said summat daft. You know how I can be on't spur of the moment."

"You haven't upset her, I hope?" said John, surprised because he believed Peter and Ellen had become good friends on the quiet along the way.

"Nay – it were just summat daft. She'll be reet. Any road, we're all too busy now for socialising. Once the mill's up and winter's done – well, then we'll see."

He refused to be drawn any further on the matter and when John, without Peter, went to the house with Len a couple of times, Ellen looked to be happy enough, managing the household affairs and spending time with Mr Stanger, receiving other visits too.

"Ellen looked well. One of their old neighbours was there yesterday," he had told Peter the next morning in the office. "We met him once walking with Ellen and her sister Sylvia. And he came to the gala on the Moor, I remember. Mr Kenneth Butterworth?"

"Oh, aye. Him," said Peter off-handedly, but his face turned darker on hearing that name in conjunction with Ellen's as he studied the plan John was sketching some details into and he said little for a while.

John said, "Never mind. It's my wedding day soon, so you'll both meet again there. And Butterworth's not amongst the guests."

Peter just grunted at that, so John, smiling to himself, left speaking about Ellen out of it for the present.

***

Ellen was in the town centre the next Saturday in the early afternoon with her mother and Sylvia, the mission being to visit the most exclusive draper's with a view to choosing material for new curtains for what would be the master bedroom after the wedding. Noel had already had it repapered for Sylvia with paradise birds in Chinese blues darting gracefully about the walls, so the existing red brocade drapes would not do at all. Turquoise silk with cream swags were thought to be the thing.

The draper had bolts of cloth and pattern books spread across the counter, involved in intimate discussion, for this would be a prestigious purchase if done locally. The threat had already been made that if there were nothing suitable in this emporium, then they would have to explore the vistas of the Bradford or Leeds drapers instead, and so very demonstrative efforts were being made that there would be no need at all for *that* by the shopkeeper and his assistant.

Ellen had grown bored and was looking out of the window where crowds of people passed by, watching busy young boys in groups or pushing barrows, women trailing bustled skirts, suited men with bowlers. There was a constant clatter of horse-drawn cabs and laden carts going up and down. She walked about the shop looking at the neat trays of bobbins with different coloured thread on them, bobbins produced by their own factory. She was attracted by the cards of silk ribbons in jewel and pastel shades, aligned by colour and ranging from bright to pale.

She turned back to see two people looking in the shop window, the man's hatted head lowered, the woman laughing. She had a saucy face with a dimpled chin under her feather bonnet, one that made you want to smile back. When the man raised his head, he was laughing too. Ellen started – it was Leonard, but who was this young lady on his arm? Ellen glanced behind but her mother and sister's backs were turned and they were shadowed in the dark interior of the shop. Her movement caught the browsers' attention and then she met Len's wide, startled eyes before he hurried his companion off.

The young woman looked over her shoulder as they went. Ellen caught her merry look momentarily and then they were gone. She was as young as Ellen herself, perhaps, or not much older. Ellen remembered the giggle she had heard in the night at Heatherfield. Had it belonged to *that* young woman? A frisson of shamed interest went through Ellen, followed by confused pity for Carrie, even though Ellen knew, from Carrie's own words to her, that she had no need of it. And yet, she *was* sorry. Carrie had run away when Ellen had told her that Len loved her and now, driven off, he was perhaps finding pleasure elsewhere. If so, he didn't wish his family to know of it. Was that a good sign? Ellen kept her own counsel when she went to join her mother and sister at the counter, a satisfactory material finally having been chosen after much deliberation.

Ellen caught herself thinking that it would be a good thing if this were some lower-class girl who presented no real social threat to Len's marriage to Carrie. And then she was ashamed of betraying, even in her own thoughts, the Clarion Club's principles which she aimed to aspire to. What did that make her feelings for Peter, in that case? Was he right in his interpretation of her hesitation? He was not, she had to admit to herself, entirely wrong if so. She sighed because it was very hard to stay true to new ideas when old ones had been ingrained into you which the rest of your world lived by! She was not entirely surprised when Len, alone, swung by later in the afternoon, soon reassured by the innocently pleased welcome he received from his mother, and even Sylvia, that Ellen had said nothing.

After taking tea and saying he was delighted to tell them the topping out ceremony of the chimney would be held soon at Stanger's Mill and he wanted his mother, father and sisters to come and see it, he said casually, "I say, Nell, come outside with me for a stroll before I go. I have missed having you with me at Heatherfield." Having contrived this private word, they walked on the broad pavement at the front of the house as twilight fell early and he said, "Nell – what you saw today – my companion…"

"Yes?"

"Well – Millicent is a great sport and we enjoy one another's company now and then but, it is a private matter."

"I see," she responded quietly.

"Do you?" he asked eagerly.

"I know that you love your wife, Len," she answered,

"and that it was not expected between you. You told me that yourself."

"You are right. I love and respect Carrie, Ellen. And..." A pregnant pause and hesitation prevented him from explaining it all.

"I won't tell anybody about Millicent, Len," said Ellen. "I promise you."

She had learned more about irregular relationships than regular ones since joining the Clarion Club and was not at all sure which were the more valid between people in terms of real feeling. It occurred to her that in Len and Carrie's case, the marriage itself was the irregular relationship.

"Carrie does not wish for children, Ellen," Len went on, frowning. "And so, things are quite understood between us."

Carrie's bedroom door remaining firmly closed to Len after the murmured refusal Ellen had overheard when she'd had been staying there came immediately to her mind, and she found herself blushingly glad that it was dark outside.

"I wonder," she found herself saying, "if, when Sylvia marries Noel, she will not wish for children either? I cannot imagine her as a mother."

"Nor I. I should not wonder at it," he answered. "So long as she has her position and all the style she wishes to assume, Sylvia will be suited well enough. You're far the better of us, Ellen, in the heart department. Does anyone claim yours yet?"

"I thought I loved Noel but I find I do not," she answered. "And not because he has proposed to Sylvia. It was only that there is something so very different about him, I think."

"He makes it look as if there is," said Len. "Which is not the same thing at all."

"Kenneth Butterworth has invited me to stay in the Lake District to keep his mother company on a holiday with him in the spring," she found herself telling him, while thinking of the one person in her life who *was* totally different and unpredictable – Peter Lumb – but she could not mention *him* to Len in that way.

"*Has* he?" said Leonard with arch emphasis. "And should you like to go?"

"Yes, I believe I would."

"I am glad of it, Nell. He is a good fellow, Butterworth, and one you already know through and through."

"I did not say he had made a proposal of marriage, Len." She laughed.

"Not yet, perhaps," he smiled back. "Time will tell."

"Oh, will it?" she mocked back, wondering, if he did make one, how she would react to Kenneth's offer, and finding she had no idea at all how she felt about it.

She sighed to herself again, for that meant, surely, that she was not in love with Kenneth either? When she thought of Peter's abrupt proposal, it made her heart thump with equal excitement and dread, a hollow kind of 'wanting to jump off the cliff with him' feeling which her reason spoke against. Still, he would not ask her again, she was certain of *that* and so the question of how she might answer him next time would never arise. On this note, they went back in and Len said he meant to ride home, but was soon persuaded to stay for dinner and spend some time in the evening talking to his father about business affairs. It was so late after this that he stayed the night and was still there at breakfast, cheerfully cracking open an egg before riding back to Heatherfield in a light Sunday drizzle.

Chapter Thirteen

The next time Len visited, he brought his wife. Ellen and Carrie were soon talking aside to one another, with Carrie eager to thank Ellen for looking after her household and her husband while she was away in Manchester.

"I have so much to tell you of Fiona's work there!" she told Ellen excitedly.

"Come up to my room to talk, Carrie," urged Ellen. "I have much to tell you too. I am just going to show Carrie my latest novels, in case there is anything she would like to read," she announced loudly to the room at large.

In reality, the books were to be passed on to Peter through Carrie, acting as go-between librarian. She hoped that this might break the ice between them again without being a direct approach, since it was an ongoing thing which he could choose to avail himself of or not as he pleased. Carrie and Ellen left the rest of the family together and went upstairs. Carrie was full of Manchester events and meetings, new subscriptions to the Women's Guild strengthening the cause of votes for women, which Fiona was now throwing herself into with Carrie fully on board.

"Fiona O'Brien and Caroline Stanger speaking, on all our printed pamphlets – imagine it, Ellen! We have platforms in many halls now!"

"That is very impressive," said Ellen, who was most struck by the formal full use of Carrie's first name and continued use of her maiden name. "I have never heard you be called Caroline before."

"It means 'free woman', you know, so it seemed fitting. Fiona told me that. Of German origin, I believe. And, of course, I use my maiden name there. I promised my activities would never bring my husband into disrepute."

This made Ellen think of the young woman, Millicent, whom she had seen Len with, and that he was perhaps being disreputable himself with a different kind of activity anyway. But she had promised to say nothing of that to anybody.

"Does the name Caroline mean that? I wonder what Ellen means?" she pondered instead.

"I have a book of names which Fiona gave to me years ago. I will look it up for you!" promised Carrie. "Fiona means 'fair' and is Scottish."

How often Carrie mentions her friend, thought Ellen, and with far more enthusiasm than she ever spoke of Len, it seemed, which did not suggest that Carrie's feelings for her husband were any stronger than before. Well, there was nothing Ellen could do about it except feel it was a pity, she told herself. Ellen was later told that her own name, of Greek origin, meant 'sunray' or 'shining light', which rather pleased her.

She now went to several books she had laid ready and showed one in particular to Carrie, with Peter in mind. It was *The Time Machine* by H.G. Wells, a book she felt would resonate with him especially in its description of workers and elite split into two utterly separated tribes, one living in troglodyte darkness underground, the other in a gentle paradise where they wanted for nothing.

She had written a short note slipped inside the cover to Peter saying, *I hope you will read this and that we may enjoy a good long talk about it one day very soon. With very best wishes, ever your friend, Ellen.*

She had phrased and rephrased it from heartfelt to bland and had in the end hit a note somewhere in between. One which she hoped might make amends for how they had parted so unfortunately before, without either of them having had chance to draw back from the brink of a rift due to the declaration – a declaration which she was in retrospect certain had been accidentally made.

"Carrie, if Peter comes to look for books, will you make sure to give him this one from me? Even if he does not ask, will you offer it to him and say I asked you to?"

"Certainly, although I have rarely seen him since I returned. He, John and Leonard are busy morning, noon and night getting the chimney and mill building finished off. I can see you are anxious about it, though and will do my best." She looked quizzically at Ellen. "Did something happen between you both?"

"It almost did and then it suddenly didn't. Peter asked me something and I made a clumsy answer, so he went away and has not spoken to me since. Oh, Carrie, I never know how to feel about things at all! It's as if I blow hot and cold without ever meaning to. There's Peter, and now there's Kenneth Butterworth asking me to go on holiday with him and his mother. I swing from liking them to resenting them when they press me to their ways of thinking and feeling. What a contrary person I must be, to be sure!"

"No, not at all, Ellen. You are simply young and only just beginning to feel your way in adult life. You cannot decide on love when you are not sure of your own self as yet."

"Love! I did not speak of love, Carrie."

"You spoke of it by implication. But there is also youthful desire to consider, Ellen, and that can fool the coolest of heads. Which neither of us would say that Peter, at least, possesses."

Ellen blushed deeply, remembering the kisses they had shared but Carrie went kindly on, saying, "Do not allow anyone to rush you for the sake of being brought up in certain ways – Kenneth, for example, and you yourself. It is even harder to resist what is socially expected of us because of what is made to seem respectable, dutiful even. It does not mean you must agree to it."

"Thank you, Carrie. I could not put it all into words as you did, but that is *exactly* how I feel!"

"Then do not worry about what you ought to do. Do what you wish to do, in as much as you can manage it with good sense."

"What a sound and practical person you are, Carrie. Thank you. I fear I burden you with my confidences. I used to talk to Libby all the time – when she was my maid, you know, and especially after the Clarion Club. But now..." Ellen sighed.

"...Now, Ellen, you have me. And I have you. I think we are both equally glad of it," Carrie said, smiling. "I will give Peter the book if you still wish it."

Ellen thought for a moment and then nodded decisively.

"Yes, I do wish it. Thank you. I want to be friends with him as we were before and I am happy to make the first move. He is so flighty and proud, you know, that he might want to do it but not be able to manage it."

"Well said and well discerned about that young man, Ellen. You are not blind to his faults, whatever there is to admire in his character."

"Oh, yes! There is. You won't know this, Carrie, but he spent much time with his friend Stanley in the municipal library, both trying to educate themselves. He told me about it, how they persevered in spite of their long working hours and all their responsibilities in having to be the men of the family from an early age!"

Carrie nodded her approval of that, smiling, and they went downstairs again, Carrie carrying a couple of volumes with her to take back to Heatherfield. A family Sunday dinner followed and the next time they all met together it was to witness the topping out ceremony of the fully restored Stanger's Mill.

***

Jane found the long journey to the boat by railway, from Bradford to London and London to Dover, both hectic and strange. Luxury train to the cross channel ferry as it was and financially exclusive to the well-heeled, the noise of so many people in the stations where they changed, with excited crowds pushing and jostling, made her afraid of losing sight of her companion, Miss Tordoff. It was unnerving to somebody like Jane, used to most of her time being spent alone or in small company.

Finally, they were travelling through the night in a bed carriage which continued to sway with the train's clanking movement, so that she slept on and off without ever feeling that she had truly been asleep at all, constantly disturbed. The carriage lights made a permanent daylight glow which woke her repeatedly. Now and again, a shrill but mournful whistle sounded in warning as they passed signal boxes and went through silent country stations, startling her nerves. The acrid smell of burning coal was in the slipstream of the train's steam, filtering into the very air she breathed. Strangers' voices talking nearby, passengers or train staff, would rouse her too, everybody restive it seemed.

Miss Tordoff herself remained something of an enigma during the journey. She made small talk about the places they passed through but disappointingly avoided conversation about Albert when Jane tried to draw her out about him. Instead, she described Paris with an enthusiasm which made Jane long to see it. Miss Tordoff said one thing in particular, though, when they reached the coast at last and boarded the channel ferry with many other passengers (for the crossing was busy, in spite of the winter season).

"I will leave you my card and my address. Keep it privately. If you find you need to, or wish to do so for any reason, you may write and come to me. There are many roads to a future, Jane, and they do not all have to lead one way. Remember that, although at present you do not believe you will need to."

"Thank you," Jane said with some feeling. "I am glad to know that I will have another friend abroad."

She put the card carefully away in a small silk pocket in her reticule and England was left behind. It was a rough passage in places but luckily for Jane and Miss Tordoff neither were afflicted by it, able to enjoy a deck view when it was safe enough to come out there. To see such a sea sky, the light in it reflected off the choppy water, made it, even on a grey day, seem a very different and wider world from the inland dullness under cloud which she had always known. Jane felt as if a heavy lid had been lifted from her spirit. They kept to themselves as they travelled, quiet together, not drawing attention from other passengers by seeming in any way interesting. Miss Tordoff behaved as an aloof employer would do with her deferentially silent companion because discretion, given Jane's real destination, had been agreed to be necessary.

After landing, they travelled in the same exclusive way by train to Paris, where Albert met them at the bustling Gare Du Nord station. It was a journey which Jane's ordinary financial circumstances would never have allowed her to make herself. Albert wore a straw boater and a light-coloured suit, looking rather summery in spite of the time of year. The sky was still grey and chilly but the atmosphere surrounding them was quite different from an English one. People's talk sounded brighter. They were more animated, more sanguine in tone and expression. The passing Parisians looked Jane over directly with an air of rude curiosity which she instantly felt conscious of. Did she look so obviously English to them?

"Albert, you look ravishing," remarked Miss Tordoff, rather startling Jane. "Paris suits you well. You see? I have brought your protégée. I hope you speak French with a good accent, my dear, or they will simply laugh at you." She tapped Jane kindly on the arm. "Here I leave you. Treat her well, Albert."

"Won't you join us for luncheon, Vivian?"

"No thank you, Albert. Henri is waiting for me to arrive. It has been quite some time and we are anxious to reacquaint ourselves."

A faint smile crossed Albert's lips.

"No doubt," he said. "You intend to stay in Paris until after the spring?"

"I do but I am sure you will enjoy your own travels moving on from here in time. Jane, the world will be your oyster, my dear. Bonne chance," she added, kissing her gloved fingertips lightly and disappearing with a porter to find a hansom cab which would take her and her trunk to her own destination.

Already, Miss Tordoff looked different, her ordinary mask lifted into a sophisticated manner. She had changed that morning into a much more shapely outfit and altered her hairstyle. The demure Miss Tordoff, who had won Jane's father over as to her respectability, was subtly transformed into a far more sensual-looking creature altogether, with a sway to her hips as she walked. The braided coil of hair pinned up was now a soft chignon under a veiled and very becoming hat. She had rouged her cheeks and lips, then strikingly darkened her eyebrows with pencil. It was quite remarkable the way all this altered her. Jane had watched with fascination as the swift changes were made. The result was that a chic woman who knew her way about the world emerged from the parochial chrysalis which Vivian Tordoff had wrapped herself about in so far. Jane had barely heard her first name spoken aloud until Albert used it..

"Isn't she wonderful?" said Albert, looking after her admiringly for a moment. Then he turned to greet Jane with a warm embrace and a kiss on each cheek. "That is the French way of greeting, Jane." He laughed. "Now here is my English one." And he gave her a kiss on the lips, right there in public, making her gasp in surprise. "We are not in Halifax now, Jane!" he said, roguish and daring, taking her by the hand. "Your trunk will be sent on ahead, I have arranged it. Let us eat and then I will take you to our apartment. You will love our rooms!"

Jane felt quite swept away and to feel his arms round her so easily after all her anguishing seemed unreal. Was this really Albert looking so pleased to see her? Her heart lifted so much that she realised she had still been plagued by anxious dread that he might not be there after all, or *not* be very pleased to see her (something which had made her bed carriage dreams uneasy ones when she had managed to sleep). She gave a spontaneous laugh of pure delight which made him laugh happily back, so that here, in this different place, it was already like a fresh start for them. Albert took her to a small bistro restaurant in a narrow street, where he ordered an odd-tasting drink he called pastis, cloudy when water was added and like an aniseed cough medicine. Jane pulled a face at its unfamiliarity when he let her taste a sip.

"I knew you wouldn't like it. Try your citron, no alcohol in that one."

Lemon with sugar, and water again, but refreshing to her travel-jaded palate.

The meal was some kind of poultry casserole, delicious to taste, cooked with wine and drunk with a glass of it and water. They had tiny cups of bitter coffee to follow and then a pastry each, sticky with glazed fruit.

Jane was so hungry that she was happy to eat peacefully with him, watching the world go by the restaurant's small window and smiling across at him. It was noisy in there and hard to speak anyway.

"Your hair is longer, Albert," she said eventually, drinking him in appreciatively as he sat across from her.

"And yours needs to be hanging loose over your bare shoulders, Jane. It soon will be," he answered, looking into her eyes with sexual mischief in his own.

"Albert!" she mock-rebuked him, with a becoming blush.

"Come! I must show you one of the great sights of Paris on our way – we will take a cab. Then you can have a delightful rest with me in your new home."

"I can't believe I am really here!" said Jane with a happy sigh.

"Well, you are, Jane. You really are. And we will have a splendid time of it!"

The streets were busy with carts and carriages, people promenading everywhere and busy about their working lives too. They were taken to a quarter where Albert handed her down from the carriage in front of a hill where sets of stone steps led up it to various passages and streets of narrow buildings. Being partly hidden from general view below, they looked mysterious and charming.

"Where are we, Albert?" Jane asked.

"We are near our apartment now, in Montmartre, the artists' quarter, Jane. There are such salons, bistros, parties and studios to visit! It is a life like no other, well, for those of us with the money to enjoy it, of course. They don't all. We have access to the more fashionable world as well as this, but here is where I have taken our lodgings. As nearby to it as is salubrious to live in anyway."

He lead her along a cobbled street to a building with several stories, rather grander than some. A wide doorway led in, up steps from the road, and a concierge came out to greet them.

"Monsieur Albert – Madame," she greeted Jane too after a beat, with irony in her tone rather than respect.

"La valise?" queried Albert, passing over the familiarity.

"En haut," she answered with a gesture from a wry neck. She was elderly and wearing a shabby black dress which had seen better days.

Albert responded with a coin in the dry, cupped palm half held out to him and gave her a wink which made her cackle with rude lustiness. All in all it made Jane realise that, in spite of calling her 'madame', the old woman was quite aware of their probable status together, in other words, unwedded.

Glancing at her, Albert saw Jane's embarrassment and as they set off up the stairs to their second floor rooms he said, "Paris is full of lovers, Jane. Trust me, there is nothing remarkable about us here. We are among the demi monde!"

Jane was not altogether sure about that, the many people on the streets had plenty of bourgeois respectability about their demeanour. Whatever the demi monde was, it was not the one those people lived in, she was sure. She was soon to discover its nature. Her reunion with Albert was passionate, in a chaotic but spacious set of rooms strewn with evidence of a vigorous social life, smeared glasses and empty bottles knocking about on tables. They spent the rest of the first day in bed together, sensuality rediscovered between them.

As darkness fell with them still in a naked tangle under the feather eiderdown, there was a loud hammering on the door and calls of, "Albert!" from several different male voices, some using the French stress on his name.

"Some of my friends," he said to Jane. "Stay here and I will see to them."

Laughing, he called to them to wait a few minutes. He got up, telling Jane to refresh herself and dress comfortably, reassuring her that there was no hurry. He would ring for hot water for her. Albert dressed quickly, then went out to greet his visitors and let them into the main apartment room beyond the closed bedroom door. Jane listened to lots of male laughter, smiling to herself as she washed in the ewer when Albert passed through the jug of water, then dressed and brushed her hair. Opening the shutters, which they had closed, she went onto the balcony, startled to see how close they were to the building opposite, where a woman with a candle could clearly be seen passing her own window. She was almost close enough to call across to. Jane drew back and prepared herself to meet Albert's new friends.

Shyly opening the bedroom door, she went across the small passage into the salon, where a litter of men had carelessly draped themselves about chairs and couches, smoking and drinking the wine they had brought. Like Albert they had longer hair than the norm, dressed in good clothes that looked nonetheless worn in, some with paint on, and they had already generated an atmosphere of loquacious dissipation. There were less of them than you might have thought given the amount of demonstrative noise they were making, about six or seven in all.

"Jane – we are to go to the ballet!" cried Albert, already looking excited himself.

"Non – Le théâtre!" called another.

"L'opéra!" said a third carelessly.

"I thought we were seeing Roget's new studio – he *claims* to be exhibiting," an English voice drawled.

There was fresh laughter at this, at the expense of Roget's notions of being an artist at all being the implication.

"Let us do everything!" cried another, "We have all night!"

He spoke English for the benefit of Jane and Albert, in attractively accented tones. They were a group dishevelled and stylish at the same time, with a confident air of standing out among the crowd. Jane later said that it was like meeting a whole set of Noel Ogdens all at once, only not so exquisitely dressed, and how annoyed he would be that he was not so unique after all, which made Albert laugh enormously at the time.

Jane soon found that this was the busy world in which Albert lived– the nights full of lit performances in the company of artists and dancers, singers and actors. There were dark little bars to sip strong, sticky drinks in and impromptu private parties in shambolic places with debauchery in their shadows. It was a louche world full of women who were far more 'demi monde' than she was. In the days, when the morning was slept away to recover, they did visit galleries, even the Louvre once, viewing a vast display of famous paintings, which were hard to take in shown all together. Albert had also sought out fellow photographers and there were other studios for life studies like his, nude portraits for artists to use. Albert wanted to encourage Jane to pose for him privately in their own apartment, where he had his box camera and the dressing room taken over to develop his plates in. The place was messy, the life was messy, and it was gradually overwhelming.

Jane rarely had Albert to herself. When she complained of being tired, he left her in the apartments alone and went out himself, so that she fretted again about other women. For these were circles in which there were many women, part of the loose groups of people Albert mingled amongst so gladly in Paris, and there was something of the bedroom and tangled sheets about all of them. It soon became evident that some of these were shared mistresses among the group of men she had first met, vivacious coquettes who called themselves names like Bonbon, Minou, and Fleur. They called Jane 'Jeanne' in rippling voices, and soon 'Tisane' for a nickname. This was because, her father being teetotal by principal, she preferred to drink one of those French herbal teas rather than the pretty liqueurs these ladies favoured sipping in tiny glasses when gatherings (which would go on late) began in the afternoons – and also because she was 'so English' they said, amused by it. They drank enough to be outrageous but not enough to be drunk like the men. They kept their lively wits about them where the men could let rip, as any world was always more dangerous to a woman on the loose in it, even this one. Jane observed a certain sharpness of self-preservation in the women, for all their carefree latitude.

This was soon born out by them introducing her, as a novice in their set, to a new form of contraception which she could use without relying on Albert's self-control or his use of a clumsy rubber condom. Through a Parisian doctor they took her to, she now had a diaphragm to protect herself with, and this brought a more complete sexual freedom to herself and Albert, which they friskily enjoyed.

At first, Jane and Albert would sometimes forget to eat when they had retreated to sate themselves upon one another in their chambers, and she had never been happier than at those times. In the morning, Jane would go out very early for a fresh baguette or buttery croissants, the air enticingly fragrant from the bakery nearby. At that hour, the streets were emptier than they ever were. She could see a green and yellow parrot in its cage inside the window of the balcony opposite, trying to sun itself as morning rays tipped over the rooftops for a bright start to a wintry day. Albert would still be sprawled sleeping on the bed, looking beautiful in the half light through the shutters. After the physical rapture of this honeymoon-like reunion, which lingered on a while, there was less time to spend in their own bed together, for somebody was always calling to interrupt their privacy. Nobody kept regular hours in Paris. At least, not in Albert's Paris.

"I thought we came to Europe for art, Albert," Jane once complained.

"Ah, but that's not what *you* came for, Jane, is it?" he said, tapping her lightly on the nose with a feathered fan he had for a studio prop (still lying about since she had used it to cover part of her modesty for a photographic pose the previous day).

Albert was as handsome as he had ever been here, living in this hedonistic dishevelment which surely, she feared, could not last. When he said things like that, on a mockingly warning note, the passionate nights between them seemed as transient as perfume, in danger of cooling as quickly as the sweat on their bare skins, and so Jane would fall quiet again. They did go out sightseeing in the city too, taking horse-drawn omnibuses to the other quarters and central boulevards, with Jane on Albert's arm almost feeling that she was really part of a couple (a thing she envied in other strollers whom she fancied were legitimised by marriage).

She had seen Notre-Dame, the Arc de Triomphe, the Egyptian Obelisk, the Eiffel Tower, and they often went out to marvel at the partly built white marble confection which was the Sacre Coeur Basilica, set to crown the hill above Montmartre. And yet, all this sightseeing again seemed done in a great rush, especially if others were with them – joining, in a way, the constant assault upon her senses. Her letters home reflected nothing, naturally, of the licentious company she was keeping with Albert. In her correspondence, the old Jane resurfaced, a Jane of the parsonage. She described the fine sights of Paris as Miss Tordoff's companion might do, two genteel spinsters together.

As she wrote of them, the things she had seen became a more vivid memory, less momentary – the simplicity of watching white swans gliding down the Seine from the Pont Neuf bridge, the mighty grandeur of Notre-Dame gazed up at from below (the central point of Paris, Albert said). Most thrillingly, there had been the trip up the Eiffel Tower. There, they had ridden in the ascending lift looking out across the great city through the iron frame of it.

On that day, at the top, she had said to Albert, with an almost nostalgic pang, "Oh, Albert, do you remember the day we all went up Wainhouse Tower together, when Noel bought it? We were stunned by the views from there, but this!"

"Ha!" he cried, heartily amused by the comparison. "Our Wainhouse Tower mill chimney folly likened to the wonder of the world that is the Eiffel Tower! Now that must be a first – wait till I tell them all," he crowed, without specifying who he meant, no doubt thinking of his new circle here.

Jane felt a stubborn and sudden loyalty to their disparaged home town, but he had at least said 'our' Wainhouse Tower.

"That tower is a fine architectural achievement too, Albert," she protested. "And Halifax boasts many outstanding buildings. What of the Piece Hall's magnificent colonnades?"

"Oh, yes, a rival to the palace of Versailles itself, my love." He laughed. "What a little provincial you are, after all. I adore you for it," he added, but more as if he simply teased her for it.

Jane loved it, though, when Albert did tease her, for then they would laugh together and he would be fond with her. It was her possessive, exclusive side that irritated him, being naturally far more sociable than she, which she recognised, but Jane still chafed at sharing so much of him with others. She could not always hold back from expressing it, however much he frowned and withdrew when she did, or made some restless excuse that there was an appointment which he had to keep with one or more of his bohemian friends. Then, he went out alone to meet them at a salon, a studio, or a café rendezvous, for more excitable discussions about their work and future directions, collaborating together.

When Albert, as he often did, enthused to them about the planned artistic community which was to be at Ogden Towers in England, he painted an imaginary scene which, even to Jane's mind's eye, presented an idyllic setting. The hills and valleys of West Yorkshire were described by him in such terms (omitting the windy, rain-fuelled weather) with Ogden Towers sounding like a magnificent chateau in gracious, sunlit grounds, that he had plenty of fellow artists eager to come and join him there when it began.

"We will make a Montmartre in Halifax, all we artists together!" he would say, regularly raising a rousingly cheered toast to it.

Jane wondered if the entire entourage might descend, the 'dancing girls', as they were politely known, coming too, but she could not imagine any of those Parisian sophisticates living in West Yorkshire, the very thought of it making her laugh in disbelief.

***

Montmartre's artistic quarter was enjoying a famous reputation at this time, and had drawn a very cosmopolitan crowd to it when Jane and Albert merged into its heady mix of creative innovators. Albert was inspired by the poster printing art which was fashionable for advertisements, those for theatre performances in particular. Women's faces and figures were idealised in figurative images of classical, nymph-like beauty, clad in soft draperies and surrounded by stylised flowers and trees. Albert was offering his photographic portraits as studies for others producing the Art Nouveau paper images. He was beginning to sell them too, because it was less expensive than paying for a live model of their own, if they had no lover to draw on as Albert did.

Their cold but big high-ceilinged apartment offered enough space for this, and Jane had been his model in various poses and outfits on many occasions. He promised her the nudes were for him alone and she had to trust him on that. The lovers of his friends, that floating ménage of Minous, Bonbons and Fleurs, or others similarly nicknamed from their shadow world of dubious reputation, also modelled for him, much to Jane's anxiety, as he would take his box camera and plates to where they could dress up for him. The knowledge that Albert frequented their shady dressing rooms, full of spilt face powder, scented rouges and heady perfumes, fretted Jane's jealousy whenever he went to them, for what else might follow on from a photographic session she knew all too well herself.

The people they saw the most often were five of the group who had crashed into their apartment on Jane's first day. Milo (Miles) Standish was the other Englishman. He and Albert were firm friends and frequent drinking companions wherever they went. Milo, with his rakish hats and rangy walk, had two regular mistresses, dancing girls called Kiki and Lulu (far too chic again to be real names, Jane thought), and they reminded her horribly of Hannah and Sarah. Sometimes, seeing Albert looking over at the trio with lenient desire in his eyes, she knew that he was reminded of them too.

Milo's gaze occasionally lingered on Jane, so that she would not have entirely put it past either of the men, and perhaps not those women either, to suggest they all took to the bed together in some libidinous liaison full of forbidden fruits. They did not, or not directly, and yet sometimes she dreamed of it, disturbingly erotic encounters in dark-coloured rooms, startling awake to find herself either beside Albert or else alone because he had gone out again. She did not like waking in the night to find herself alone.

Then there was an American, Vernon Greenbank, a young man of Scandinavian height and colouring. He had flourishing blond moustaches and, by reputation, an even more flourishing bank balance courtesy of 'the governor'. He was a fellow traveller seeking art's civilisations abroad, presently indulging his bold, experimental brushwork in Montmartre.

Guillaume Artois, a quick-witted native Parisian, had the self-designated role of introducing newcomers to all the thrills of Montmartre, successfully bankrolled in his own painterly endeavours by those on 'the tour' whom he plunged into that society. His bar and restaurant bills were often on their tabs and he was always in the midst of everything socially.

Patrice Thibault, square and dark, was poorer, hailing from a peasant countryside in the south which he painted, even in Paris, over and over from memory in vivid, eye-crashing colours, with an unforgiving sun beating down on bent backs in fields. He was an intense, garrulous talker full of egalitarian ideas.

A courteous Austrian artist, Lukas Wolf (whom everybody, of course, just called Wolf), leaned towards a softer, still more impressionistic palette, where Paris was hazy with misty air and pearlescent grey skies. Jane liked the restful nature of his reflective temperament. He was less janglingly loquacious than the others and did not thrust himself into the competitive limelight as much.

Christmas and New Year came and went in Paris. Christmas day brought an early snow in the morning. Icy crystals furred the balcony top like iron filings on a magnet. Their apartment being colder than ever, they walked out into the snow-minted streets of Montmartre, exchanging cheerful greetings with others. They stopped to watch proficient street jugglers with audiences of other laughing people. Albert bought Jane a bird whistle from one of the many vendors, since they seemed to be all the rage on that Christmas morning in Paris. Later, crowds of people were heading for church, especially to get to the Madeleine, as they learned when they asked where everyone was going. It was an unusual building with a temple-pillared frontage in the next district, which seemed to be the fashionable gathering point for a service today.

"Do you want to go to Church on Christmas morning too, Jane?" asked Albert lightly. "You *are* a vicar's daughter!"

"A *Catholic* church, Albert?" exclaimed Jane, adding with a rare giggle, "What would my father say? No. I have no need of worship."

"None? Then we are scandalous indeed!" laughed Albert.

This was one of their happiest mornings together, wandering the eclectic streets of Montmartre on Christmas morning in the snow. It concluded back in their apartment with food they had bought in to eat the day before, everywhere being closed for the public holiday. For once, they ate and drank quite alone, toasting one another with watered wine which the snow light shone through in ruby tones. It was so cold, in spite of the French stove they had fuelled with coal, that they soon retreated to bed again for part of the afternoon, and then it was time to go to the lodgings of the American, Vernon Greenbank. He had laid on a great feast for everyone, with a cook in his employ to make a splendid roast goose dinner and provide everything needed for the generous table. It was a very convivial gathering and one at which, it being Christmas, the artists refrained from the rivalry and squabbling which their party sessions could sometimes descend into.

By the new year, Jane's French had begun to improve quickly, although some of their group increasingly spoke English, partly for the benefit of those of them for whom it was the first language, and partly because they wished to learn it. With them, Jane began some of her first steps into teaching English to others, soon mastering enough, along with better French of her own, for Albert to suggest she advertised lessons. They were not living in luxury, far from it, but they were extravagant spenders when out and, as Albert said, 'the old man's allowance falls a bit short by the end of the last cheque', although he had no qualms about asking for more from that quarter if he needed to.

Through word of mouth, Jane began to garner some pupils and feel she had a role of her own too. Even if, apart from modelling for Albert, it was not an artistic one. As they grew more familiar, some of the other artists asked Jane to sit for them too (because again it saved paying a woman to model if you had someone to do it for free from within your own circle). Already disinhibited by posing for Albert, although she drew the line at full nudity with them, she began to enjoy it. Albert himself made no objections because, after all, he was taking portraits of their own mistresses too. Besides, he had the assurance that she remained clothed while doing so. When they were out and about, Albert sometimes bought souvenir trinkets. They were not all for his family, for a certain little smile played over his lips when he wrapped them carefully in tissue paper and laid them aside to be taken home eventually.

"Who is that for?" Jane asked, as he purchased a delicate silver anklet she could picture all too clearly around Sarah's slender leg, which she had seen revealed in the photograph of Hannah washing Sarah's arrogantly poised foot.

Albert glanced round at her from tucking the small gift carefully into a pocket of his waistcoat and said, "For the people I left behind."

"Your *mill* women, you mean!" she flashed out.

"Hannah and Sarah, your friends at the Clarion Club," he returned coolly. "Who once showed you more than kindness, I believe." Jane flushed deeply, with shame at herself for her continuing resentment and shame, too, that Albert knew Hannah had tended her. He had never mentioned it previously. "Be careful, Jane," he added. "Your green eye is showing and at a time when they, and not you, are the ones alone!"

"But you will go back to them, won't you?" she could not prevent herself from saying, that sullenness he so disliked distorting her face and mouth.

Albert looked at her for a moment and shook his head slightly, as if a person disappointed once again. "You are proof yourself that I do not abandon people, Jane. Are you not?"

She looked down, biting her lip and unable to reply,

the ready tears threatening because she had spoiled the moment instead of affecting not to notice it when the gift was put away.

"You cannot expect me to pretend I do not know!" she burst out hotly, unable to stop herself.

"When have I ever expected you to do that?" he retorted and he walked away from her into the crowds from the little booth on the city bridge he had made his purchase from, leaving her to walk on or take an omnibus back to Montmartre as she chose.

It was not like him to be so ungentlemanly, however provoked, as to desert her on the open street and so she knew how irked he must be. When would she learn to hold her tongue, she asked herself? Albert was not at the apartment when she returned and she soon made a tour of the bistros, bars and cafés they frequented, fretting for forgiveness but hating feeling in the wrong at the same time because she knew there was injustice in the whole situation. She found him in none of them, only Wolf in one place, sipping a beer in contemplative silence in a corner spot. He was watching the street scene in the reflection of a mirror above the bar and studying the different play of light and perspective it gave, as he explained when he had stood up politely and asked her to join him.

"Have you seen Albert?" she asked at once.

"No. You are not together today?"

"We were but I lost him in the city and, well, we had a misunderstanding..."

"I see," he answered, studying her in his serious way. "Jane, have you considered, that this might not make you happy, being with a young man such as Albert is?"

"Oh!" she dismissed irritably. "Everyone tells me this!"

"Then there must be something in it. Something

everyone sees in *you*, perhaps."

He spoke quietly, gently, without any judgement in his tone, so that she apologised for being abrupt but was restless still to be off and find Albert.

"I must find him to make my peace."

"As a man myself, I advise you not to do it. Let him wait. As a supplicant you will be taken completely for granted, if you are not already. I apologise if I intrude further, but I believe you are a clergyman's daughter and I am a pastor's son. I know how such daughters are raised. I have sisters. Be dutiful, be subservient, do as the men in your life tell you. From father to brother to husband to lover."

"I don't do that!" she exclaimed, raising her look proudly. "I am here alone with him, on my own terms."

"No, Jane. You are here on his terms," Wolf answered. "There is no point in deluding yourself about that."

Everybody, including herself and Albert, used that phrase, 'terms', about their relationship, Jane thought, and yet there was no contract, either formal or informal, between them. Jane looked aside and, out of nowhere, remembered Miss Tordoff's long-forgotten offer and the card secreted in her reticule. The ghost of a smile crossed her lips, enigmatically attractive, so that Lukas Wolf looked at her with a questioning smile of his own, wondering what she was thinking of.

"Thank you, Wolf. I have a place to go if I decide not to remain on Albert's terms, as you put it. Besides, Albert himself has suggested I may wish to stay supporting myself here if I choose to."

"Hmmm. And why is that, I wonder? So he can please himself too, I expect. I may mix with all the artists here but I don't agree with everything they do. You can't create a paradise without consequences to people in *this* world."

In that, Jane had to agree with him and she stayed quietly by for a while as he explained more about what he thought he wished to capture in his painting from the scene outside, instead of chasing further after Albert that morning. Wolf even persuaded her, rather than going to wait alone in the apartment for Albert to come back, to go to his own studio to look at the works he had done most recently and give her opinion on them. She enjoyed having her view sought and gave the paintings serious consideration. When he asked if she would sit for him for a head and shoulders portrait, she agreed to it.

"That expression you had in the café for a moment when you smiled to yourself thinking of some private knowledge – I would like to capture it…"

"I don't know what expression you mean," said Jane, made shy by being noticed in this way.

"Ah, but I do," said Wolf. "Let me take a charcoal sketch now and I will show you."

He placed her by the window and she kept very still, as she knew how to do, her head turned as he had wanted. When he had finished the drawing he showed her a young woman whose face was alive with intelligent warmth and lit by a slight smile.

"Is that really how I looked?" she marvelled.

"It is. And I will paint you so that it shows your inner life," he promised. "There is more to your character than to Albert's, Jane, if you did but know it," he told her. "I will show it to you and when you see it, it might help you to decide what you want."

"Albert is what I want," she told him firmly, so that he laughed quietly.

"Well, we shall see," he said.

"And what about you, Wolf? What do you want? Will you go to England to try the new artists' community with Albert?"

"No, Jane. I have my studio here in Paris and I prefer to work alone than as part of any movement. Life is exciting enough for me here. Did you know that in Paris this year, a tornado sprang up right in the middle of the city? At least seventy people were killed or hurt, but it never touched Montmartre. Here, we did not so much as have our hats blown off. Such a thing was never known. Have you tornadoes in Halifax?"

"No! But I don't believe you, Wolf. People always think they can tell me such stories!"

"Well, in this case it is quite true. Ask anyone." He shrugged. "Now, Jane, if you can, come back later today, while the light is still good in here in the afternoon."

Jane left to go back to the apartment and felt no embarrassment because Wolf had not spoken in any way other than his usual matter-of-fact one. She had never seen him flirt the way all the others did, serious in demeanour where they were flamboyant. There was a certain dignity about Wolf's commitment to his art, even as he smiled indulgently at the antics of his friends. When she went back to the apartment, Albert was there, sorting through his photographic plates in a box. Looking up, he asked her where she had been.

Making no reference to their earlier disagreement and pleased not to have been found waiting at home till he saw fit to return himself, she said, "I met Lukas Wolf and he asked me to sit for him. He made some very good charcoal sketches to begin a portrait."

"Did he indeed?" said Albert, sounding surprised.

"Yes. I am going back to him later in the afternoon today so he can continue sketching."

"Are you? Oh. All right," said Albert and, being hoist by his own petard, could not himself bring the subject round to earlier on, so as to enjoy an abject Jane being drawn back into his forgiving arms, as usually happened.

This was something which, Jane realised with some pleasure, rather threw him. Wolf was right, Albert should not take her devotion for granted! They went out for luncheon without any more being said about it and then Jane went to Lukas Wolf's studio, leaving Albert to his own devices for the rest of the day. Albert seemed a little put out to find that he was not deciding on what *he* was doing first.

Lukas Wolf's painting, when he had done it, was full of light in white oils, with greys folding in the background like shadowed velvet. Jane's skin was almost translucent, the expression Wolf sought to capture delicately rendered. Her hair was coiled above a reflective, open gaze looking directly at the viewer, with a hint of a smile at some private thought.

Albert said dismissively, "Hah! the *Mona Lisa* by Renoir," when he saw it.

There was an echo of both in Wolf's rendition and not by accident, as the artist himself pointed out, clearly annoying Albert by being delighted with the success of his intended effect rather than wounded by the slight that his work was imitative. The artists (amongst whom Albert counted himself) were not given to easy praise of one another's work, especially if they saw it as any kind of challenge to their own talents. They called this honest criticism but it was always rather more nuanced than that.

"Ah, so you do see it, Albert?" Wolf answered happily. "That is what I saw in Jane's face one day when we met in the café. She had come in alone, you know, from the city, and I happened to be there. We talked a little and something Jane thought of made her smile like that."

"What was it?" asked Albert, his reaction further tinged by jealousy that Wolf had seen some magic in Jane as muse that he had missed in his own photographs of her.

"I do not know. She did not say and I never asked her," said Wolf.

Albert relaxed at this and turned a complacent eye upon his lover.

"I know what day that was, I think," he commented.

"The day perhaps, yes, Albert, but not the thought," answered Jane.

"Mysterious girl!" he said, smiling, but they all knew he believed her inner thoughts must have been of him and she did not disabuse him of it.

When the others moved on from this latest exhibit, saying it was time for a glass of something before supper somewhere, Lukas Wolf said, "So, Jane – you see yourself now?"

"I do, Wolf," she agreed. "And I thank you for it."

"I will show this painting and if I do not sell it, if you make your mind up to leave, for that was in your head I believe, I will give it to you one day."

"Thank you. If that day ever comes, Wolf," said Jane, but already her eyes trailed after Albert knowing that, flattered again, he would be desirous of her after supper tonight. Following her look, Wolf said no more of her leaving just then.

"Did you ask about the tornado?" he said, changing the subject.

"I did."

"And I told you the truth?"

"Yes."

"I am not a joking man, Jane. I meant all I said that day. Look at your picture again before we go and remember what that was."

Jane looked and did remember, as she heard Albert laughing carelessly at some witticism of Guillaume's. Her picture seemed forgotten already, nor did Albert look back to see if she followed.

"You see?" said Wolf. "If I were you, I would not leave him thinking it was he who put that secret smile on your lips. You did not have Albert in your thoughts then, did you?"

"No," Jane agreed. "We were talking differently then."

"We were," agreed Lukas Wolf. "Good. Then let us go to supper with that in in mind."

Locking the door behind them, Wolf offered Jane his arm and she took it to follow the chattering group surrounding Albert as they continued on down the street. Something happened, however, not very long after this, to change things and to prove Wolf right when he had said you could not create a paradise in this world without consequences. There came a day when Milo did not appear as expected, then several days. Albert, returning after going to ask after him and his whereabouts, abruptly decided it was time for them to go to Venice. Albert looked anxious when he told Jane this.

"I am very happy to travel there but what has happened, Albert?"

"Milo must take the cure," Albert said. "He has been too careless in Paris, or elsewhere."

"The cure?"

"Mercury." He shuddered. "Thank heavens you are chaste to me, Jane. That is one thing your being so in love has saved me from. I wondered if some of these handsome fellows here might not have tempted you a little."

"Never," she averred.

"I know – I had hoped to give you a little more taste of freedom but it is as well you did not attempt it."

"And – and you, Albert?" she asked wonderingly, not at all sure what he meant, although surely he referred to sexual matters.

“Whatever you may think, or I may have let you believe because you cling so, I know enough to avoid such easy temptations and I choose my lovers with care”

“Your lovers…” she repeated, the plural trailing painfully off her tongue.

“You are my lover in Paris, Jane,” he said. “Only you.”

“And yet, you are anxious that something may be amiss?” she pursued, puzzled as to what exactly.

“Not at all but it has shaken me a little, I admit, Jane. It is a dreadful prospect if the cure does not take for Milo. I have grown fond of the foolish fellow, of them all, but they may not have kept their magic circle intact between them, or done so too late.”

“And – you have done so, Albert?”

“I have,” he assured her. “This disease, it – it comes about from reckless congress, Jane. You need have no fears for yourself.”

Jane asked no more because she found the whole subject distastefully disturbing and the word ‘syphilis’ was never mentioned between them. In less than two days, they were packed and gone again. That whole demanding world which had consumed Albert’s time there was shaken off with such ease that Jane wondered why he had thrown himself so much into it when he could have been alone tasting delights with her instead. She knew better now, though, than to say it. Besides, there were friends made, in Wolf and even among those colourful parakeets of women, whom she too would miss.

After the busy intimacy which had been Paris – a whirligig of bright dresses in garish lighting by night, crowded streets, the apartment so uncomfortably close across the way, the people they endlessly met and talked to – the cool lagoons of springtime Venice were a great contrast. There was a dreamlike quality to the shabby palaces by the water, a different light over the islands and in the church-filled plazas, an enigmatic history to the bridges arching tightly over dark waterways between buildings. Venice was quieter by night too, less uproarious altogether than Paris had been.

They were thrown together much more by day and night in discovering this extraordinary place. As a result, their relationship entered a new phase of relying on each other's company without the relief of that of others after intervals alone together. There were languorous nights, certainly, and days of wonderment in exploring the treasures of Venice, enjoying the romantic novelty of travelling in gondolas instead of busy horse-drawn omnibuses on crowded streets. But sometimes, too, for the first time, there was the boredom of a couple who lacked affinity, something which, being mostly apart before Paris, or when there in the company of others, had always been concealed. Albert began speaking of inviting some of the Paris crowd and when they were out he cast about among fellow tourists for new acquaintances.

Then Jane would think of one of the days she had spent in Wolf's studio being painted for her portrait and a conversation they had had when she had asked, "What did you mean, Wolf, when you said there was more in my character than Albert's? I do nothing but accompany him and sit for people, when he is the photographer, the dreamer of a new art movement in our home town."

"I meant that you have a strong passion for life, but it is turned in and not out. You have confined it to love alone."

"Surely that is the essence of life and all that it should be about? As an artist you must feel that, Wolf?"

"Not only that. And it is a miserable thing to attach all your feeling to one capricious individual."

"Capricious? Is that how you see Albert?"

"He is a sensation-seeker, Jane, and so, of course he is. How much have you taken in of Paris when your every waking thought is about him? Free your mind to the beauties of Venice and Rome when you reach them, I beg of you. It will enrich the abilities in you. Jane. You are a natural studier and there is much to learn of art, culture, nations and history."

"A studier!" she exclaimed.

"Yes, but you make Albert your single subject. And Albert – Albert needs an audience and company, ladies to flirt with and be admired by as a young man. Do you deny it?"

"No."

"I wonder, when you are quite alone together for a while, just how interesting you will continue to find him? As a man, I mean, and not as a lover? Forgive my candour but you asked me a question and I always make an honest answer where I feel one is deserved."

"Albert is wonderful company!" Jane had loyally protested. "And we are in no need of any other when we are together!"

Wolf had said no more, continuing his brush strokes as he seemed to look through her rather than at her, perfecting his painting with concentrated skill. Wolf did not waste his breath, any more than he held back from speaking the truth as he saw it when asked what he thought, and Jane was flattered rather than offended at the time. She did not believe he would think so well of her, though, if he knew how her jealousy had brought her close to poisoning her rivals and so near to her own death. And yet, Wolf had spoken of her love being turned inward, so that he saw something of it, that dark, inverted side of her love for Albert, one which she did not want to remember now.

Here in Venice, she did find her interest widening out

from Albert himself because she had the security of his company already. She absorbed all she could in their tours of magnificent buildings such as the Basilica, St Mark's and the palaces of Doges. Her spirit, which had been like a clenched muscle under strain, began to relax and breathe in inspiration of its own. They attended musical evenings with plangent quartets playing and this gave her a new, deep pleasure, whereas Albert, attending them as somewhere to dress up and look for new society among the audiences, did not especially enjoy the music itself.

One day, they were in a gondola together crossing the lagoon to see one of the smaller islands. They had eaten a platter of tiny baby octopus, a local delicacy, and after lunch decided to go to the island, one they had not seen. They had reached the more open water, full of other gondolas gliding through, the colourful uniforms of the gondoliers bright in the sunny haze over the water, when they were hailed from behind. Jane was facing Albert, who could see who it was approaching. An English voice was calling, "Albert! Albert Dewhirst!" in ringing, mellifluous tones.

"Noel Ogden!" Albert, looking delighted, called back. "And Sylvia Rastrick, looking as beautiful as ever!"

"Rastrick no longer!" boomed Noel. "Sylvia is Mrs Noel Ogden now!"

Jane stiffened.

"What shall I do?" she murmured to Albert. "I shall be recognised too!"

"Let me think," said Albert. "Stay turned to me for the present. We will decide whether or not to be open about your being with me in due course."

Jane bowed forward under the parasol protecting her face and Albert shouted, "Tell me which is your hotel and I will call upon you when my passenger and I have returned from our trip."

"Certainly!" called Noel, as their gondola approached closer under his direction. "We are just returning from our own first sightseeing on the lagoon. We are in the Baglioni Hotel Luna!" he called across, as they came briefly parallel.

Jane, her head lowered, was now a side view and she was aware of Sylvia, a gossamer figure against the light, in a white dress and with a white hat, tied with gauze ribbon, shading her eyes. As their gondola departed, she heard Sylvia say, her voice carrying quite clearly across the quiet water, "Noel, who is that lady with Albert?"

"Some Venetian beauty he has met, I don't doubt," returned Noel as they floated off. Albert and Jane looked at one another, laughing because Noel did not seem to have recognised her any more than Sylvia had done.

"Well, that is our peace and quiet over for now!" Albert declared. "Noel and Sylvia have arrived on their honeymoon."

Jane smiled at him wistfully.

"Well, I dare say you are glad of it, Albert," she said. "I am quite happy alone with you but I know that *you* are eager for some lively company."

"Jane, you are quite lively enough for me," he returned gallantly. "But let us take it carefully so news does not get back to your father that you are in my company, and with Miss Tordoff nowhere to be seen! You have plenty of books to study now if you must hide in our room. And how quickly you have picked up doing that in French and Italian too!"

"Oh, thank you!" said Jane, pleased to be praised for a facility she had discovered while abroad, her once reasonably proficient schoolgirl French having developed swiftly.

She had taken the opportunity as well to begin to learn

Italian from some of those living in Montmartre, in preparation for travelling to Venice and Rome. Her education had always born in mind that a clergyman's daughter might one day need to turn to governessing, and training in learning lists of vocabulary was standing her in good stead. In truth, a natural talent for picking up a spoken language in its own country had surprised her and given her some of the confidence Wolf had suggested she should allow herself to build up.

"I will tell him all about the artists I have met and will persuade to join us at Ogden Towers," Albert said, brightening up completely at the prospect.

"All men," said Jane. "And yet there were women artists in Montmartre too."

"There were, I suppose, but they were not of our party," said Albert.

"No – you were all so busy vying to be the best of the new that you did not acknowledge them, since they were not dancers or sitters for your own portraits."

"*You* met them, Jane?"

"I noticed them. That is not quite the same."

"No. I suppose not," agreed Albert absently. "We will have people to go dancing with now, Jane, and take supper together."

"Yes," she agreed. "Or at least, you will, Albert."

It occurred to Jane to wonder if Albert had known exactly when Noel and Sylvia were due to arrive and had timed their own stay to coincide with it, concluding that of course he would have done, as one of Noel's oldest friends. Albert sent correspondence to England too and received letters in return. He came back in due course from Noel and Sylvia's hotel lively with stories of the wedding day and of how, since he had been in Venice a short while already, they had appointed him their tourist guide.

“It is only for a week or so, Jane, then they travel on to Lisbon. Since they are on their honeymoon I am sure that they will not require my constant company.”

But Jane found herself their shadow, following unseen as Albert, Noel and Sylvia wandered around Venice and seeing how, when they paused for refreshments at a table somewhere, Sylvia’s face turned to Albert’s like a flower towards the sun. Noel struck up acquaintance with other travellers, animated with them, laughing with parties of young men they encountered en route in the city and waterways. He was as exuberant as ever, and quite as careless, while his wife hovered, exquisite as a hummingbird, on Albert’s arm.

One night, before the newly weds departed for their next destination, there was a public masked ball, something very popular in Venice, which they attended with Albert. Jane flitted in after them, her face disguised by a mask she had bought that very morning, determined on pursuing them. She had no difficulty in tracking Albert and Sylvia among the crowds, while Noel, hidden behind a gold foil Zeus mask, strode about just like a god himself, attracting attention as he loved to do.

Jane held back and got closer at the same time, close enough to see Albert and Sylvia embrace in the folds of a curtained window as once Jane herself had done with him, and to hear him say, “Now you know what married love should be, Sylvia”, and close enough too to hear Sylvia’s reply.

“My husband does not offer it as you do, Albert – only a shadow of it.”

“He cannot help how he is made, Sylvia, no more than we can help ourselves how *we* are made. You are too beautiful to waste yourself upon it. Did I not tell you so once?”

“No, you said why choose Noel when I could choose

you. The reasons I did so remain."

Albert laughed quietly. Her answer pleased him, suggesting that as she was not in love with him an intrigue might continue, without risk to either and to their mutual pleasure, as Jane bitterly perceived from his next words.

"I will be near to you at Ogden Towers, Sylvia, and even more so when the artists come. Noel might not be complaisant of a lover at home and we will have to be discreet. Unspoken understanding is one thing but display another."

"Yes," she agreed, looking flirtatious and intimate. "Oh, I know they will come, Albert. Noel longs to be a grand patron with his own circle of artists and craftsmen on his grounds."

"They will indeed, and it will benefit a whole new movement of modern work, Sylvia."

Jane had heard enough, burning up in the shadows so much that she expected to catch fire there and then in a spontaneous combustion of jealous despair and, yes, jaded disappointment too. She slipped away, for she would not lower herself to confront them and as she did so she faced her reality, that living in the Ogden Towers artists' group would be, for her, an impossibility. Sylvia would be there and clearly she and Albert had every intention of continuing their affair. Hannah and Sarah would not be far away, either. There would be others. Albert had never dissembled about his belief in free love and Jane's early hopes that being alone together would change his mind about that had not been realised. He had remained chaste to her in Paris for safety's sake as, in truth, she had realised at the time he spoke to her of Milo's plight. Angry and hurt, she acted now on the spur of the moment.

Jane remembered what Wolf had said about her

leaving, what Miss Tordoff had said about going to her and, without giving herself any more time to think about it, she dashed off a letter to Miss Tordoff. She addressed it from the card she had kept secreted and, while still alone, packed her trunk. In the early morning, Albert slept on unawares, not having come in until dawn had broken. She went out to make her arrangements, had her trunk collected and was on the boat away from Venice to get on the railway again before he had even arisen.

When he did so, it would be to an unexplained absence. Jane had left him no letter, only the mask which she had worn to the ball, so he would know that she had been there and what she must have overheard. She wanted to tantalise him, punish him, make him want her back and to escape away from the distress all at the same time. Jane would go to Miss Tordoff first and after that she would return to her father. As if some delusion had fallen away, she realised the impossibility of leaving her father completely and felt what a cruelty it would have been to abandon him through a deception. No. She would go home and give herself time to plan her own future while Albert remained abroad.

In the heat of the moment, she found she had the strength to go through with it. As she travelled and regret, of course, soon crept in, she still believed she had done the right thing. She had some money from her lessons and she would earn more if necessary. If Miss Tordoff would be kind enough to shelter her in secret for a while, she could make her own way home, she told herself.

Chapter Fourteen

Prior to all these events abroad, in Halifax the proud day had finally arrived for the topping out ceremony of the new chimney for Stanger's Mill. Ellen had not seen the final stages of construction and she was excited to see it now. A crowd of workers and builders were already assembled, along with invited businessmen and town dignitaries, the lucky elite who would go back to Heatherfield for a celebration luncheon with the owners. The builders had been fortunate in a quiet, cold spell that did not have ice and snow leaching the salts out of the mortar to stain the brickwork, or heavy rains to prevent it drying. The gods had been propitious with the weather for building work and it was hoped this was a good omen for this phoenix, literally risen from old ashes. They had managed to get the project finished, as hoped, before Christmas. The topping out ceremony was the final symbolic moment before the mill reopened with all its new machines installed. It was fine but overcast, so that everyone could look up at the plank platform around the pinnacle without being dazzled.

Peter, used to climbing as a fireman, had been given the job of clambering up the flimsy looking workmen's ladders to that high platform to do the honours. John's hands were not strong enough any more for such work and he had stood down from the volunteer fire service too. Just now he was beside Leonard, who was waiting to give the signal from below. Peter's figure looked very vulnerable climbing higher and higher up the enormous chimney, so that the crowd was in hushed suspense in case he fell, sure-footed as he seemed. Finally at the top, he raised his arm to show he was ready with the trowel in his hand and Leonard fired a single shot into the air from a pistol to announce the moment. The last brick laid,

Peter raised his arm again and John ran a flag up the flagpole which would fly on the main building itself. It sported the name *Stanger's New Mill* on its banner. The crowd applauded and cheered.

The tall chimney was banded with yellow, red and black bricks rather than being finished with stone like the rest of the building, so that it would stand out and be recognised, a brand for Stanger's New Mill. Its top tiers of arched windows were pointed up with decorative coloured tiles, lending it the Italianate grandeur which John and Peter had envisaged for it, like the ones Peter had seen in Lancashire. It was, in its own right, a beautiful thing. Leonard explained to the watching audience that it was to be regularly cleaned to maintain it from soot damage destroying its splendour, designed to be visible from all surrounding hillsides. Peter, after descending, was so elated that he forgot all about feeling awkward with Ellen and she with him.

"See that?" he exclaimed. "Nah then. Where's your Wainhouse Tower in comparison wi' *that*?"

"Nowhere to be seen!" Ellen loyally replied, although she did not really think that the magnificent folly had been outranked. "The Dean Clough Mills' chimney is nothing to it either, Peter. Just a great plain thing with a crown on its top!"

"Aye, that's right!" he said gleefully, clapping John on the back in delight and shaking Len's hand vigorously. Turning to Ellen again, he said more quietly, "And I thank you for the books, Ellen", so that she was happy to know Carrie had managed to give them to him.

Carrie's father had been brought down in his bath chair to see the ceremony. The sight of him, their respected employer for years, brought applause from the crowd of mill workers. It seemed to please him, his craggy face (all nose, chin and crevassed cheeks now) lifted in an answering smile.

He regarded the new edifice with some wonderment and said in his old, caustic way, "Well, Leonard, I hope we can cut our cloth to suit the outlay, my lad, once we've made some worsted for it, that is!" But then he added, approvingly, "It's a fine new mill you've made between you and I've high hopes of the new machines."

"They'll not have seen t' like of that round 'ere Mr Stanger, sir," said Peter.

"No," said Mr Stanger. "And they're not likely to miss it either, are they?"

"I hope not, sir" said Len. "The grander the building, the better the firm's standing is. When Peter showed me those Whitworth Street cotton warehouses in Manchester, built like mansions, I grasped entirely what he and John Henderson here had a vision for."

"I think it's quite beautiful, Father," said Carrie, looking up at the chimney again. "A remarkable achievement, John and Peter. I congratulate you on it, and Len above all for having the courage to persuade us both into the venture. Isn't that right, Father?"

Leonard glowed, very happy to receive her praise, giving her a beaming smile of great affection. Then he turned to speak loudly to the crowd.

"You'll be walking in there on Monday morning, everybody who is on our workforce, and a Christmas bonus with our first wages to you will be in all your pay packets – without fear or favour!" he added with a humorous rhetorical flourish.

Another loud cheer and laughter went up at this and Peter said, "Without fear or favour! You cheeky beggar – that's one of mine, that is", in a joshing tone.

"Yes, it is," agreed Len, "When you're on your soap box about injury compensation and suchlike."

"Aye, well, I'll let you laugh at me today," conceded

Peter. “But I’m right and you know it.”

Len laughed back, quite unoffended as employer, since they were on partly informal terms now after working together so closely as young men, and also because this was a special occasion in which the three of them had triumphed.

“Let us round up our guests for the table and get some investors interested, not to mention drumming up a few orders,” he said.

Carrie and Leonard moved off among the more influential of their audience and, as the crowd broke up, those invited made to return to Heatherfield for an informal celebration of the opening. Peter was caught in a group of men wanting to shake the hand of their new manager before they started work on Monday. He walked aside among a cheerful crowd of well-wishers hoping for their mutual success in Stanger’s New Mill.

“John, well done,” said Ellen to him. “What a wonderful design you have made and carried out.”

“Inspired by Peter’s ideas,” he tempered her praise with.

“Nobody can draw like you and Cyril,” she said. “You could be an architect as well as a stonemason and sculptor, John!”

“And maybe I’ll need to be. I can use a pencil where I haven’t the strength always for carving now.”

Ellen turned her face aside a moment, for of course the opening of the new mill and seeing Peter climb the chimney could only recall the fall of the old, with Peter and John stranded so perilously on the burning, collapsing structure.

“Do you find it hard, John?” she asked, full of sympathy.

“I do,” he answered honestly. “Very hard. I feel the failing of my old skills that I took so much for granted.

Not that I hadn't worked hard to get them. I miss being a fireman too. The excitement of it, the camaraderie, the doing something *grand* to help, you know. Not that Libby isn't pleased about that. 'I don't want my future husband tramping soot everywhere,' she says. 'I'm a maid, so I know all about cleaning floors'." He smiled. "She's not one to let me feel sorry for myself. I'm a very happy man in my own life, Ellen, and I expect my hands will improve more. Doctor didn't think I'd use them again at all. And I can and do. It took a long time but I finished that angel monument, didn't I? Sculpture will come back to me. And I'm getting wed in two week. You'll be there?"

"I will, of course I will!" she said. "Libby is bound to look lovely as a bride."

"Aye, she's made that way," John answered, as if to say, that was just Libby's luck in life and nothing to boast about.

"So she is," said Ellen, laughing and thinking how typically local that deprecating dry humour was.

She could not speak much with either John or Peter again as her mother and father were, naturally, present at the ceremony among the notables and came to toast Stanger's New Mill at the luncheon.

Noel and Sylvia arrived fashionably late to that after some wedding-related appointment of their own, full of apologies, as Noel put it, "That I missed you playing bricklayer, Leonard."

His poetic licence went uncorrected, for Peter and John, being among the workforce, were not at the Heatherfield luncheon for dignitaries and the mill-owning class. If they had been, Peter for one, Ellen thought, would certainly have put him right. Her parents had been busy mingling with those who should be impressed. If they had noticed Ellen speaking to Len's architect and new manager for a moment, it was not remarkable in the circumstances of the topping out ceremony occasion and so nothing was said about it.

***

John and Libby's wedding took place in one of the many chapels dotting the hillsides. They dated from the Wesleyan preachers' zealous heyday earlier in the century. These were bare, minimal places of worship, stranded amongst the winds blustering down from the tops and where sermons on temperance and restraint blew equally strongly over the heads of the congregation below. Seeing Libby and John together in such an austere setting, both looking the epitome of earthly vigour, made Ellen fancy that some puritanical cleric might call out against them for looking so indecently glad to be alive. None did and their wedding vows were quietly and quickly made, with rice showered over them for luck when they came out again. They made a handsome couple whom everyone was happy to toast at the Speckled Hen inn, hosting their wedding breakfast later on. Peter and Cyril were there. Or at least, Cyril had been at the church but Ellen could not see him at the inn. Eustace and Hannah were here from the old crowd too, although Sarah was absent. Leonard and Carrie had come with Ellen to wish the designer of Stanger's New Mill all the best, and had quietly financed this small wedding feast to launch John and Libby in their new lives together. The other guests were John and Libby's families.

Ellen saw that Eustace and Hannah seemed to have arrived almost as a courting couple themselves. Speaking to them, she learned that Hannah had been persuaded to do some work in the orphanage school. Ellen herself had not been going of late. She had not got around to it after her long visit to Heatherfield, although she kept intending to. Ellen felt there was more to this new pairing between Eustace and Hannah than that, however, and being curious she drew Hannah to one side.

"Have you and Eustace become particular friends, Hannah?" she asked.

"We 'ave that. He's a good man to be beside," confirmed Hannah, with a significant nod.

"Then, are you are considering a future together, Hannah, like Libby and John?" ventured Ellen.

Hannah nodded again.

"You are surprised *he* would," she stated cannily.

"I, I don't truly know. Does he know – what of Albert?"

"Eustace knows. Of course he does. Same as you do. Any road, Albert's been away and will be for months to come…" (So who knew what might happen with him when he returned, was the inference.)

"I heard that he had gone travelling," said Ellen, who had been surprised to learn of it from Noel when she came home from Heatherfield.

"Aye – a 'Grand Tour' 'e called it, for art, courtesy of his father," said Hannah disparagingly. "Reckon 'e's being got ready, me and Sarah do."

Which meant that she was right in thinking Hannah and Sarah were not sure where they might stand in his life after he came back, Ellen supposed, depending on what plans were made next as Albert reached his majority in the next year or so.

"A 'Grand Tour'!" she scoffed in return at this aristocratic-sounding pretension, which was not at all Clarion Club like.

Ellen felt she understood more now why Hannah might be responding to Eustace's attentions and she could see, knowing him better herself these days, that Eustace might not judge Hannah for her situation, for all that he seemed so moral in his own conduct. Hannah would be a good companion for Eustace too, Ellen thought, calm and capable as she was. She would certainly not be challenged by the kind of children he taught, either, having been a workhouse girl herself once.

"Did you know that poor Jane Ellison has lately gone abroad too, as a companion to a lady?" she asked after a moment, as it came to mind again in present company (Jane was now always 'poor Jane Ellison' in Ellen's mind).

"Aye, I heard," replied Hannah. She shook her head, knowing what Ellen alluded to. "For t' best, mebbe."

Ellen thought they had spoken discreetly but Eustace had caught Albert's name and part of their conversation.

"Albert Dewhirst has no moral compass! A young man who presses young women into things they ought not to be persuaded into!" he exclaimed, for his ire on Jane's behalf was still easily raised, not to mention how he must feel about Hannah being one half of Albert's two mistresses.

"Why bring *him* up at John's wedding?" objected Peter, who was nearby, speaking in far too rough and ready a manner than was warranted.

He had never taken to Eustace particularly, in spite of the man's kindness in fetching the Clarion Club subscription money up to his mother and Stanley's when they were both in hospital. In fact, Peter had felt sorely shown up by that then and was still aggrieved about it now because Eustace had taken Ellen with him. She had met Peter's mother and seen the poor place where he lived without his being prepared for or agreeing to it! Peter, having been trained in the Methodist Sunday Schools as he learned to read and write, rarely drank and neither did Eustace, but this was a wedding, so they had both taken some drink. As bumpers were raised their voices were too, unawares. Eustace flushed, riled at once by Peter's taking him up in that way.

Inhibitions lowered, he burst out angrily, "And as for *you*, Peter Lumb! You are no better! Ellen is your loyal friend but you have influenced her to act against her better judgement with you. I *know* that you caused the mill fire at Stanger's Mill. Far from being the hero you claim to be!"

He spoke far more loudly than he had intended and voices fell silent in shock as Peter, without denying it, cried rather wildly in return, "Do not blame *Ellen*! No! The fault was all mine – Ellen did nothing, knew nowt!" He gazed at Ellen fiercely not to contradict him now that they were publicly accused. "It were *my* doing alone to set that fire. And I cannot bear the guilt of it to this day! My dearest friend dead after it, my other, that I'm best man to today, maimed! It weren't meant to catch like that! I've done my best and my damnedest to make amends for it 'aven't I? I've raised a new mill and John designed it wi' me, didn't he?"

"What?" cried Len, appalled by this outburst. "*You* committed arson, Peter? *You* of all people, who have stood by my side these many months? The one who raised the alarm about it? I can't believe it! And you admit it?"

But Peter, now the long-kept secret was out so unexpectedly, wasn't looking at his employer, he was looking at John. The bridegroom's stricken face showed that he was, for the very first time, having to believe that his best man today (Peter and not Cyril, as Ellen had been surprised to see) truly *was* the author of his misfortune. This Clarion Club comrade, fellow fireman and, latterly, close workmate, had been deliberately responsible for the fire that had disfigured those skilled hands with which he had hoped become a sculptor of renown one day.

"John!" Peter cried out to him in an anguished plea but it was Libby who responded.

"Peter Lumb! This is our wedding day. Mine and John's. *Our* day!"

"Then I'll leave you to it, and Stanger's New Mill to go to hell after the last one along of *me*!" shouted Peter in incoherent distress.

Pushing violently past people who stood amazed, he burst out of the Speckled Hen and ran away to his bicycle before anyone thought to follow. When they did, it was Len who said, "No, leave him! This is a celebration day. The rest can wait."

The celebration, though, was soon over now.

"Eustace, how *could* you?" wept Ellen, longing to go after Peter but knowing that it was useless to try.

"I'm sorry. I am. Truly," apologised Eustace. Aghast at what he had done, he cast aside the drink in his hand with horror. "I had no intention of revealing what I long suspected."

"You tried to implicate my *sister*?" exclaimed Len in disbelief, rounding on him and trying to console Ellen along with Carrie. "How dare you even think of it! Ellen – you are never to go to that school again or find yourself in this man's company! But come, we must not spoil the wedding. Carrie, let us take Ellen back to Heatherfield. John, you and Libby have our very best wishes for a happy future. Please enjoy the rest of your celebrations on your marriage day."

With that, their little party left and the rest of the revellers, John and Libby, together with their families and friends, did their best to rally and enjoy the food and drink laid ready for them. Eustace and Hannah left too, with Eustace offering his profuse apologies to anyone who would listen before being taken away, still slightly drunk, by Hannah, who was far better versed in dealing with such awkward situations than he was. Only Ellen, out of all those present, knew that what Eustace had said was true, but she could not give him the relief of admitting it without finding herself cast out of her family, as Peter had once said she would be. Her heart was very full, knowing that when it came to it, Peter had completely taken the blame. He had proved himself to her completely today but only in time for her to lose him, she feared.

Carrie persuaded Leonard to leave Ellen with her when they finally arrived back at Heatherfield, while he himself made straight for Peter's cottage to have it out with him, even though it was unlikely he would be there now. Ellen was distressed as well at being, if quite unintentionally, partly responsible for blighting the wedding breakfast.

"Libby will never forgive me for it!" she cried. "And, oh, Carrie, we were once very close, you know. We used to talk privately all the time at home and knew each other's secrets. Well, that is, Libby knew mine, such as they were. And poor John, knowing what happened now when Peter worked so hard to make up for what he did!"

Carrie looked at her with thoughtful solicitude.

"Ellen," she said quietly, "you did know, didn't you? I always felt there was something between you and Peter which was more than friendship or attraction. Oh, I know that was there, and I could see that on your side you both liked and drew back from it. And you half-spoke of that to me only recently. But there was always something else, something that held you to him in some way. Tell me the truth, Ellen. Did he confide in you?"

Ellen bowed her head, the impulse to tell all and reveal the full extent of her guilt dangerously close but then she remembered Peter's warning look at her. He had spoken truly when he said setting the fire had all been his plan and he had, as Eustace alleged, twisted her arm to do it. He had acknowledged that between them in his look at her before fleeing and she knew he meant to make amends for that part, now it had all come out, by keeping her, at least, safe. She prayed that he would get away before the forces of the law were sent to get him.

The thought of Peter hung, that all of his impatient, feeling and difficult nature could be snuffed out in one instant was incredible but all too likely to happen. Stiffening her resolve, she repressed the instinct to unburden herself. A confession from her now would not aid Peter, she told herself. She had best remain innocent and try to persuade Len not to have him pursued if she could. Raising her head, she denied it.

"He did not. But you are right about our attraction, Carrie. Peter – Peter asked me to marry him one day but I gave him a foolish answer and hesitated. Now it will all be too late. And now, now that it is, I know that I do love him. Whatever he did, Carrie, I didn't know about it. But I do know that it was some misguided ideal that led him to it. I *know* Peter!"

Carrie gave her a rather steady look and then softened.

"We have talked about his irregular temperament, Ellen. He is a hot-headed young man given to unconsidered impulses. I am sure setting that fire was one of them. I will not press your loyalty to him further but I will say this. If you only know you love him now that you think you cannot have him, question that feeling. It may not be founded on reality. And you know that, after this, it cannot *be* a reality."

"I do," agreed Ellen with another sob. "But, Carrie, he has worked so hard to make things right again! He cannot be punished after doing all that! Please help me to save him at least? He would be executed!"

"I will speak to Leonard. I do believe Peter regretted it

at once, given how hard he fought the blaze. I believe too that he did mean to redeem himself by rebuilding the mill and make what amends he could to John Henderson. I see now why he pressed to have John be employed with him to do it. I fear your brother, though, will see Lumb as a man who wormed his way in under false pretences. I will endeavour to persuade him not to have Peter chased down. But I cannot promise it. Len's professional pride and his personal trust will each be deeply wounded."

Ellen blushed, very aware of her own betrayal of Leonard and Carrie in keeping silent about her part in things, but Peter's self-sacrifice could not go in vain. He would never have spoken up if Eustace had not accused her too. That had been the spark that ignited the dangerous firework of his public confession. Eustace, that mild and conscientious man, for him of all people to burst out so! But then again, it was because his own principles were outraged that he had done it, Ellen knew. She thanked her sister-in-law, trying to be calmer, and was so by the time Len returned a short time later.

"There is no sign of Lumb. I will have a watch put on his cottage here and have the police visit his mother," he told them angrily.

"Len," petitioned Carrie. "Perhaps spare the mother that shame before all her neighbours? She is a poor widow, I believe?"

"Yes," confirmed Ellen. "I am sure taking trouble to her would be the last thing he would wish to do."

After a moment, Len nodded, conceding it would indeed be a cruelty to innocent parties. He was clearly shocked to the core, however, that the young man he had trusted, had worked alongside for months on such familiar terms, had set fire to the mill in the first place. He clearly felt played for a fool.

"Lumb has been thumbing his nose at all of us,

Carrie!"

"Len – let us not act too hastily. Think of what he said. It was never meant to end in that disastrous inferno. Think of what he has done since. He regretted it and felt the pain of what happened to his friends because of him. Now he has lost his friends, his position and his reputation, all in one blow. We have a brand new mill just opened. One as modern as ever you hoped to persuade my father to update his old one to. Why, without that fire and without Peter's ideas…Yes, it's true, Len, *Peter's* ideas, you would not have this shining, modern, very grand mill to call your own. And it *is* your own, Len," she urged him to remember.

Len paused in his angry pacing, his colour hectic at the thought that Peter had fled before he could be held in any way to account.

"And what about your poor father?" he said. "Was *he* not a victim too? The blow of that fire brought on his attack!"

"It hastened it," Carrie said. "Yes, it did. But the doctor has been quite plain with me that my father's condition is one of a gradual sinking. His collapse one day was inevitable. We should not add that to Lumb's crimes."

Ellen bowed her head in private shame again, thinking of the letter Peter had persuaded her to write to Mr Stanger. Fortunately, her brother was looking at his wife and not her. Now he spoke with an odd resentment.

"How reasonable you are," he frowned. "You always are. I *suppose* that is a good thing." But he did not sound as though he really thought it was.

"Len," cautioned Carrie gently. "We are not speaking of ourselves."

"I'm sorry," he said at once. "That was uncalled for. Well – let us not react as hastily as Lumb acted in the first place. We have our own reputation to maintain. Arson suggests a vendetta against the owners, which might spread vile rumours and thwart success with the new mill. Accidental fire is sheer bad luck and common enough. Our venture needs to begin with good fortune and not bad. *Why* did he do it?" he demanded helplessly.

"Peter once had radical views about how only action would force things to change. He told me so in the hospital," said Ellen, fudging the truth again. "I did not know what he meant, he seemed very confused then. Perhaps it was to do with those views, why he did it? He said he had a different vision now. And he brought it to you, Len. Didn't he? What happened changed Peter too, I think. What will become of the plans for the workforce?"

"We will honour them, of course. Contracts are drawn up. Why – I might invite John Henderson to manage them for me," said Len. "He was party to all those discussions and, in the light of those, he designed the mill as it is now. Many windows for daylight to work by and good ventilation for the lungs, space between machines for safe working."

"I think that is a capital idea, Len!" said Ellen, brightening. "He cannot work as he once did so successfully. But – John is a sculptor," she added doubtfully.

"These are all things we can talk about later," said Len, looking decisive. "No. No, I cannot let it rest entirely. Those at the wedding heard it all!"

"Perhaps, but if the owner does not act rashly in response it gains no credibility and then disaster need not gather momentum. Would you see him hung?" asked Carrie starkly.

"He deserves to be," answered Len after a pause, but less heatedly, so that Ellen had hopes that he would not set the full wrath of the law upon Peter's heels. "But I agree that he tried to make up for his criminal act, although he also did much to better his own condition through it! Perhaps he played a longer game than you think, Carrie."

"No, it's my belief he acted as an impetuous young man might do, without thinking of the full consequences to all. I think he has matured since then thanks to working under your direction, Len," Carrie said, flattering her husband's confidence in himself as leader and owner.

She could understand, even sympathise with Peter's violent sabotage to an extent, far more than Len or even Ellen could do, due to the more hard-line activists she knew who were fighting for women's suffrage in Manchester.

"Possibly," he conceded reluctantly. "I will have a watch kept for him though, and it is bound to get out that he has fled. Ellen – as I said, no more good works at the orphanage school for that fellow. Falsely accusing you in drink! Lumb at least defended you to give himself away like that! An arsonist! Ellen, do not tell Father, I beg you! I cannot have him doubt my credibility in business. Nor any of the folk who came to our opening day!"

"I think, Len, given that he has gone of his own accord, you will have to say to the workforce you regret his going but will move on with a new manager. Explain nothing but simply speak with authority as if it was an entirely personal decision of Peter's which concerns you not at all," said Carrie.

"I will make no public statements other than that," Len agreed. "Fortunately, since it was a small gathering held away from here, there were none at the wedding from the mill apart from Lumb, the groom and ourselves. I will speak to John but as for Lumb!" He breathed heavily, emotional again at mentioning Peter's name. "He ran away like the coward he must really be! If he shows his face, I *will* report him to the police and have him taken up directly. I cannot fail to do that, in all conscience!"

Carrie and Ellen were unable to move him from that course of action. He clearly felt his honour as a man had been completely undermined by what he saw as Peter's secret treachery in coming into his employ at all, and so there they had to leave it. Only Ellen knew that it was not cowardice but selfless courage that had taken Peter away from all he had just achieved, and what it must have cost him to do it. Back at home, Ellen hoped for some secret word by note or letter from Peter but none came. She waited through suspenseful days waiting to hear if he had been found and caught, but no word of that came either.

How changed everything was, she felt, from those early days in the summer! Even that strong alliance between Hannah and Sarah looked set to separate if Hannah *did* marry Eustace one day. She longed to see John and Libby, to speak to John, but her own conscience about the fire made her hang back from that. That, the risk of being questioned about Eustace's bizarre outburst and knowing she would be intruding on newly weds, kept her away from their new home.

Finally, she cycled down to the stonemasons' yard again, one bitter afternoon when solid skies threatened snow showers. But the ornate metal gates were locked, a great padlock and chain across them. The only occupants behind the ironwork were silent statues turning indifferent faces up to the wintry grey skies. Even Cyril was not there. He might still be living up at Ogden Towers while he worked on Noel's circle of memorial tablets in the garden, or perhaps he was out with John meeting the newly bereaved who wanted memorials of their own?

Ellen felt very lonely without them, and loneliest of all without Peter. Even when she had not seen him at

Heatherfield while she kept house for Len, she had known that he was busy nearby and, although estranged after his proposal by their mutual embarrassment, she had not felt separated from him. Now she felt that connection gone and it was a very sad loss to her indeed. She hardly ever went to Heatherfield now, where the sight of that grandiose chimney rising from the valley was such a reminder of Peter's triumph and joy, so soon to be snatched away from him. Nor did she go again to the Crossley and Porter Orphan Home School at the top of the Moor's gracious green space. She could neither face Eustace nor forgive him and believed she never would.

It was around the same time of Peter's disappearance that something happened which added to rumours as to why he had left the town among those who knew of it. Noel's habit of carrying large bank notes on his person (which plenty had remarked upon as just asking for trouble) was thought to be the cause. Coming away from his club in town in the dark, before he reached his carriage he was felled by an assailant and robbed of all the money. Briefly concussed, Noel had no memory of either incident or attacker, but somehow it became whispered that Peter, in need of funds to run away, had robbed the rich man he had met at the Clarion Club.

Rumours circulated, dark ones about the mill fire and that Peter Lumb, arsonist, had now turned murderous attacker. No official source, either Noel or newspaper, confirmed it, but mutterings reached Ellen's ears through the Clarion Club to distress her further. Poor Peter, she mourned, would he never be able to return? Part of her (an unworthy part she told herself) even wondered if he could have done it. Peter had an angry contempt towards Noel in general. Further, he harboured resentment that Noel was able to help Stanley's family due to his social and financial standing whereas Peter, due to his, was not.

Peter could flare up and lash out and he had an angry pride, that upside down sense of injustice she had seen go sour before. But no, he would never do that! Would he?

***

Christmas was celebrated at home and at Ogden Towers where Noel, fully recovered from the incident, held a ball for New Year's Eve. Leonard and Carrie were unable to come, both afflicted by heavy seasonal colds and remaining with Mr Stanger, who had been laid very low by the same. But Kenneth Butterworth and his mother were among the guests and Ellen danced with him several times during the evening, when he spoke again about the proposed visit to the Lake District in summertime. Ellen looked forward to it more than ever, she thought. It would help her to get away from home and her conflicted feelings there, where she missed Peter and felt more bereft by the day that he had sent no word to her. Perhaps he dared not but courage was one thing he never lacked and that look he had given her at the last had been a very speaking one between them. His continuing silence made her fear that some accident had happened to him, then that he might have despaired altogether, but this she could not believe, for the life force was very strong in Peter.

At the ball, Sylvia wore a gown of pale pink satin which warmed her complexion under the candelabra candles which scattered soft diamonds of light on the company's finery. Sylvia had a serene radiance about her, the poise of a confident beauty. Ellen was standing watching at the side, alone for a time while Kenneth attended to his mother with refreshments. Cyril Raynor appeared at Ellen's elbow, very elegant in a full evening dress suit, so that she barely recognised him.

"Cyril!" she greeted him with pleased surprise. "I am so glad to see you. I have had no chance to speak to you since that time at John's wedding. I have wanted to and to John too! Oh, but then – I saw you at the wedding, only not later on, at the Speckled Hen?"

"We had a falling out over him asking Peter Lumb to be best man instead of me. He felt obliged to, he said. By then I'd been up here working and he'd been at Stanger's – and we hadn't seen eye to eye about either of them things either."

"Oh – that is sad, Cyril. Are you friends again now?"

"Aye, of course. It were a foolish bit of jealousy on my part about not being best man. I went to their wedding in't church any road, didn't I? Just ducked the rest." He looked across at the dance floor where Sylvia twirled elegantly with Noel. "Look at your sister," Cyril said, in a tone like bitter aloes. "It won't be long for her now. Will it? Another wedding…"

His voice fell away a little as he mentioned it, jealousy still clearly in his mind.

"Yes," said Ellen, "but you will still be Noel's friend, Cyril. You are a guest here tonight, after all!"

"Perhaps," he said with a private, cynical smile. Changing the subject he said, "John's wedding – you meant what happened with Peter Lumb, of course. John was distraught when he told me. In fact, it was how we made up again."

"Yes? Oh, it was dreadful, Cyril! I never dreamed for a moment that *Eustace*…!"

"Eustace Horsfall was not the only one to guess the truth. *I* did on the very day itself but Stanley defended Peter to the hilt. What's more, Ellen – what is it?" he asked, as she looked taken aback, then realised he only meant the truth about Peter himself.

"Oh, nothing, only, you startled me by saying that."

"Well – it's not the only fire Peter's been involved in, is it? What about that flour mill, Bradbury's? I've heard his talk often enough, Ellen. He's a madman when he lets his temper take hold of his wits. Talks himself into going berserk, then does it. Tells himself it's *for* something but it's not really, is it? It's because he wants to do it. And then there was Noel getting knocked out and robbed when Peter left. I'm not saying it *were* 'im but who knows? He's got a violence in his soul, Peter Lumb has. That's why he looks goes looking for trouble."

"You wrong him!" protested Ellen.

Although she had perceived much the same herself previously, she had a far more rose-tinted view of Peter's volatility now that he had thrown himself to the wolves for her sake than previously, even if she *had* briefly wondered herself about his being Noel's attacker.

"Ah. Do I, though?" said Cyril darkly. He regarded her with that bright-eyed intuition of his which missed little. "And you, Ellen Rastrick, you've got romance in *your* soul. A dangerous beast. Trust me on that subject. I caution you to go steady. Stick with that respectable fellow, Butterworth, over there. He's a decent sort."

"Decent!" said Ellen, as though this were a very damning indictment of Kenneth's character indeed, even though, again, Cyril only spoke aloud what she had often pondered over to herself.

Cyril just smiled, then said, "Well, one good thing has come out of it. John has been asked to take Peter's place as manager at Stanger's. Did you know? He has taken it on to begin with but only until the venture is fully launched. In this winter weather his hands are too bad for working long as a mason. By summer, we hope to be here sometimes to take part in Noel's new artists' community. John believes he will sculpt again then as he dreamed of."

"I very much hope that he will!" said Ellen fervently, glad that Len had followed through the suggestion he had made to her and Carrie on John's wedding day of making

John manager in Peter's place.

"As do I," agreed Cyril. "John has great talent for it."

"So do you, Cyril!" she exclaimed.

"Not in the same way." Cyril laughed. "I'm a craftsman, not an artist. I'm to design moulded plasterwork for Noel's new domed orangery which he plans to build next. I am making the drawings for it now."

"Then you *will* be here!" Ellen said, pleased for him.

"Aye – as a grafter, I will," responded Cyril, but, just then, Noel gestured over to him with a smile of invitation to join him by the fireplace with the guests he was talking amongst.

Cyril gladly hastened over to him and was greeted with a friendly arm about his shoulders as Noel said, "And here he is! The creator of my latest garden wonders, with many more planned for you all to see."

Cyril responded with a look of such warmth that Ellen was fleetingly reminded of Jane Ellison with Albert Dewhirst, but soon forgot it when Kenneth returned and swept her off to the dance floor again. They were both capable, if not gifted, dancers and so they made a good match for the sets. She was glad not to think of anything but pleasure in the moment for a while, once again appreciating Kenneth for offering what he did not realise was a distraction to her from wondering where Peter was.

Her mind turned once again to travelling to the world of the poets, as Kenneth called it, and more than ever, she thought how much she might enjoy it. It would give her time to think, not of men and possible marriages but of herself and what she wanted in life, as Carrie had said to her before. Ellen imagined solitary, reflective walking through inspirational scenes, for surely she would enjoy that in between being social with Mrs Butterworth and Kenneth, she thought? Noel politely claimed her for a dance before the end of the evening.

"How well you look tonight, Ellen," he remarked but then added, rather unfortunately, "My way of lighting a room affords everyone the best possible advantage, you know", somewhat taking away the effect of his compliment.

Instead of being offended, however, or wounded as she would have been earlier in the year, she was only amused by noticing the way Noel could not pass a mirror, or any reflection in a window, without looking at himself in it.

She imagined Peter saying, "Look at that great ninny fancying himself!" and laughing heartily, which made her think of Peter again and miss his downright humour, among all the other things she missed about him.

Where was he? she ended the night wondering, just as she had begun it. Finally, it was time for the carriages to roll them all home again.

***

The short winter days were full of busy activity, for in spite of months of preparation, it seemed there was still much to be done for the wedding to take place on the first official day of spring in March. Sylvia's dowry had to be arranged by Mr Rastrick. The wedding feast, so fussed about, was to be paid for as the father of the bride and gone through over and over again in great detail by Mrs Rastrick. There were wedding rehearsals in church.

The parish church of Halifax at the bottom of town was to be where Noel and Sylvia got married. Ellen sat by her father in the old wooden pews, hand-worn smooth. With long stretches of sitting in between rehearsals, to pass the time she was idly studying the tattered military brigade flags hung on poles from the ceiling and wondering what battles they might have seen. Mr Rastrick grumbled to her as they waited again in between their roles as chief bridesmaid and father of the bride.

"Why did they not go the whole hog and book Westminster itself for the nuptials? I am sure Noel would have had no qualm about it. Self-deprecation is certainly not one of his failings, is it, Ellen?"

"I thought he had enough money and position not to have *any* failings, Papa," she replied with a smile.

"As far as your mother is concerned, that is so, I am sure." He smiled. "But there is too much peacocking about in my view for him to be a serious man of business."

"He does not have to be one, Father," pointed out Ellen. "Noel inherited so much from his wool merchant family that he can play gentry. And likes to do it."

"Aye, that he does," agreed Mr Rastrick. "But I'll wager his money's running through his fingers like sand. I must caution him as his father-in-law, since he has no parents left of his own."

Ellen privately wished him luck with that and, besides, Noel had shrewd business investors taking care of his pockets, or so he always claimed.

"He is going to be a patron of the arts, Father," she said, watching Noel and Sylvia practise their vows at the altar again with the vicar.

"Good Gad!" exclaimed Mr Rastrick in reply as Sylvia returned to the church entrance, gesturing for her father and Ellen to join her there. "Sylvia," complained Mr Rastrick, rising with a groan, "I have given you away more often today than is seemly for any parent. May we call a halt to proceedings for decency's sake, I beg of you?" But Sylvia remained implacable and the rehearsal continued with them marching solemnly down the aisle, Ellen holding up her sister's pretend train.

The wedding day itself, when it finally arrived, was full of that kind of strain always attendant on too many anxious arrangements which had to be perfectly timed. Nobody was relaxed at the house due to Mrs Rastrick's highly strung moments of panic. Sal volatile was required by her more than once and, in Mr Rastrick's exasperated case, an invigorating whisky or two. Finally, their carriage set off for the church, where Noel waited looking resplendent and enjoying everything hugely, as he did every public occasion which he figured in.

"Sylvia, you look heavenly!" he approved as she shimmered up to him in white silks and veils.

Even Ellen had to admit that she truly did. After that, the prestigious wedding banquet with all its guests, flourishing commerce represented among family, neighbours and friends, seemed to go on forever to Ellen. It was a dreamlike procession of waiting, food, more waiting, and speeches which culminated in a cake. Noel and Sylvia cut it, the final toast was made to bride and groom and, at last, it was done. For something Noel was involved in, the whole affair was remarkably respectable. There were no baroque theatrics to enliven it, for this occasion had been the bride's family's duty to provide for and Ellen's father was given to none of that kind of thing.

Ellen became aware during the celebrations that her sister-in-law kept trying to catch her eye. She gave a wry grimace back at Carrie from time to time, to show that she also found it tedious beyond words. It was enough to put Ellen off the idea of getting married at all, quite apart from the question of who any bridegroom might be! Afterwards, though, Carrie manoeuvred her way round to her and contrived a private moment.

"Ellen," she said urgently. "I am sorry not to have seen you of late."

"I know, I just – after –what happened," Ellen stumbled. "And Mamma with Sylvia's wedding…"

"I have some news for you."

Ellen drew an apprehensive breath. She knew Carrie meant Peter. Had he been caught after all this time?

"What is it?" she asked.

"I know where Peter Lumb is. I have not uttered a word to Leonard and nor will I. I have seen him. He came to find me in Manchester when I visited Fiona last. He has joined one of the affiliated groups linked to the old Chartists, he said. Our Guild was speaking at a meeting about women's suffrage and it was a mixed audience. He was there deliberately and came up to me afterwards to beg my forgiveness for the fire. He said he would never do it now and that solo acts were pointless in matters of political action."

Ellen gave a little smile.

"That does not sound like a complete conversion."

"No – but would you expect it of a young man like Peter? He's a firebrand in more ways than one, Ellen."

"I know – but is he well? Working? Is he…?"

"He is employed, he said, and since he only asked of you, then I think you can be reassured as to your other question."

"I did not ask if he was courting, Carrie!" said Ellen in instinctive reaction, but she was, of course, deeply pleased. "Why has he not written to me? I could have told him how I did myself."

"Peter does not want to compromise you in any way or be discovered. 'I wouldn't trust a servant or her mother not to be opening her letters now!' he told me."

"How rude!" said Ellen, secretly relieved that there was a reason for his silence.

"I did not reassure him. He might be right, Ellen. Len did have a discreet word with your father after John Henderson's wedding. I could not prevent him from believing he had a duty to do so about the Clarion Club, given Horsfall's conduct on that day. And you have said yourself you have been much kept to the house."

She had, Ellen realised, and not just due to her own withdrawal into her shell. There was always some reason now, or had been, why she must be with her sister or her mother.

Her father had indeed asked her if she meant to go any more to do charity work at the school above and she said no, at which he harrumphed and said, "Just as well, too much rain and bad weather for you to be out and about, especially on that damned two-wheeler of your brother's!"

In fact, the last time she had gone out to have a forlorn look at the carved names on Albert Promenade and round their old routes, she had walked to The Rocks. She had had to push back the grass which had crept across but in the end she did find the names, J.H. Henderson and C.J. Raynor, with the date, 1896. The inscription conjured up the feeling of that hopeful day when they had all first been together, before she had any guilt to feel.

"You are right, Carrie!" she said, realisation dawning. "They *have* kept me much at home and perhaps they *would* check any strange letters if Len suggested I were vulnerable to wrong company. Oh, I am so very glad Peter is safe! Can I get word to him?"

"No, Ellen. He left me no details of where he lived or worked, or could be found. And, given Len's threat, I told him he must not return to Halifax or he would be arrested. I let him think he was already a marked man to keep him away. I think pride would anyway, after that public humiliation."

Ellen digested this and saw the logic of all Carrie had said, asking then, "What about the group he came with?"

"I don't know. I only saw Peter, and he did not name it."

"How maddening and elusive!"

"Better so. I wanted to reassure you of his wellbeing, that is all."

"Thank you, Carrie," said Ellen after a pause. "It is very good of you. I have thought of him often."

"Forget Peter, now you know he is safe. He made his own troubles and must *deal* with his own troubles. Let your mind fill with other things, Ellen. There is a whole world out there, you know."

She squeezed Ellen's arm gently and then they had to rejoin the crowd. Len, of course, had been busy as best man and now came to speak to them, pleased with how it had all gone.

"What a show!" he crowed. "Mother is like a cat with two tails. Even Father hasn't gone off to find a newspaper to hide behind yet. Come on, ladies – we must see them off in style! Away to Rome and Venice in the spring. Lucky newly weds, indeed! We should go away ourselves, Carrie."

His enthusiasm died back as she answered, prosaically, "We cannot. There is the mill and Father, and my work in Manchester with Fiona."

"Of course," he answered after a short, offended moment. "Duty first. Pleasure later…Ellen – you must come and visit us again soon to break our monotony at Heatherfield."

Ellen remembered about Millicent, the young woman she had seen him with and the giggles she had heard at night, thinking that Len had found pleasure later already, then blanked it out again as another entanglement which she did not wish to dwell on. It reminded her of Albert with Hannah and Sarah and then of the unlikely betrothal between Eustace and Hannah, if such it really was.

"I should like to do both again, if I may," she answered boldly. "Visit you there and go with Carrie again to Manchester. May I?" she asked of Carrie, turning to her, adding. "You know it will simply drive me mad at home now. There will only be me to accompany Mother!"

"I will speak to our parents," Leonard assured her, with a laugh of acknowledgement that she would be so called upon. "And I will do my best."

Now that she had news of Peter, Ellen felt she could go to Heatherfield, and of course Carrie knew why she really wanted to go to Manchester but made no protest about it just now, only saying that an extra hand would be very useful. There was a great deal of want following the winter months in the big city and even more need of the charitable works she supported Fiona's group of ladies in doing, she said. Next, they went with all the guests to see the happy couple depart. There were, of course, none of the Clarion Club comrades, and certainly not Cyril, present, all the guests being of suitably bourgeois credentials to satisfy Mrs Rastrick after her great disappointment in Leonard and Carrie's wedding.

***

Sylvia had been swept away into Noel's 'enchanted palace' at Ogden Towers and Ellen was duly left at home. The wedding success brought in its train a flurry of return invitations from the affluent and influential. As predicted, it was now Ellen who had to pay house calls with her mother, or attend dinner parties with both of her parents. Her visit to Len and Carrie was fretted for but could not be agreed on by her mother for a month or so, until the invitations fell away again that the family must accept. Occasionally, Kenneth Butterworth called in. Their talks about books, going to the lakes, occasional walks and once, another trip to the bookshop, were a welcome distraction for Ellen. Even so, Kenneth was part of the old Saville Park world and it seemed a long time since she had feared losing his good opinion at the gala on the Moor.

Ellen chafed for the freedom which she had known with the Clarion Club and for that broader future which it had seemed to hold out. She promised herself it would all return to her somehow. Enough time had elapsed for her to persuade her father it was good for her to get out, code for escaping her mother's social demands, which he sympathised with as long as she promised not to resume reading at the school, which she happily did. Secretly then, she again managed her escape to attend a meeting of the Clarion Club, for these were resuming now that the spring was here.

She went partly in hope that someone there might know where Peter could be contacted and also to see if any of her old friends were there. The business of the meeting was to try to rally membership for the coming seasons and organise deliveries of the paper more widely again, along the valley and among the hill-dwelling hamlets and villages above. When she entered the rooms of the Liberal Club, where a carved head of Gladstone oversaw the entrance with severity in its stone gaze, she looked around both eagerly and with her heart thudding.

Her first hope was realised. Libby and John *were* here. Her second hope was that Eustace would *not* be present, and so far he was not, but Hannah Robertshaw and Sarah Greenwood were side by side as of old. Felix Sykes was in deep discussion across the room already, provoking debate by being deliberately controversial about something. It was the stance which he had always affected here but which Ellen now understood better after seeing him liven up Jane Ellison's father in the same way.

She smiled to herself at hearing him announce, over the heated responses he was receiving, "Nay, I merely play devil's advocate, friends! If we cannot convince ourselves, how may we hope to convince those opposed to us?"

Ellen caught Libby's eye and was greatly relieved when she came over at once with the old familiarity.

"Ellen!" she cried, giving her a hug. "Where have you been?"

"I so wanted to come and see you!" Ellen replied, looking at her with guilty affection. "But after that day, I felt so awkward...and then Sylvia's wedding took up every moment until it happened. My mother has scarcely let me out of her company *since* Sylvia got married!"

"Yes, she will miss her. But *you* had no need to feel that way about coming to see us, Ellen."

Ellen realised that Libby was already fuller in face and figure than she had been on her wedding day several months ago.

She had a certain bloom and Ellen said, to change the uncomfortable subject, "Libby! Are you and John already blessed?"

"Yes," said Libby. Looking pleased and rosier in the face than usual too, she squeezed Ellen's upper arm and then hooked hers into it to draw her over the room. "Come and speak to John. See? He is smiling there waiting to greet you."

It was only now that Ellen dared turn tentatively towards John Henderson, who nodded at her as she searched his face to see if his smile reached his eyes and was not altogether certain that it did.

She joined him with Libby, and John said, "Now then, Ellen."

Was there a little distance in his deep voice?

"John – I – I believe more congratulations are in order. I am very happy for you both," said Ellen.

This broke the ice enough for him to look proudly at his wife.

"Yes. We will be a little family soon enough. And no more being a maid for Libby since we were wed, of course. I have been standing in Peter's place at Stanger's. Did you know? You haven't been to see your brother and sister-in-law lately, have you?"

"Yes, I did know and I'm glad you are, John. No, I haven't been able to visit them. Sylvia's wedding meant Mother would not spare me at all from the house and since it I have had to be her companion at all the calls my sister paid with her. You would not credit the amount of five course dinners I have been forced to go out and eat with my parents," she added, relaxing briefly. She thought at once what a gaffe this was in present company, among those who had to work so hard to even provide their own meals. "Oh, I am sorry…"

"No apology needed with us, Ellen. You came from your world to join ours. That's credit enough to you," said John. "You should come to visit us, Ellen. We are in the same cottage Peter Lumb had. His few bits are laid aside. Even his dad's pipe were left behind and it meant a lot to Peter, that did. All he took were the bicycle he left on from our wedding breakfast."

"The same cottage?" wondered Ellen, adding, "Then he really never did come back at all…" Although she had known he must not have done, the thought of Peter's few cherished items being abandoned was poignant to her.

"No – nor should he do," John answered shortly, his face darkening at that suggestion. "A man I believed in, for all his cranky ways! If I'd have known what he did, I'd have left him to get down from that chimney himself if he could and be damned if I'd help build him another!"

This smote Ellen's heart dreadfully, of course.

"But you built it for Carrie and Len really, John, not Peter." She faltered, looking fearfully up into his face.

"John!" Libby scolded, hitting him on the arm. "You

are making Ellen feel badly. Don't! Ellen, Eustace Horsfall had no right to say you knew about it. Poor girl, to go away so upset before we could stop you."

"He didn't say she knew about it," said John. "He said she were forced into helping Peter Lumb somehow. Is it true, Ellen? *Did* he make you shield him?" he asked sternly.

"I – no," said Ellen, looking very uncomfortable.

"It's not her fault she were a bit sweet on him in't end, John," said Libby, who knew Ellen all too well. "That's why she looks like that. Why, poor Ellen had never been out in't world till we came here to the Clarion Club. How could she see what a fellow like *him* were made of? Or any of them? If he did put pressure on her, no blame to Ellen. He'd have made her feel she owed *him* a living for simply being who she was!"

"Aye, that sounds like Peter Lumb." John's look softened a little. "Ellen, we were good friends last year. We still are. Libby's quite right. Who in their right mind could blame *you* for anything? Whatever Peter Lumb did or said about owt to do wi' it were down to him."

Here, he shook Ellen's hand, renewing with the gesture the pledge between them, as handshakes had done in the past, that all was well between them as friends. 'Poor Ellen' wanted to say that she was not 'sweet' on Peter, as this sounded embarrassing and juvenile but it was safer not to deny it, with Libby laughing at her naivety just the same as she had done at Ellen's one-time attachment to Noel. Feeling furtive, guilty and undeserving of their renewed trust in her innocence, she looked about herself nervously now, her eyes flitting across Hannah and Sarah, seated together in front in the rows of benches which were beginning to fill up to hear the meeting once it began. Their backs were to her. John correctly interpreted her anxiety.

"Nay, he's not here – Eustace. Do you know that him and Hannah Robertshaw are an item, of all things?" And he laughed in his naturally loud, hearty way again. "What will young Dewhirst make of *that* when he comes back from his gallivanting, I wonder?"

"None of our business," said Libby smartly, cracking him on the arm again. "Those girls have to take care of themselves. You know that. *He* won't when it dun't suit any more."

"Maybe he will one of them," said John. "Word was he'd live over t' brush wi 'em and keep them women as servants of his own when he's of age to do it."

"Sarah's clever," mused Ellen. "And I think she likes to be part of some devious delight a lot more than Hannah does. He won't own Sarah, if he does do that."

"What would *you* know about it? Devious delight, indeed!" exclaimed Libby. "You've been at too many of them novels of yours, you 'ave, young Ellen. Come on, let's sit down to the meeting. It's starting."

Ellen was pleased to find herself sitting beside them and stopping feeling like a worm wriggling on a hook every time Peter Lumb was mentioned. She was also very glad to have got it out of the way and not be blamed, even if John did have his reservations that Eustace had some kind of foundation for what he had said. Peter had wanted to save her from that and she owed it to him to keep the faith with his self-sacrifice. Besides, she still feared there would be retribution for him one day. He could not stay away from his family forever, if he really had done so already.

Her next plan was to brave visiting his mother and to do it alone. It was not a place she *ought* to go to alone, of course and nor did she feel comfortable in doing so, or expect to be well-received by the grim Mrs Lumb when she did. Nevertheless, she was determined upon it. There was nobody at the meeting who knew a thing about Peter. They all knew even less than she did already, thanks to Carrie. Before it ended, though, a set of motions having been proposed, debated on and some agreed, she spoke to Felix Sykes and then Hannah and Sarah. She asked Felix if there were any news of Jane at the vicarage. He reported that Mr Ellison, from her letters, believed her to be very happy in her journeyings with Miss Tordoff.

"Miss Ellison has been in Paris and they are soon to travel to Italy. That was the last he told me. He hopes for her return in the summer but that is yet to be confirmed. I was glad to hear that she is so well, at least."

"So am I," said Ellen, detecting some offended reservation about Jane's journeyings in his tone. Perhaps Kenneth had been right about Felix Sykes having had some interest in Jane, but now he either disapproved of her travelling or felt her departure repudiated him. "My sister and Noel Ogden will be in Venice for part of their honeymoon," she continued. "How strange if they should meet there of all places, although I suppose it is unlikely they would travel to the same city at the same time."

"It would be strange indeed," agreed Mr Sykes, dismissing the notion. "Oh, excuse me, Ellen. There is a fellow over there I simply must take to task about what he said in the meeting. I cannot agree that we should be haranguing the good people of the town like common hawkers! The *Clarion* should be distributed like any newspaper. We should seek that for its circulation and let the newsboys do it along with other broadsheets!"

He moved on and Ellen found Hannah and Sarah right in front of her.

"She's coming back then, is she? That Jane Ellison," asked Sarah.

"I don't know," said Ellen, not liking her caustic tone. "I am sure you stood close enough to overhear what Felix

Sykes said of it, didn't you?" she added.

"Oh, pardon my manners," said Sarah.

"Where's Eustace tonight, Hannah?" asked Ellen, turning away from Sarah's blunt sarcasm.

"There's a bad do with scarlet fever at the school. They're all shut in so as not to spread it. Poor man's nursing 'em along with others. I just hope he doesn't sicken too."

"I am very sorry to hear it and I pray he is not infected," said Ellen, taken aback, for she certainly did not wish Eustace any ill even if she did not wish to see him.

"He were sorry, you know," said Hannah. Ellen gave a short, silent nod because of course, she knew what Hannah alluded to. "He's not used to a glass or two and Peter goaded him. He were always like that, Peter Lumb."

But this was a step too far for Ellen, who leapt to Peter's defence.

"Eustace put Peter's very life at risk!" she protested. "He's lost everything."

"Not his life, though. He ran away quick enough, didn't he?" derided Sarah, crossing her arms to show she stood with Hannah.

"Aye and it were Peter who put lives at risk in't first place, weren't it?" said Hannah, her eyes going significantly across the room to John Henderson, where he was busy chatting to others with Libby and clearly receiving more congratulations on their coming event.

"And he weren't the only one who did, were he, Ellen Rastrick?" pushed Sarah.

"Sarah!" hushed Hannah instantly. "Eustace had no business saying that."

Hannah looked full of consternation, as did Ellen, who flinched. Her additional personal guilt about writing that letter to Mr Stanger, which had initiated his first collapse, was something she would never forgive herself for either, fire or no fire. She had been so weak to give into Peter on both matters she castigated herself, not for the first time.

"He did, though. You told me so," accused Sarah, defending herself to Hannah.

"I know but he were a bit too drunk to get his words out straight. He didn't mean that."

"If you say so," said Sarah, eyeing Ellen darkly. "Where is he now, then? Peter, like? If anyone knows, *you* will."

"I *don't* know!" declared Ellen, realising that she was beginning to be a good liar thanks to Peter and not liking that one bit, since she never had been. "How could I?"

"Let her be," said Hannah in her calming voice.

"All reet," relented Sarah, but still looking Ellen over critically. "Where's t' rest of your sort tonight?" she demanded. "Apart from that cleric, there's only you."

"But I *am* here," Ellen said. "Aren't I?"

"Aye," agreed Sarah, with less antagonism. "Tha's here."

"I must go," said Ellen, both because she should and also as she had had enough. "Hannah, I hope Eustace keeps well."

Hannah nodded soberly. Scarlet fever could be a killer and not only of children. "He lives simple, so let's hope so," she said.

At the door, Ellen promised that she would see John and Libby soon at Heatherfield, for she was intending to come and stay there in the near future and it was almost arranged. It had been a difficult time attending the meeting, being challenged about Peter and what had happened, but she had come through it unscathed again. Feeling guilty about that as well made her feel even more obligated to try and find him. Carrie had told him he must never return as if he were actively being searched for by the law. But he wasn't. Not as far as she could find out. Ellen didn't want Peter to continue living in fear of that. She determined again that she would go to see his mother.

***

It was a week or more before she could get out alone again, on a day of sunshine and late-blooming daffodils which was a good enough reason to say she was going to go for a bicycle ride in the morning. She was soon cycling by the rows of yellow flowers massed on either side of Saville Park's grass verges, a sweep of cheering optimism which made her feel more hopeful herself. At least, it did until she was coming up to the tiny, soot-blackened terraces of back-to-backs which she had last visited with Eustace. Reaching Peter's house, its scuffed door almost bare of whatever paint had once decorated it, the whole street equally weathered and poor-looking, she knocked. It was a depressing place, even on such a day.

A totter went by with a virtually empty cart, calling out, 'Rag Bo-o-ne!' as he passed.

Nobody had anything to throw here, not even that, and his call, plaintive and lonesome sounding, went unanswered. Ellen's heart sank as she waited. The door was opened grudgingly and Mrs Lumb stood there, holding it half-open in that way she had of looking as if she were about to slam it closed again in the face of bailiffs.

"Oh," she said. "It's you today, is it? Where's '*e*, then?" she asked with a jerk of her head behind Ellen. "Can't 'e come?"

She looked expectant. Whom did she mean, wondered Ellen? Peter?

"I – I came to see if you had heard from Peter, Mrs Lumb," said Ellen hesitantly, after first making sure nobody else was about listening. Nobody was.

"Oh aye?" said Mrs Lumb trenchantly. "Took you long enough for *that*, didn't it? I'll give you t' letter in a minute. That were for you. I thought you'd 'a brought that club benefit an' all. *He's* coming wi' that again later, is 'e? For't rent, like?"

Light and incredulity dawned on Ellen together. Peter *had* written her a letter! She had never thought of coming here to ask. And surely the 'he' his mother spoke of was not Peter at all but…

"Do you mean the man I came here with first, Mrs Lumb? Eustace Horsfall."

"Aye, of course! Who else would I be on abaht?" demanded Peter's mother, sharp and impatient as ever.

"Erm, he is unable to come due to illness at the orphanage school." Ellen ferreted hastily in the purse attached to her belt and pulled out several higher value silver coins. "This will pay the rent and…"

Mrs Lumb cast a longing look.

"That's too much."

"Then it will pay for more weeks. Eustace may not be able to come for a while. It's a contagious disease. The school's quarantined because of scarlet fever."

The woman pursed her lips and drew breath, shaking her head.

"That's bad. Aye, it'll pay a few weeks for us, will that. I'll wait to 'ear again?"

"I will make sure you do," promised Ellen.

"Good," said Mrs Lumb, speaking quite as if this were her due and reminding Ellen rather forcefully of Peter's less attractive traits. "I'll fetch Peter's letter. I'll not ask you in, if you don't mind."

Her tone suggested it did not matter much if Ellen did mind, then she vanished back inside to get it. Ellen realised, as she waited, never having thought of it at all, that Eustace had been taking care of Peter's abandoned family by himself, no doubt feeling culpable for their being in need and acting out of his own kind nature as well as his sense of honour. What's more, he had been doing it from his own wages, for there *was* no club benefit raised for Mrs Lumb. Now that the Clarionettes were meeting again, ought there to be? Ellen could not leave Eustace out of pocket. If anyone ought to help Peter's family, *she* ought to do it. And she would push for regular money for them from the club collections too.

She pictured Eustace, his homely face red from exertion, labouring conscientiously on his bicycle from the school in all weathers, as he must have done these past several months! Once again she realised how much, like everybody else, she had underestimated him. Eustace quietly did the things other Clarion Club members heralded as their virtuous intention. He had kept his silence about the fire at Stanger's Mill for a long time before John's wedding, even though he had let Ellen herself know long before then that he suspected the truth, and even offered his confidential friendship if she needed it. She had never said she did and he honourably never raised the subject with her again.

Hannah had spoken truly, too, no doubt, when she said that Eustace had not intended to speak out at John and Libby's wedding feast like that. He and Peter had both been at fault – Eustace for inappropriately criticising Albert's morals there and Peter for blasting Eustace, in that chippy way of his, about doing so. For once, Eustace had retaliated by speaking his mind entirely and disaster had followed. Here, Mrs Lumb reappeared and gave Ellen a grubby-looking, folded note.

"I can't read it and kept it 'idden. Don't be telling me owt. Least I know, least I can give away. I don't believe what I've 'eard from others and one day Peter will tell me himself what 'appened. Until then, we leave each other alone."

She closed her mouth with the fierce set which Ellen remembered, so Ellen simply took the note and put it in her purse bag to read by herself as Mrs Lumb closed the door very firmly in her face. Peter's brothers would be out at their apprenticeships and bringing some little in for food and fuel, Ellen thought, but she would make sure that she helped with the rent, as Eustace had done. He would be worrying about that, she realised, now that he could not get out. Did Hannah know? Probably not, Ellen thought. He would not want to tell anybody what he was doing for Peter's family.

Perhaps, after all, she *would* forgive him in part and perhaps, also, she would write to him at the school, she decided. Just a note to tell him she had taken over paying the rent for the family and that she would continue to do it if necessary, but the Clarion Club was meeting again and she would seek a benefit for the innocent dependents who should not suffer.

Ellen freewheeled back downhill with a soaring feeling. She would do right by people too, to make her own amends, and she could not wait to read Peter's letter! Once she had got through the town's busy main streets, avoiding carriages, cabs, delivery boys with handcarts and other general traffic, she reached again the peaceful green and yellow stretch of Saville Park's daffodils and carried on to Albert Promenade, the only place where it felt right to read Peter's letter.

Leaving the bicycle propped on the low wall by the broad pavement, she climbed over to the flat-topped columns of dark rock where John and Cyril had carved their names last summer. Pulling away the rough grass which had crept across their inscription once more, she looked at the chiselled letters and date for moral support.

The sight of them gave her again that happy recall of the day out when they were all new together and rested here, although even then, she smiled to herself, Peter had complained of the ridiculous extravagance of Wainhouse Tower's existence. Taking out the note she read the following:

Dearest Ellen, for so you are.

Stand fast. Let none accuse you. Never defend my name. I must leave my family but I know I can trust you to do for them what was done for Stanley's. Be glad you never said yes to me and can stay safe away from my disgrace. Mine alone. Remember that.

Yours ever,

Peter.

She sat looking across the valley for a long time. The minute she read his words, all thought of Peter's having been Noel's assailant left her. It just went to show how easily rumours got into your head, even if you couldn't possibly believe they were true, thought Ellen. The sound of sheep came faintly across to her from the shadowed green fields slanting down Norland's hillside. Hooded crows gave their garrulous, clicking calls in the canopy of Scarr Wood's holm oaks on the slopes below her. Wainhouse Tower, currently owned by Noel, looked impossibly tall, dark and unique against a blue sky creamed with high cloud. It seemed incredible that she had once stood at the very top of it. A train chuffed below on the line travelling through to Manchester, steam rising and catching her eye. She looked along the deep cleft of Calder Valley after it, towards where the bare hilltops of Saddleworth Moor were the palest golden brown in the far distance and where, somewhere beyond them and below, Peter was today.

She had never given a thought to his family's plight at all and he had put faith in her that she would! Only

Eustace had done so and that, she thought, was *her* disgrace. She would make up for it now, she told herself. She would look forward to the day when she could tell Peter that Eustace himself had stood by them first, while she was stuck at home with her parents and Sylvia's dreaded wedding. Yes, she would tell him! All she had to do was get to Manchester. Peter was there somewhere and he had found Carrie to tell her that he was, which meant that he wanted Ellen herself to know. She did not ask herself how she might find him. She just told herself that she would.

***

She cycled back home and hid Peter's note very safely away among her own treasures, later writing the letter to Eustace which she had promised herself she would. In it, she said that she had met Hannah at the Clarion Club and learned of his predicament. She hoped very much that he would stay well. She had called upon Mrs Lumb to see how the family fared and learned of his kindness to them. He was not to worry, she wrote, as she would take up that responsibility now that he could not and would petition for an allowance for them from the Clarion Club. Peter had been a member and his family was not at fault in any way for his having deserted them. She remained *Your friend, Ellen Rastrick* and found that she sincerely meant it as she sealed the letter and stamped it.

It was not long before he replied and, mindful of what Carrie had told her Peter had feared, she checked her letter was still sealed when she collected it from the morning post. She had got into the habit of being the earliest riser while waiting for some communication from Peter to get to any letter first so that, knowing Eustace was likely to write, she was even more vigilant. She had not given her parents any cause for anxiety in recent weeks but even so she was pleased to snatch the letter off the silver salver in the hall before either of them noticed she had received one. Ellen had breakfasted and read it before her parents appeared.

Dear Ellen,

I am so glad to hear from you. I very much regret my unfortunate words before Christmas and believe me when I tell you how much more I regret their effect. I deserved to lose your regard and feared I had done so entirely. I did not intend to endanger Lumb, or for him to lose his position, which I know was hard earned, whatever had gone before. My small efforts to help his family were what little I could do in recompense. I have been deeply troubled that I could not continue to do so due to sickness at the school. Believe me most grateful indeed that you have discovered the need for yourself. Please do apply to the Clarion Club on their behalf if you are able. We have lost some of our children here already and the outbreak is far from over. We do our best for the poor souls. Thankfully, I stay well and can help with sitting up and nursing them.

With best wishes and warmest regards,

Eustace Horsfall.

Very pleased to hear from him and be re-established as comrade friends, Ellen was equally sorry about the situation in the school. She had taken to some of the youngsters more than others. Ellen remembered how they had let loose in the playground cheering Eustace on. Privately, she cheered Eustace on herself, hoping he would stay safe, even though she did still blame him, of course, for denouncing Peter and implicating her.

After breakfast, she wrote to the Clarion Club secretary and treasurer, putting the case for a subscription to support the family of a former member who had had to leave due to circumstances beyond his control (the whole world did not need to know what they did not know of already). After a moment's thought, she wrote next to Felix Sykes, asking that he second her in this proposal to aid a widow with two sons of only apprentice age and insufficient means to pay the rent. He had not been close enough to their circle to know Peter well, nor had he been at John's wedding, so she hoped he knew nothing of his downfall. She felt terribly for Peter, who must be in great distress at being unable to support his mother himself. She wished she were able to tell him that her petition had been successful when the Clarion Club duly agreed to a regular amount to be raised for the Lumbs, collectable by one of Peter's younger brothers rather than being delivered to the door, for discretion's sake.

***

Ellen was soon at Heatherfield again. She was shocked at the change in Mr Stanger, who was shrunken in his bath chair and slept most of the day away by the fire, nursed at night by the manservant who cared for him. Len and Carrie were not spending a great deal of time together, he busy at the mill and she planning her work in Manchester with Fiona in a constant exchange of correspondence. Again, Len was often out for most of the evening after dinner following the first few days of Ellen's visit.

"If you are to come with me, Ellen," Carrie warned, "you will be quite as busy as I told Len you would be when you proposed joining me. We will not be searching for Peter Lumb. Nor will we have time to do it, if that is in your mind."

Ellen, naturally, said that it was not. She felt in part that Carrie was keeping so ferociously busy because it kept her mind from dwelling on her father's decline and understood it. There was no immediate danger, or so Carrie determinedly said (although it did not look to be the case), and plans were going ahead to visit Manchester. Ellen called to see Libby in the daytime at the cottage, changed in its interior from bachelor sparseness to a more comfortable setting, although Libby said they would be moving to a different place before the baby came.

"John is set on his sculpting again in the summer. How he'll get on at Ogden Towers for that, I do not know. We're to have one of t' groundsmen's cottages, thanks to Noel, when he finishes here. If he goes ahead wi' it."

"John is a good influence on my brother," commented Ellen. "Len uses terms like the Clarion Club itself does now – enlightened employer, pension rights, compensation for injury."

"In fairness, that were Peter too," replied Libby.

"It was," agreed Ellen, and changed the subject to tell Libby she was to go to the Lake District in the summer with Kenneth Butterworth and his mother.

"Are you now?" said Libby, with an archly interested look. "That's a change for the better, Ellen."

"I am looking forward to seeing the mountains and the lakes. It is poets' country, you know," said Ellen.

"Oh. Is it?" said Libby. "And what is Mr Butterworth looking forward to, I wonder?"

"The same," said Ellen with a smile. "So you can stop your speculating. I'm in no rush for a wedding with *anybody*, Libby! I had enough with Sylvia's."

"Hmm. I'm looking forward to seeing her in her glory at Ogden Towers," mused Libby. "That Noel. It weren't what I expected for her."

"No," agreed Ellen. "Nor I. But she's Mrs Ogden now."

She saw John when he called to the house to see Leonard in his study and, one day, she did go down to see the mill again. She was shown proudly around by Len and John, admiring how light and airy it was inside with all its windows. But it made her privately sad as well to see that statement of a chimney, the crowning glory which Peter could no longer boast of. Perhaps, she reflected, if he had done less showboating to Eustace and been more amenable, this would never have happened. Eustace irritated the Clarionette men, not because what he said was wrong but because he was stiff and diffident, seen as prosy. Peter was not alone in showing it.

The way Eustace had burst out when his inhibitions were lowered by alcohol at the wedding showed how much self-control he had used not to react to them before. Ellen supposed she should admire him for it and yet, oddly, she found that she did not.

Albert and Peter's behaviour, although reprehensible enough in their different way, was more manly somehow, she felt, more open and immediate. Then she questioned her reaction. Why would she think this when Eustace had shown himself to be such a considered, good and kind person with the maturity to control himself? Later, she mused over these contradictions between emotional reaction and rational perception with Carrie, although not in direct relation to Albert, Peter and Eustace, of course.

Her sister-in-law enjoyed such debates with her and said, "It is good that you question it, Ellen. We are all emotionally trained by our upbringing to judge what is manly or not, what is womanly or not. But reason rather than feeling begins to tell you it is not so clear cut a matter, doesn't it, Ellen? You will hear all these things debated in our Manchester Women's Guild meetings."

"I wonder what Len makes of it all?" Ellen teased, knowing full well that such emancipated conversations were only enjoyed between her and Carrie privately.

"I do not spell it out with your brother, Ellen. Leonard is having his eyes opened through being married to me, I hope," Carrie had said with a smile and Ellen thought that, probably, he was.

***

Ellen arrived in Manchester this time feeling rather under false pretences because, of course, whilst being warmly greeted as a guest again by Fiona and welcomed into the Guild's gatherings, she *was* really only there to try to find Peter. They were staying for two weeks, during which Ellen sat through many busy occasions full of debate and helped to give out soup kitchen foods to the destitute, of which there were a frightening number amid the industrial might of the city.

Children with old faces and old people without hope crept out of the shadows of Ancoats at dusk. Worst of all was when they ventured to Red Bank's Angel Meadow. A less aptly named place it was hard to imagine. There was a Ragged School and a Church and there were the St Michael's flags, the graves of paupers laid over a one time plague pit. Otherwise, it was an urban abyss of the deepest poverty, not safe to venture into. The police did not dare to enter it, so if you were attacked and robbed you were most certainly on your own. Besides that, territory was jealously guarded here by gangs of dangerous young men who had nothing else to fight over but that. They were known as the Scuttlers, notorious in the poorest districts of Manchester and Salford, Ellen was told. So here, they stayed on the margins near to Cheetham Hill Road and Ellen felt quite afraid after all she had heard. There was no faulting the courage of the members of Fiona's Women's Guild, who also tried to persuade those who came for food to come and listen to free meetings.

Around here, they were accompanied by men from one of the sympathising groups, for their safety. While talking to the men, Ellen discovered that they were linked to the old Chartists. Was Peter among their number?

Checking that Carrie and Fiona were not in earshot, she asked if anyone knew him. Nobody seemed to but, not quite giving up hope, she asked if word could be given back through their groups, if he were among anybody's associates, that she would be attending a concert of the Halle orchestra at the Free Trade Hall in a few days time. If he could come, she, Ellen Rastrick, would be very glad to see him.

"You see, we were in the Clarion Club in Halifax together," she explained. "Peter left to work in Manchester, but I would dearly like to wish him well."

"We are not so many that if he is in one of our groups somebody would not know him. We'll pass the message on," one of the men she asked assured her. "We know where our radicals work."

"Oh, he will most certainly be one of those!" Ellen said, knowing instinctively that Peter would be.

The night of the public concert was their last in Manchester, a treat from Fiona, and Ellen was still very hopeful that Peter would come. She looked about the people outside as they came to it and then as they queued to make their way slowly in. Peter loved music. She was sure this orchestra would be a draw to him and that he would have been before. Would any message have reached him? It was a big city and yet a small one too in the circles he would be moving in. He had managed to find Carrie. Surely, Ellen would be able to find Peter? Carrie and Fiona were ahead in the group gradually moving forward to go and seek out their seats, whilst Ellen hung back looking about. All at once, she thrilled to feel a hand on her arm.

A familiar voice said, "Ellen, lass", very warmly.

She drew a sharp breath as she turned to see Peter himself. A baggy flat cap shadowed his face but the voice was unmistakably his.

"Peter!" she exclaimed gladly.

They did not have to say any more to know how each of them felt.

"Come aside before you sit down – I see Carrie there," he urged.

"Yes!" And eagerly she drew back with him to edge of the entrance vestibule, where they spoke in low, urgent voices. "How are you? *Where* are you? And what have you been doing all this time?" she asked.

"What a barrage of questions!" He smiled, pretending to recoil. "Well enough, thank you and working – in a textile mill – cotton instead of wool, though, and just on't machines again." He gave a wry smile at this. "We're looking to make a union, if we can. Folk here are worse off than ovver theer, if anything. I'm hopping beds on shifts in shared lodgings. Word came back to me you were asking for me on't soup run, Ellen. My mill's up that way."

"Oh, Peter, it all sounds…" (Dreadful, she thought, but did not say). "You have to know this! I must tell you at once. You are *not* a wanted man. Len was persuaded not to go to the police. Only – if you were to be seen openly back in Halifax…"

"He might do yet?"

"I don't know but I don't think so, Peter. He was persuaded to keep all quiet for the mill's reputation and it has all died down. Oh, and I saw your mother – Eustace has been helping with her rent. You know, his conscience smote him, and he has a good heart. The Clarion Club is going to support her with it."

"I'd have come back if I'd known I could! Why did *she* not tell me when I saw her?" he demanded, firing up at once and indignantly pointing to the concert hall. Ellen knew he meant Carrie. "I've money saved for the family!" Then he pulled himself back. "But – no – of course I know why. The fire. And I beg your pardon. Thank you, Ellen, please and thank Eustace for me too. I were 'igh-handed with 'im and we'd both been supping. It weren't all his fault, you know."

Ellen hadn't expected him to either see or say that, given the outcome. Peter had matured since they set the fire in Stanger's Mill, she thought. They found they were clasping each other by the hand, reaching for one another's touch without thinking about it.

"I have to go in," said Ellen reluctantly. "Will I see you at the interval, or afterwards?"

"Nay – I've no ticket and I wouldn't be welcome wi' Carrie coming in alongside of thee, would I?" Ellen had to shake her head, knowing it was true. "Best not show me face, then, eh? Besides, I'm on nights in't mill. Going there next."

"Oh! We go back to Halifax tomorrow," she said, disappointment flooding in. "I am so glad I found you, Peter. It's why I came to Manchester."

A smile brightened his face at this unguarded and transparent truth. He looked pasty and tired from long working hours, poor food and bad living conditions. The glad animation of his success at Stanger's New Mill was gone from his expression but this smile belonged to *that* Peter.

"I'll come back – secret like – and I'll see you there. I promise you, lass."

A moment's hesitation and then, stooping, very quickly, he kissed her briefly on the lips and was gone. She turned back to follow the stragglers of the crowd in and saw Carrie and Fiona looking round for her, standing up in the stalls. Waving, she went across and said she had got caught up and held back by the press coming in. It was a full concert hall and the music was Beethoven – stirring, full of emotion, a reminder of the concert she had taken Peter to in Halifax. Now he was excluded, and by fear of being found out by Carrie, of all people! Still, he was right. Carrie had told her she must not look for Peter and that she must never expect to be with him. She had kept his secret when he came to her first, apart from telling Ellen, but she might not again if Ellen pushed the agenda too far.

And yet, those few moments of talk with Peter, long awaited, were so fleeting that she felt stressed and let down, resentful of the two women friends sitting there so contentedly together. If it were not for Carrie, she thought (knowing too that this was irrational and unfair), she and Peter would have been in the concert together, able to talk for hours! She let her imagination roam free and picture him at her side. If Peter asked her to marry him again she would accept, she suddenly knew. She scarcely realised that it was by becoming an outcast that Peter had won her heart.

How brave he had been to leave all he knew and start again somewhere else, with nobody to help him but himself, even if he had been the author of his own downfall! That gave the lie to everyone who said he thought the world owed him a living, Ellen told herself proudly. And anyway – it wasn't that at all, really, was it? It was because he knew everyone deserved better than they had as workers. His ambitions for those at Stanger's Mill showed that and so did his wish to form a union in his new workplace now. He was committed, feeling his cause, as he did everything else, with very strong emotions. Look how he had mourned Stanley, she said to herself. If he didn't have such feeling, he wouldn't be so headstrong and go off the deep end the way he did, would he? Ellen believed that she understood him now, her cautious inner voice of reason, which sounded like Carrie's these days when it spoke in her head, silenced.

Would he come to Halifax and when would he, if he did? No mention had been made of letters, just that he'd come back secretly one day and see her there. Oh, this was torture now! She was so quiet after the concert that Carrie and Fiona were concerned, but she just said she liked the music to stay with her and if they would excuse her she would go early to bed ready to pack in the morning. Touched by how moved she seemed to be by the concert, they did not press her. Ellen said goodnight, turning with her candle to see their heads bowed together across the lamplight, already talking away again and completely at one. She envied their closeness. They were like sisters, she thought, and far more so than she and Sylvia had ever been.

Just now, Ellen felt very alone, hugging the knowledge that Peter was somewhere in the city but knowing also that, by now, he was exhausting himself working through the night on a hated, clattering loom, with his energy and intelligence going to waste and not even a bed to call his own at the end of it. She did not want him to spend all his life at the bottom of the ladder fighting for the rights of those sharing that lowly rung. Let him do it from a better position, one that she could offer him. Whatever her mother said, or a possibly furious Len might object to, she was sure her father would never cut her off completely. Didn't he love her too much for that? Peter had managed Len's mill. If she married him, he could help her father with Rastrick's Bobbin Manufacturing in the same way, and make *him* a modern, forward-thinking employer too, looking to the future ways! Surely that would benefit the family enterprise overall and give Peter fulfilment, too, wouldn't it?

Sylvia and Len had brought money and position into the family by their marriages. She was the youngest child. She could bring talent into it through hers. It was a happier thought to fall asleep with, even though she was quite unable to share it with Peter himself. But she had seen him! That surely meant better things were to come now, and that luck was back on their side.

Chapter Fifteen

In Venice, Jane's disappearance, when he realised that this was what it was, came as a great shock to Albert. He had awoken late with a languorous stretch, a beam of sunshine playing over his eyelids from between the shutters, which were still closed. He recalled, with a smile, the success of the masked ball and his clandestine words with Sylvia. Noel would be glad of having Sylvia distracted at home where Cyril was, too, thought Albert, conveniently for him. For the present, Sylvia had been too ensorcelled by her dalliance with Albert to notice what Noel was doing on their honeymoon. Noel himself had said in a mocking murmur, brushing past Albert last night with a beautiful youth in tow, "Libertine!"

Sylvia had still been a virgin when she first lay with Albert because Noel's love-making was that of kisses, embraces and stroking with her and she, having known no other and not being especially awakened to sensuality, had not thought it strange. Sylvia would pose no risk to Albert as a lover, something he had a renewed awareness of following Milo Standish's recent misfortune. He soon realised, however, that she had already posed a different kind of risk.

"Jane?" he called out idly, rolling over and looking about the apartment.

She was not in the bedroom with him, nor, when he padded through naked into the saloon (something she usually liked to see) was she sitting there reading and waiting for him to rise.

Bless her for letting him sleep on, he thought, returning to lounge in bed. She must have gone out on her own to look around. He was impressed by how independently she could act now, having begun to do so in Paris. Noel and Sylvia would be leaving next week and

Jane had been very good at keeping out of their sight. They had laughed together about it. It was only as the day drew on and he began to be hungry, expecting her back to eat at lunchtime, that he began to wonder as he dressed. Then to realise that it was several days since he and Jane had laughed about her hiding from Noel and Sylvia and that he had not spent much time asking her what she had been doing.

Looking about the rest of the apartment now for any kind of letter, he noticed instead a full-face mask with ruby red cupid lips and eyeholes, set on a gilded stick, which was laid on a small table. It was not his. This, then, was her only message and Albert knew immediately what it meant. She had followed him, seen him with Sylvia and must have heard him with Sylvia! Alerted, he looked behind the curtained alcove where their travelling trunks were stored. Hers was gone. But why a silent departure? Where were the hot tears and upbraidings she would burst out into and he would so expertly coax her from, persuading her that it was she who still needed to release herself from needless jealousy (something which Albert believed that *he* truly believed himself)? Where was she? The possibility that she might have gone to Sylvia and Noel and created a dreadful scene there occurred to him, so he hastily left and headed across to their far more prestigious hotel.

They too had slept late after the masked ball and were only just taking a light luncheon in the restaurant before going out on a gondola trip again. Both were pleased to see him and, clearly, Jane had not been here, so he could not say anything to them. He thought at once that she must have gone back to Paris. A surge of possessive anger passed through him as he thought of her fleeing to Wolf, the man who had painted her! He was not immune to such feelings as a man, even though he believed that in a future of free love, both sexes should strive against them.

"Take a glass of port, Albert," urged Noel. "You have not picked up yet after the ball last night and look peaky. Would you like to join us on our gondola? We are in the last few days in Venice on our honeymoon, you know."

"I – thank you but I have come to tell you that I find I must leave here earlier than I expected myself. Let me tell you why. Noel – our artists' community is already building. I meant to keep it as a surprise but here it is. I have met some wonderful people in Paris who are just ripe for the venture and doing exciting work. May I have your permission to invite them to Ogden Towers? They are about six in number, if they all join us."

"Oh, certainly! Sylvia, are you ready to welcome them to our new world in Ogden Towers?"

"Yes, if they do not intrude on us too much," she answered, with a complicit smile at Albert.

"Oh, no. They will have their quarters in the unused wing and the tower rooms which we do not use. We shall be quite as private as you wish and also quite as sociable as you wish," teased Noel. "I am sure you would not like a dull life, would you, my dear?"

"It would not suit me, no," she answered demurely.

Noel flicked a playfully wicked glance at Albert, remarking, "Then we are quite agreed. Albert, are you going to Paris immediately?"

"I had a letter today asking if my offer still stood before other commissions are taken," Albert lied smoothly. "I would like to go and assure them that it does. My own tour is almost done now and I may arrive back in Halifax as soon as you do, or shortly afterwards, with my artists alongside or to follow."

"Excellent." Noel beamed. "We must take them up my Wainhouse Tower and ask how it compares with the

Eiffel Tower," he joked.

This reminded Albert, who experienced a sudden pang of the heart due to it, of Jane saying the same thing. He took his fond leave of them, kissing Sylvia's hand, embracing Noel and promising that he would see them again very soon in England. He hastened back to the apartment with an unusual scowl on his handsome features, hoping very much that Jane might have returned as unexpectedly as she had left, but she had not. The strength of feeling which moved him to hurry back to Paris to go after her surprised him. If she were not there, then she would have run away back home and he would find her at the vicarage. He must not have his rescued reputation in Halifax put at risk, he told himself, realising that in fact this was the least of his worries. Albert did not want to lose Jane. In her abrupt departure, he found Jane's real value to him.

It piqued him afresh that he had begun to realise, just before the advent of Sylvia and Noel, that on occasion Jane had looked bored in his company, rather than he being restless in hers. It was not a thing which Albert was accustomed to finding in women, and certainly not in Jane. Perhaps, in part, he had seduced Sylvia to subjugate Jane again. It was not a pleasant thought and not in keeping with what he believed his principles about free love were. Instead of that, though, Jane had found the strength to abandon him instead. Yes, abandon him! And without a word! He was angry, aggrieved and distressed beyond measure, all comfort in his success with Sylvia lost for the present. Jane had loved him more completely than anybody had ever done and he wanted her back. She was meant to be part of *his* world now. He would not let her know this though, of course, when he found her again, because that sounded like a wish to possess, the very thing he strove against.

If she were in Paris, he would say that he had returned to persuade his comrade artists to join him in England. If she were in England, it would be that he had returned from his tour and to bring himself, triumphant with his clique, to the new art movement at Ogden Towers. Moreover in England, Hannah and Sarah would be waiting to welcome him home. Let Jane regret her decision at leisure! This was what he told himself, whilst flinging things furiously into his trunk and instructing a servant to get him the first possible booking for the boat and then the train to Paris – actions which were hardly in keeping at all with that sentiment.

***

Albert did not find Jane in Paris, however. None of the artists had heard from her. Or so they all said to Albert. Wolf still had the portrait of Jane in his studio window and Albert bought it from him for a good sum. When he found Jane again, he would show it to her, as a demonstration of his belief in the fineness of their love, which her running away had shown such a disregard for. In fact, it was quite a strong likeness of her at her best in character and he found he longed to have it, if he did not have Jane herself. He did not admit to anybody that she had left him, only saying that they were following different travel paths for a short while and had loosely said they would meet again in Paris. Jane was seeing a little more of Europe with their mutual friend, Miss Tordoff, while Albert returned to rally the artists to come to England as he had promised. Or so he said.

Only Wolf did not seem to believe Albert. He did not deign to say so, though, just giving a fleeting, dismissive smile when Albert tossed out his casual explanations to the group of artists. It suggested that Wolf knew more about Jane's intentions than he thought Albert deserved to know. It entirely maddened Albert, who had put himself in a position of not being able to ask Wolf anything, thanks to his false story.

He tried to visit Miss Tordoff to ask if she had heard anything from Jane, but she was not to be found at her Parisian address and did not reply to him from her English one, so was probably away elsewhere. After waiting a while, Albert was left with no recourse but to return to England himself. He did so with several of the artists he had already persuaded to join the new movement. He and Noel had christened it in Venice before the masked ball, over several glasses of champagne together one night after dinner.

Each notion was more outlandish than the last until, reminded of their fellow Clarion Club members' shared inspiration for the artistic community, they came up with, 'The Clarionistas'. This sounded like a group of partisans in a revolutionary movement forging ahead with a new vision, certainly, but it also embodied the word 'Clarion'. Noel wanted to be a patron of the arts, yes, but he had no intention of his artists being allied with any Royal Academy stuffiness.

"We will have a battle on our hands to get established with our new group, no doubt about it. Let's have a battle cry for a name, then!" Noel had proposed and Albert, carried away too, had agreed.

"Peter Lumb would like that, wouldn't he?" remarked Albert. "Not that he's an artist."

"No, but his fellow firemen are. John Henderson, that is, and Cyril Raynor, of course."

"Oh, yes, of course, *Cyril*," answered Albert drily, raising his glass again in toast of absent friends. "I expect our friends will all be waiting for us."

"I expect they will, Albert. Hannah and Sarah – oh, and Jane Ellison too for you, no doubt."

"Jane Ellison? What makes you mention her?" asked

Albert warily.

"Oh – nothing at all!" said Noel airily. "Nothing at all. By the by, what *did* become of that mystery lady in the gondola? Usurped by my wife, perhaps?"

"I have no idea what you mean," said Albert stiffly.

"No?" said Noel. "Of course you don't. Another toast to our Clarionistas, then!"

He had smiled easily, letting Albert off the hook he had only half bothered to catch him on, and the Clarionistas were duly christened.

***

It was a fine spring day, with daisies sprinkling the grass of the Moor, when Ellen received a message from Peter. It came by way of a hand-delivered note with the small parcel of a book. The package arrived as if it were from the bookshop, so there was nothing remarkable in that since Ellen received such parcels at intervals. Ellen, who had ordered no new book, initially thought it must have come from Kenneth. She had unwrapped the brown paper and opened the book before awareness dawned. A small square of paper inside the cover was in Peter's hand, a quick scrawl written just now, it seemed! *Here. At the rocks. Meet me? Yours, P*, she read.

"Another book, Ellen?" Mrs Rastrick reproved, looking up from writing answers to some invitations which she had been exclaiming gladly over shortly before.

"Yes, but I am not going to read it now, it is far too nice a day to stuff indoors," Ellen said with a bright smile, closing the book hastily. "I am going to take a turn outside while you are busy and will look at it another time." She hurried off, ignoring her mother's half-hearted protest that she had been thinking of calling on Mrs Butterworth with Ellen later that morning. Turning a deaf ear was the easiest at this point. "Yes, later, Mamma!"

she called back, closing the door on her mother.

She pocketed Peter's note, took the book upstairs and put on her outdoor things to escape. She did not go along the tame pathways round Saville Park for her morning airing, however, as was deemed acceptable. Ellen knew exactly where Peter would be waiting for her, on Albert Promenade. There he was, a bicycle on its side next to him and sitting with his legs and feet dangling over the edge of the flat rock where John and Cyril had carved out their initials, surnames and 1896 in the summer of the previous year. He was looking out across the valley, his back to the roadside.

"Peter!" she called gladly.

"Ellen, lass."

He turned, smiling, and reached his hand out to steady her as she sat down beside him. Below them was a steep drop to the narrow pathway of the top walk of Scarr woods.

"I remember watching you climb up and down these rocks with John and Cyril," she said.

"Aye. I remember that day too," he said.

"How did you know I would be at home this morning?" asked Ellen.

"Because I'm a psychic," he answered, glancing sideways at her, then laughing a little. "I asked if you were in," he said, "before I left t'book. Said it were ordered."

"You came to the house?"

"I did. I'm that bold," he mocked himself. "Nay, no servant except Libby knew me, did they? Took a chance on Len not being there."

"No, that's true! They didn't and it was a good job he wasn't! Oh, I'm so glad to see you, Peter!"

"And I you."

They still held hands and, here, he turned to kiss her in

the tender warmth of the spring sunshine.

"Ellen," he said, "I asked you a question once and I never gave you a chance to answer. I want to ask it again. Can ah?"

"Yes."

"Will you marry me? One day?"

"Yes!" agreed Ellen, making his face brighten up as completely as the sunny day and they kissed again. Ellen could not wait to tell him about her half-formed plan. "Peter, you could be manager in my father's mill instead of Stanger's. He hasn't got Len there much now and – and we can persuade him of all your ideas just the same! He's a kind man. Father just stays set in his ways of handling things because it's how it's always been."

"Let's not run away wi' ourselves," said Peter. "Remember what Eustace said about the fire. I don't know how much word spread abaht it. I miss that place," he added. "Stanger's New Mill. Nobbut what I'm sure John's done well as manager. I'd like to see him – make my peace with him if he'd let me."

"Don't talk about that. Not just now!" Ellen pleaded, wanting only to be happy in the moment. "Where are you staying, Peter? Have you seen your mother?"

"I have and I've brought plenty for 'em to manage on. I've been working hard ovver theer and spending nowt. All my time's gone on campaigning."

"Did you make a union there, Peter?"

"Aye, I did." And he gave a rueful grin. "Had the usual result for me. Got the sack for being a trouble maker. So my job was done both ways round."

"Then – you really *are* back here?" exclaimed Ellen, delighted.

"Lying low, like, yes. I'll have to get took on somewhere. My brothers are doing well as apprentices, you know."

"I'm glad."

"Ellen, I'll be working when I wed you. I promise you that."

"I know. But, Peter – I was serious about my father's bobbin mill. I'm his favourite, you know. Oh, he never says it. But I am. He would stand by me, whatever Mother or Len said. I need to get Carrie on my side to persuade Len!"

"I'm not asking you to wed me for that," said Peter, looking uneasy.

"I know!" she said impatiently. "It's my idea but think about it, won't you? Let us see Father alone first. We must get you a good suit again!"

"Oh – you reckon me turning up like this won't impress him, then?" laughed Peter. "I still have a good suit. It were packed away up in't pawn shop by Mother. I told her to when I legged it. I've already got that out. And what if he says you cannot marry me, Ellen? Let our engagement be secret between us for now until I've got a position sorted. I'll not turn up a beggar for his daughter's hand in marriage. I must be in respectable employment if we've a hope of talking him round to it."

"I don't care about that!"

"Then you ought to, daft head," said Peter fondly.

"If you do as I suggest, Peter, you would have the position you ought to have, and by my side!"

He looked at her with more consideration.

"You mean it, don't you? And you've thought about it before," he added, a pleased realisation dawning. "I'm ready to brave it if you are, my lass. And – Ellen – I won't let you down. I'm not the madman who forced your hand that day at Stanger's Mill any more. It were the wrong road, that. I know it. And I apologise to you with all my heart for making you a part of it."

"I made my choice that day, Peter. And I make my

choice today. I love you. And I want to be with you."

"I love you too, Ellen – and you will be. Let me first do as I said – it'll not be long afore I'm in work. It never is. I have to earn for Mother and the lads. After that's done, then we'll go to your father. And I'll be just as fancied up as ever you please for it!"

"You don't have to be fancied up for me, Peter."

"I know it, lass" he said. "You're fancy enough for both of us."

Ellen laughed, blushing, and pleased to be complimented in Peter's particular way. She was deeply happy with the promises they had made between them and she was able to let him go, this time, knowing that she would soon have word from him again.

"We'll meet," he said. "And I'll write. Don't fret on that. It's thanks to you I knew I could come back. And it's only for you that I did."

They leaned their foreheads together, still hand in hand, and with one last kiss for that day they parted, with their only witnesses being the strangers passing on a promenade walk in ones and twos. These gave them passing smiles, seeing sweethearts sitting innocently together and admiring the view. How they would truly overcome the fact of what had been done at Stanger's Mill, Ellen could only think of covering up somehow again. She would have to work on Carrie and Len to persuade them that Peter had not meant what he said, but had only defended her, out of the love between them which nobody else had known of at the time.

Ellen, being romantic, hoped that this would be enough to convince them, and she was more than prepared to lie about it. If she could stop Carrie from objecting to Peter for her and persuade her to calm Len down in advance, Ellen would try to convince her brother too. But first, she determined to get her father on side with Peter by taking him completely by surprise. As for what she would do if her father refused to give his permission, well, although she was under twenty-one, she was of marriageable age. She and Peter could simply run away, only they would do it together the next time, she concluded. But Ellen did not believe there would be any need for that to happen.

They met secretly on Albert Promenade several times after this and Peter told her about how he had fled in panic after John's wedding. He had thought at once of Manchester as being far enough away for safety but his journey there had been fraught with the fear of being caught. After a hasty visit to his mother (where he had left his note for Ellen, never thinking it would take so long as it did to reach her) he had headed down to town and made for the Ripponden Road across the moorland to Manchester, keeping off the main highways until he reached it. He had not dared go by train, lest he be arrested at the station or along the way. It was heavy work on the bicycle, the only thing he had taken, slogging up the steepest inclines between boggy ground among bleak hills.

This was an inimical landscape, especially in winter, a barren grandeur above tree and snowline whose heights showed no life on them then, not even grazing sheep. He had struggled on for thirty-five miles and more, drenched occasionally by showers which he could see approaching in slanting, smoky columns dropping down from the clouds coming over. He followed the way west and the sinking winter sun on the road, not venturing to leave it for shelter or rest among rocks, even overnight, in case he became lost or died of exposure up there. He was only thankful that there had been no snows yet. Eventually, in a dark dawn, he saw the smoke stacks of Rochdale and Oldham below and left the strange, lonely world of

Saddleworth Moor to lose himself in the city of Manchester, soon able to beg lifts from passing carts to take him there. The stress of that journey over the tops had been such, he told Ellen, that all other thoughts had been numbed out of existence, survival being his primary human instinct.

"I were glad of it," he said. "It were punishment and relief as well, since I hadn't any energy to think of owt but getting through it. I were sick of feeling things all t' time – angry, guilty, flung from being 'appy to in despair all at once. And then that damned wedding. I can't explain," he finished, impatient at himself for his inability to define such layers of emotion adequately.

"I understand," said Ellen, who had felt many of the same things herself at different times.

All because of one act, done so quickly but one with such enormous consequences both to them and to others, consequences they were helpless to influence but were affected by. She was horrified by what he had endured, even as he dismissed it all as over now and not for dwelling on.

Soon afterwards, Peter got taken back on at Bradbury's Flour Mill, which was back up and running. He counted this a great success, as it meant no rumours had spread to there about him. Ellen was very pleased too when he met her on a fine Sunday afternoon, their usual time, once more at Albert Promenade.

"It gives the lie to Eustace's accusations made in Len's hearing, and we can use that if we have to. I will, when I speak to Carrie in private," she said. "I will be meeting her for lunch next week. Are you still at your mother's?"

"Nay, no room up there now. Lads are getting bigger. Besides, best I'm not too obviously about till we're in the clear. I've taken a room in a lodging house again, down along by Bradbury's. It's nowhere near Stanger's Mill. Room and board this time, so it's much better than in Manchester. Landlady's got a big house for paying guests, widow of a manufacturer that went bust. Quality, like," he joked. "I want somewhere decent to court you from. I had to take the cheapest in the city before, so I could save what I got for my mother. And, Ellen, thank you again for what you did for them all. When I knew that, I knew you'd stayed loyal to me."

"Of course I did, as soon as I realised," exclaimed Ellen, all her doubts about Peter in the past bowled clean away by their new circumstances now. "But how do you find it back in the flour mill?"

"All reet. I know the people and they know me. And," he said, looking modestly proud, "Mr Bradbury were at the opening of Stanger's New Mill, so he knows something of what I did there but nothing about why I left. I told him I went to Manchester to advise another factory owner as my work at Stanger's was done. He's took me on as foreman and asked me to look at safety in there too. That's how I got my lodgings. Mrs Crabtree only takes in by recommendation and Bradbury gave me my reference for her."

"But, Peter – if he knows Len and Len speaks to him?" demurred Ellen, rather fearful again.

"No, he doesn't. Not directly. Don't forget, we invited all the manufacturers of note in the area to come and be impressed. Seems like yon Bradbury was. The fire *did* make him think on about how old and risky the place were as it was. Not that I'm saying it were right of me to do that there, either. The Clarion Club's taught me about acting as an organised group to get anywhere. So did setting up a union. And I learned a bit from the Women's Guild in Manchester, women that are right up against it to find any voice at all. But they're finding one now. You get nowhere alone and reform's best done with them owners on board, like I did with Len."

"You're right, Peter," Ellen agreed, impressed by this new level-headedness.

"Mind you – it takes a right good kick up the backside to get 'em started." He grinned. "And I did do that, didn't I?"

"Peter!" she mock-scolded and they embraced, each time they did so wanting each other properly more than ever. "When can we go to my father?" asked Ellen, full of a thrilled desire for him. "Let us do it this week. I want our engagement agreed before Sylvia and Noel return and they are doing so very soon now. I don't need my sister backing Mother up in any objections."

Peter agreed to this now that he had a good situation, saying with a smile, "I'd best not be on my high horse that day, then, had I?"

"No!" replied Ellen firmly.

"He might not like it, lass. You know that, don't you? And you must have his permission to wed before you're twenty-one."

"We will persuade him, Peter."

"And if not...?" he asked, an anxious cloud crossing his face.

"We will be engaged in secret until we marry and leave," declared Ellen roundly. "Plenty of women work for a living. I'm not afraid to."

"Only at summat decent," cautioned Peter. "You're not brought up for it."

"I can teach," said Ellen. "I already have done at the Orphan Home and School."

"Aye, now that's a notion," agreed Peter, adding drily, "Well, let's see what he says, like, eh, before we go running off to Gretna Green?"

The time soon came when Ellen sent a note for Peter

to meet her once again on Albert Promenade and to ready himself for coming to see her father that night. Ellen had carefully chosen this evening for it as her mother was to be out at a select private supper for those ladies who were wives of a gentlemen's rotary club, which let Ellen out of attending. It was nominally to arrange a charitable function but really, of course, it was so as to be seen amongst the right people.

Ellen and Peter met on a fine Saturday afternoon at their trysting place on the rocks. Once again, there were strollers along the Albert Promenade who looked indulgently at two young sweethearts embracing, if perhaps a little too freely. They forgot to be discreet entirely when Peter asked Ellen once more to marry him and she happily agreed, the two of them falling into a standing embrace.

"Best be sure I'm wanted before I start pestering your father in his own house for your 'and," he teased her before tender kisses were shared between them.

Peter's body, back to the street, had concealed Ellen's figure as they stood together. It was their parting which revealed them. Among the strollers admiring the fine view that afternoon was Kenneth Butterworth. The sun cast a milky golden haze over the hills opposite and, like others, his attention was caught by the couple's romantic moment against such a setting. The man's clothes, even in Sunday best, identified him as lower class, and while the display was unseemly to the respectable promenaders who saw them, it did not impinge on standards for their own kind, so they took no particular note of the individuals.

Kenneth, in fact, had been walking and thinking directly about Ellen. He had left his mother visiting and taken a lengthy stroll here to consider things. He was not a man to rush matters but he felt now, possibly, that he was ready. He had been surprised and pleased by Ellen's acceptance at Heatherfield of taking a holiday with him and his mother.

Whilst he had observed, with caution, her interactions with that man, Lumb (then working for her brother), due to his station Kenneth did not view him as any kind of aspirant for Ellen's affections. It was not that but the social impropriety of their propinquity which concerned him. Ellen's membership of the mixed cycling club, where clearly she mingled with some others of that man's ilk, was something he disapproved of as inappropriate. Cycling for women was contentious in itself, improper even. It made Kenneth wonder if Ellen were becoming too 'modern', as he thought of such things.

On the other hand, he had known Ellen from early girlhood. Her general shyness, interest in discussing books with him and pleasing deference to his suggestions of what she might like to read, together with an easy friendship between them of long standing, still offset that concern, however. He had also been impressed by how generously Ellen had spent time with her sister-in-law's ailing father, which seemed entirely appropriate to Kenneth. Yes. He would see how they fared in the Lake District together, for she must, of course, suit his mother too in the same way as a companion, especially in future years. And it was high time that Kenneth himself got married.

He admired beauty in women, true, and Sylvia's beauty, particularly, was captivating. But such beauty, to whomever it belonged, was merely an aesthetic ideal. Ellen's face was not as symmetrically pleasing, certainly, but she was slender, unencumbered by those womanly curves so in vogue which Kenneth found unappealing. He continued to stroll and consider his own suitability. He would not, he believed, be a cruelly demanding husband.

He was appalled by the number of pregnancies and risk of death in childbirth that so many married women suffered. No wife of his would have such a life inflicted on her. Kenneth aimed for a high-minded union, a marriage founded on shared sympathies. Ellen, he now felt, could meet him in that.

Being fastidious and principled, Kenneth had not, like so many of his peers, lain with any prostitutes or taken lovers. His curiosity about the female form led him no further than to have a vague notion of a nude purity as smooth as that belonging to a classical female statue, pudenda only delicately defined, or with carved drapes for suggestion. He had grown up with no sisters to imagine that anything else might lie beneath a decorous gown. For all his wide reading, Kenneth was a repressed innocent who had always lived with his widowed mother and lost his father very young.

Standing on the promenade with these comfortable assessments passing through his mind, Kenneth noticed the entangled couple kissing. In public! Then, he saw them part. The man made to go down the pathway to the woods and the woman was revealed as – Ellen herself! He felt an almost physical shock as, in that instant, Kenneth also recognised Peter Lumb – the one who had been on the run! The arsonist wild man who, rumour still had it (and Kenneth was drawn to rumour), had destroyed Stanger's Mill! An extraordinary rush of feelings went through him. Most strongly, nothing to do with Ellen at all but, strangely, relating to that almost elemental game of Knurr and Spell on the moors. When Peter had called him back to shake his hand as a good sport after what had been a grudging battle between them, Kenneth had been disarmed by the manly generosity of the gesture, even moved by it.

Now, just as Kenneth recognised Ellen, he recognised

Peter too and, bizarrely, felt betrayed by them both. How dare this reckless ruffian, this lout, in whom he had seen a brief glimpse of honour amongst men, impose on his own nearly betrothed? And she, so gently courted by Kenneth, to be pressed by such a fellow! He felt a knightly nobility rise up in him to deal with it. But, instead of going to Ellen, who was walking away up to the Wainhouse Tower end of the promenade, he found himself plunging across the street to follow Peter down the path into the woods, only moments after him, although it felt like a stunned lifetime to Kenneth. He caught up with Peter on the pathway along the top of the woods, at the very spot where he had first seen Peter, as a volunteer fireman, climbing dangerously on ropes as they practised their drill. They were brave and selfless men to act as firemen. Surely, he could appeal to that better spirit in Peter now to resist the low inclinations of his class with Ellen?

"Lumb!" he called out after him.

Peter turned, the sunlight's play through overhead leaves catching his fair hair and strong, straight features in one of those clear moments which, like the handclasp on the moors, Kenneth knew, strangely, that he would always remember. Peter saw Kenneth with surprise.

"Butterworth! What does *tha* want wi' me?"

The blank aggression in his tone was a clear rebuttal of Kenneth's perception of them both having been, briefly and unforgettably, connected as kindred male spirits after their contest on Rishworth Moor. Peter's rough address showed no recollection at all of the brief respect which had flashed between them on that day. Worse, he glared as if Kenneth had no right to speak to him at all!

"What do you mean by your conduct, Lumb?" Kenneth burst out. "I thought you a man of honour!"

"And so I am!" shouted Peter, instantly in a rage at such words, even though he did not at once comprehend the reason for this sudden attack on him. "Let any man who denies it stand up to me here and now!"

Again, to Kenneth, there was that something splendid about Peter as he spoke, squaring up immediately to battle the accusation with force as well as words. Kenneth stood amazed, stuttering to a halt before Peter's fists-up stance, his intended rebuke about Ellen's character being compromised dying on his lips, his thoughts too incoherent to be expressed. Peter dropped his fists with a contemptuous shake of his head and strode off, plunging down the cobbled cat steps towards Copley Road below. Kenneth found himself shaken. Great heavens, but he was no ruffian to sink to that scoundrel's level, was he? Of course he had not responded to the challenge to fight!

Pulling himself together, he headed up the path the other way and emerged at the top end of Albert Promenade. Again, scarcely any time had passed and across the main road he could see Ellen, walking down the green length of Skircoat Moor towards both their homes at the bottom of Saville Park, lost in her thoughts. Should he speak to her directly, Kenneth wondered? Instead, he followed back down at a distance, for he did not feel quite in command of himself.

He must not accuse Ellen in default of Peter, for the man was always the real culprit in Kenneth's view. If he had hesitated to speak up to Peter it was because, unlike Peter, he was a gentleman who prided himself upon acting like one at all times. It was only Peter's being such an uncouth, raw being that had disabled him from doing so, he told himself, and yet Kenneth's legs still trembled a little beneath him in reaction to the brief confrontation as he followed behind Ellen. He was careful not to catch up with her but rather watched over her as a careful chaperone, unobserved.

His clear duty was to speak to Ellen's father. Kenneth knew his duties and he would do it. Kenneth was only thankful that he had made no proposal to Ellen as yet, and in that he found a kind of relief that he was no longer obliged to do so. He sighed. Perhaps it remained that marriage, after all, would not be for him. His further thoughts about what he *would* have said to Peter in the woods, and done physically too if he had not held back from it, did not provide much balm to his wounded sensibility. Clearly, Peter now believed Kenneth to be a coward and a lesser man than he had thought him before.

Bitterly stung by all these considerations, on his return Kenneth immediately penned a high-toned, astringent letter to Mr Rastrick. He expressed his disappointment that as a family friend and, he had begun to hope, rather more than that, he felt obliged to report what, as an innocent bystander, he had witnessed that afternoon. He asked Mr Rastrick to explain to Ellen that, as a result, his own intercourse and friendship with her must cease. He had once explained to her that his good opinion, once lost, would not be regained. He found himself now in this most unhappy position, he regretted to say.

It was his sad duty to tell Mr Rastrick, he wrote, that Ellen should be protected from herself by being prevented from meeting with a most unsuitable fellow. Ellen's own honesty would, he was sure, bring her to tell her father who this person was. If not, he would feel honour bound to disclose this himself at her father's request, due to the man's reputed character. He hoped, nay presumed, even, that this letter would be taken as one sent with the most honest of intentions and that his own relations with Mr Rastrick, in business and as neighbours, would remain entirely unaffected by any of this. There was, of course, no further question of a holiday being spent by Miss Ellen Rastrick with his mother and herself. He was happy to leave it to her father's discretion to explain matters, as he did not wish to cause her any direct distress. He remained, *respectfully yours, Kenneth Butterworth.*

The letter was sent by hand directly to Mr Rastrick, to be opened privately in his study at his earliest convenience. There it was left on his desk, where such letters awaited his attention in due course. Business and more social letters were sometimes sent between the two men in this way for ease of communication and so there would seem nothing odd to the rest of the household in this one's arrival. Kenneth, even in the heat of his indignation, did not want to cause a hullabaloo for Ellen with her mother. Let her father, much the better half in Kenneth's view, deal with the matter as discreetly as he preferred. Kenneth decided that he would not write to confirm any of the rentals he had been looking at in the Lake District. Or, on the other hand, maybe he would, and hire a companion for his mother for the duration. He would commune with Wordsworth alone in the hills and be all the better for it, he concluded, still trying to feel noble.

Mr Rastrick was taking his wife out for an airing in their carriage at her behest when the letter arrived. It being nothing out of the ordinary, the servants did not bring it to his particular attention, as his habit was to remain with his family during most of Saturday and he might not enter his study until late. That evening, Ellen's mother spent an age fussing over her dress, the sit of her hat and the fit of her long evening gloves, for the occasion of her supper outing. Ellen was in agonies for her to leave before Peter arrived. Finally, Mrs Rastrick departed.

Mr Rastrick sat down with a contented sigh to his

newspaper when Ellen interrupted him with, "Father, we will have a caller tonight and I very much want you to speak to him."

Her father looked up, seeming to take in the import of this at once.

"Oh? I will be very happy to speak to Kenneth Butterworth," he responded warmly, not yet having retired to his study to receive that gentleman's heated missive of earlier in the day.

"No, Father. It is not Kenneth."

"Not...?" her father answered as the doorbell rang.

Moments later, Peter, very smart in his suit and looking his energetic best but also with a touchingly hopeful air, entered the room. He crossed it in quick strides with his hand eagerly outstretched.

"Mr Rastrick. I'm Peter Lumb and I am delighted to meet you properly, sir."

His approach took Mr Rastrick by surprise but he instinctively responded by standing up and shaking hands with Peter in return, saying, "Good evening. You are an unexpected visitor, Mr Lumb?"

"I know it, sir, but Ellen and I very much wanted to speak to you."

"Together?"

"Aye, sir. She must speak her own mind too."

"I have never prevented it," answered Mr Rastrick, raising an ironic eyebrow. "But I must confess to being taken by surprise, if I understand you both correctly."

"Sir, I believe you do. I have asked Ellen to marry me and she has done me the great honour of accepting me this very afternoon. I asked her before and we became engaged privately. I asked her again today for her to be absolutely clear in her mind."

"I have accepted him, Father, and very happily."

"I'm not of your station, I know," Peter hurried on,

picking up on Mr Rastrick's instant appraisal of him and reacting with a prickly defence of himself. "But we all make our own way in life, do we not? I'm a foreman at Bradbury's Mill now, sir, and..."

"But – forgive me – how are you both acquainted to begin with?" interrupted Mr Rastrick, frowning at his hastiness.

"Peter," warned Ellen, and Peter subsided, cooling his manner instantly. She decided to bite the bullet. "Papa, Peter was Len's manager at Stanger's New Mill and he designed the new chimney for him that is the talk of Halifax. Not only that, he is the reason why they have the best new machinery in the area, and such good working conditions that people are fighting to work there now. Len has the best workforce in Calder Valley thanks to Peter."

Now it was Peter's turn to say, "Ellen!" as his heart sank at her words.

They were all still standing and Mr Rastrick said slowly, "I believed I had heard your name and of course, I saw you at the opening of Stanger's New Mill. You raised the flag! I recollect you now although we never met in person. Len spoke highly of you at one time. But I believe you left him without warning! Hardly a steady prospect for my daughter, even if I favoured you as a son-in-law."

Here, both Ellen and Peter breathed a small sigh of relief that Len had not told him all, the potentially damaging secret about what had happened at Stanger's Mill before having been kept close, they hoped.

"Peter left because his work was done there, Father. He is improving Bradbury's Mill now and just think – if you were to take his advice too – how modern and advanced Rastrick's Bobbin Factory might be?"

"Ellen!" objected Peter. "Mr Rastrick – Ellen's

enthusiasm carries her away. I do not suggest any such thing myself. It would be a great presumption."

"It does. And it would be," replied Mr Rastrick. "I must thank my daughter for her confidence in her father's own business abilities." But he did smile at her here as well. "Ellen is a great moderniser. And I can see she is not the only one. It is no bad thing to be looking to the future, young man. Leonard's success has shown me that, and if he has you to thank for it, that is a good thing too. But *marriage*? Ellen has only just turned eighteen and has her head in books all day long. She has no notion of keeping house, my dear fellow. Quite apart from anything else."

It was in the last phrase that all his reservations really lay, they both knew, those of Peter's class, but Peter ploughed fervently on anyway.

"Sir, if you will forgive me? It's natural for a father to see his daughter as just a girl still. But Ellen's a right good lass and with plenty of sense. More than I've had at times, I can tell you. We have known each other many months now and I cannot say how much I admire and respect her. I will provide a very good home for her. And I don't doubt we will manage it together very well."

Mr Rastrick regarded them, struck by the hope in their ardent faces and by the obvious feeling radiating between them.

"I see that this is a real attachment," he said eventually. "I have listened and I will speak to both of you alone next, if I may. Mr Lumb, come with me into my study. Ellen, wait here for me. Mr Lumb may wait then, while I speak to you."

Ellen and Peter exchanged a look and then he went out with her father. Peter had conducted himself well so far, with dignity but not the defensive antagonism of old, after that one brief flash of it which he had instantly repressed. Ellen knew how much he was keeping himself in check there. She was also pleased by how well his confident intelligence was showing, and without conceit. Her father would appreciate that, as well as Peter's canny ambitions to improve the industry, which had already proved successful for Stanger's New Mill. Her father was a competitive man in that way and he would certainly want to equal his son's success if the family bobbin mill could be advanced too. She could only hope that she had not rushed into those statements, which were bound to be discussed with Len. She must get to Len first and determined to do it when she went to see Carrie the next day. There would be no time to lose. Mr Rastrick now found Kenneth's letter on his desk, just as Peter entered.

"One moment, Mr Lumb. I have a letter here which I had not seen earlier."

Peter bit his impatient lip while Mr Rastrick opened the letter, recognising Kenneth's writing and expecting it to be some social or business note, for Kenneth often made recommendations about investments. He glanced through it with some initial puzzlement, then realised that Kenneth must have witnessed Ellen and Peter together and judged what he saw by Peter's station. Before referring to it, Mr Rastrick asked Peter what he had to say about his prospects, which he happily outlined and they had a lengthy and lively discussion about various matters concerning them. After this, Mr Rastrick handed him the part of the letter referring to him, leaving out the rest about the withdrawn invitation. Peter turned very red upon reading it.

"Mr Rastrick, the embrace he saw was the seal on my proposal to Ellen today, which we told you of! I asked her on Albert Promenade, in full public view of all t' world and respectable as you like. The occasion when she was so generous as to say yes to me again. I swear to you that I have been a gentleman in every possible way towards your daughter." He looked directly at Mr Rastrick as he spoke. "Whatever that mealy-mouthed Butterworth has written there, he'd have heard t'truth from me if he'd been man enough to ask for it. He followed me dahn to the wood and challenged my honour. I dared him to tell me what for and he had no words. Just stood there like the nincompoop he is!"

His posture and manner left Ellen's father in no doubt as to how Peter might have defended that honour and his blazing honesty of feeling impressed Mr Rastrick with his sincerity.

"Well, I am thankful for it, Peter. Had I read it alone and prior to your announcements, I might well have feared that Ellen had fallen an unlikely victim to some dastardly rakehell, and on Albert Promenade, too, of all places!" Peter gave a shout of laughter at this unexpectedly humorous response and Mr Rastrick joined in. "Poor Kenneth," he observed after a time. "He is an old-fashioned soul, you know. And you must forgive him as our family friend. What a relief that Ellen will not have Mrs Butterworth for a mother-in-law. Although I hardly think she would have accepted his proposal, should he have finally brought himself to make one, that is," he added drily. "I find myself glad of it."

"I hope you are, sir," said Peter, still laughing in relief, whilst also thinking that Mr Rastrick might think better of that emotion when he met Peter's own mother in person.

"First Sylvia and now Ellen lost to him. Where will he turn to next, I wonder, for I find myself quite out of daughters for him to seek to measure up to his expectations?"

"Ah've only brothers, sir," Peter attempted to quip back and Mr Rastrick smiled, shaking him firmly by the hand.

Peter thought for a moment and then said, "Mr Rastrick, there's implications in that letter about my character."

"He judged you as he thought he saw your position in society to be, I presume."

"Mebbe, and mebbe by gossip too, sir. I were known to 'ave – views, sir. Active ones."

"Active views," pondered Mr Rastrick. He sniffed. "I make my own judgements and they are not based on rumour." He looked Peter steadily enough in the eye for Peter to know that he knew what rumours were meant, and to know that even Mr Rastrick might have heard of them. He flushed dully to realise it but Mr Rastrick surprised him again, saying, "My son employed you at Stanger's Mill, did he not, Mr Lumb? The new, raised Stanger's Mill?"

"Aye, sir," Peter responded.

"Then no further talk on it is needed," said Mr Rastrick, leaving Peter uncertain as to whether this meant bygones should be bygones, whatever the truth of the matter about the fire, or that his employment with Len dismissed such accusations automatically.

Peter resisted opening up any further. There was brave truth and there was reckless endangerment. He had done enough of that all round in the past. He simply nodded, rather too overcome to speak and that, in fact, did him no disservice in Mr Rastrick's view. "We may understand each other, Peter, with no more said on the subject," Mr Rastrick concluded. "Now, we will go back to Ellen. I would be grateful if neither of us referred to Butterworth's note. I will deal with it in my own way, since he has announced he will be keeping his distance now."

"Agreed, sir," said Peter, readily, for he certainly had no wish to broach such a subject with Ellen.

Peter came back in to Ellen after what seemed to her like a very long interval and her father called her to him directly, without giving them chance to speak together first. They could only exchange another look, and that fleeting. Peter gave her an encouraging nod but looked stressed, she thought. Her father closed his study door behind them and indicated that she should sit.

"Now, Ellen," he said, looking grave. "You must consider yourself carefully. Kenneth Butterworth has invited you to go and stay with him and his mother in the Lake District and you have accepted. That and your general relationship with him suggests an understanding which your mother and I fully expected you had agreed to. I did not see it as a passionate connection but certainly one of shared interests and equal station. Have you given your word to him before you did so to Mr Lumb?"

"No, Father!" declared Ellen vehemently. "There is nothing but friendship between us, I assure you! Kenneth sought me as a companion for his mother for the holiday. And any wife he does have in the future would have to perform that office too. Believe me when I say that I *never* would do that!"

She spoke so indignantly, jumping to her feet, that her father laughed.

"I am delighted to hear it," he said unexpectedly. "The thought of listening to that woman's vagaries as well as your…but never mind," he added hastily, before indiscreetly naming his own wife in the same criticism. "Butterworth is a sound man, however?"

"Kenneth wanted to make an offer for Sylvia, Father, and not to me. We all knew it. Then Noel Ogden asked her first."

"Ah, yes. Noel. An interesting kind of son-in-law, but your mother is happy about it given his position."

"Then that will have to do for her. I shan't marry to

please my mother, you know."

"Or your father?"

"I hope I will marry to make myself happy, Father, and that you would be pleased because of it."

"You judge correctly. Peter will suit me far better than Noel Ogden has ever done. But the question is whether Peter Lumb is the man to make *you* happy, Ellen? It will not be the life you have been brought up to live so far. He's always been a working man, whatever he reaches for now."

"Peter has no wish to ape a gentleman and I respect people who work for their living, Father."

"He has character and force. Vision too. I'll grant him that. And however you came to love one another, I see that you do. Still, you are very young and untried, Ellen." Mr Rastrick walked about a little, hands behind his back. "To me, so is Lumb. Here is my offer. I will accept your engagement on the understanding that he proves himself as good as his word. I have offered him a trial position with Rastrick's and he was glad to accept it, but is bonded to Mr Bradbury for the next several months. I respect his loyalty in holding to that commitment, I must say, for my offer that he leave early was testingly generous. We set a later date. Then we shook hands upon it."

"Then, Father – you agree to his proposal?"

"Now that I am assured you have not made any prior commitment, I do. Let me tell your mother in due course. Leave Kenneth Butterworth to me, my dear. I must say, I never cared for the assumption that he would transfer his interest to you so easily, as it did not bespeak deep feeling, nor did I see any on your part. What will he make of it, I wonder? And Noel Ogden!"

Mr Rastrick gave a bark of laughter, for he always found Noel challengingly affected.

"I agree that they are not at all alike, Father," said Ellen with a smile, not revealing that Peter and Noel already knew one another. Their acquaintanceship through the Clarion Club had bound so many of them happily together, she thought, and quite unexpectedly! "I shall not go away with Mrs Butterworth and Kenneth now, Father, of course. Peter would absolutely hate it!" she added.

"Of course you will not," her father agreed. "It would be wholly inappropriate. You had better go and reassure him on that and all scores relating to Butterworth, then."

"Father – you did not suggest...?" cried Ellen, horrified.

"No – but it does a man no harm to think he might have had a rival. I let him know that one of our neighbours had long been paying court. I said that your choice came as a surprise to me but I could see where your heart truly lay tonight. I told him that this was a man of excellent character, long known to the family." (All things which he had proceeded to tell Peter about Kenneth Butterworth.)

"And what did Peter say?" asked Ellen anxiously.

"He said, 'I can see I have a mighty amount to live up to, sir', as dry as you please," Mr Rastrick chuckled. "He stood his ground well enough, I must say. He'll do. If he's all he's cracked up to be," he added, looking at Ellen meaningfully. "No wedding for at least six months after I take him on. That takes us up to this time next year. So that's plenty of time for us all to find out about one another."

They were not entirely comfortable words to Ellen, knowing what might be found out, but she was delighted that her father had agreed to things at all. She ran to him and threw her arms around him.

"Thank you, Father. You won't regret it!" she

promised.

"Let us hope that neither of us do," he answered.

"But, Father! We could not bear to wait so long. And I cannot agree to him being on trial with you to see if he suits you as a manager before you allow him to marry me! It is not a commercial transaction and very unfair to both of us! Why – it will be almost as if we are not engaged at all! I am old enough to marry without your permission, you know, Father? Peter will not care if I come with a dowry or not and has no thought of such a thing, if that is your concern!"

"Perhaps he will not. But I will. I do not want my dearest girl to live in a poorer situation. It would not be a happy start for either of you to struggle. You are not used to it."

"Then perhaps I should be!" declared Ellen hotly, tears stinging her eyes already. "And I will marry him without money as happily as he will do me!"

"I already know that," said Mr Rastrick. "The young man was quite forthcoming upon the subject!" Ellen was between a sob and a laugh at hearing this. "Dry your eyes. You have both said enough to convince me of your decision and that your promises between you are heartfelt and genuine. Very well. I put no conditions on your union. Oh, and of course I will give you a dowry."

"I cannot believe you put me through all that to see how much I meant it, Father!" exclaimed Ellen.

"I owed it to both of us as your father. Now, we must join the young man again, who has probably worn a hole in our best rug in front of the fender pacing about waiting. He isn't the sitting still kind of fellow, is he?"

"No, he isn't," agreed Ellen, laughing.

Together, they went in to find Peter, as expected, restlessly on his feet walking about the room. Mr Rastrick went across to shake his hand again.

"I welcome you as my son-in-law to be. The rest, we already shook on."

"That we did, sir!" exclaimed Peter, looking quite transported and, unable to help himself, he grabbed Ellen into a bear hug of delight before releasing her and saying, "I beg your pardon, Mr Rastrick."

"Now, young people. You must be prepared for resistance from some of the rest of the family, I don't doubt. Let me say this, though, Peter. I might be a gentleman in standing now but my own grandfather was a handloom weaver in Bradford once, so you may realise that I know, too, what hardship the coming of the machines gave to people like my own family. It's ability and commitment that carries you into success in my view. Chance too. I think you've made your own luck, Peter, and so that stands you in good stead with me."

"Thank you, sir," said Peter gratefully, being careful to address Ellen's father with full respect throughout the interview.

Mr Rastrick rang the bell for sherry to be brought, and they toasted one another with a small glass of it each, even Ellen. After this, Peter left and Mr Rastrick said, "Perhaps I might be allowed a read of my newspaper now, Ellen. Your mother will be back any time and at this rate I will lose the opportunity altogether. Might we wait until tomorrow before telling her the news?" he pleaded.

"Of course, Father! Better still, let us wait until Noel and Sylvia have returned and she will be quite distracted anyway," laughed Ellen, running up to her room to write to Peter immediately, even though they had only just parted.

The following day she went to Heatherfield, joining Carrie for lunch and to spend the afternoon. Her mother's continuing reluctance to see Carrie meant that Ellen going was seen as smoothing the way in family relations between them all. Over lunch, she told Carrie about Peter's return, his proposal, her acceptance of it and her father's agreement to their marriage.

At first, Carrie was as silent as she had been on first acquaintance, so Ellen pressed on with, "I am speaking to you now, Carrie, to ask that you stand by me when I talk to Len. He said he would come up to meet us for tea after the office. Carrie – I assure you that I marry for love."

A dark colour stained the bottom of Carrie's cheeks, a crimsoning flush of feeling.

"Yes. That is something which *I* could not do," she said softly, looking aside at the green, sloping field angling up outside the window. "Very well." She sighed. "I had hoped that you would give yourself more time in life before tying yourself to any marriage, to say nothing of the man himself."

"I am not like you, Carrie. I do not have some driving ideal carrying me forward. Or if I do, only alongside the person I love."

Carrie gave a small smile at those words.

"We are more alike in that than you believe, Ellen."

An unexpected image came to Ellen of Carrie and Fiona, their heads bent close together in intimate and eager talk over the candle flame. A glimmer of understanding came to her, but only with the thought that however deep their friendship was, it could not equate with her own feelings for Peter.

"Father has agreed, Carrie. I *cannot* have Len telling him what Eustace said that day. He has not done so yet but I fear he might do at this news. Whatever Peter said then, it was because Eustace implicated me. Peter's only thought was to protect me and he gave none to what it might cost him. He achieved so much here, Carrie and had such hopes!"

Carrie said, after another long interval, "Ellen – only

you and Peter know the truth between you." It was Ellen's turn to colour here. "But he did create a whole new mill and Len is having great success with it already. Let that stand now and I will back you with Len today. I agree that it is best to tell him at once."

"Thank you," said Ellen and she and her sister-in-law (who was not demonstrative in general) exchanged a rare embrace.

Leonard, when he appeared, however, did not arrive alone. To Ellen's utter amazement, Peter, again in his best suit, was with him.

"Come in and sit down, Peter," Len said.

Ellen looked between them in astonishment. Peter came to take a seat beside her on the couch and said, taking her hand, "Ellen, I came to see both John and your brother here today. It were time. I can't go skulking about when I've already spoken to your father. John's forgiven me for barging out of his wedding like I did and..." Here he looked across at Len, with a hopeful light shining in his eyes.

"And I've listened to what Peter had to tell me," said Len. "The past is done with already, whatever led that teacher to make his accusation."

"Aye, and when it were Stanger's New Mill, I never stinted an hour of work or effort on your behalf to make it the best it could be for everyone," Peter said, unable to prevent that slight note of swaggering challenge from creeping into his voice, for all he tried to repress it, especially at a nudge in the ribs from Ellen.

But Len broke into an unexpected smile.

"No – you did not – and John Henderson will be glad to get back to his masonry and sculpting. He's faithfully followed on from you, Peter, but it's not his wish to stay at it. The day you left, we all discussed it here and Ellen spoke out for you. She said that it was her name being called into it that led you to make that confession. I believe entirely in the truth of that part and let us leave the rest unsaid, whatever it might be."

"Thank you, Len!" cried Ellen gratefully.

"Welcome to the family, Peter. I wish you and Ellen all the luck in the world. And I hope you will manage *both* of Rastrick's mills into a better future."

"Whatever happened when the mill was my father's alone," said Carrie, "and it *was* in a poor condition by then, with old machinery and the place crammed with flammables cheek by jowl with it – Stanger's New Mill was built by the two of you and John Henderson. I am very glad that Peter has come back to join us again. If my father were still able to do it, he would thank you himself."

Peter and Len shook hands and then he shook hands with Carrie, who gave him and Ellen a steady look, one which spoke volumes about the silent knowledge which lay between the three of them. Len had an air of some relief that Peter would return to the role which had given him such solid support. Ellen, who had been quite prepared to battle with her brother that day, was delighted their old fondness for one another would not be compromised in any way now. Of all the three siblings, she and Len got on together the best. She also realised that both Carrie and Len were adepts at not confronting what could be avoided to ensure a pragmatic concord and successful relationship. She knew that this, today, was supporting her and Peter. But she did not want to think of those shadows of deceit lurking in the background. In her case, she had been forced to lie to protect Peter from any punishment, and thank goodness, too, that they had already persuaded her own father.

***

What she did not know was that Peter had already met privately one night with John and Cyril before he came to the mill that day, at an inn tucked away in the side streets near the top of the new Borough Market. *They* thought they were meeting a supplier of marble and were amazed when Peter walked into the tavern instead and got straight to the point with them.

"I'm back to make my peace, if you'll have it, John? We were fellow firemen and comrades a long time. I beg your forgiveness for what happened. There was no intent of it and I'll take my punishment now if you think it's due to me?"

"You did it, though. *You* set that fire!" declared an incredulous John, amazed to see him.

"Aye, but only to disrupt, never to destroy t' place."

"And Bradbury's?" murmured Cyril, for even though they were private in the snug they kept their voices low.

Peter flushed uncomfortably.

"It were the wrong road. I know that now."

"And coming back to fight the fire, playing the hero? Did you glory in it, Peter? Was that part of it for you?" pursued Cyril.

Clearly stunned by this suggestion, which turned him pale with shock at the dishonour of such an idea, Peter visibly fought back his natural inclination to blaze up, shout denials and storm out full of wounded indignation. Mastering himself, he spoke with low and feeling vehemence.

"Never that! Never. I sought only to stop what I'd started. I thought I knew what I were doing but it were wrong. All wrong! And John, I tried to put it right for you after, wi' t' chimney at Stanger's!"

He was unable to go on, overcome by emotion. John looked back long and hard, saw the tears of shame and regret standing in Peter's eyes and eventually put out his hand to be shaken in forgiveness. Peter looked, with a guilty stifled sob, at the damaged but healed fingers, pink with scar tissue, and reached his own hand out to clasp John's gently back, afraid of hurting him further.

"Aye, it *were* wrong," said John. "But you fought that fire like a demon. It were me that went up after you when you told me to stay back. You tried to stop me. But it's a good job I did when you fell in the rope." Peter nodded, deeply moved. "Time's passed. I'll sculpt again. I know that now. If you *have* changed, then I do forgive it."

"I promise you that I have," said Peter fervently. "Thank you. Thank you both, indeed. I must go. You can't be seen wi' me yet. Not when you're working as Len's manager. Ellen told me."

"Ellen!" exclaimed John in surprise.

"Aye." A prouder smile crossed Peter's face. "We're promised to one another and I'm to speak with her father. But I had to speak with you first, John. Make things right between us if I could."

John and Cyril exchanged looks and nods which silently said they would keep this to the three of them, although Cyril had shaken his head a little at the announcement about Ellen, while not looking entirely surprised.

"You should come to see Leonard Rastrick after seeing his father about getting wed to Ellen," suggested John. "I know he and Carrie kept quiet on all t' rumours, even as far as Mr Rastrick senior was concerned. They wanted to keep Stanger's reputation sound. As temporary manager, I were in on all them discussions. I don't want to keep that job on. It's thy job if tha wants it back. I'm going back to my own work with Cyril and to my sculpting. If I shake hands before Len with you, Peter, and you make a full denial of the accusation, all may come good. Eustace can't prove what he said and he were aghast that he had done so after my wedding. Besides, he's in quarantine in that school as it's full of scarlet fever."

"Lie again?" said Peter. "I ran before rather than do it!"

"Nay – you spoke up to save Ellen's name. We all knew that. And she denied all, of course. As if a girl like her would have to do with your daft antics!"

They all smiled at that and Peter knew that this was an offer to let the waters finally close over the truth of what had really happened on that day. He gladly accepted it because Ellen's name did indeed have to be protected.

"I'll do it, John, and I'm to speak to her father any day now."

"Well – I wish you luck, but I don't know how you might fare wi' the father."

Peter wanted to say that they would marry either way but refrained from it. He contented himself with shaking hands heartily with both his old friends instead, before leaving as a visibly much happier man than the one who had first come in.

"Ellen and Peter," remarked Cyril. "We'd better wish her good luck then, John. She'll need it wi' that one."

"She will," agreed John, as they clinked halves of mild in an ironic kind of toast to their young friend.

***

Full of the day's success at Heatherfield now, Peter took tea with them all and then Ellen asked if they might walk around to John and Libby's cottage because she wanted to tell Libby herself now that the news of their engagement was known in the family. She wondered what John would think and if he would be happy for her. To walk round arm in arm in the open felt like the wildest indiscretion to both of them, knowing that anyone who was passing, or looking out of one the other cottage windows on the row, might see them.

"You do realise that you and Noel will be brothers-in-law, Peter, don't you?" Ellen teased him.

"Aye, I'll have to refrain from calling him a great ninny now, won't I? At least if we're round a table together. And what will your hoity toity sister make of it, I wonder? Don't you let her be gibing at you because of me, Ellen."

"I won't care a jot!" returned Ellen. "But she'll make eyes at you now. You know that, don't you?"

"Me? Whatever for?" exclaimed Peter.

"Because all men must admire Sylvia first, that's why. She will flirt with you because you are engaged to me. She even looked kindly at poor Kenneth Butterworth again when she thought he had begun calling on me."

"Oh, *him*! I could tell you about *'im*!" exclaimed Peter, in a richly derogatory tone which made Ellen feel, rather warmly, that he did not like to think of Kenneth visiting her.

"And what precisely, do you think you could tell me about Mr Butterworth?" asked Ellen, laughing.

"That I'm the better man at Knurr and Spell for a start!" said Peter, grinning. "Nay, he's nobbut the loser now, is he? If he were ever going to be a winner."

"Not with me," said Ellen, squeezing his arm but remembering, not wanting to lose that good regard of Kenneth's which he had told her once lost was gone for good.

Now, sadly, it was. Her father had thought it best to show her Kenneth's letter and she was very sorry about it, whilst blaming him for writing to her father at all and for his rigidity. True to his word, Kenneth no longer called when Ellen was at home and she missed his friendship while realising that his withdrawal of it was inevitable now she was engaged to be married to Peter.

She had been relieved to learn that he had taken his mother away to the Lake District with a hired companion servant and they would both be spared the difficulty of meeting for a month or two.

John was already at home when they arrived and had just finished his own tea. When they knocked on the door, it was clear that Libby already knew. Ellen had not seen either of them now for a while, especially not John, and felt suddenly shy, but both of them shook hands with the couple in congratulation and Libby gave Ellen a kiss on the cheek.

"I'd say the Clarion Club has a lot to answer for, Ellen, wouldn't you?" She laughed. "Me with John and you with Peter. John has told me all about it and that you came to the mill today, Peter."

"I did and John was good enough…"

"John was glad to shake hands," interrupted John. "I don't deny I had bitter thoughts and plenty I wanted to say at one time but not now. Time's passed, I've healed and I've a new life. I'll be a sculptor again at Ogden Towers soon enough."

"Aye," agreed Peter, relief at old friendship restored on both their faces. "And I believe congratulations are in order for both of you too, with a little 'un on the way," he added, grinning and, with that, they were all able to be at ease with one another.

Libby produced a parcel carefully packaged up for him – the teapot and pipe wrapped up with his few abandoned clothes.

"Kept by for you, Peter, against your return," she told him, and he thanked them both, very touched by the gesture and by having the precious keepsakes restored to him.

When Peter and Ellen eventually left to go back to Heatherfield, Peter said, a little bitterly, "That preaching

Eustace has his fair share to answer for, doesn't he?"

"But he doesn't though, Peter. Does he?" answered Ellen. "It was true. We must be glad we have concealed it. And he tried to make amends by taking funds to your mother from the club when you had to leave because of what he said."

"I suppose so," agreed Peter, who had begrudged this act too as a piece of charity born of guilt when Ellen told him of it. "But it galls me to let it go."

"You must, though," Ellen urged, stopping and laying her hand on his arm to look up into his face with entreaty to overcome his natural instinct to have things out with everybody.

"I will, lass. I made you a promise to behave missen, didn't I?" he answered. "And I will."

Back at Heatherfield, Peter collected his bicycle to return to his lodgings and Ellen was sent home in Carrie and Len's carriage, smiling all the way back.

***

Noel and Sylvia swept back into Ogden Towers, and soon to Saville Park, with a train of souvenirs in their baggage to adorn the two houses and its occupants. Mrs Rastrick was in transports of delight at both of them and everything they brought. There was nowhere as splendid as Ogden Towers, she would tell anybody who might listen.

At a welcome home dinner party for them, when Noel had feasted them all on a host of recollections and anecdotes, Mr Rastrick finally said, "This is as fine a time as any to announce some other family news."

"Oh, but Harold, Noel has not yet finished telling us about *gondolas*," objected Mrs Rastrick, as if these were things newly discovered by her son-in-law himself.

"Then you must possess your soul in patience to hear more about them, Mary," said Mr Rastrick. He rang the bell and their manservant quietly ushered Peter in, again looking well in his dark brushed suit. "Sit here, my boy," invited Mr Rastrick, offering him a chair at his side. "This place is set, not for a missing guest but for an expected one. Raise a glass please one and all – to Mr Peter Lumb, who is to marry our dearest Ellen, with my very good wishes for their happy future."

The butler, as he was speaking, quietly poured some champagne into the flutes he deftly set on a tray and handed them round.

Mr Rastrick stood and raised his glass. Len and Carrie did the same and, looking highly amused, so did Noel.

"Great heavens, Ellen! You are to marry our very own firebrand!" he exclaimed naughtily. In the moment's awkward silence which followed, he gave a bellowing laugh. "Mr Lumb is Leonard's radical manager, Mr Rastrick. A man with *quite* a reputation!" he said, with a wink at Peter and Ellen.

"I believe I know of it," replied Mr Rastrick equably. "And hope to benefit as Stanger's New Mill has done from it. How is Mr Stanger, Carrie, my dear?"

"Failing but comfortable, thank you," she answered. "Congratulations to the happy young couple," she hurried on to say.

"To Peter and Ellen. And welcome home again, Noel and Sylvia!" toasted Len.

Sylvia was not looking at all pleased to have the centre of attention removed from herself and Noel as the happy couple and favoured Peter with one of her most beguiling looks.

"I believe I have had the pleasure of meeting Mr Lumb before. Did I not see you climbing rocks most daringly with the volunteer fire brigade last year at Albert Promenade?" she asked, with the little laughing thrill in her voice which she could produce so effectively.

"Aye, that you did, Mrs Ogden," said Peter warily, rather thrown by all the flummery and foxed by Noel's words.

Either Noel hinted at the Clarion Club, or worse had somehow got wind of the rumours and accusations against Peter too. But this was Noel, who enjoyed making mischief for its own sake and now moved on from unsettling Peter.

"Sylvia, my love, Peter cannot remember it. He has been quite bowled over by your sister. Felicitations, my dears!" said Noel. "How absolutely fascinating. To complete the evening, all I need now is for Albert Dewhirst to walk in with Jane Ellison on his arm and announce that they are to be wed too. Is he invited?"

He gave one of his sideways, flirtatious looks at his wife, alight with knowing suggestion so that, looking discomfited, she took refuge in raising her glass to Ellen and Peter too.

"Albert Dewhirst?" frowned Mr Rastrick, not seeing the relevance of this to any of the proceedings. "No, he is not invited tonight. This is a family party only."

"Pity," said Noel reflectively, smiling to himself. "I expect he is still rampaging around Paris on his tour anyway. He's bringing a batch of artists back to Ogden Towers, sir, where we are to begin a new movement. We shall be the flower of the county. But don't let me detract," he added serenely. "Peter, old chap, you must call often as we are to be relatives. My door is always open to you!"

Noel was fully aware, naturally, of how Peter talked about him but here Peter surprised him by saying, "I have never forgotten the kindness you showed to my friend Stanley and his family, Noel. Thank you for your invitation."

He spoke with a simplicity which appealed directly to

the best in Noel, who dropped his mannerisms at once to say seriously, "It was a very little that I could do. And I was more than glad to it."

"May a *mother* speak?" enquired Mrs Rastrick in tones of outraged dignity. "When was *I* to be consulted on the matter?"

"It is customary for a father to be asked for *his* permission," answered Mr Rastrick. "Rightly or wrongly. And I have given it, Mary. I do not recall any such question being asked by you when Noel requested my permission to marry Sylvia."

"But…" began Mrs Rastrick helplessly. Good manners forbade her to go into too much detail in company. "But I already knew Mr Ogden."

"And Leonard already knew Mr Lumb very well indeed. So there we have it. And now, you *do* know Mr Lumb, Mary."

"I must apologise for taking you by surprise tonight, ma'am. No offence from me is meant towards you for it," Peter said.

"And none is taken. Is it, Mary? The invitation to join us came from me," said Mr Rastrick with a rather glacial smile.

It was an expression he rarely wore but it was enough for Mrs Rastrick to say hastily, "Of course not." Pulling her dignity together she added, "I look forward to hearing all about it from you, Ellen. Congratulations to you both."

The ladies withdrew to grill Ellen, and the gentlemen remained for a short while after which Peter, having come in to make his farewells, made his relieved departure. Much as he wanted to be in Ellen's company, being in everybody else's was rather a strain. Ellen felt much the same and was very glad when her father, Noel and her brother joined them again to relieve the pressure. Still, she had very much enjoyed putting her mother and sister at such a disadvantage and it was worth enduring their astonishment afterwards for that alone.

***

Noel himself had always seemed oblivious to the story which had circulated about the night he was attacked and robbed. It was possible he had never heard it because it had not formed any official enquiry at the time, of course. He had merely reported that he had no memory of either assault or assailant. Relying on that, Ellen had not repeated it to Peter. She was still too ashamed that she could have considered it a possibility to wish to bring it up in any way. Besides, it would make him furious and it had all died down now.

Peter's return to Bradbury's Mill, however, had set all the rumours about him flying up once more like a flock of startled birds. Peter was aware of certain jealousy towards him due to his new and more superior position there (a jealousy he would formerly have felt himself towards anybody else who was so elevated) and worked all the harder to ensure good working conditions for his fellows. But he soon noticed how he would be looked at askance, how people drew aside and whispered when he passed by. Being Peter, he tackled it head on in the only way he knew how to, by singling out the next strong fellow who scowled at him and boldly demanding to know the reason for it, risky as that was.

"What's wi' your dirty looks, Cartwright? Let's 'ave it out in't open, man if you've got owt to say!"

"We all know where tha's really been these last months," the man flashed back. "In jail for setting on yon Ogden in town and robbing him to run off."

Peter responded to this with an outburst of laughing disbelief, a hot denial and knocking the man down, offering the same to anyone else who said it.

"Aye? Noel Ogden's to be my brother-in-law any day!

So why would I rob the man? He were my friend in the Clarion Club afore that too. That's right!" he called out to the lookers-on. "What other daft heads have we got 'ere, then? Come on, let's have t' rest of it. You've all known me long enough to spit it out."

His opponent got up from the floor as someone else shouted, "You've always been trouble, Lumb! And there's no smoke without fire!"

Some low laughter followed this sally, although in truth any scandal about the mill fire emerging from anybody who had been at John's wedding was garbled and unclear. Besides, the key players had all closed ranks to protect the good names of both Stanger's New Mill and Ellen Rastrick, any open suggestions being very firmly dismissed. Peter stared them all down.

"What's that supposed to mean?" he demanded. "Say it straight out or don't say it at all." Nobody did because he was foreman manager after all and nobody wanted to be dismissed. Following up his advantage, Peter said, "I'm 'ere to mekk a good place out of what were a bad 'un. After that, I'm off to do the same at Rastrick's Bobbins. So how's that trouble for any of you? A safe workplace, better working conditions, better pay! You're all getting it, aren't you?" Subdued nods and agreement followed. Peter concluded the business by shaking hands firmly with the man he'd knocked down. "Now let's 'ave and end of it and get on. I've never been in prison in my life and I never intend to be. Trust me, I were working me socks of ovver in Lancashire, just like I said. And what I learned, I've brought back to all of you here."

While people did not exactly cheer, the atmosphere eased up, as he had indeed brought better times along with them being back in their old workplace again. Peter's open laughter at the idea of his attacking Noel settled that issue, as well as his claims of intimate association with the man. It was another very close shave, though, and Peter spoke of it to Ellen in one of their private walks together.

"There are things we will just have to live down, Peter," she said seriously. "We both know that, don't we, and who really paid the price for it all? That's our secret. And it will always have to be. Remember, you've been forgiven. That's the main thing."

Peter agreed that it was but he was still uneasy about having gained a social leap by being engaged to Ellen, so they also talked of future days doing other, grander things than being part of Rastrick's Mill. Nobler things, standing up to be counted for people's rights in different ways, just as when he'd started the union work.

"I might be an MP one day!" he suggested.

"You won't be if you don't have business standing," said Ellen astutely. "So you'd better stick to having one while you make your mind up."

"I suppose so. Imagine it – anyone like me in Westminster. That'll never be the day."

"You'll have to settle for being an Alderman in Halifax, then, get all fat and have a big watch on your waistcoat," said Ellen, which made them both laugh again.

He had no serious political ambitions beyond his drive to change things and, being practical, he was really happier doing that on the ground, so to speak, he said.

"Good," said Ellen, not sharing how difficult she had found the campaign meetings with Carrie and Fiona in Manchester. "Don't go stirring it all up again by challenging more gossip, will you, Peter?"

Only when he had to, was all he would agree to there, with which she had to be content for the present.

***

The artists, or a few of them at least, not including the

unfortunate Milo (under further treatment somewhere), Vernon Greenbank (gone back to America) or Wolf (remaining in Paris), arrived at Ogden Towers with Albert to introduce them. Noel had arranged for rooms to be prepared for them in the towers and, as he said with largesse, the whole garden could be their studio. If it were raining, not an unlikely prospect, the attic rooms had a steady north light on their side of the building. John Henderson would have a sculpting studio among the stable buildings to use in between working at the monumental masonry business he had rejoined Cyril in now, and Cyril would also be continuing with design at Ogden Towers. Albert, talking to Noel, made light of Hannah's defection.

"Can you believe that she has become engaged to our earnest Eustace Horsfall? And I cannot sway her!" he said mockingly.

"So, you had only the fearsome Sarah to greet your homecoming?" answered Noel, noticing that Cyril and one of the Parisian group seemed to have an instant sympathy and not liking that at all.

His attention was only partly on Albert, covertly watching the artist and Cyril talking with great animation in the garden outside the window of the drawing room.

"Yes, but I cannot complain about my welcome home," said Albert, with a certain smile of recollection.

"I don't doubt that my wife will be delighted to see you too," remarked Noel casually, turning his back on the annoyance outside. "I will find her for you – oh, by the way, old chap, Miss Ellison is back at the vicarage. In case you are interested," he added, with an insinuating glance.

He went away and, shortly afterwards, Albert saw him break into the tête-à-tête in the garden between Cyril and the artist, with a crashing insistence. Sylvia, all lace and grace, fluttered into the room like a summer butterfly. Albert allowed himself to enjoy her beauty and be flattered by her attention. But he was not wholly satisfied by it. Not now. Very soon, he made his excuses and left. He was delighted to hear from Noel what he had thought he would have to try and find out about Jane himself.

It was not long at all before he called up at the vicarage, thinking it best to take Jane by surprise with his presence, rather than writing a letter asking to see her which she might refuse. Jane happened to be at the window, arranging some flowers she had gathered from the garden, so she saw Albert approach. The sight of him, that so familiar handsome face and figure, made her catch her breath. Seeing her too, he smiled with delight, tipped his hat and the next thing she knew, the doorbell rang. What should she do? Confused feelings ran through Jane and she felt her resolve wilt.

She could hardly refuse to see him even if she wanted to, which she didn't, and she heard her father emerge from his study calling, "Mr Dewhirst! Come in! Do come in!" when the day servant opened the door to Albert.

Albert faced a begrudging look from this woman because, being a servant about in the background of things, she had guessed at more than anyone knew about the cause of her young mistress's former distress. The vicar, however, gladly welcomed Albert with a handshake and brought him into the sitting room where Jane was.

"Look who is here, Jane! Well, well, so you are both returned for the present from your adventures abroad," he said, looking between them both with innocent pleasure.

"We are indeed!" returned Albert gaily, noting the 'for the present' with interest. "Miss Ellison, I hope I find you well?"

"Very well, thank you," Jane replied with veiled

composure, not responding to his solicitous tone.

He felt at once that she did not love him as she had done before. Surely that could not be so, though? On the contrary, she had left him because she loved him so much! Albert was sure of that. Doubtless, she had been torturing herself with jealousy ever since, when she should not have been doing so at all, if he had taught her anything! Albert bowed to Jane, looking into her eyes and smiling, then was invited to sit down by the vicar. Tea was brought in. Albert charmed Jane's father, knowing that Jane was watching him and being reminded of his good looks. For Albert's part, he thought Jane *wa*s looking very well, her figure as desirably supple as he remembered. It seemed very strange to be sitting and taking tea like this in the vicarage once again but he rather liked the game.

"Did you enjoy Europe's treasures, Mr Dewhirst?" asked the vicar. "What a rare opportunity you have had."

"I did, thank you, sir, and I have brought one or two back with me in the form of French artists!"

"French artists?" exclaimed the vicar, suitably taken aback.

"Only as guests at Ogden Towers, sir. Mr Ogden has the notion of a new school of art being established there and has invited them to stay with him."

"Extraordinary," said the vicar, shaking his head at this news. "A new school of art, you say? I expect that will make people sit up and think."

Albert laughed aloud at this gently prosaic surmise.

"Oh, yes, sir. I expect it will." He turned now to Jane. "You have left Miss Tordoff as her companion, Miss Ellison?" he asked, with subtle meaning.

"I have," she replied. "I could not abandon my father any longer."

"And yet, you found that you could happily

abandon Miss Tordoff without a qualm?" he pressed reproachfully.

"Miss Tordoff has many other friends and interests to occupy her time with," said Jane. "Ours was a happy interlude amongst them."

"Oh, surely more than that?" Albert exclaimed.

"I saw beautiful cities and great wonders which I never should have done without her company," replied Jane. "I even taught my own English classes, Mr Dewhirst. It was a taste of independence. And I have learned from it," she added, with some firmness.

Albert placed his cup back in its saucer, saying, "Well, I am glad to hear it. Since we have both been on our travels, won't you take a walk outside with me? It is a beautiful day to share tall tales and we must not bore your father with them."

"Oh, not at all, not at all." Mr Ellison beamed. "But of course you must take a stroll together."

Jane had no option but to agree or make things awkward, and besides, she detected a certain complaisance in Albert's carefully playful manner which she was determined to address. He believed he could win her over if he wished to.

"Let us go into the garden," Jane suggested. "Our rhododendrons bloom late but we have a fine display I can show to you."

"Certainly," Albert agreed, with a happy smile at the vicar.

Jane went to fetch her wrap. They stepped out and round into the relative privacy of the shrubbery, alight with colourful blooms as Jane had promised, whites and pinks in a glorious profusion.

"Beautiful!" Albert admired. "As are you, Jane."

"No. It is over between us, Albert. I cannot live as you do. Will not!" she declared, stepping back from his hand reaching for hers.

"But you love me, Jane," he protested, unable to credit that her adoration of him had really faded, although he read it in her face.

"That is not the same as you saying that you love me, Albert. Is it?"

She looked at him with such candour that he dropped his own eyes a moment, even as he said, "Love is freedom, Jane. You had no need to leave me as you did."

Jane shook her head.

"Freedom for you if you think of it so, Albert, but not for me. I told you, Albert. I cannot live like that. Will not!" she repeated.

Sylvia's name hung between them but Jane would not speak it nor Albert defend himself about that.

"Then I am sorry for it," he answered at last, meaning her decision and not any apology for himself, she knew, yet there was regret in his tone. "Jane," he pressed her. "We cannot part like this. I came back to find you."

She gave him an odd smile, resolute, even angry, but sorrowful.

"Not just for that, Albert. You came to bring your artists to Noel and yourself to Ogden Towers..." Again Sylvia's name hovered unspoken. "Your father no doubt expects you back at the dye works. You also have Hannah and Sarah to return to."

Albert did not tell her about Hannah's change of allegiance. He had no right to object to it, he knew, but even so pride kept him silent on that subject. Instead, he brushed Jane's words aside.

"What we have stands alone. You *know* this, Jane," he said, as he had done of old, but it was no good this time.

"I have told you. I cannot live like that. Will not!" she repeated with a passionate defiance.

There was a moment's silence, during which many

more things were left unsaid between them and then Albert tried once more to appeal to desire.

"Then I say again that I am sorry for it, Jane. Surely you remember Paris? I bought your portrait from Wolf, you know," he said winningly. "I will keep that if I cannot have you." She said nothing, although it was an effort not to, he could see. After waiting another moment or two and seeing she would not bend even to this, he asked, intrigued by the new purpose he sensed in her, "Do you have plans, Jane? To go away from here again?"

"I do."

"But you will not tell me of them?"

"No, Albert. They do not include you visiting me when it suits you to travel."

"Then you are going back to Paris?" he pounced. Jane said nothing to confirm or deny it and, in spite of himself, Albert could not help saying, "You will not find what you are looking for in Wolf, Jane." Jane just shook her head in impatient dismissal of that and gave him such a steady look that he was momentarily ashamed. After a pause he said, "I will bid you good day then, Jane, and if I *can* only wish you well in the future, then believe me that I do it most sincerely."

Jane watched him go, trying to collect herself. Even though she had found the strength to leave him and refuse him now, it broke her heart again to think of losing him completely, for she had loved him so. Even as she thought it, she realised that what she had said was true. It *was* over between them.

For his part, Albert, as he walked away, felt a mixture of things. He was hurt, yes, he was, and disappointed, deeply so, but he also felt relief at being released from Jane's intensity. Being with her again, if only briefly, had reminded him how exhausting and irritating he had found that. Such a sombre devotion, exclusive and demanding, was the opposite of his nature and beliefs and yet…and yet he regretted the loss of something between them which he had not experienced elsewhere and might not again. Whatever else about their love affair together, Albert knew that at least.

The irony was that by finding her own self-respect and acting upon it, Jane had gained Albert's respect for *her*, but he did not quite know it yet. He thought about what she had said about 'a taste of independence' and having learned from it. Well, if it hadn't been for him, he thought, validating himself once more, she wouldn't have done. Would she? What had she really meant by it, he wondered? Where did she intend to go? He would have been astonished, in fact, to learn of the plans she had already begun to make, but Jane did not wish to tell him of them. Her feelings for him were still too tender to trust herself with doing that and compromise her future liberty by seeming to invite him into it.

***

When she had left Venice so hastily, Jane eventually arrived at Miss Tordoff's Parisian apartment in a state of angry defiance against Albert. Miss Tordoff listened but, as before, would not discuss Albert in person herself.

She allowed Jane free reign to express her feelings for a day or two and then, over a sunny luncheon, with peaches and apricots glowing in a cut glass bowl between them, she laid down her knife and fork to say, "Jane, that is enough. You are raking over a past which you have turned your back upon. That was your decision and now we must help you to move forward from it."

This was spoken with such practicality that Jane did stop, and apologised for her self-indulgence. Miss Tordoff waved that away and had a suggestion to make. This was that she could make an introduction for Jane to teach English in a private 'pension' for the children of diplomats. It was outside the city itself in pleasant grounds, and Miss Tordoff would be able to recommend her to one of the diplomats who was key to the school's status and funding. She picked up her napkin to wipe her mouth delicately with a small, reminiscent smile.

"We met again here only recently after a long interval. I am quite certain that he will be happy to assist any friend of mine with absolute discretion," she said.

Jane demurred at first but with her new facility in languages discovered, and demonstrated to Miss Tordoff, who praised her greatly for it, was soon persuaded that she ought to capitalise upon it, both on that and on her newfound independence. A successful arrangement was soon made with the school, as Miss Tordoff had suggested it might be. The position would not begin until later in the summer and so Jane returned to her father first, introducing the subject over time to see how he regarded the idea. The contract would be for six months and, if suited, for a further such period. She would return home regularly, for visits during the school holidays, she told him, but would board there.

In fact, Mr Ellison was greatly relieved that she would have a source of income available to her, being older now himself and not well off as a clergyman. He was, besides, faced with adamant pronouncements that she had no intention of marrying and desired an independent life. Mr Dewhirst did not call again, much to the vicar's disappointment, whilst Mr Sykes had stepped back before Jane left, his tentative advances ignored. Finding her confident and altered on her return, he did not renew his former attentions either. Jane was in no need of the tender sympathy she had awoken in the curate when she was a docile invalid and an adventuring wife was not at all what *he* sought.

Nobody could have been more surprised than Jane was

herself to find that her former infatuation for Albert had lifted. In Venice, she had begun to realise their incompatibility. When he came to the vicarage, talking so confidently to her father while she looked on, she saw a handsome young man whom she had once adored but did so no longer. She had realised it with such clarity that she wondered how she could have felt so consumed by love for him before. After he had gone, she remembered Miss Tordoff's words.

"He was your first love, Jane. That is all. Remember the best of it and let him go now. Allow yourself to be happy."

After seeing Albert again Jane would, she knew, be able to do so, in spite of the deep physical attraction she still felt towards him. She would exist as her own person in her own self-determined life. However Albert, or Miss Tordoff, or others like them lived, that would never suit Jane and Albert must have known it, whatever he said! Yet in his way he had, as he had promised to do, set her free, just not quite in the way that he had intended.

She was to leave again for Paris with Miss Tordoff in secret only a few weeks later, having begged by letter to go earlier due to Albert and the artists being at Ogden Towers. Jane kept to the vicarage, meanwhile, studying her language books. She did not want to risk seeing those who had known her in France with Albert, even if they were a few miles away and safely on the other side of town. She kept well away from the Clarion Club too and felt an unexpected calm because she had made such a firm decision to completely avoid Albert.

As time passed and no word or hint came to him from Jane, Albert knew for certain that her infatuation with him was over. He had recognised it in her, being so much more experienced in lovers than she was, but he had never known such complete devotion before. Much as he had chafed against its faults as being disproportionate and overwhelming, inevitably lacking in joy for Jane because he remained the man he had always told her he was, Albert found that he missed her belief in him. His clandestine liaison with Sylvia palled, lacking in that very intensity which he *had* experienced with Jane, and also because Noel knew and did not care so long as it were not a public matter. What cynically selfish creatures he and Noel really could be, Albert sometimes felt, whereas before he had confidently believed them to be the true standard bearers of bohemian freedom. He still believed it but found himself less convinced than he had been before.

Instead, his life with Sarah, the most fierce among his women, began to draw Albert in more deeply. With her, he found that darker, complex side of love again, but in another way. Sarah had a dangerous sensuality. Alone, they began to explore it and punish each other with it together. To Albert, this new element seemed somehow fitting. His photographic plates began to express something of this. He portrayed Sarah bound in chains as a slave princess, or as a warrior Boudica, her foot on a prostrate male face down before her – Albert, naked. Now using the new clockwork timer with his folding box camera, the latest in photographic machinery, he was able to participate in his own tableaux.

When Sarah found him looking sometimes at the pictures of Hannah that still hung on the walls, fair and buxom where she herself was so differently made, she laughed at him for being such a fool as to lose what he had in two women for the sake of another that he never cared for while he had her. When she found him looking at plates of Jane, though, Sarah must have deliberately left them out to fade in the light, although naturally she professed to know nothing of it. When he protested at the destruction she said, arching one wanton leg to push him in the face with her bare foot, having wandered in wearing nothing but a shawl over her shoulders…

"Tha's got what tha deserves wi' me nah, Albert. Tell me you don't like it," and he was drawn back at once into rough sexual play with her.

He kept the painted portrait of Jane in his photographic studio, draped if he had sitters, taken down before any sessions photographing Sarah. He was not entirely certain what she would do to that image if she saw it. Sarah's lack of boundaries both excited him and left him half afraid of what often felt like a primal excess. He had never doubted that women knew animal passion as much as any man but Sarah's response to him now could be savage, born of the violence in her early life, a hard one. Above anything else that passed between them, this opened a window for Albert into a far more troubled world than the one in which he had been lucky enough to take his pleasures for all his life so far.

"I never knew such things in you before," he said.

"Best you know t' truth o' me then, for ah've always known t' truth of *you*, Albert Dewhirst," she retorted. "We're alone nah. No Hannah to soften up t' edges."

"I am not sure I am flattered," he said, slapping her on the behind.

"Weren't meant to be," she answered, with some contempt in her tone. Flinging his hand aside, she bit the soft flesh of his inner arm in a nip that was less than playful.

"Stop it, you minx," said Albert, sitting up. "I tire of this."

"No, you don't," she replied but she got up to dress herself, careless of him now. "I'm on shift soon. Get aht nah and down to thy father in't office, like a dutiful son."

Albert laughed.

"You really are the most disrespectful…!"

She looked back over her shoulder, dark hair still tumbled down.

"I told you before, Albert," she said. "Tha's got what tha deserves wi' me. While I'll stand it."

Half-joke as he believed it was, Albert could not help but feel, uneasily, that she meant it and perhaps it was time to draw this liaison, too, gradually, to a close. Things were not the same without Hannah there and the balance of things was getting skewed. When he finally heard that Jane had really gone abroad again under her own initiative, he was impressed and disappointed in equal measure. It was time he made sure of his own future, instead of being left behind or dominated by his own women, he began to think!

For the present, Albert continued on in his studio, as well as visiting Noel's mansion and getting involved in the new art movement with his photography. Locally, Ogden Towers and its strange group of itinerant artists and local artisans was viewed as one of Ogden's eccentricities, another extravagant foible. Since he was rich, he was still partly to be boasted of as a novelty in the area, full of folly to any with a clear business head of course and of dubious reputation, naturally, due to foreigners present, but intriguing nonetheless. Besides, Rastrick's pretty daughter Sylvia had married him, bringing more proper money to the door through the manufacturing world. Still, many reservations were felt. This summed up the general disapproval felt by many Halifax burghers, including Albert's own father, who told him he expected him to settle down after his sojourn abroad.

"You've sowed some wild oats, my boy, maybe more than most. There's a family business you're part of here and if *you* want a part of it, it's time to put your back into it."

Albert was not at all sure that this was a choice he was ready to make yet, but it was 'yet' rather then 'never' now in his mind.

Chapter Sixteen

When Ellen and Peter married later in the summer, it was a quiet affair. Due to Peter's lack of connections, Mrs Rastrick was happy to allow it to be so, still basking in the glory of Sylvia's wedding after the disappointment of Leonard's. Mrs Lumb, for her part, refused entirely to be persuaded by Peter's new circumstances to leave the street and neighbourhood she lived in for a more comfortable home near the house he and Ellen would be renting.

"Besides," Mrs Lumb said with a snappy glare when it was proposed, "how's Stanley's mother to get on without me next door to keep her going? It's me as keeps them all going round 'ere!" she declared.

Her indignant energy, the wellspring of Peter's own, angry in adversity, also came from being needed by others, Ellen realised, warming to her because of it. Discovering that Ellen was engaged to Peter meant that his mother did not feel the need to be overburdened with gratitude towards her. The money which Ellen had formerly given to her for the family was even more a duty than charity in the circumstances, according to Mrs Lumb's view of the world and people's position in it.

By way of a welcome for Ellen into her own family, Mrs Lumb said, when Peter had introduced her again as his wife to be, "We'll see what tha makes of thissen, then, lass", giving her a gruff kiss on the cheek.

It was an unusual endearment, Ellen realised, understanding too the indication that, being more softly born, she would need to prove her mettle. Ellen had no doubt of that but she could happily believe that she had already proved it to Peter. The modest celebration over, they were finally together. Their first home was within reach of the Rastricks' factory, cycling distance for Peter, who was used to a long trek to work. It had that view across the Calder Valley which Ellen loved, just alongside Albert Promenade itself, where short terraces had been stepped into the hillside. They could see Wainhouse Tower from it very clearly. Peter would ride out with Len in his carriage to Stanger's New Mill too, and sometimes he and Ellen would stay at Heatherfield. With regular meetings planned between Len, Mr Rastrick and Peter, it was felt that all could be smoothly managed across both concerns in this way between them.

Mr Stanger had quietly slipped away without distress in his sleep shortly before the wedding and the mill was now Leonard's to run. Carrie told Ellen that she would stay at Heatherfield until after the wedding and then begin spending more time in Manchester, campaigning with Fiona as planned.

"I will not vanish altogether, Ellen. Len and I are quite in accord about our arrangements and we are the greatest of friends."

Leonard, when she spoke to him, said that Carrie was as honest as she had always been and that he respected her determination.

"I am very fond of my wife, Ellen. She tells me I am free to separate whenever I wish. I do not wish it. Not yet at least. In spite of our pledge ending with her father's death. There are different forms of love and we do hold it for one another in our way. She will have my name as long as she wants it and the freedom to live as we please. She may fight her good fights with her beloved old friend. Thick as thieves, aren't they?" he said lightly, leaving the discussion with Ellen about it at that.

Ellen and Peter honeymooned, courtesy of Mr Rastrick, in the elegant spa town of Harrogate. They stayed at one of the splendid hotels there, finding themselves at the height of the fashionable spring and summer visiting season for those from well-heeled, or even aristocratic circles. Walking through the beauties of the landscaped Valley Gardens one afternoon together, Ellen said, her arm through Peter's, "How different this all is from Halifax, and how grand we are here, Peter!"

"Aye, for now," he said, wry as ever.

"Trust you to say so." Ellen laughed at him.

"Trust me for it being so," he returned.

"I know. And I want our proper, ordinary lives to start too, Peter. We *will* carry on being Clarionettes as well, though, won't we? I should hate to lose that."

"Of course we will, Ellen! Tha's wi' me now. No hiding away or permissions needed from your father and mother. We'll be at the centre of all that's going forward in the Clarion Club."

"I want us to promote a general subscription for working people to get to the music concerts, Peter," Ellen said, repeating an idea they had had before. "I have never forgotten how much it affected you hearing Beethoven at the Halifax Theatre."

She looked up at him fondly, squeezing his arm.

"Aye, that it did. And it's a grand notion, Ellen. Here, come on, let's take some of them famous spa waters. T' Royal Pump Room's dahn theer."

The small round pavilion, with a domed cupola roof, was at the bottom of the hill outside the gates of the gardens. A noxious, eggy smell enveloped them as they went in and paid to be served a glass of the Harrogate spring water which was so renowned for its health-giving properties. They laughed together, spluttering at the sulphurous, mineral taste of it.

"Reet! I reckon we're set up for life now," grimaced Peter. "We'll both live happily to a hundred at least. We deserve to after drinking that mucky stuff!"

***

Jane was already back in France before their wedding, so that Ellen was saved from any need to invite her to it. Jane, and the very idea of Jane, had always continued to discomfit Ellen after the melodrama of the other girl's attempted suicide. They had not renewed any friendship when Jane returned to Halifax and now she had gone abroad once more to teach English to the children of diplomats in Paris. A very privileged position, or so everybody was assured by her proud father. Since he was their vicar, many people naturally came to hear of it.

Miss Tordoff travelled back with Jane, who stayed with her benefactress and mentor for another couple of weeks again in her rented Parisian apartments. She dined with Miss Tordoff and the diplomat 'friend' of hers who had secured Jane the post. Nobody was so indiscreet as to suggest in any way that he was Vivian's lover or, like Albert, one of them, but it was implicit. Monsieur Laurent, for all his important position in the world and well-dressed air of knowing his place in it, treated Vivian with a poised and tender courtesy at all times. This was a sophisticated relationship, one of long-standing mutual respect and affection, it was clear.

Monsieur Laurent introduced Jane, over other dinners, to the parents of some of the children being privately schooled in the pension, so that she would enjoy a more elite status among the staff when she began there. Vivian told her that it was important not to seem of lowly foreign origin but to appear as a lady of personal means who was teaching English in a select establishment by choice while improving her own French. Jane demurred at first, the Clarion Club's ethos making her feel that to claim an elevated social standing was wrong. Vivian, however, persuaded her that otherwise she would be belittled as a poor clergyman's daughter, barely above being governess, and thus likely to be put upon and refused independence from the pension.

"If you wish to be more free to come and go about Paris, as I know you do, then you must appear to be a very desirable employee, there by choice rather than necessity," she told her. "It takes subterfuge to be modern in any society as a woman. Surely you know that, Jane, after all your adventures?"

Jane agreed that she did and, put that way, it did not seem to be wrong to present herself as Vivian suggested. She soon renewed her acquaintance with Wolf, too, and with him she dined in the shabby bistros frequented by the artists. They only had one conversation which concerned Albert, on the first night they dined together.

"You are quite sure in your decision?" Wolf asked Jane.

"Oh, yes. I am," she assured him.

"I thought you would be, if it came to it," he said. "Did you know that Albert bought my portrait of you?"

"Yes. He told me of it," she said.

Wolf studied her a moment.

"Well, then, I will have to paint another for myself," he said.

They smiled at one another with the comfortable intimacy of those who know each other well without many words being needed between them. This too felt like the beginning of something new to Jane, even though she and Wolf did not know each other very well at all. Or at least, they did not do so in depth yet. Somehow, she felt that they would.

No, she would not be lonely in her teaching at the pension while she had a friend in Wolf to turn to, she knew. Secretly, she had been touched by Albert's purchase of her painting from Wolf, which made her think a little better of Albert's alleged feelings for her than she had done when she fled from him. It had been hard to resist Albert when he called at the vicarage. Physically, he attracted her as much as ever, but his opportunistic betrayal of her with Sylvia had opened Jane's eyes to the careless reality of his promiscuous ways, so alien to her own nature. Once again, she bade farewell in her heart to her first love and began her new life, with a job of her own and a foundation of support in Vivian Tordoff, Wolf and the other people she would make friends with during what she hoped would be a year in France.

***

Sylvia and Noel's artists' community brought them a different kind of prestige in the region as its reputation began to be made, hosting salons as well as social occasions for the right people. When Albert drew aside from her, Sylvia was doing the same from him, her elevated and queenly role requiring her character to be maintained without a stain, just as before, in her view. And besides, Noel was more attentive to her doings here as his constant hostess. What she had learned from Albert livened up their own marital bed, for Noel was quite conscious of her beauty and his duties as a spouse, attracted to women too. He was rather grateful to Albert for teaching her to know what she was doing, which made her far more desirable to him than she had been as the virginal bride who just succumbed to his advances without any notion of how to meet them.

She had no real understanding, naturally, of his interest in young men and he confined that to Cyril outside of their marriage. Because Cyril loved Noel, he endured it and because Cyril was only a stonemason who had done work for them, Sylvia did not really notice him anyway. Noel was flamboyant and had always been so. She saw no difference in him there. He treated Sylvia with exquisite politeness at all times, intrigued by the inner coolness about her which made her so usefully incurious about his other doings. He looked forward to children, imagining small creatures as beautiful as they were who could be delightfully dressed up. It was no more real to him than that, at present at least, nor to Sylvia, the new bride.

At Ogden Towers, among the artistic movement they had named the 'Clarionistas', Cyril had a new proximity to Noel which he had never enjoyed before. Although he was just as challenging to Noel in private, angry at him for marrying at all, it had, as John had long ago said, always been an inevitability. Their sexual love affair had been a secret one out of legal necessity and it was newly exciting to them both now, hidden behind Noel's public marriage, a dangerous pleasure. If John guessed at the relationship's continuance, as surely he did, he said nothing to Cyril, who had chosen to be held to Noel. Whatever frustrations might come from that were his own to manage, having made that decision. Cyril had the comfort, though, of knowing that Sylvia and Noel were not at all in love except with an image of themselves as a golden couple. Cyril's love was real, even though he knew that Noel was one who allowed himself to be loved and, at bottom, did not deserve his devotion, so Cyril granted himself carte blanche to give Noel a hard time of it for his frivolous ways and vanity. Since this was how they had always sparred, things were no different there.

Cyril's sense of himself now was also influenced by the influx of people from a different milieu, the artists being in the main far more decadent than anything Cyril had known before (apart from Noel himself). He had a new set of associates amongst whom he was a fellow artist, with a standing which he had never enjoyed as an artisan mason. They absorbed him into easy fellowship, forays into town drinking at the inns together, impromptu parties on the louche side of life, which they seemed able to create easily around them. The fact that Noel, as patron, for all his efforts to be part of it all, was slightly excluded, gave Cyril considerable satisfaction and Noel some jealous pique of his own, which was no bad thing in Cyril's opinion. Somewhere in his consciousness, he was aware that one day the choice would be his to part from Noel and that, one day, he might be ready to do it.

Noel, naturally, took the artists as a party up Wainhouse Tower. They were very impressed by it and the vistas they could see from it, exclaiming and excited. They walked around the storied balustrades as the Clarion Club members had previously done.

Luc, the artist whom Noel had first seen Cyril talking to in the garden, a lively Parisian with animated ways, threw an arm around Cyril's shoulder up there, crying, "Ah, now you see, Cyril, how you must come back with us to Paris in the spring and see the wonders there! Your art will be inspired by our own monuments."

Others gathered round Cyril too, clapping him on the back and saying that yes, he must indeed go back with them! Cyril smiled back at them while Noel, standing by, looked annoyed and momentarily surprised.

"Spring?" Noel asked, rather sharply.

"Yes, some of us plan to go back, Noel. You knew this," said Luc.

"But I – the Clarionistas are becoming so well-established!"

"It is a beginning, my friend, but we have our Parisian art world too. We will come and go, others will join you. That is the way of such things in a free art movement. It must grow and change, as we do."

Ordinarily, Noel would not have demurred but his resentment about Cyril flared.

"Cyril chips out gravestones," he said with light

derision. “What does he want with the Arc de Triomphe or the Eiffel Tower? Besides, I refuse to allow any of you to leave!” he added affectedly. “You are all *far* too precious to me.”

“Nonsense, Noel,” said Cyril, seeing through him as easily as ever. “And if that is how you value my work after all my efforts in your garden for you, then I need to broaden my perspective!”

“*You* will not go to Paris,” Noel scoffed, still trying to keep a light-hearted tone, but Cyril just looked him straight in the eye and said:

“Oh, I might, Noel. I might do just that. Why not?”

He turned, laughing, to Luc and the others, who clapped him on the back again and said, “Bien sûr!” and “Courage, Cyril!” exclaiming jovially around him.

When they all descended again, it was Cyril’s supposedly forthcoming journey to Paris among the artists which they toasted with teasing humour, raising bubbling glasses of the champagne which Noel had supplied, with cheers and hoots. For once it was Noel who was rattled and in his face was an uncertainty rare to see when he looked at Cyril. While Cyril was secretly pleased to note it and felt it served Noel right, the idea Luc had laughingly suggested began to appeal to him in reality as the champagne and laughter influenced him. Perhaps he *would* go back to Paris in the spring with them after all, he thought to himself, and if he did, who could say what changes that might make in his own life? It was rather beyond his immediate imagination to see himself transported there but spring was a long way off and there was plenty of time to see if he could get used to the idea.

***

When Ellen and Peter returned to Halifax and the Clarion Club too, although many of their original members remained, relationships between them all had changed. To celebrate the anniversary of their first year of membership, as many of them as possible gathered to cycle again to Sunny Vale in Hipperholme. Peter and Ellen, Albert and Sarah, John and Cyril, were all there. It was perhaps fortunate for Peter's temper and Albert's amour propre that Eustace and Hannah (already privately married) were unable to be present due to other commitments at the school, where they were now housed in the tiny lodge at the gates in return for pastoral and care-taking duties when Eustace was not teaching. Libby, gallantly escorted by Noel in his carriage, awaited them in the Sunny Vale Pleasure Gardens, being in no condition, so near her time, to travel any other way.

Some of Noel's artists had joined them too, a raucous crowd who generated a newly careless spirit amongst them all as they enjoyed boating, roller-skating, strolling and even riding on donkeys, before taking tea and buns together at the Pavilion. This helped to echo the atmosphere of their first outing together last year. Noel loudly decided that his next sculpting commission from John would be one to adorn a public space, portraying the Clarionettes themselves. He envisaged a marble frieze promoting fresh air and exercise though a carved relief of a man and woman cycling together. Anything more political would be too inflammatory for the town's worthies to approve.

"The sight of that will set their pulses racing quite enough," Noel said with a wicked smile. "No pamphlets needed." He looked around the company and his eye settled on Albert. "Albert, my friend!" he called in his carrying, attention-seeking voice. "We have not seen you lately at Ogden Towers among our artistic community? I am sure that *Mrs* Noel Ogden would be very pleased to have you entertain us by calling again."

"Of course," replied Albert smoothly, well-versed in Noel's various tactics to needle and embarrass. "It will be my pleasure to do so."

The answering barb brought a small smile to Noel's face. Ellen, so recently returned from her happy honeymoon with Peter, caught something in the exchange, and also heard Sarah say, with defiance in her narrow dark looks, "Tha won't be leaving *me* in't lurch by going up theer wi'out me, Albert. Not now. Or I'll do it first. Like Hannah."

"Oh," he said. "Will you now, you hellion?"

His tone, like Sarah's, was provocative, private and with blush-making undertones in it of sexual teasing. Ellen glanced at Peter, unable to help it, for now she knew full well what really lay behind those physical delights hinted at which she had so longed to know of last summer.

As if in tune with her thoughts, although as usual he had paid no attention to either Noel or Albert, Peter said, "Nah then, Ellen, lass. Time to pay a visit to that tree we once sheltered under 'ere. Remember?"

Of course, Ellen did. The lightning kiss, as she had always thought of it, the first time when they had truly felt that there was something between them, something special. Going away from their party, they walked up the knoll to the privacy of the tree's low boughs. They stood under it hand in hand, on the other side of the trunk from that facing downhill this time and under a very different sky, with nothing but white summer cloud in it now. When they kissed again there was nothing to constrain them from taking every pleasure in it, man and wife in a private embrace. Peter patted the tree's trunk affectionately when they broke apart again.

"That's one of our anniversaries celebrated, Ellen," he said. "Best get on wi't other 'un dahn theer since folk are so set on laiking for nowt."

He spoke as broadly as possible to provoke and raise a smile, for Ellen often accused him of exaggerating his local accent out of devilment, particularly in her mother's company. She said he meant to irritate Mrs Rastrick's snobbery by sounding as uncouth as possible, and more especially still if they were all round a dinner table with Noel and Sylvia. When he protested his innocence, Ellen pointed out that he did not do it with Len and Carrie.

"No point in that," he admitted with a grin. "They wouldn't give a damn, would they? Besides, it gives Mr Rastrick summat to enjoy with them particular guests about."

"Papa is quite as bad as you are where my mother is concerned!" Ellen had retorted, laughing about it herself.

Now, Ellen batted him on the arm as he gave her his broadest possible local dialect and they strolled back down to the Pavilion, laughing happily. More than one person, seeing their approach, thought that they made a very natural and handsome couple, grown into a new maturity together. Various of the Clarionettes came up to congratulate them again on their recent marriage, wishing them all the best for a very happy future. Peter and Ellen, of course, had no thought that they could possibly have any other kind.

THE END

Acknowledgements

My very grateful thanks to those who helped me in writing this book – my family, friends and all at Blossom Spring Publishing, with particular thanks to Publishing Manager Claire Voet, Editor Dave Holwill and Artist-Editor Laura Cosby for their invaluable expertise and patient support.

Reference – Malcom Bull's *Calderdale Companion*

About The Author

Ruth Enright is from Halifax, West Yorkshire. She enjoys holidays in Whitby, Scarborough and the surrounding area; with Robin Hood's Bay and Whitby being the inspiration for her debut novel *Seahaven*. Her second book, *Button Box*, is for children and young adults. A young girl finds herself living in two worlds – the modern day and a dangerous Victorian past in 1850s London.

Ruth studied English Language and Literature at Reading University and has always had the ambition to write herself. She lives in Manchester with her family and works for local government, where she has held a number of posts. She is now an Information Governance Officer. Ruth came to Manchester as a graduate trainee in Librarianship with Manchester Polytechnic before changing career paths and training for a certificate in teaching lipreading to adults with acquired deafness in Adult Education. Ruth then had her daughter and later became a local government officer.

Ruth has always kept on writing and started a blog a few years ago for her poems, stories and other items. Encouraged by readers, she has recently succeeded in having five short stories published by *Yours Fiction* special short story quarterly magazine.

Ruth loves to read and enjoys writing in both historic and modern settings, experimenting with different genres. Ideas for her writing come from many sources, for instance the name of Robin's uncle Jorfant in *Seahaven* came from researching her partner's family tree!

Ruth lives with her partner Jack, and a cat called Margot.

Ruth is delighted to be a published author and is looking forward very much to writing more novels.

Website: www.r-enright58.co.uk
Facebook Page: https://www.facebook.com/ruthwriting
Twitter: Ruth Enright@2382a72570c7409
LinkedIn: https://www.linkedin.com/in/ruth-enright-9272ba227/
https://www.patreon.com/ruthenright_writings

Printed in Great Britain
by Amazon

27122820R00306